# Been Clever Forever

# Been Clever Forever

Bruce Stone

HARPER & ROW, PUBLISHERS
Cambridge, Philadelphia, San Francisco, St. Louis,
London, Singapore, Sydney
NEW YORK

Been Clever Forever
Copyright © 1988 by Bruce H. Stone
Typography by Joyce Hopkins
1 2 3 4 5 6 7 8 9 10
First Edition

Library of Congress Cataloging-in-Publication Data
Stone, Bruce.
    Been clever forever.

    Summary: A brilliant sixteen-year-old oddball,
having trouble adjusting to his conventional high
school, clashes with an emotionally disturbed
teacher and comes upon some important truths
about life and his place in it.
    [1. Gifted children—Fiction.
2. Teacher-student relationships—Fiction.
3. Emotional problems—Fiction.   4. High
schools—Fiction.   5. Schools—Fiction]
PZ7.S875945Be 1988      [Fic]      86-45774
ISBN 0-06-025918-3
ISBN 0-06-025919-1 (lib. bdg.)

for Mary Jo

# Been Clever
# Forever

# Chapter 1

To begin, I should explain that I am afflicted with a
congenital disease, a birth defect less treatable than
heart murmur, curvature of the spine, or kidneys
made of bad cheesecloth. Mine is a most uncompan-
ionable complaint, a scourge, a curse, a blight, a
randy albatross, stigmata incorporeal, a cross unbear-
able, a heinously Cain-ish mark, a markedly Twain-
ish spark, a . . . See. There goes. I am smart, is the
problem. Some would affix "aleck" to the simple
Anglo-Saxon descriptor. I have endured them all, all
the whispered, snickered, niggling cognomens that
collect in my wake like brown bottles and cast-off
candy wrappers. They go like this:

> Smart mouth
> Smart guy
> Smarty-pants
> Smartass
> Smart, smart, the big brown fart
> and worse . . .

The problem with being smart, besides all the cat-calls from the nose pickers and terminal droolers, is that people have certain expectations for you. And the trouble with all these great expectations is that someone's always telling you how to act, think, speak, dress, comb your hair, and best of all, what to do with your life.

It's like The Amazing Kreskin has written down your every move for the next five years and sealed it in an envelope. When time's up he opens the envelope and reads it off. Then you say, "Sorry, Amazing, it didn't go anything like that," and he clears his throat and the audience squirms in their seats and suddenly you're such A Disappointment.

I mean, it's like just because you're bright, you're supposed to Amount to Something, for god's sake. So get busy, sucker, and cure cancer or harness tidal energy or write an epic poem reconciling the nutritional schisms among the four basic food groups. What no one seems to accept is that extraordinary intellectual endowment is no guarantor of greatness. I mean, look at Barbara Walters.

I was never classically precocious, though. Rather than play the piano at four or master Basque verb tenses, I worried. In first grade I handed the appropriately named Miss Means a prospectus of what I thought should be a proper course of study:

1. Why do men have nipples?
2. Why are all magazine subscriptions sent to Boulder, Colorado?
3. What do those South American countries do with all that flax and jute?

4. What is riboflavin, really?
5. Why is Scotch tape made in Minnesota?
6. Where has Donald Duck left his pants?
7. What becomes of the roaches you flush down the toilet?
8. Why are oranges called that? Coincidence, or what?
9. Why does all the canned corned beef come from Argentina?
10. Why is aluminum foil shiny on one side and dull on the other?

Two days later Miss Means held forth for my parents and Mrs. Flatner, the guidance counselor.

"Stephen is a divergent thinker," Miss Means declared.

"Your son is obviously bright," Mrs. Flatner chimed in, "but these questions suggest a curious turn of mind." My parents studied their photocopies.

"Bent, not turn, Mrs. Flatner. I think it's bent," my father said.

"Please, not bent. She just meant somewhat unusual, didn't you, Mrs. Flatner?" Miss Means explained. Mrs. Flatner agreed I wasn't certifiably bent.

"No, phrases have turns, minds have bents—'turn of phrase, bent of mind,' like that," Father instructed.

"Of course they do," consoled Mrs. Flatner, her lips pursed in a comforting moue.

"Well, he's always been a nipple freak," my mother offered. "He puts Lifesavers on them and

5

walks around bare chested. The sticky kind, what are they, Wilson?"

"Butter Rum, I think," said Wilson, my father, failing to add that it was his idea in the first place.

Mrs. Flatner thanked my parents for allowing the school an opportunity to "register its concern." Everyone agreed that it was important to keep the lines of communication open. She would do a workup of the conference. It would represent the first installment in my folder, my personal school record, which in eleven years has come to rival in sheer bulk the collected case studies of Herr Sigmund Freud.

By the end of that first landmark conference I had failed a dressing-for-assertiveness quiz I had found in the pages of their office copy of *Psychology Today*. I got marked down most strenuously for my Winnie-the-Pooh windbreaker. Mother took the magazine away from me as we were leaving and replaced it on a corner table. But not before I latched on to one of those blow-in subscription cards. I had decided to skim off some of my milk money and subscribe. And where would I send my skimmed milk money? That's right, Boulder, Colorado.

# Chapter 2

The what-shall-we-do-with-Stephen conference came at least once a year, usually by October. The teachers changed, the counselors came and went. Principals sometimes got involved. But Mom and Dad remained the constant, even if their marriage did not. By fifth grade they were separated, by junior high divorced. Still, dutiful and doting, in they trooped with the regularity of the autumnal equinox. Thus did we have our family reunions: no baked ham, no potato salad, no Frisbee on the beach.

It was during the Year of the Pig that everyone decided my strangeness had slipped into dementia. I called ninth grade the Year of the Pig because that's the year we were forced to read all the pig books. Don't ask why. We read *The Pigman* about an old guy called Mr. Pignati who collected glass pigs even though he was really enraptured by a baboon. Then we read *A Day No Pigs Would Die* about some crazy Quaker pig farmer and the son who feared him. Then came *Lord of the Flies*, which I renamed *Lord of the Pigs.* Some boys go wild on an island and hunt pigs, also wild, and roast them. Then they kill a boy named Piggy and everyone worships the pig's head because it will keep the beast away, which is the pig in everyone. Anyhow.

I read most of Thomas Hardy that year just to stay sane, and when they caught on they bumped me into the enriched ninth-grade English class, even though I was barely pulling a C. So what did we do? We read *Animal Farm*, in which two pigs named Snowball and Napoleon become tyrants over their animal brethren.

I was so pigged out that year that by the time we got to an unpiggish book called *A Separate Peace*, I snapped. Instead of writing about the friendship between these two guys at prep school during World War II, I wrote my own porkish version of the book.

I wrote *A Separate Pig.* Two young pigs, Lean and Finicky, spent their days casting themselves off the top of their sty into a great ooze of mud below. Until one day Finicky is given an envious pigly nudge by Lean and takes a bad tumble, thereby shattering a cloven hoof. Guilt, anguish cloud the relationship until both pigs are sent to France to snuffle truffles behind enemy lines during World War II. They turn up weeks later—on two great platters during D-Day as *porc au vin.* General Eisenhower sups on their succulent flanks and pronounces them mighty good. Finis.

"You should be ashamed," pronounced Mr. Cheddaster, principal, after reading most of my 172 pages. "And the language . . . unacceptable."

I assured him I was only trying to capture the ambience of pig talk, things overheard at the trough.

"Still and all, a clever piece of work, don't you think, Mr. C.?" Mr. Mustero, enriched English teacher, had taken my work to Cheddaster not in betrayal, but in pride. "Why, the fluency, the dialogue . . . it's rich. The boy has promise."

"Hogwash," sputtered Mr. C., pigheadedly keeping in the spirit of things. "Let's get the parents in here."

Again we went round and round. Presiding at this affair was Miss Ramseur, recent graduate and acolyte in the church of B. F. Skinner. She saw all life shaped by a matrix of rewards and denials, reinforcement both positive and negative.

"This is a learned behavior," she said. "We must reinforce those behaviors Stephen displays that are more compatible with the acceptable norm."

"Dog Yummies or monkey pellets, name your poison," Dad mumbled with a wink in my direction.

"Really, Mister . . . Mister . . ." Miss Ramseur groped for a name.

"Douglass . . . two *s*'s, with a burr if you please." Dad was proud of his ancestors.

"Well, anyhow, Mister Burr Douglass, here again you're only reinforcing your son's behavior with your comments and your sly little winks."

"Just Douglass," I threw in. I had learned back in sixth grade to speak up for justice and truth. Miss Ramseur wasn't connecting.

"The name is Douglass, the last name," Mom added, the third line of defense. Even in disarray, our

9

family rallied to the cause. "He meant pronounce Douglass with a burr, a Scottish accent. 'DOOOG-luss,' like that."

"Oh, my mother's got some Scotch in her," said Mr. Cheddaster, waxing jolly.

"Shouldn't we all right now, if we had any sense?" said Mr. Mustero, closing ranks with the Douglass family, bewildering Cheddaster and the Ram. It was four against two, Mustero making a surprise ally.

"So, where are we?" Mr. C. attempted, throwing out his arms in a gesture of conciliation and love. He had no idea, and wanted to start over. Good fellow, that Mr. C. I was ready for a fresh start, too.

# Chapter 3

"Why not give us a hand?" asked Mr. Mustero the next day. It seems he had a handpicked blue-ribbon committee of enriched kids primed to put on the annual graduation and awards ceremony. Weather permitting, it was to be held at the high school stadium. That would give everyone a sense of the approaching grandeur of high school life and would save immeasurably on air-conditioning and janitor fees as well.

Nu Tran Banh—the droolers called him Neutron Bomb—showed us the program he had designed, a marvel of calligraphic virtuosity with lettering as precise as the teeth on a comb. The cover showed a generic kid from the back, mounting some golden stairway to the future.

Amber DeVoto, the golden princess, was refreshments. "I am refreshments," she announced, snapping a crisp new steno pad onto her desktop. "Right. First. Punch. Floating Paradise. Twenty gallons. Zarex syrup. Flavor. Tropical. Ginger ale. Right.

Twenty quarts. Pale golden. Check. Sherbet, ten gallons. Crushed fruit, twelve cans, eight ounces. Hold it, let's go back to the sherbet. Okay?"

No one protested.

"Right. Sherbet. Ten gallons. Okay, flavor on that is pineapple, make that pineapple." She underlined pineapple on her pad.

I looked around to make sure no one was taking notes on this. No one was. And there was more: doughnut holes, stoned-wheat wafers, processed-cheese-food snack spread, punch bowls, cups, twenty boxes plastic sporks, crushed ice. And then she asked for feedback.

Feedback was unforthcoming.

"Sounds like a bunch . . . how much is it costing?" I said.

"Mostly donations, Stephen," she answered patiently. "I've contacted all the local merchants. And no, we figure maybe what, six to seven hundred people once you count all the relatives."

"What are the sporks for?" I pressed on.

"Good point, Stephen. We really don't have any need for sporks. Everything's finger food, except for the cheese spread. Maybe, at most, some nice table knives," said Mr. Mustero.

"Check," said Amber, a touch of bruise in her voice. She scratched out the spork entry on her pad until a small black rectangle glistened on the page.

Next up was Peggy Klecko, she of the waist-length honey hair. It hung just about to the full rise of her dimpled undercarriage, which was a marvel of gluteal tone proclaiming her bondage to the rigors of the stretching bar. Peggy, see, was a dancer, and it showed. Plus she wore these ballet slippers all the time, and leg warmers in June. Finally, you had to admire Peggy for her extraordinary collection of buttons. My favorites included "Eat the Rich," "TV shits in color," and "Smile—your gums are bleeding."

"How are we doing on the ushers, the seating, the sound?" asked Mr. Mustero.

"We're doing great," said Peggy. "The high school janitors will set up the risers at ground level, connect the speaker system. Plus I've got sixteen ushers lined up from seventh and eighth grades. All set." And then she smiled and snapped her honey hair with the authority of a Clydesdale.

Was I in love?

Then came Roy Bedoya, or RoyBoy to his friends. He was the only specimen still extant of an adolescent who groomed his hair with Brylcreem. Plus he wore tasseled loafers on all public occasions. It was rumored in some circles that RoyBoy's apparent lifetime exemption from phys-ed classes derived primarily from his mother's inability to find for him a pair of tasseled gym shoes.

"The diplomas are printed, in boxes, in the office," boomed Roy in a surprising baritone. "And Mr. Cheddaster has the list of award winners. Maybe we should make a backup list with all names spelled phonetically, just in case."

"Good idea, Roy," Mr. Mustero agreed. Cheddaster's abuse of family names was legend. Ned Szymycywcyz (say Simswits) was once paged to the office by Mr. C. to meet his mom. Thenceforth he was known in school as "Suzy Ma Q Zee," at least until he showed up one day in a Solidarity T-shirt.

"All that remains now is for us to put the program together. We need a speaker, a presentation, something to make it all sort of special and . . . well, memorable. If you remember last year's program, we had the Reverend Bilney talk on surviving in the bush. And we've had nuns, the water commissioner, even an Iranian once, I think it was. . . . Stephen here has consented to help me with the program." I made a gesture of consent. "But we need your ideas, your support, to make this a worthwhile whatchamacallit."

A stone-cold silence followed Mr. Mustero's appeal. No one seemed bristling with good ideas. The room filled with a fluorescent hum. From far-off corridors came the hollow pop and rattle of those last few lockers slamming shut. All eyes turned to me. It was my cue. As latecomer to the committee and know-it-all, I was clearly expected to propose something brilliant.

I searched the walls of Mr. Mustero's room. In an effort to conceal the expanse of concrete-block drabness, he had invested heavily in posters. They hung in irregular patterns across three walls. To my right, Charles Dickens gloomed back unconsolingly. To my left, Earvin "Magic" Johnson drove for a layup. Behind us, Mark Twain tinkered with a cigar.

"How about smoking, dangers of, some formative-years stuff?" No takers.

"Too gloomy, too preachy. Try again," said RoyBoy.

14

Above the pencil sharpener Michael Jackson snarled in mid step.

"How about something musical, a chorus or something?

"Better," said Mr. Mustero.

"Bad acoustics," said Peggy Klecko.

"Try again," said Nu Tran, with relish.

Above the chalkboard Jesse Owens froze in his blocks, coiled for a sprint that would never come. "Anyone know any famous athletes?"

"Dozens," said RoyBoy.

"Someone must know somebody," said Amber.

"Let's ask around, someone might. Has promise, Stephen. We've done enough for now. Let Stephen hear from you if you get any leads. Now go ahead and have a good afternoon, what's left of it. Thanks for coming." With that, Mr. Mustero stood, signaling an end, and we all bolted for the door.

"Oh, Stephen, hold on," he added, his voice pulling me back from the hall. "Check in with me tomorrow. . . . We've got to get going on this, or we'll come up empty-handed. Ten days isn't much time."

# Chapter 4

By the next afternoon, it became apparent that no one had any leads. Mustero and I conferred. "Make a list," he suggested. So politicians, educators, librarians, architects, surgeons, ministers, police, generals, and real-estate tycoons all in a row tumbled onto my list.

"Now, let's cross off those categories that've done it before," he said.

"And the boring ones," I said.

Having eliminated the entire list, we decided to call the State Arts Council. They had two potters and a hammer-dulcimer player available for the evening in mind. Only in a pinch, we decided.

Then I called the Natural History Museum. They had a guy who did a program called "The Poison in Our Midst." They assured me it was riveting. He did school programs all year long, always in demand.

"What is it? Dope, booze, something like that?" asked Mr. Mustero.

I hadn't asked.

The next day, I phoned Dr. Rasmussen, the speaker himself, and discovered that "The Poison in Our Midst" was a program on common toxic vipers indigenous to our region.

"Could you sort of adapt it to a junior high graduation ceremony, give it a sort of transcendent twist, if you know what I mean?" I implored.

He assured me that he would do his best, reminding me that he was a veteran of countless school assemblies.

Mustero was so beamish to hear that everything was set I hated to tell him the viper part. So I didn't.

The days sped by like bullets shot downhill, and come that Friday evening in June, students, parents, and a residue of teachers assembled at the high school stadium. Parents sat in the bleachers, home-team side, while their kids arrayed themselves in an arc of folding chairs set up on a makeshift stage at ground level, just inside the oval track that circumscribed the playing field. At the front of the stage, a podium, a microphone, a row of empty seats awaited the dignitaries. Between the stage and the stadium, Amber fussed over the details of her refreshments. Steno pad brandished on high, she walked the length of three adjoining picnic tables, running a last-minute check on her doughnut holes.

Nervously, my classmates took their seats on stage.

I stood by the gate of the chain link fence leading into the stadium. From there I could keep a lookout for Dr. Rasmussen when he pulled into the newly paved parking lot just beyond the brick refreshment stand. I was assigned to usher him onstage and seat

17

him up front next to the podium, if he ever showed up. By then, I had concluded that maybe it would be no great tragedy if he didn't. He could spend the whole evening in the breakdown lane of the Memorial Expressway for all I cared. I would just as soon collect my diploma and be gone, with three glorious months to recover.

Back at the stage area, Mr. Mustero fiddled with the microphone, running a sound check. Peggy Klecko fluttered beside him, pointing to amplifiers perched right and left on the edge of the platform. Then suddenly Mr. Mustero bolted from the stage and sprinted down the track toward me. He stopped, throwing his arms above his head, palms up, shoulders scrunched in a shrug. "Where is he?" he pantomimed with his mouth.

I gave him back the shrug. "Beats me," I mouthed. Mysteriously then, Mr. Mustero started bouncing up and down and pointing with a cocked wrist over my head.

I turned, and sure enough, out in the parking lot a blue pickup bumped its way slowly over the curb and rattled across the rough stone walk leading down to the fence. It stopped barely a hundred yards away, and a man stepped out of the cab.

I raced to the truck. "You must be Dr. Rasmussen," I said, my hand extended.

"Sure am," he said, pumping my hand. "And you're Stephen. Come on, give me a hand with my stuff." He led me around to the truck's bed, where he lowered the gate and slid two long black metal boxes in my direction. Each box had a brass handle and what seemed like vents on the sides. "You get these, son, I'll get the rest."

"The rest" included two worn canvas bags drawn tight at the top and knotted with their own drawstrings. Dr. Rasmussen also carried what appeared to be a walking stick until I noticed that at one end it was fixed with a metal extension bent into the shape of a question mark with a flattened top.

"Try to hold these steady; they've had a rough ride," said Dr. Rasmussen. I guess I knew what I was carrying but was trying not to think about it.

"These dangerous?" I asked, trying to keep stride with the doctor as he giant-stepped his way across the track. I was not reassured by the knee-high leather boots he was wearing.

"What isn't?" he chuckled, eyes twinkling behind steel-framed glasses. "No, seriously, they're kinda shy if you know how to respect 'em."

"Oh, I respect 'em," I said. Dr. Rasmussen just snorted.

By the time we reached the front of the stage, all eyes had fixed on us. Curious skeptical stares. Even the gum chewers sat at attention for the first time, bolt upright, their jaws suddenly frozen in puzzlement. As we set Dr. Rasmussen's gear on the platform, Mr. Cheddaster commandeered the microphone, cupping his hand over the mouthpiece and summoning Mr. Mustero to his side. Now seated in the dignitary row beside Dr. Rasmussen, I watched with everyone else as the two men pretended to be having a civil word. Yet the intense bobbing and twitching of their heads, almost nose to nose, meant

19

trouble. Occasionally, stifled bits of Cheddaster's angry words reached us in the front row: "absurd . . . irresponsible . . . twenty years in public schools . . . unthinkable . . . these children . . ." and so forth.

Finally Cheddaster withdrew his hand from the mike. Mr. Mustero kneeled beside me and whispered something to Dr. Rasmussen, who nodded in agreement. Then, voice trembling with controlled rage, Mr. Cheddaster addressed the audience.

"Ladies and gentlemen, we are going to make a slight change in our program for tonight. Because of the unusual . . . uh . . . nature . . . uh, of tonight's special program . . . we are going to go right to the presentation of the awards and diplomas. As your children receive their diplomas we ask that they proceed from the stage area here and join you in the stands. As a special precaution, we ask any of you who are taking pictures to stay on the track surface and not approach the stage itself, heh heh. Thank you."

The audience buzz didn't stop until finally the diplomas were presented. Mr. Cheddaster stood stage right, by the steps, dishing out diplomas and shaking hands. My classmates left the stage, one by one. "Stephen Alexander Douglass" rumbled at me from across the stadium. My turn. I stood, nodded to Dr. Rasmussen, and crossed the stage to where Mr. Cheddaster waited. Unable to look him in the eye, I fixed him with a waist-level stare. The left hand plucked a diploma out of a box sitting on a folding chair at his side. The other hand floated upward from his thigh and reached out straight at me. I took the hand offered and the diploma. But he didn't let go.

20

"This is all your doing, isn't it, Douglass, smart guy?" I looked up at last and shivered at the stiff grin twisting his face. "Just keep it up, Douglass. You'll come to no good, no good at all."

I crossed the track and climbed the stadium steps, finding a seat in the front row down at the end. Behind me somewhere, up in that mob of proud mothers and fathers, sat my parents, separately, each probably wondering if I would join the other. But right then, I didn't need company—I needed summer vacation and a cave to crawl into.

# Chapter 5

By the time Linda Zagouris got her diploma and joined the rest of us in the stands, Dr. Rasmussen sat alone on an empty stage among 142 Samsonite folding chairs, one podium, two boxes, and two bags of snakes. Mr. Mustero had already disappeared into exile, and old Cheddaster paced the painted white lines on the track like a man taking a sobriety test.

It was a stalemate. The proud moms and dads wanted to bolt with their kids for private celebrations somewhere else, somewhere with air-conditioning and pizza and salad bars and pitchers of iced tea. Cheddaster wanted to lock up and go home to his coffee. Amber wanted to unload her doughnut holes and get her punch bowls back to her mom. And Rasmussen, poor Rasmussen, probably wanted to vaporize right up there on the stage, knee-high boots and all.

Sadly, and with biblical resignation, Dr. Rasmussen stood and approached the mike.

"Well, folks," he sighed, almost in apology, "looks

like it's just me and you." Some muffled sympathetic chuckles, some polite applause.

"My name is Dr. Orrin Rasmussen," he continued, "and I'm curator of reptiles at the Natural History Museum up in the capital. Guess they asked me here tonight 'cause they couldn't get Ralph Nader." More polite applause. "Anyway, when young Mr. Stephen Douglass called me, he said I should try to make my talk appropriate to this wonderful occasion in their young lives." I could feel myself shriveling like a slug in a salt mine.

"Course that's hard when all's you got to show people is a couple bags of poisonous snakes." The crowd rumbled like water coming to a boil. Girls squealed with disgust. An outraged voice behind me growled, "Good lord, what's Cheddaster thinking of, anyway?" That was hard to answer right then, for Cheddaster was gone from the track.

Under the hot lights and a gathering storm of moths, Rasmussen groped for his point. His glasses twinkled as he swiveled his head like a blind preacher broadcasting salvation. His text took shape and he carried us through centuries of serpent lore: Knowledge is freedom, and ignorance is fear, he proclaimed. He spoke of superstition, of tribal rites and cultish worshippers, of sects that made the serpent a sinister squirming vessel of poison and death.

He said: "And all these creatures really want is what we want too—a frog, a mouse, a place to shed their skins. And so as you young folks shed your skins, remember, you might leave behind the shapes of your youth, but you carry with you the creature you have been and will become." Rasmussen was really trying to make it all work. His face glowed white and pale under the stadium light. Dark stains widened under his arms.

Finally he had arrived at the moment of climax, the moment for which he had really come. He stopped and unfastened the top of his first black box and gingerly lifted out a shimmering length of living reptile. Holding either end in his hands, he lifted the snake above his head and approached the mike again.

"This little lady is a three-foot diamondback rattler—maybe four years old. Like all rattlers, she has a toxic venom with which she can kill or paralyze prey. She mostly picks on small rodents and other reptiles, however, and will avoid man like the plague unless she's absolutely forced to defend herself." With that he pinched behind her head with his right hand, holding her at chest level, and made like a cobra with his left hand. He darted and lunged at her with his cobra hand until she flexed her mighty jaws and set her rattles to work. Chilling. The crowd, as one, swallowed hard.

Dr. Rasmussen had them where he wanted them—at last. "Not to worry, folks. I been bit by these critters over twenty times and can claim almost total immunity to their venom. In fact, snake venom is used in medicine and research both as antitoxins and as the principal constituent of several sophisticated remedies." He stooped to the box once again and retrieved a large plastic cup.

"How many of you-all ever seen a snake milked?"

The audience craned and scanned each other until maybe five reluctant hands shot up. "Well, really ain't much to it. Let's see what we can get out of this little lady." Poor unwitting snake, before it could know what happened, its upper jaw was locked over the rim of the cup. The audience couldn't see a thing. "Well, you'll just have to take my word, there's about a quarter inch of venom at the bottom of this cup. Can you see that up front?" He walked to the edge of the stage and held the cup straight out toward us at eye level. A smattering of applause settled the matter. He was losing them again.

"Tell you what let's do," Dr. Rasmussen blurted, now back at the microphone. "Since this is a special occasion, it deserves a special extra something. Now you promise not to run for cover, I'll show you what I was talking about immunity. Now just watch here closely." Suddenly he dropped the snake at his feet and then plucked her up by the tail, dangling her there, then bumping her up and down against the stage. When the snake was good and angry he lifted her up and offered her the fleshy part of his other forearm.

The creature attached itself almost delicately to Rasmussen's forearm, as if reluctant to join in with the curator's shameless grandstanding.

"See there, folks, nice and solid," Dr. Rasmussen said. He held his forearm straight out at his side and the snake, still clamped on, dangled loose, its body curling with the effort. "I'll have me four nice clean puncture wounds, but don't forget, she's fresh out of venom. No charm, no harm."

25

The audience was aghast, I was sick, yet no one dared move. What had this evening become? What strange compulsion could make a rational scientist like Dr. Rasmussen turn into a show-off nincompoop for a captive audience at a high school stadium on a warm evening in early June?

Finally, he reached up with his free hand and dislodged the snake, again pinching it just behind the jaws. He raised his arms in a triumphant V and I half expected a pretty blonde in pink tights to come out of nowhere and hand the old fool a wand. Still he held the pose. Did he want applause? Groans of whispered disgust flurried through the stands. Did he want his picture taken? No one offered.

Still he held the pose, snake aloft, as he shuffled from behind the podium frozen in his V of triumph. He stood over the black box but made no effort to replace the snake. Then, drunkenly, he pivoted on his heels and faced the empty seats. And he held that pose, it seemed, for hours, rigid, until, as if with the impulse of an unseen wind, he swayed backward on his heels and crashed to the stage, his right hand catapulting the snake out onto the grassy infield where Amber's refreshments waited to be served.

# Chapter 6

So, now I was starring in some impromptu documentary on emergency medical procedures. See, I wasn't ready to have a dead guy on my hands. It might tend to make my personal school folder a little more dreary reading than it already was.

Without hesitating, I vaulted the railing along the front row of seats and took off across the infield, circling wide to avoid tripping over the rattler. I plunged onto the stage headfirst, not bothering to take the extra few seconds to use the steps. Grabbing Rasmussen by his boots, I dragged him full onstage so his head wouldn't be dangling over the edge and tried to pump his lungs with a little mouth-to-mouth.

I puffed and I wheezed and pinched his nose and cleared his mouth and double-checked his tongue. I was one breath short of hyperventilating when a hand grabbed my shoulder and asked how it was going—Mr. Mustero. "Not so good," he answered for himself. He went to the microphone and appealed to the audience for a doctor, then kneeled beside me,

27

checking Rasmussen for a pulse. I stood, tried to catch my breath, and searched the stands for reinforcements.

Sticking closely to the graveled walk, fathers, mothers, and offspring darted for the parking lot and escaped in their cars. Finally someone sprinted across the no-man's-land that separated us from the stadium. He was wearing a striped seersucker suit, and his head seemed held down by a pair of glasses nesting atop his pinkish dome.

"What have we got here?" he asked, ripping Rasmussen's shirt down the front and lowering his head to Rasmussen's chest. Then he pulled back Rasmussen's sleeve and examined the forearm, barely speckled with four small points of dried blood. "He seems okay. Breathing's rough, though. There should be an ambulance soon." He folded Rasmussen's shirt closed and knelt on one knee, keeping two fingers pressed against the jugular.

Mustero and I set to work pulling off Dr. Rasmussen's boots. Suddenly the parking lot swarmed with blue and red lights and the dying shrill of sirens. In another minute stretchers, oxygen tanks, and lots of stainless-steel stuff with wheels crowded the stage. Brisk little men with flag patches sewn to their sleeves scurried like gnomes. Soon they whisked away Dr. Rasmussen and all their paraphernalia, too. Police with flashlights big as bowling pins scoured the grass, prowled the stadium, and pronounced the snake "not in the immediate vicinity."

"A night to remember," said Mr. Mustero as he joined me on the edge of the stage. We sat, architects of disaster, as assorted janitors and the remnants of our blue ribbon committee dismantled the rest. Below us, Amber glowered over her punch bowls. RoyBoy joined her for a sullen toast, dipping two cups into the wilted sherbet brew. He assured her that it had not been mixed in vain.

"Go on home, Stephen—we'll finish up. I think someone's waiting for you." Mustero nudged me. "Your mother, maybe."

"No kidding," said my mom right on cue. She grabbed me by the arm and nodded with her bravest smile at Mr. Mustero. "Who else would claim this?"

Hooked arm in arm, we made our way to the parking lot. Here is what my mother said on the way: "Stephen, Stephen, Stephen, Stephen, flesh of my flesh, blood of my blood," followed by more Stephens, and so on.

"Here's from your father, Stephen," she said when we had sealed ourselves into her front seat. "He said to hang loose. Typical." She thrust a small package at me. I tore off the gold-foil wrapping and opened the box.

Inside were a pair of eyeglasses and a paperback. I picked up the glasses and read the tag. "X-Ray Spex," it said, made in Hong Kong and guaranteed to see through anything. I tried them on and looked at Mom. Her denim pantsuit was still denim and blue and eminently opaque.

Oh well, maybe the glasses needed batteries. Maybe the prescription was wrong.

"Now what?" said Mom, snapping up the book with her right hand. She transferred it to her left and held it angled toward the window. As we slowed for our first stoplight, she saw what I had already discovered. On the cover two blondes and a redhead had draped themselves suggestively all over some guy with all the animal magnetism of a postal inspector. He was smiling for dear life. He had obviously read the book himself. It was called *How to Pick Up Girls.*

"Girls!" Mom hissed. "The man has no shame, no shame whatsoever," she affirmed to the heavens through the roof of her Volvo. Then, both arms braced against the wheel, shoulders back, she drove on through the night, seeking another mantra for a June evening. This is how it went: "Typical, typical, typical, typical, typical, typical."

# Chapter 7

So much for clean slates. That's what they always told us we would enter high school with, but even after a summer of monastic seclusion, I found myself as a sophomore at Cable Hall High School a marked man. Even though Rasmussen had recovered from his collapse, his pitiful decline was followed closely by our local paper. Blood pressure was the problem, plus a sort of progressively "unstable, unprofessional attitude." So he was canned at the museum and given early retirement. What clinched it was when his wife confessed to a reporter that he had been bringing snakes home for weekend retreats and feeding them in a local park troubled by declining populations of squirrels and ducks.

"See what happens when you push things too far? Your old Rasmussen's just another show-off," said Mom. She never missed a chance to hammer home the old object lessons.

As for Mr. Mustero, he left town with the locust, sometime in August. The school board terminated him for lack of professional responsibility, while admitting what a fine teacher he was. All they wanted was a scapegoat, and since I wasn't available, Mr. Mustero would have to do.

And so I became "the kid that got that teacher fired back in junior high." I heard it first in homeroom, day one, when Miss Armias read my name off the printout. I walked to her desk and she handed me my schedule. "Aren't you the kid that got that teacher fired back in junior high?" she asked. I had hardly gotten out a weak "not exactly" when Jenny Chatauqua, aspiring cheerleader, burst forth, "That's right, Miss Armias. That boy, Stephen, he's the snake boy." There followed a chorus of general acclaim in which my homeroom mates officially dubbed me the snake boy. And so the legend lived on.

Little could Jenny Chatauqua and my classmates have known that my father had anticipated their affectionate label by weeks. Mom and Dad had traded months—that is, Dad agreed to take me for July and August so that instead of taking my usual alternating months of Mom/Dad/Mom/Dad custody, we would go two and two. The court no longer cared, and Mom and Dad were very progressive. So it happened that one July morning, as I sat eating my Pop Tart and contemplating my two webbed toes through the top of Dad's Lucite dining table, he held forth on the lessons to be gleaned from my infamy.

"Remember, Stephen, that every action has a consequence. For every action there's an equal and opposite reaction." He stood above me yawning into a box of cornflakes. "And when you set a course of action, it's important to consider what possible directions that action can lead. You follow?"

"Sure, I follow. You're talking about repercussions."

"Exactly right. I'm talking about repercussions."

He sat across from me, his short terry-cloth wrap riding up far enough to reveal that he still adhered to the manly pursuit of sleeping in the raw. "Cover up, Dad. I'm trying to eat my breakfast over here." I would have to talk to him about that Lucite table sometime.

"Oh, sorry." He laid the box of cornflakes flat in his lap and continued. "My point is, Stephen, that with your intelligence and all, maybe you see the world too simply, or too clearly, or . . ."

"Different, maybe," I tried to help.

"Sure, and with that, you can lose sight of what might happen, how people might see you. Always stay in control. Make sure you know the worst that can happen—then you'll be on guard. Like this snake thing. You can't just let loose a snake and let it crawl off into the high grass somewhere. You gotta know where it's going to go."

"But I didn't . . ."

"I'm not talking snake snakes, I'm talking like snake ideas, snake actions, wild things you let loose and then *fffffttttt*. . . ." He loosed a spray of soggy cornflakes in my direction.

"Figurative snakes, you mean," I said.

"Right, brilliant, ya punk." And he reached across and practically snapped my nose off, a tweak of love and pride. "Right. And so my point is, when you let the . . . this figurative snake loose, ya gotta watch it and see where it goes. Damn straight. Ya gotta keep your eye on the snake. . . . *Keep your damn eye on the snake.* Right, Stevie?"

"Absolutely, Dad. Keep my eye on the snake. Will do." How the Douglass family wisdom and folklore made a quantum leap that July morning! In greeting, in farewell, in simple daily discourse, my father made that simple phrase his anthem, our anthem, so that even on that late-August morning when school at last beckoned once again, he sent me off with nothing so comforting as "Have a nice day," or "Take care and be good," but instead with "Keep your eye on the snake."

And so, on that first of 180 school days, during that first of my high school years, I embraced my snakehood. I turned derision into celebrity. I could, as my mother always proclaimed, be just about anything I wanted to be. . . . Why not a snake?

"Jenny Chatauqua, honeybun, precious temptress," I hissed. "Come feel my fangs. Let me sink them into your flesh." I flicked my tongue menacingly at her from across the aisle.

"Seeeee, you're plain crazy." She clasped her new duofold laminated Trapper Keeper across her breasts and crumpled in her seat.

"That's enough, that's just about enough, thank you very much." Miss Armias floated up our aisle, between us, intimidating through the sheer bulk of her sundress overflow and her Pine Sol cologne. She finished handing out schedules and announcements.

When the bell finally sounded, we all dispersed to our several classes, and so the news spread. Glad tidings of the Stephen Douglass story traveled far and wide. By seventh period my name was already writ large in the annals of Cable Hall High School.

# Chapter 8

Jab, jab. The soft end of a pencil poked into the tender meat between my two favorite ribs. I turned and there sat Peggy Klecko, adjusting her stool beside mine. We sat behind a large black slab of table in the accelerated biology lab.

"So you bit a girl in homeroom this morning? Is it safe to sit here?" She flashed a wicked grin.

"Depends," I told her. "Did you order your school insurance yet?" She was sporting a new button for the occasion: It showed Princess Diana in a spiked dog collar. Obviously she had been to England over the summer.

"So this is the best of the sophomore crop. I suppose that we shall see, in time. Hello, little ones, my name is Mr. Truelove and spare me the jokes because I've heard them all by now in my years in this sludge pot of a school." That pretty much set the tone for seventh period as Mr. Truelove hovered among us, wheezing in labored breaths through his nose, a sinister apparition in a starched lab coat. Hands thrust into the pockets, thumbs hooked over their edges, he stalked the classroom, fixing each of us in turn with his dull gray eyes. His pale face sagged like a caul, then tightened as his lips clamped slowly into a grin of clownish glee. We had become his new specimens.

Further discussion of my homeroom assault on Jenny Chatauqua would have to wait. Truelove had us on the run. "And today I begin my quest anew, my yearlong mission of intellectual search and destroy. Some of you will make it, and regrettably, some of you will not. But isn't that always the way?" He fixed us with a rhetorical smile. Then, from a counter behind him, he picked up a quart bottle and unscrewed its top. "Take a whiff of this, youngsters." He passed from aisle to aisle, holding the bottle just below our noses. I took a bold whiff. . . . From somewhere just south of my spleen there rippled forth the quivering of violated organs. I was going to heave. Memories of past excesses—chili dogs, beef jerky, bowls of raw cake mix—danced in my head.

"That, students, is formaldehyde, elixir of death and preservative *extraordinaire*. Learn to love it. After three weeks in this lab, your entire back-to-school wardrobe will be saturated with it. By June you will wonder how you ever lived without it."

He then settled into a recitation of the glories of dissection. Worms and frogs and grasshoppers and starfish. As accelerated students, our good fortune would also take us into fetal pigs, cats, diseased human organs, and, if we got lucky and showed an aptitude, maybe a primate now and then. He finished with a walking tour of pickled oddities, bottles

37

of sludge and slime-covered things whirling uneasily in their jars as he held them aloft. Dust stirred from the lids of Truelove's bottles, sifting through the slant of afternoon sun to settle in our hair, our eyelashes. Thus were we anointed as budding biologists and day-old veterans of high school life.

"One final thing," Truelove announced. "Come back tomorrow with a lab partner, and be ready to go to work. Now get out of here."

The bell hadn't rung. Was it a trick? Uncertainly, we stood and filed out the door. Truelove spit into his wastebasket and fiddled with the window shades. Finally, halfway down the hall, we exhaled and took stock.

"Is he a maniac or what?" asked Nora of the eternal braces.

"I bet he subscribes to *Hustler*," said Buddy Autry, outstanding scholar-athlete from junior high days.

"I say he's lonely and bitter and hates us all 'cause we don't love formaldehyde the way he does," Peggy offered by way of psychoanalysis.

"Naw, just first impressions," I said. "Scare us shitless right off, see. Then it's always easy to soften up later on. It's the ones start nice that get in trouble. Remember Miss Torgeson, taught art in seventh grade? Let us go outside the first day to draw weeds. She was done by Thanksgiving."

"Oh her," said Peggy, squinching up her nose. "But I don't think she ever bathed. They had to get rid of her."

We concluded that it would be wise to consult some upperclassmen on the matter of Mr. Truelove.

With that, everyone scattered to buses and lockers. I trailed along behind Peggy, admiring her inverted form reflected in the polished linoleum underfoot. Almost three summer months of unchecked buffing had given it the sheen of freeze-dried obsidian.

"Hey, Peggy, wait up," I called as she veered right and disappeared down another hall. I hurried around the corner myself and practically knocked her over.

"Uh . . . I was just wondering if you'd like to be my . . . uh . . ."

"Valentine?"

"Well, for now I was gonna settle for lab partner."

"What if I say screw off?" she answered.

"Don't be cold. Think of the miles of intestines we could unravel together. Think of the ganglia—"

"Tell you what. I'll think it over. Call me tonight. . . . I might have a proposition for you. I'm in the yellow pages. Right now, gotta dance." And so Peggy Klecko bounded off down the hallway.

Was I in love?

# Chapter 9

That evening I sat nursing a Reuben sandwich in the
Mother Won't Know while Dad replaced the fluorescent bulb in the tropical-fish tank. The Mother Won't
Know was more commonly known simply as "the
Mother" to the undergraduates who had made it the
preeminent bar in our small university town of Cable
Hall. For seventeen years my father had been its
owner and presiding barkeep. He had bought it as a
present to himself for finishing first in his class at law
school. He took occupancy the afternoon Mother announced she was pregnant. On the day he was scheduled to take the bar exam, he instead hung a
makeshift plywood sign spray-painted with the new
name over the entrance and declared himself open
for business. This was the first grievance my mother
logged in those early years of the marriage.

"There, wanta give me a hand with this planter rig,
Steve?"

The planter rig Dad referred to was a custom-built
cover for the aquarium, on top of which sat a spray

of plastic ferns in a cast-iron kettle. It was his design, a shield to spare the fish untold indignities. Many an undergrad, tender of stomach after a nightlong revel, had cast his curdled offal over those troubled waters. Dad went through gouramis like they were Kleenex.

Finally, the top was in place. "Let's try it out," Dad said. He switched on the light to reveal a fresh assortment of tropical specimens. They were striped and spotted orange and pink and yellow phosphorescent like ornaments hand-painted in Hong Kong.

"Looks nice, Dad. Hope they make it 'til June." For nine months the university students laid siege to the bar, drinking gallons of beer and keeping my dad rich, something he had always been anyhow.

"Hell, I can always stock it with minnows."

I returned to the bar to finish my sandwich. Dad drew himself a mug of beer and joined me. Otherwise, the bar was empty. Summer session had been out for two weeks. It would be another two weeks before the university fall semester started.

"So how did it go today?" Dad asked, nerving himself for the big question. He was a firm believer in giving me what he called my "own space," but I think he secretly ached to know everything that went on in my head. He took up a bar rag and started polishing the ashtrays, at pains to be casual.

" 'It' meaning school?" I asked.

"Of course, 'it meaning school.' What else would 'it' mean?"

"It went fine," I answered. I saw his face shrivel with frustration in the bar mirror. Delicately, he

41

stacked the ashtrays and went behind the bar. It was his fortress, his sanctuary. Like a captain at the bridge of his ship, he became the genial bartender, all happy-hour happy talk.

"Hey, how about those Braves? Go to L.A. and leave their bats at the damn airport. Swear to god, I think they have a team meeting every time they go on a westbound plane and vote to have a slump. If Murphy could stay healthy one August, they might have some chance, but jeeze, if Lasorda doesn't have a voodoo doll for the entire lineup stashed away in his locker somewhere, then I don't know what his secret is. Tell you one thing, though, buddy, they keep it up like this, you'll never see the Braves on cable in this bar again come next April. And old Ted Turner can take that little yachting cap he always wears and shove it right up his porthole . . ."

"Dad—"

". . . I mean, he put Atlanta on the map, sportswise and all, but I mean—"

"Dad, school was fine. It'll be all right."

"It will? That's good. Can't ask for more than 'all right.' "

"Well, I mean it's going to be . . . the same, only bigger. They don't like to let you off the hook too fast, that's all."

"What hook?" he asked, running the rag back and forth across the bar in front of me. I expected to see sparks leap from its varnished surface.

I explained the incident in homeroom, how Miss Armias blamed me for the firing of Mustero, how I got pinned with the snake label.

42

"Weeell, that's bound to happen, Stephen. People like easy targets. Takes the heat off them. You can let them get at you, you can ignore it, or you can prove them wrong."

"Guess I just wanted, you know, to start off fresh, leave all that crap behind me. People laughing at you all the time gets old real fast."

"Sure it does. But look, most of that laughing is from confusion or fear. People don't know how to deal with something, they laugh. You'll see."

"I know, 'They laughed at Edison, they laughed at Marconi—' "

"And at me, your old man. And they still do." Dad shook some crumbs out of the bar rag, folded it in half, and blew his nose. "Most folks look at me and see an educated fool. I pissed away a career in law, sold out my brain for a saloon, *yak yak*. Why do you think all your blue-blood relatives stay on the other side of the Mason-Dixon line? Why does your mother wither every time she passes this place?"

"Well, if you must know, she says . . ." I checked his face for that look of pinched anger.

"Says what?" he urged.

"She says you're afraid of success. She says you feel safe down here in your little bar, away from your family, all the surgeons, and Connecticut Yankee lawyers up north, and old women collecting antiques and dried weeds."

"She say that?" He broke into a huge grin. "That's pretty good, that's damn good, in fact."

"You mean you agree?"

"Sure, why not? Sounds as good as anything else.

43

Why not feel safe if you can? I consider this bar my calling. Who needs any higher mission in life? Excellence in the pursuit of the trivial—there can be no finer purpose." Pinching the tip of his tongue between his lips, he wheezed and squeezed until something of a chuckle escaped like trapped gas.

"If you can spare me, I think I'll go upstairs and make a call." I took my plate around the bar and dropped it in a gray plastic tub and headed toward the office where a set of stairs led up to Dad's apartment.

"If it's your mother, tell her a big *touché* for me. Tell her I owe her one." He had followed me into his office and plopped into a La-Z-Boy, the only piece of furniture he had claimed during the divorce.

"Wrong party. Don't be so paranoid," I told him. "Just someone from school. A girl, if you must know."

"She hot? I bet she's hot. Stephen, you're gonna be all right."

I closed the door behind me and climbed the stairs, letting Dad drool his approval into the Scotchgard finish of his reclining lounger.

# Chapter 10

Dad's apartment dated from the divorce, when he had bought out a printing business upstairs and re-modeled it for a bachelor apartment. That was dur-ing the days of burlap wallpaper and shag rugs thick as Johnson grass and built-in wooden bookcases that held everything but books: stereo, tennis trophies, chambered-nautilus shells, sextants, and porcelain bulls. All very masculine, calculated, I suppose, to wow the impressionable coeds that Dad now enter-tained as an exercise of his newfound freedom. It was not lost on these young acquaintances, either, that my dad bore a striking resemblance to Paul Newman from before his salad dressing days.

Despite all this showroom opulence, Dad's apart-ment still smelled of printer's ink, a sharp, pleasant smell that tickled the throat. Entering his apartment, I ritually sucked in a deep breath of the inky air, and it carried me past his moldering kitchen and the grand high muskiness of the bathroom. My room, the "spare" bedroom, boasted all the appointments that a generous dad considered necessary for the further-ance of my career as a teenage American male child. Cassette recorder, earphones, desktop computer, video recorder and TV, set of weights, exercise unit crouching in the corner like the hind legs of a giant metal cricket, and all sorts of Japanese whatnots with digital readouts. In the midst of this electronic debris stood sturdy bunk beds of Danish walnut, proclaim-ing Dad's faith that at some time I would have a friend over to spend the night. The bottom bunk was a sleep-rumpled nest; the top bunk gathered odd-ments, mostly instruction manuals to all the equip-ment. And a telephone.

I hoisted myself to the top bunk, found *Klecko* in the phone book, and dialed. At the sound of the first ring, I hung up.

I sat on the bed and tried to stare down the phone. It grew, it pulsed, it throbbed, it hummed. An hour passed. I went to the bathroom. I went into Dad's room. I put on his snappy Irish-tweed, kiss-my-ass, country-squire hat. I sat on his bed and dialed Peggy's number.

"Hello?"

At last. "Hello, Peggy, this is Stephen. I was just sitting here after my workout and it suddenly oc-curred to me that you mentioned something about giving you a call tonight. As I recall, you said some-thing to the effect of having some sort of proposition to make, as I recall, and so I thought I'd give you a quick ring before it got any later."

"I'm sorry, but Peggy's not in right now. Can I give her a message? Can I have her call you back?"

"No . . . you shouldn't," I said, and hung up. Then I turned out all the lights, put every blanket Dad owned on my bed, and crawled underneath them still fully dressed. It seemed like forever before sleep would come. Finally, I heard my dad enter the apartment, and I listened as his steps found their way to my room. Another thirty seconds passed before I felt his hand clamp my left ankle where it stuck out over the edge of the bed. He gave it a soft squeeze. "Chilly, old man?" he said. "Just sleep."

# Chapter 11

At lunch next day I sat alone at a corner table in the cafeteria probing the crust of my tuna-noodle casserole. I would be ready if Truelove hit us with our first dissection. But I wouldn't be ready to sit next to Peggy Klecko until I figured a way to salvage my self-esteem. I only hoped that her mother hadn't recorded my call on tape.

The cafeteria was nearly empty. Most kids strolled the quad out back.

The cafeteria walls rippled like an underwater world. The bottom half was painted aqua, the top, sky blue. Brilliant white porpoises in clusters of three leapt in and dove along its length and width.

"Enough to make you seasick, isn't it?" Peggy Klecko asked, placing her tray opposite mine.

"Oh, yeah, hi," I gurgled. There went the suspense of facing her seventh period. "I was trying to figure out the inspiration for the artwork."

"Inspiration might be stretching it," she said. She lifted a solitary bowl of peach slices off her tray and a paper cup of water. "I'm sure it's some art class's beautification project. You remember the black bathrooms at junior high, don't you?" They had been painted black as a class-service project to fight graffiti. Two weeks later the walls had been filled with obscenities scribbled in whiteout.

Peggy gulped the cup of water, then drained the peach syrup into the empty cup and started eating her peaches.

"That's your lunch?" I asked.

"Dancers have to watch their intake," she said. "See that juice? All corn syrup, like glue. It's everywhere."

"Is it?"

"Yeah, it is. Why'd you hang up on my mother last night?" She caught me with a piece of tuna crust lodged in my esophagus.

*"Mmmmmffff,"* I replied. "I didn't hang up exactly. Just didn't have anything else to say. I was gonna see you in class. Where were you, anyhow?"

"Oh, the university had a colloquium on battered wives last night. Mother said you sounded deranged."

"She must be a good judge of character. Is wife battering a big problem in your house?"

"Naw. I'm preparing myself for my role as a woman. Raising my consciousness."

"Oh. I thought it was pretty high already." She gave me a look and swallowed her last peach. "So have you made up your mind about lab yet?"

"Lab? Oh, partners. All right, but don't expect me to do all the work. No screwing off, no snake tricks. Okay?"

"Jeeze, can't we drop the snake bit? All right. Part-

49

ners." I lifted her cup of syrup. "Here's to our partnership in the service of Truelove." I threw back my head and swallowed the sweet liquid.

"You are deranged, honestly." We returned our trays to the slop window, and as we turned back to exit, I could see a glimmer of a smile tugging at the corners of her mouth. Finally, the whole mask crumpled in glee. " 'The service of true love.' God, who will rid me of this fool?"

And together we went out into the quad to spend the rest of the lunch period digesting under the sun.

Together. I hope you got that. A milestone, if you must know.

# Chapter 12

"Here, quick, read this." The Truelove hour was about to begin. Peggy thrust a sheaf of papers, dog-eared and badly soiled, into my lap as I sat at my designated stool behind the lab table. It was Peggy's little "proposition." Truelove had already started droning the class roll, his nose stuck into the class register. I held the papers flat on my lap, below the table edge, and read as Truelove bulled his way through our alphabetical surnames.

CABLE HALL HIGH SCHOOL PETITION FOR STUDENT GOVERNMENT ELECTIONS
We, the undersigned, petition in behalf of Stephen Douglass for the office of president of the sophomore class.
(30 signatures required)

1. Amanda Middour

2. Kirk McClister

3. *Steffi Lopez*

4. *Carlton Van Rossum*

5. *Tiffany Roberson*

6. *Hardy Mueller*

7. *Kari Lynn Davis*

8. *Aaron Sussman*

9. *Andrew DeFriese*

10. *Claudia Owen*

11. *G. Hill Harrison*

12. *Angela Sue Ludlow*

"*Stephen Alexander Douglass.*"

"What?" My name, coming from . . . up front.

"*Are you here among us today, Mr. Douglass?*" My god, it was Truelove!

"Yessir, I am . . . among us, that is."

"In what sense, pray tell, Mr. Douglass?" snarled Mr. Truelove.

"In the common sense, sir," I answered, all sincerity, while dropping the petition between my knees to the floor. They laughed, of course. The whole class jiggled with hilarity.

"And what is the common sense, Mr. Douglass? Please explain," he roared over the laughter.

52

"Sorry, sir, I just meant I was here, that's all."

"No, Mr. Douglass, that's not all. You fancy yourself a clever fellow, don't you, Mr. Douglass?"

"No, not especially, not really."

"Oh yes, I think you do just that." He circled nearer, lowering his voice as he approached.

"Stand up, Mr. Douglass. Let's have a look at you," he whispered. I searched the class for sympathetic faces. Mostly I saw terror.

"Up, Mr. Douglass," he ordered through clenched teeth. I rose. What could he do?

"Now approach the board and face the class." I scraped my stool under the table, pushing the petition underneath as well. I walked to the board and turned. My classmates had dropped their eyes. No one had the heart to watch whatever use Truelove was going to put me to.

"Now, class, today we have our first specimen, our first phenomenon, if you will. As we will learn this year, the scientific method involves the close observation of phenomena, of organisms, of . . . of things. Mr. Douglass falls into some such category, agreed?" No one dared challenge.

"Fine. All experiments, all dissections this year will require of you lab reports—a record of the scientific method. Please record this procedure in your notebooks. Today, entry one. Subject, Mr. Douglass."

The class fluttered with paper noises as twenty-seven notebooks were produced and turned to page one. Truelove unbuttoned his lab coat to reveal a paper-thin yellow shirt. Through it I could see his sleeveless undershirt. His breast pocket held a plastic pouch. He withdrew from it a piece of chalk poised in a metal holder, and then turned to the board. Jabbing in angry strokes, he wrote:

## HYPOTHESIS: STEPHEN DOUGLASS IS A CLEVER FELLOW

"There now," he exhaled gleefully. "We have a hypothesis based on preliminary appearances or behavior. Now, if our purpose is either to prove or disprove this hypothesis, how shall we proceed?"

No one offered a thought. Truelove wasn't inclined to wait. "Fine, children, then I'll tell you. We may dissect, but that doesn't reveal cleverness. We may observe future behaviors, but for now I rather doubt we have the time. We might concoct an experiment to ascertain his cleverness—say, put him through a maze or lock him in a crypt and see if and when he makes it out. Of course, such an experiment would require what we call a control. That is, we would need to lock up other subjects, other rats, or better, other young fellows of, say, quite normal cleverness. Then we could measure by comparison how much more or less clever Mr. Douglass turns out to be. Yes?"

Still no response. The class sat, some with heads bowed studiously into notebooks, others focusing intently on the chalk scrawlings dead ahead.

"Yes," Truelove answered himself. "But for today's purpose, that too would require too much time. Good experiments take planning. But what we can do, the very bedrock of the scientific method, my dears, is gather data, collect observations, and record them. So much of good science is simply observing

54

and noting. Now, what have we observed of Mr. Douglass?"

I pressed my back against the board, hoping it would grow soft and let me ooze through to another dimension.

"How many of you have ever shared a class with Mr. Douglass before? Hands? Don't be shy." Reluctantly, seven, then eight, nine hands floated to ear height. Finally, Peggy's hand rose among them.

"Excellent, let's begin with you." He pointed to Carl Rose, pale as cream cheese, who had shared many a reading group with me in grade school. "Based on your previous encounters with Mr. Douglass, can you recall any incidents in which our subject revealed any particularly memorable moments of cleverness?"

"Well, I don't know . . ." cringed Rose, a reluctant witness.

"Try harder," urged Truelove. "Can you recall a year . . . a class?"

"Well, there was fourth grade."

"Good. What about fourth grade?"

"Well, Stephen won the class spelling bee," Rose recalled correctly. The word was broccoli. "And then . . ."

"Yes? And then what else?" coached Truelove. Rose squirmed as I scoured my memory of fourth grade for incriminating behavior.

"Well, there was the claw. We called it the claw."

*Aaaaaaiiiiiigggghh.* Rose betrayed me at last. It all came back, fresh as pie, my little indiscretion lo those many years ago. Rose described in some detail a science project, a hand in fact, I had constructed of balsa wood, wire, and strapping tape. The thing really worked, every finger flexed, even the marvel of the opposing thumb recreated in loving detail.

"And so comes the night of the science fair, and Douglass is up there getting his blue ribbon for the claw, like, with all the moms and dads and stuff, and of course we all have to tell about what we made. So Douglass has this claw, see, with all these wires hanging loose where the wrist should be, and I guess he wants to show everyone how good the thing works. So he just kind holds the claw up and starts tugging on these wires, and all these balsa fingers kinda twitch around like, until suddenly the whole audience realizes he's, like, flipping us the bird."

"The bird?" Truelove said.

"Yeah, the bird. Like he's giving us the finger, I guess you'd say."

Truelove spun in my direction, brimming with delight. "Really, Mr. Douglass?"

I stood dead still. I could almost feel a nail slide through my feet, pinning me tighter to the floor. I shrugged dumbly.

"Crackerjack," Truelove exploded. Again he jabbed at the board with his chalk:

1. 4th grade spelling bee
2. Claw gestures obscenely

"And what else?" Truelove asked. But he had gotten his pound of flesh. Rose shrugged and shook his head and shriveled studiously into the task of getting

56

his board notes, his betrayal, recorded in his lab note-book.

But now the momentum was with Truelove. Once he had gotten the inquisition started, it became quite easy for my former classmates to offer up a catalogue of minor highlights from my sad career in the halls of learning. Separately, the incidents were no more than small breaches of good taste and classroom propriety. Yet accumulating in Truelove's frenzied chalk scrawl—7, 8, 9—they seemed symptomatic of a pathological screw-off, a social misfit.

So my peers poured forth with a litany of "cleverness" turned most foul. They told about the human heart model I had made in sixth grade molded from cherry Jell-O, with flavor straws for arteries. Everyone had a taste. They told about my cycle of erotic haiku in seventh grade and my report on India in fifth grade, when I had photocopied illustrations from the Kama Sutra and told everyone they were wrestling holds. They told about my nutrition project, when I had fed a box of roaches cafeteria food for two weeks, and half died and the other half escaped in the cloakroom. They told about the time the teacher let us take our math workbook home one weekend before Thanksgiving. I finished the whole thing and spent the rest of fourth grade mastering Chisanbop, the Korean art of calculating on the fingers.

And of course they told about my epic parody *A Separate Pig*, and the ill-fated junior high graduation ceremony, and the decline and fall of Rasmussen and Mustero. And even my threatening to bite Jenny

Chatauqua. By then Truelove was up to number eleven. Only Peggy hadn't testified.

Right then, I wasn't feeling any too clever, just totally numb and wanting to leave. Only seven minutes remained. I had gotten through shock, through humiliation. I could stand there all afternoon and endure the slaughter if it made Truelove feel that he had gained his sadistic little victory. All that remained was hatred, and by now even that was dwindling, replaced by a kind of amazement, awe really, that a grown man, entrusted with the job of teaching fifteen year olds the miracle of life or whatever, could dredge up from somewhere inside himself this poison. Hadn't his own need to be clever turned him into a freak? I glanced upward to the pine shelves along the wall. There sat rows of Truelove's pickled grotesqueries. He belonged up there among them.

"Now you, dear. I believe you had your hand up," Truelove purred, pointing at Peggy.

"I think you've got plenty to prove whatever it is you need to prove," she said, managing to sound quite polite.

"You're quite right, dear," Truelove whooped joyously. "But then again, let's rely on observation for our final proof. For example, the gentleman was sitting next to you, Miss . . . Miss Klecko, is it? Yes. And you are, by all objective measures, a sweet young thing. Yes, quite appealing, a . . . mmm, help me, children—you are a fox, a chick, a hot ticket—you are a prize, Miss Klecko, a trophy of the species."

Peggy shot up from her stool. "And you're a . . . sick, disgusting, filthy, old—"

58

*"Enough,"* Truelove bellowed. "That's between me and my doctor—*now sit down.*"

Peggy collapsed to her seat, smoldering, and packed her books.

"Leave her alone," I said, the words dry and scratchy in my throat.

"Aha! Exactly my point!" Truelove continued. "The young buck claims his doe, the prize, the choice vessel of procreation. And the species continues, stronger and smarter, clever forever."

Truelove surveyed the class, triumphant, his chalk poised once again just inches from the board. "Need we go on, children?" In generous capitals, Truelove wrote:

CONCLUSION: Gloriously CLEVER
MR. DOUGLASS.

And so, precocious even as a specimen, I was honored with an epitaph and twelve degrees of cleverness.

"Remember," Truelove trumpeted, ecstatic in summary, "it's as simple as hypothesis, observation, conclusion. Now go forth and forget."

# Chapter 13

It seemed that only when the bell rang did I dare exhale for the first time. Truelove fled to the back of the room, to his desk, like an animal to its burrow. I slid down and collapsed, still with my back against the wall. My classmates and accusers marched sheepishly past me. Then I was staring into a pair of knees, Peggy's knees. "We'll get the bastard, don't worry," she whispered. "He should burn for this, the sexist sicko."

I just stared at her knees. Her voice seemed so far away. "Stephen, get up," she urged. "Come on, let's go, before he finds you here and . . ."

*"Did you drop a contact lens, Miss Klecko?"* came Truelove's voice from the back of the room.

"I . . . no . . . I thought I saw . . . something," Peggy stammered.

*"I'm sure you did,"* he answered. *"Please close the door when you leave."*

I waved a hand limply toward the door. Peggy spun and tiptoed out. The door clicked shut behind her.

I pushed myself away from the wall and slid, back first, across the floor to the first row of tables—counters really. There, in a space like that underneath a kitchen sink, I folded myself sideways and nestled in among the pipes that drained the lab-sink overflow down through the floor. Bottle brushes, bent and red with rust, clustered beneath my elbow among the crumbling roach pills left from earlier years. Cobwebs and clots of dust dangled from the U joint just above my knees. I could taste the dust, in my throat, my lungs, with every breath.

My legs trembled involuntarily, the knees shaking just beneath my chin. Then I heard it—the squeal of a strange animal, starting as a small point of noise and growing, filling the room with asthmatic glee.

And again the silence. I hunched more tightly under the sink, forgetting the numbness of my legs and breathing in small bursts. I relaxed, my breathing settled into a rhythm, my head once again cleared. Nonsense. I would stand up, walk out the room, make the long walk home, collect myself. I could find Peggy's studio, visit her dance class. She would want to console me. We would talk. I would see someone in the morning about the class, about Truelove. Get out of it. I didn't need honors biology, didn't need the grief.

From where I sat, I now sensed that Truelove was moving slowly around the room. He squealed like a trampled pig with each breath. I squeezed more tightly into my hiding place, bent at every joint, ready to wither and dissolve. Fear filled me, fear and a kind of disgust. I was not afraid of Truelove, not afraid of any harm or pain or strange new dissection

61

he would inflict on my accordioned body. It was more the fear of discovery, that he should know I had been spectator to his strangeness.

A green and mossy stone, moldering and much neglected, had been overturned somewhere at the center of a very dark forest. Something vile and deformed had slithered out, a small blunt head twisting, its red eyes sunken and blind, toward the new light.

Suddenly a chant began, slowed, paused. It was followed by grunts and the noise of some new effort. Metal chair legs scraped the floor followed by more labored breathing. Finally the chant began again, the voice this time coming, it seemed, from midair.

"M.D., M.D., M.D., M.D., M.D., Doctor Truelove, Doctor Truelove, Doctor Truelove, Doctor Truelove, Doctor Truelove . . ."

And then *"Unnnhhhh,"* followed by an explosion, a hollow, liquid "pop" somewhere in front of me. Then "M.D. . . . *Uuunnnhhh,"* and again an explosion above my head. Across from me the chalkboard and the wall darkened with a large wet stain. Fragments of glass, shining wet under the fluorescent light, scattered and settled on the floor in pools of liquid. Again came the "M.D. *Uunnnnhhhhh,"* and *Pokkkkk* exploding off the board. This time, among the wet glass bits, something spun to a stop just inches from my feet. Glistening gray and pink and strangely smooth, it lay on its side, a fetus barely the size of a baby's shoe.

Sheep, or pig, or even human, I don't know. It lay on its side, drawn into the classic fetal curl, mocking my own bent shape beneath the sink. It stared without seeing, accusing and questioning at the same time, with small fleshy bumps, optic buds, where one day eyes would have been. I shuddered and turned away. It too was something never meant to be seen.

The room filled with the pungent stench of formaldehyde. Sharp and sickening, it probed like a finger at my gut. Overwhelmed, I was slow to recognize that the barrage had stopped. I had lost count of the specimens, fetal and otherwise, that had hit the wall during Truelove's tirade. He had laid waste a significant number of his pickled oddities. The thickness of the smell, the stillness of the room . . . had he gone? Was it over? I had lost track, was about to crawl out from my sanctuary when the lights snapped off, and the door opened and then closed with a solid, institutional click. At last!

After sitting tight for another couple of minutes, I scuttled out from beneath the sink and tried to stand. My legs collapsed under me, and I fell to the floor, catching myself with both hands. A fragment of glass slid into the heel of my right palm. I removed the glass and watched as a thin red arc blossomed. With my other hand, I finally pushed myself upright and walked to the door, crunching bits of glass under my feet.

The hall seemed empty, so I slid out the door and headed for the main corridor, down toward the office where green felt letters stapled to a gray corkboard said, "WELCOME BACK, LET'S HAVE A GOOD YEAR."

"Drippin' on my floor, boy" came a voice from behind me. I spun around, maybe too quickly, and

63

saw a janitor, poised like a colossus at parade rest. He stood with legs apart, one hand clasping the handle of his push broom, the other waving, finger pointed, at his side, front to back. "All up down like that," he muttered, nodding at his hand. I squinted at the floor where his finger was pointing. There, sure enough, every three or four feet, a drop of blood drying nearly to black described my path down the hall.

"Sorry, must have cut myself," I apologized, still looking at the floor. I jammed my right hand, now a fist, into my jeans pocket and turned back toward the main entrance. Finally I was out, across the bus loop turnaround, past the rising banks of azaleas and lugustrum, onto Moorhead Road into town. Two miles of walking, and I needed every inch.

# Chapter 14

It was after five when I reached downtown. I went straight to the Mother Won't Know, but it was locked. Dad was out. I could have let myself in with my own key, of course, but right then I wasn't feeling like playing latchkey child in an empty saloon. Instead I strolled the length of Mifflin Street, enjoying its emptiness, imagining it as it would appear in two weeks, swarming with freshmen, coeds trying out their back-to-school looks on the uninitiated. Storefronts would be newly scrubbed, windows filled with Go Hornets T-shirts. The Central Picdmont Bank would roll out its old sandwich board announcing "Hornet Student Complete Banking—Talk to Us First!" Even the Food Lion would unfurl its Hornet-gold "Welcome Y'all" banner and set up card tables completely covered with fluorescent study lamps on the walks. The same lamps each year. "Only $19.95. Visit us for all your student needs."

The shadows of buildings had stretched from one side of the street to the other by now, and the air hung thick and unmoving between, like the stale breath of an animal.

Occasional cars prowled. Windows down, they belched small chunks of FM rock. A pickup rolled by. An elegant Detroit sedan, Turtle waxed and Robo washed, blared like a sound truck.

I needed sanctuary. But not home. Not, that is, above the Mother Won't Know. There was solitude there, but no peace. Only my empty room and the chance to think back through the day's events. And it was thinking that I most needed to get away from. I found my sanctuary in the Campus Twin Cinema. I sat twelve rows back, on the right aisle, "my seat."

The Empire was striking back for the umpteenth time—endless summers of striking back in endless revivals of the old interstellar whizbang. The theme music swelled up its brassy overture, and I slid down, hooking my legs over the seat back in front of me. I was glad for the familiar companionship of this movie. It was safe and comfortable, a celluloid uncle who came to call each year, full of the same old jokes and lunatic charm.

But it was old hat. Where was the moral complexity, where was the emotional subtlety? The human beings were decoration. They wore tunics and capes and nifty leather bandoliers, but they were there just to fly the ships and crack the jokes. They babbled about good and bad, about light and dark forces, about empires and rebel alliances. But they had all chosen sides two episodes ago. The good guys hung on to their swell hair and their buttermilk complexions. The rotten guys wore bureaucratic uniforms or

66

black capes and masks with built-in antiasthma devices that kept them from strangling on their own spit. And then, somewhere, came the unmaskings. The ugly face of evil was always blotted with lumps and boils and pores the size of storm sewers. And small collapsed mouths like turtle beaks. And eyes pink and small and staring blank and wicked. Those same universally wicked fetal optic buds of eyes, hardly eyes at all.

It was all snake oil, far as I could see. Technology and talent and fortunes and reputations, all spent on this technicolor comic book. Why bother? "Excellence in the pursuit of the trivial." That phrase came to mind. My dad's phrase, it had suddenly occurred to me, explaining his life. And mine. "Excellence in the pursuit of the trivial."

# Chapter 15

I let myself into the Mother Won't Know and crossed the empty tavern to Dad's office. I snapped the dead bolt tight once more and climbed the stairs to his apartment. "Home." I went straight to my room and flipped on the light. My bed had been made. The mess on the top bunk was gone, piled on the floor in the corner. A maid? Not likely.

"That you, Wilson?" came a woman's voice.

I stuck my head out into the hall. The bathroom door was shut, water was running. I hadn't noticed.

"Not Wilson. Stephen, son of Wilson. Who are you?"

"Hello, Stephen, son of Wilson. I'm Jamie, friend of Wilson." So Dad was starting early this year, getting a jump on the fraternity boys. Maybe Mother was right, maybe the man had no shame.

"He said to expect you," came the muffled voice. "He'll be back late. Went to the coast. Something about business." The water stopped, the door opened slightly, letting the voice out, clear. "Hope you don't mind my staying over. Wilson said you wouldn't. He said you're a neat kid, and you'd understand."

"Sure, no problem, neat as they come," I answered. "Make yourself comfortable," I added. Then I closed my door and locked it. I had had enough surprises for one day.

In homeroom next day Miss Armias handed me a sheet of pink paper folded once lengthwise and stapled around the edges. I pried the staples apart and read the note. It said, "Memo from Howard Wilfong, Principal, Cable Hall High School." Below that someone had written in green ink, "Report to the office during homeroom." I flashed the note at Miss Armias and excused myself, slinging my Mountain Trail backpack over one shoulder.

"Go right in," said the secretary in the main office. She waved to the door behind her desk. I circled her station and went through the door.

"Close the door behind you, son. Air-conditioning." It felt twenty degrees cooler than the office outside. I shuddered and closed the door. There behind a cluttered desk sat a trim little man with a great pelt of beard, wheaten and graying, and half-moon lawyer's glasses perched, of necessity, at nose's end.

"Have a seat. I think you know some of these folks already." Wilfong had a folder in his hand, my folder it would turn out, and waved it imperially in the direction of his seated guests. Five chairs curling in a semicircle held, in order, the colossus janitor, an elegant woman heavily pearled, my mother, and a thirtyish guy in khakis and running shoes. The last chair was mine. Wilfong pointed at it, and I sat. "Stephen Douglass, this is Thomas Parks, head custodian. Miss Collums, your counselor. You know your mother, of course. And this is Stephen Switzer, city police juvenile officer. Stephen, meet Stephen. Heh heh."

I ignored that and looked at my mom. She grimaced and rearranged her legs, tucking them back underneath her seat.

"Let's begin. Now, Thomas, take a final look. You're sure this is the young man?" Wilfong handed the folder to Thomas, who looked at my ninth-grade mug shot stapled to the outside. Thomas gave him a quick nod, setting in motion a multitude of chins.

"Sure is. Bled on my floor. Drippy droppin' right out of one twenty-one. Truelove's room, like I said." He leaned back, his large brown face turning away in disgust.

"Let's see your hand, Stephen. Which is it?" Wilfong asked.

I had forgotten myself. I held both hands in my lap, palms up. The crescent creased my right palm. I raised it toward Wilfong's face.

"Want to tell us about that cut, Stephen?" said Wilfong.

"Well . . . not much to tell." I suppose Wilfong wanted a confession. Why all this coy business with the cut? "Just a piece of glass. It'll be Okay."

"That's good," continued Wilfong. "But of course you know why we're here, don't you?"

"None of the above," I muttered. Wilfong snapped bolt upright in his seat.

"Again, please, Stephen. Didn't catch that."

70

"Stephen said, 'None of the above,' I think, Mr. Wilfong," my mother volunteered. "Please, Stephen, we haven't got all day."

"Let me try," offered Switzer of the running shoes and the police department. "Stephen, it's called vandalism. The biology lab here was messed up pretty bad. Specimens smashed all over, chalkboard ruined, floor tiles peeling up, books, lots of stuff. Talking maybe thousands. Thomas and his crew here all night."

"Damn straight," shot Thomas, forcing a yawn.

"And the whole school reeks. Or didn't you notice?" added Wilfong. In fact, I hadn't noticed. My nose was shot from the first go-round.

"And all the evidence points to you. Can we call it evidence, Lieutenant Switzer?" asked Wilfong.

Switzer shrugged.

Wilfong continued, "You've got the cut. You're the one Thomas saw coming out of the room yesterday. You have biology seventh period. Don't make us run a blood type on you. We could run a blood type, couldn't we, Lieutenant?"

"I suppose we could," answered the lieutenant.

"Where's Mr. Truclove?" I asked.

"Home. He's taking some days. He was very upset at the news. It might be weeks before his room is ready again. We'll just have to see." Wilfong pushed his glasses up on his nose.

"Blood type! Hold on a minute. If it's a matter of money, we can take care of that. We're perfectly willing to . . . settle this thing, if it's the money, you know." Mom fluttered through her purse seeking . . . what? Credit cards? Traveler's checks?

"It's hard to put a price on class time, on one hundred and twenty students, times one hour per day, times two, maybe three weeks." Wilfong handed the folder back to Miss Collums and continued. "Learning time is a precious commodity, Mrs. Douglass. Can't put a price tag on how much this sets back our tenth-grade science program."

So it was settled. I was clearly the phantom of the lab. Barely three days into the school year, three days into high school, no less, we were solemnly convened to consider *my problem*. And suddenly I couldn't take my eyes off Wilfong's beard. It's funny how beards, especially those big bristly beards like Wilfong's, never seem to move at all, how they just hang stiff as plywood while someone talks. Wilfong's little mouth just kept saying these things about valuable learning time and precious commodity and the beard just hung there, totally immobile while his lips babbled and danced like two eels trapped in a bowl of shredded wheat. I searched his face for seams or rivets. Just above the line of beard above the jaw the skin was florid, pink and pitted with a delicate line of scars. The poor guy was a victim of problem skin.

"Such promise, such promise," Miss Collums was saying. She was sifting through my folder, quoting the usual test scores. She kept bringing her index finger to her lips, moistening her finger, and shuffling to a different page. Her nails were unreal, sculpted long and pointed and painted iridescent to match the pearls around her neck. I was afraid she was going to cut herself.

"It might be appropriate to give Stephen the Waddell-Franklin battery," Miss Collums said, closing my folder. "Can we try that, Mr. Wilfong?"

"What's the Waddell-Franklin, for god's sake?" asked Mom. "He's had them all by now."

"Attitude survey. Find out what are Stephen's inhibitors to learning," explained Wilfong.

"Stephen doesn't have any inhibitors. The only inhibitors are sitting right here." Mom fixed Wilfong with a look, as if to say Take that.

"Gotta be going now," said Thomas, excusing himself. Suddenly the bell rang to announce first period. The school rumbled with distant noise. It was nice not to have to run off to class right away. Wilfong's office was really quite pleasant, in fact, with its walnut paneling, framed certificates of accreditation, and this huge collage of old *McGuffey's Reader* pages up on the wall behind his head.

"Well, the bottom line is that this is a disciplinary matter, first and foremost." Wilfong was getting to the point. "Damage has been done, a student has been identified. It's all pretty straightforward. Everyone wants what's best for the boy. Of course they do. But first and foremost there are guidelines, clear-cut guidelines. This little book," and he pulled a small yellow handbook from his top drawer, "this little book is the student handbook. It was put together three summers ago by a committee of teachers, administrators, and yes, students, I might add. It's an attempt to be fair, to make all parties accountable. Let me quote from page seventeen paragraph two:

73

"Our school is our home of learning. Like our home, our school must be a comfortable and valued environment. Any student who damages, destroys, or defaces our school or school property commits an offense against our home of learning. . . ."

I really liked the part about damages, destroys, or defaces, with all those terrific *D* sounds right together like that. I was thinking of other destructive *D*'s to add to the list—devastates, disintegrates, debilitates, decimates—when Wilfong got to the part about suspension.

". . . usually two or three days in vandalism cases, plus restitution where possible. Of course, we've never seen students involved in a case of this magnitude. I think Stephen in this case should be held accountable to the full extent of the district's code. I'm asking two weeks. Plus damages. Whatever that comes to."

"Then you want to handle this more or less yourself?" asked Switzer.

"No use staining a young boy's reputation. Okay?" Wilfong answered.

"Fine by me," said Switzer. "Of course, I still need to file a report if you handle this through insurance."

"Of course," agreed Wilfong, humanitarian.

"So that's it. Two weeks out and damages. How's that work?" asked Mom.

"Up to the student's ability to pay, of course. Not right away. Given the magnitude, maybe a graduation time frame would give Stephen more of a chance to make a dent in the overall price tag."

Graduation time frame! Three years! Suddenly I was an indentured servant.

"We can help place him in a job after school, if you'd like our help," volunteered Miss Collums.

"No, thanks just the same," said Mom. Then pulling me by the strap of my backpack, she practically lifted me out of my chair and toward the door. "Let's get out of here," she said. "I've heard enough."

# Chapter 16

Twenty minutes later I was unpacking B-complex vitamins at the Whole Body Fitness Center. After the divorce Mom had given up family counseling to ride a swelling tide of flab to fame and fortune. She had started as partner in a new exercise salon and slowly had seen the enterprise bulge to include three spas, a vitamin/health-food emporium, and a deep-muscle-massage therapy center. She had bought out her partner just last year to become sole proprietor and supreme tsarina of the whole shebang.

"Labels out, please," she warned, as I stacked the little bottles row by row on a shelf behind the counter. "And pack up those Formula G grapefruit things before the FDA SWAT team shuts us down."

I suppose I was doing penance, at least to Mom's way of thinking. We had driven back from school in the enchanted blue Volvo. Mom carried on a one-sided dialogue with her dashboard, something to the effect that I was a lost cause as far as high school went. "It's hopeless, utterly hopeless," she told her

76

odometer. "17472," replied her odometer. "When will he ever learn? When, when?" she asked the tachometer. "2700," replied the tach. "What can we do with him? What will ever become of him at this rate?" she asked the temperature gauge. "Cool," replied the gauge.

What the car never wondered, and what I had not had the heart to suggest, was that just maybe none of this was my doing. Not Wilfong, not Switzer, not Collums, not Thomas the colossus, and not even my own dear mother, none of them even for an instant doubted my capacity for doing the foul deed. To the others, it was probably a matter of evidence, an airtight case, and all their Charlie Chan mentality couldn't let them see otherwise.

For Mom it was probably just more evidence of the declining curve my life had traced ever since those first few weeks of kindergarten. By now she had probably developed a certain immunity to shock or disappointment when it came to my checkered career. Apparently, in her scheme of dwindling expectations, anything was possible.

But still. Destroying a classroom. Was that part of the old Stephen A. Douglass smartass syndrome? Wouldn't that take a deeper, darker urge, a deliberate streak of out-and-out malice? Maybe that was a part of me as well.

But nobody even wondered why. That was the worst. Here I was taking the blame and enjoying the luxury of an extended vacation from school with a perfectly clear conscience. And it had never occurred to anyone to ask why I had done what they all assumed I had done. I mean, I had motives. Just ask seventh period, they'll give motives to spare. Revenge. Pride. Humiliation. Madness. But that never entered into the discussion. There was complete justification for what I had done, come to think of it. For what they thought I had done, I should say. They owed me one. So maybe I could take the blame—and the credit. Laugh at the snake boy all you want, but don't dare to call him wimp. There is danger in his blood. Don't tread on me.

"Want these here?" I asked, placing the box on the counter, beside where Mom was totaling up yesterday's receipts. I had taken all the Formula G Weight Control Tablets off the shelves and put them in the empty B-complex boxes.

"On the floor for now," she said. "Have you got a thing for beards, by the way?"

"What thing for beards? Who said I did?"

"That Wilfong guy. They were giving you the old one-two, and all you could do was sit looking at this guy's beard. I really wonder about you, Stephen. Where's your head sometimes? Sometimes I don't think you're all there."

"I might not be all here, but I'm usually all somewhere. I just got interested in his beard. It seemed, I don't know, out of place, like it had been transplanted there or something."

"A man with a beard is making a statement about himself, that's all." Mom could never shed the psychoanalytical approach. It amazed me that she had such a paltry understanding of me. Or maybe it had never occurred to her to bother.

78

"I think Wilfong's statement is simple, if you ask me. He doesn't want anyone to see his gross complexion."

"There, see, the old smart mouth just won't quit." She spun around and gave me the index finger to the sternum. "See, the problem with you, Stephen, is that you think you know more about people than you really do. You seem to think that anyone over seventeen is engaged in a career of masquerade and high deceit. That people skulk around in beards and raincoats as if they're hiding something, as if they're conspiring against you personally."

"Well, as a matter of fact . . ."

"Don't talk facts to me. Just listen for once, Mr. Wizard. Maybe you'll learn something." She pounded the top of the vitamin box. The bottles of Formula G rattled like rocks in a lunch pail. The something I was supposed to be learning I had heard before. Mom said that she was a sixties person. She was the first girl at Barnard to burn a draft card. And on television. On the national news. Trust no one over thirty, she had believed. She had kept a vigil the night Bobby Seale was jailed. He was a panther, she said. Something about the barricades at Columbia. I was losing her thread. She was losing her thread.

"Listen to me. We all grew up, is the point. We learned to compromise, however much it hurts. We got jobs, took on responsibilities, had children. It happened to us. But—are you listening? because this is a key point—we all knew that we stood for something. We came out of a context. We had a social-moral-political context. You have nothing. You have no context. You're drifting. Aimless. You can't just float, Stephen. You need a context, for god's sake. Get yourself a context."

I promised her I would get myself a context as soon as possible. Then she started talking spiritual values. Fortunately, I was saved by Rolf.

"Rolf, so early. Rolf, you know Stephen, don't you?" Mom chirped an introduction, bouncing on the balls of her feet and throwing back her shoulders into a comely military brace.

"Yes, we know Stephen, don't we, Stephen?" Rolf had a curiously awkward sense of pronoun usage for someone who had lived in America for over ten years. He had come from Germany to study physical therapy. Like a well-bred Doberman pinscher, Rolf was a study in lean, Teutonic sinew—long of limb, full in the trunk, sharp and feral around the nose and ears. He favored electric-blue running shorts, the kind with the racy little vents up the side, and end-less permutations of those fishnet tank tops that look sort of corny on most guys.

"How about we run some? Stephen can open up today, yes?" The mall would open at ten thirty, but the fitness business was pretty slow until after lunch.

"Oh, Rolf, you're unquenchable." Mom giggled. "Maybe just a short one. We have to be ready for the show by one." A "short one" meant from the mall to downtown, across campus, and back out Mifflin Street to the mall again. Maybe four miles. Mom always considered a run with Rolf as business and pleasure. They always ran through town because Rolf had the sort of body, with a strange European tan, butterscotch, the color of his hair, that even men stopped to appreciate. The business part was advertising. Mom was the prime artificer of what had come to be known around town as "the spa body," and her little public runs served as inspiration and inducement to all the fitness delinquents intent on giving it one last shot.

And then there was her show, *SpaTalk*, fifteen minutes on local AM, chock-full of fitness and beauty, holistic health, and fine-tuning the bod. Each show included a special community guest who received a free treatment from Mr. Massage. That was Rolf. Mom got the massage in the first segment. "Live on tape," she panted and moaned and cooed over the airwaves as Rolf talked her through the major muscle groups.

"Here's money for the register," said Mom, coming from the back of the shop. She was wearing an all-pink running ensemble, and she held a pouch of change for the cash register.

"Don't take any wooden nickels, eh?" Rolf said. That German wit was hilarious stuff. He pinched me on the back of the neck, then leaned against the wall, pushing with first one leg, then the other. Mom joined him. Then, their flexing done, they bounded out the door. "Have a nice run," I called after them, but I don't think they heard me.

At ten thirty I took the lock off the door. I put money in the change tray and turned the store's stereo to 96.5, Morning Masterworks. They were doing a special program on the sons of Bach. Bach was prolific. All his sons were composers. They had applied themselves. They had a context. I wished I had been a son of Bach's. I liked all that *tumpty-tum* harpsichord stuff. I could really go for Baroque.

It was after noon when Mom woke me. I had fallen asleep on the floor behind the counter. Mom, now fully dressed in a formal sweat suit, was checking the cash tray in the register.

"Well, thank god they didn't clean us out."

"Who didn't clean us out?" I asked.

"Anyone who wanted to, that's who. You're about as responsible as a . . . a . . ." But Mom couldn't think of anything irresponsible enough to finish her sentence with.

"Pretty slow around here. What'd you do with Rolf?"

"Rolf's lubricating the Nautilus machines at Spa Two. He's meeting me at the station for our show. Wanna come? See a taping?"

I really didn't want to, not with Rolf around. So I said I'd watch the store.

"Well, watch it from a distance because Donna's coming in at twelve thirty, and I don't want her to think she has to baby-sit for you."

# Chapter 17

I hung around the Whole Body shop just a little while after Donna showed, maybe half an hour late. Then I left and just cruised the mall, messed with mechanical Robotronics in Radio Shack until a uniformed security guard came by and asked why I wasn't in school. I mumbled something about going away to a private academy and excused myself. They had been cracking down on teenage gangs loitering at the mall that summer, she explained. I wasn't a teenage gang, I replied.

So I left the mall and headed back up the endless stretch of University Avenue toward town. Condominium developments had been sprouting the length of University for most of the summer, spilling orange clay onto the sidewalks and uprooting the rows of crape myrtles that would have been blooming by now. I stopped at one point where a huge rectangle had been gouged to watch as workmen poured the concrete footings. Down in the orange rectangle, two workers in hard hats ran in tight circles, shaking bright silver cans and laughing, spraying each other with beer.

Farther up University Avenue I passed the small white bungalows that line the steep grade of the road as it climbs finally into Cable Hall.

A yard sale offered three rows of detergent boxes overflowing with good junk. A Clorox box was filled with lacrosse balls, knee pads, and a catcher's mask.

"Good mask," said a guy dressed only in shorts. He was as tan as the Clorox box. "Old style, real metal, none of that high-stress molded plastic. My old man took that mask to the regionals in Charlotte."

It was a fine old catcher's mask. The leather over the padding was pale and cracked, but you had to admit it was a good old mask. Of course, I didn't play baseball, and if I had I wouldn't have been a catcher anyhow.

"Try it on," the guy said, so I did. "Perfect," he said. This guy was desperate for a sale.

"I'll take the mask," I told him.

"You like girls?" he asked. He pulled me to another box full of "men's" magazines. "Mint condition." I slipped the mask over my face and told him no thanks. "How much you want for it?" I asked.

"Hey, no charge. Enjoy it." He gave me a big grin. He had a mustache. Guys with mustaches were making a statement, too, I supposed.

I left the guy to his yard sale and walked the last couple hundred yards up University Avenue to town. I turned right at the post office on the corner of Mifflin and looked along the main drag through the barred quadrants of my mask. Upper right: lampposts, treetops, sky. Lower right: Campus Twin marquee, storefronts, sidewalks, parking meters, brick tops of buildings, and so on. Neat, manageable, precise as a bombardier's grid.

"Looking for a pop-up, sonny?" I practically knocked the old man down. I decided to keep my sights through the lower quadrants. Finally, the Mother Won't Know loomed in my lower right. I pushed open the big plank door and went in.

As my eyes adjusted to the darkness, I heard a chorus of voices swelling up from the back. A bunch of people back there were singing "Hail to the Chief" and clinking spoons on the bartop in perfect time. Actually they weren't singing "Hail to the Chief" as much as they were humming it, since "Hail to the Chief" doesn't have any words. I made a mental note of that. I would write some lyrics and send them to the president.

I flipped the catcher's mask on top of my head and walked along the bar. There sat Peggy Klecko, Nu Tran Banh, Dad, and a lady, mid-twenties, in an oversized, zebra-emblazoned pajama top.

"Hail, chief, how's it going?" Dad yanked the mask off my head and tried it on. "This is to keep the mosquitoes away or something?" He filled a mug with iced tea from beneath the bar and plunked it down in front of me. "Here, sport, wet your whistle, then tell us all about it."

I told them the short version. Peggy had already done the lab replay and the Stephen humiliation passion play. They seemed to know most of the details about my morning conference, too.

"Bad news travels fast," said Nu Tran.

"Not bad, Banh, good," said Peggy. "Look at this!" She whipped the same much-crinkled petition onto the bar in front of us, the same petition I had last seen playing across my shoe tops twenty-four hours before when Truelove had called me to the board. But stapled to that sheet were four more filled with signatures. "You're a lead-pipe cinch, a shoo-in, a sure thing. It's destiny," Peggy announced.

"Looks like you've trashed your way to the top. From what Peggy tells me, the guy had it coming." Dad drained the rest of his mug and refilled it. He stood, trying to drink through the bars in the mask. "Wish I'd known, is all. Shoulda been there for this morning's go-round. First one I ever missed. Did your mom hold her own?"

"She was a force," I said.

"Good woman, your mom," he said. "Don't worry about the suspension. We'll have that overturned in days. I've got a buddy with the ACLU who's looking at your case. No due process. We'll burn their ass."

"I don't want to burn anything, Dad. Can't we just let it slide, like?" I looked at the whole bunch of them. They glowed back at me, seeing me as some budding boy icon, watching me for some divine sign, basking in my aura.

"Stephen, you're the giant killer, don't you see?" Peggy tried to explain. "Everyone hates his guts. It's no secret. It's just that you're the first guy to ever, well, fight back. God knows, he drove you to it. Look at this," she said, flipping through the pages of her petition. "This whole page is our seventh-period

86

class. Even Carl Rose, that creep." She pointed to his penciled scrawl at the bottom of the sheet.

"So, big deal," I said. "Sooner or later, someone would have done it. It just happened to be me." There. Let's play this thing out. If I was destined to be the Silly Putty of the gods, then I might as well play it with style. Peggy Klecko needed heroes, and I needed Peggy Klecko.

"So the class presidency is yours for the taking. At first you were a long shot, a black sheep."

"Dark horse, you mean," I said.

"Sure, a dark-horse candidate. I couldn't see someone like Roy 'Mr. Wonderful' Bedoya getting everything like usual, him and all those prissy little . . ."

"It's a chance to turn things around," said Dad. "Use this to your advantage. Seize the moment. Who knows, you might surprise a few people, maybe even yourself."

"It's just a big joke, all that class officer stuff. No one takes that seriously except the jerks that run for those things," I said.

"Don't be so negative. Remember, you're a Douglass. That counts for something—or it used to." Dad pushed a stool in my direction. I pulled it to the end of the bar and sat looking back at my brain trust.

Peggy slid down beside me. "We've got a little media campaign all planned. Can't fail. Show him, Banh."

Nu Tran pulled a scroll of paper out of his lap and unrolled it across the bar in front of everyone. It was a takeoff on the old Save the Whales routine. In the same lettering, it said "Save the Snake," and underneath that legend was a giant viper—coiled, fangs bared, and ready to strike. It was really pretty good.

"Swell," I said, caving in. "What do we do with it? Posters and all that?"

"Kid stuff," said Peggy. "Tell him, Mr. D."

"Same as that," Dad said, pointing to the wall-length mirror behind us. "Doing them in Mother's greens and blues." Hanging from the mirror were the famous Mother Won't Know T-shirts, with the bar's name across the top and a matronly figure bound and gagged in a rocking chair. "The people over at Sunshine silkscreen are doing four hundred with Banh's design. And more if needed. Courtesy of yours truly."

"No kidding, you guys are amazing," I told them all. "But why not sell them. I could use the money. They're making me pay for the lab." I explained the terms of my punishment, and they agreed to give it a try.

"We'll call it the Stephen A. Douglass Defense Fund. Anyone who's ever had to put up with True-love for biology is bound to buy one," Peggy said. Nu Tran agreed strenuously.

So we sat drinking tea and beer and planning the campaign. I explained about being sort of a lame-duck candidate, since I couldn't even show my face in school until after the election: Voting was to take place in homeroom on Friday.

Not to worry, said Peggy, assuring us that she had plenty of campaign workers lined up, and the halls would be covered with our posters. Come Monday, our T-shirts would be the uniform of choice. It sounded simple, until I reminded her that I wouldn't be in school next Thursday either, when all the candidates gave their speeches at a morning assembly.

"Shit," she exploded, then quickly added, "Sorry, Mr. Douglass."

"I'll give your speech," she suggested. "Write me one if you want. Campaign by proxy. It'll just remind them, that much more, of your suspension. Like you're on a hunger fast in a Belfast jail or something. We can work on that angle."

"Really, Peggy," I said, "maybe it would be easier just to run yourself. What's so great about me?"

"You're a *cause célèbre*, that's what. I can get you a special pass for next Thursday. Just show up, give your speech, leave. Sort of like a parole. They can't stifle your First Amendment rights, can they?" She pounded the bar with her fist, and everyone rose to huzzah. Then she left with Nu Tran to "attend to details," as she chose to call it.

"There's the old fight, the Highlands pluck," roared Dad, his voice thick with perhaps one too many beers.

So take that. From such humble beginnings do spring the political impulses that topple governments, that shake the monuments of empire to their very foundations, that loose the hounds of revolution on the smug and lounging patricians, the Roy Bedoyas of this world. Or something.

Anyhow, I had become their best hope. Dad must have seen in my campaign the chance for personal redemption and family ambition. Let the word go forth that the Douglass blood runs strong; that although it might have taken a generational hiatus in the service of innkeeping and philandering, the Douglass banner will once again fly high; that generations of Douglass magistrates and Connecticut blue bloods have not died in vain. Hallelujah, we are back.

For Peggy, radical of the ballet, I was a surrogate champion of counterrevolution, a teenage Trotsky in the rough. Or maybe I was just a pathological mess of a lab partner, a chronic cosmic goof, and she had singled me out for reconstruction.

For Mom, who knows? Maybe I had only become a nuisance, a hanger-on, a slight embarrassment at most. She was preoccupied with her business, her Rolf, her muscle tone. She never simply lived, as much as she fine-tuned her lifestyle. And nothing in her subscription to *New Woman* magazine quite explained my place in the bigger scheme of what they called the "Total Woman's Gestalt." Still, she wanted me to get a context, and here was a context, after all.

# Chapter 18

"That Vietnamese kid does nice work," Dad said. He walked the length of the bar until he found a felt-tip marker stashed underneath in an old marmalade jar. Then, returning to the drawing, he wrote: "T-shirts coming soon. All sizes, $10."

"There, that should help the defense fund. We'll see how it goes." He returned the marker to its jar and refilled his mug from the tap midway along the mirrored wall.

"So you and Jamie have already met, sport?" He winked in the direction of the girl, or woman, Jamie. She smiled back, gently, warmly. She had still not uttered the first word.

"Well, sort of. We kinda talked through the bathroom door last night. That's about it." I turned toward Jamie and nodded. "Hello, Jamie, pleased to meet you." It was sort of hard to take seriously someone who thought p.j. tops were high fashion.

"Good to meet you again, Stephen. Sorry it had to be through a bathroom door, as you say." She had a great voice, raspy but not rough, just deep and with an edge to it, especially now that I was hearing her talk for the first time without the water running.

"Jamie really wants to get to know you better," Dad said, again with the wink. "You might say she has a vested interest in your future." Oh god, here it comes, I thought. They're going to get married. It had all the earmarks of the future stepson-stepmother setup. Spare me.

But no, not quite. Jamie was just an old employee of Dad's, three, four years ago in her undergrad days. Now she was back at the university in grad school— education. Writing her thesis. On "Patterns of Giftedness in the Male Student." I could see the handwriting on the wall. It said "guinea pig" one more time.

"Gee, that sounds familiar," I said.

Jamie laughed, a deep hollow chuckle, really, uncoiling in her throat. "Your dad says as much. Says you've been scrutinized and analyzed three ways from Sunday."

"And it all comes to nothing much," chimed in my dad. "Mostly it's a kind of absolution for the schools. They give him a test or sit him down with a psychologist for an hour. Then they churn out another one of those 'profile' things. Zap, right into the folder it goes, and they've done their little bit for humanity. And of course, nothing ever comes of it. Just into the folder and wait 'til next year, and on and on."

"What are they supposed to do, anyways, Dad?" I asked. "They can't plant electrodes in my brain."

"Stephen's right, of course, Wilson," Jamie offered in my defense. "That's where my study comes in. Some kids just don't fit comfortably in the usual school environment. It's nobody's fault. That's why my research is going after attitudes."

Jamie described a project she was working on with the university. Sounded like they had rounded up all the misfits in the state and brought them to Cable Hall in a laboratory school. And the clincher was that I was to be her homegrown specimen, assuming, of course, that I fit her "profile," that word again. So I told her sure, maybe, okay, and other such noncommittal stuff. She seemed pleased and said she'd schedule an admissions interview for the next week. Dad seemed pleased, too. And I was pleased that they were so easy to please.

"And now for the annual anointing of the bar," Dad boomed, disappearing into his office and returning with a gallon paint can in each hand. It was time to polyurethane the bar, the last ritual of preparation prior to the return of the beer-swilling undergrads. Dad handed out brushes and pried the lid off one can. We spread the thick gluey substance up and down the length of the bar, careful that our brushstrokes overlapped nicely. The bar, great planks of oak initialed and etched by the first clients at the Mother Won't Know, was the central artifact and drawing card of my father's establishment. By renewing its clear hard finish each year, Dad felt he was somehow enshrining and preserving the impulse that led to the bar's creation. "Returning to my roots," he liked to say, only half joking.

By now the wood seemed suspended beneath thickly transparent layers of the hard finish, forever unreachable but still right in front of your nose. "Peace and Love" said one carved legend on the bar. "Power to the People" said another. "Hornet Heaven" and "Wilson Douglass is a beerhead" were scrawled side by side, and so on. It was sort of like the Rosetta stone.

Dad and Jamie asked me to join them for pizza out, but I declined their invitation and sat in the darkened bar watching the polyurethane dry. When that got old, I went up to my room and sat at the computer. I decided to do my "Hail to the Chief" lyrics. My best version came out like this:

No kings or princes, no barricades or fences
Can stop up the voices of people speaking free.
No tyrants claim us, no nations rich or famous,
None could e'er blame us for singing *"Liberty."*
So lift up your voices and now proclaim your
    choice is
One from among us, one of the free.
And all hail the chief, yes, and hold to the belief
That one among many stands for you and me.

Well, it might be a bit short on ramparts and rockets' red glare, but this was the twentieth century, more or less, and you sorta had to make do with what you had. So I printed that out and addressed it to 1600 Pennsylvania Avenue and all, and enclosed a little handwritten note about how I thought it might be nice to have some lyrics in case anyone ever wanted to sing the darn thing, since it seemed to put so much wear and tear on military buglers all the time.

Two days later I packed up my clothes and my computer and moved back to Newgate Estates for September with Mom. Newgate Estates was one of those upscale developments where they measure your status by the density of trees and the length of your driveway. It also helped, this being the South, if you had lots of columns along your exterior facade, even if the trees made them barely visible. The Newgate name was an attempt at a vaguely British sense of elegance by a developer who probably didn't know that for Londoners, at least, Newgate meant prison.

Still, it was home. I was raised there and had watched our family home go through many incarnations.

## A SONG FOR MY HOME
I was four when the pool was built.
Five when the deck went up.
Six when the Tiki lamps circled the patio.
At seven, two atriums swelling like blisters beside
   the Greek dining room: one his, one hers.
At eight came the tennis court.
At nine it was waterproofed, enclosed for the
   winter months, safe from the cold.
By ten we were gardeners, abusing the rototill,
   feeding our compost pile eggshells and fat.
Eleven meant hot tubs, saunas, and steam rooms,
   and guests for the weekend dressed only in towels.

Here my song fades, for during my twelfth year the house itself became the central object and bone of contention in the property-settlement phase of the divorce. I had already been parceled out simply enough, one month at a time, but then I was transportable, and the house was not. So Mom got the house, and Dad got reduced child-support payments, and I got a set of Samsonite with retractable wheels.

After that the house came more and more to mirror the changing lifestyle of my mother. Mirror, literally, because in two weeks a crew had denuded my dad's basement billiard room and lined the walls and ceiling with mirrors, so that Mom could have her dream exercise studio. And she mirrored two walls of her bedroom as well, a sinister turn of events that roughly coincided with her hiring of Rolf as resident spa masseur.

Dad's study became an office as her business grew, and the kitchen became a museum for the cutting edge of Western appliance knowhow. Only my room remained intact, untouched and untouchable, a sacred shrine to Mom's idea of what my childhood had been. Even my great stuffed Babar was not to be removed under penalty of death. I think she refused, still refuses, to acknowledge that I have ever lapsed into any chronological age that can be described by more than one digit.

Most of the time the house was pretty empty, as were most of the houses out there. People who could afford homes in Newgate rarely got to enjoy them. They were usually out accumulating the money it took just to live there. In Mom's case that meant classes, workshops, fitness and nutrition forums, and close personal supervision of her body shop. All that, plus a frantic neo-single lifestyle of hopping from gallery to tennis to melon bar to skiing weekends, left the place pretty much to me.

For most of the following week, I worked on my campaign speech. I was torn between the usual teen-age political oratory and a stirring call to action. Nothing seemed quite right.

By Tuesday the first run of T-shirts had arrived from the silkscreen place. Dad gave me a call and I went down to the Mother for a preview. Peggy and Nu Tran joined us for a campaign fashion show. The shirts were every bit as spectacular as we had hoped, green or blue with black or white graphics, Nu Tran's huge serpent writhing in 100-percent cotton as we moved. Dad tacked two above his sign on the mirror, and we divided up the rest, a few to sell in the Mother, the others for a precampaign blitz at school. Peggy reminded me to get there first thing Thursday morning, as the election assembly was to be held right after homeroom. I would be there, I promised, with my Save the Snake T-shirt waving on high.

# Chapter 19

Peggy obviously took that comment to heart, for when my bus pulled up in the turnaround come Thursday morning, the first sight to strike me was a small circle of students clustered at the base of the school's flagpole. They were standing, heads cocked toward the pole's very tip, gaping in wonder at the blue and green truncated pennants—two of our T-shirts—hanging limply just beneath Old Glory. I could see instantly that my campaign suffered from a lack of staff discipline.

Nu Tran grabbed me as I walked through the front door. He shoved a piece of yellow paper into my hand. It was a visitor's pass, identifying me as Peter Klecko, visiting from Detroit to attend classes with my cousin, Peggy. It bore the rubber-stamped signature of Howard Wilfong.

"This is no good," I told Nu Tran. "Where's Peggy?"

"Peggy's in the auditorium. She said not to be sweating it. We'll go there now."

I followed Nu Tran through the main corridor, out the back door by the cafeteria, and across a covered walkway to the auditorium. We walked half its perimeter until Nu Tran found a side door marked "Emergency Exit." He knocked sharply, three short bursts, and the door swung open. Two kids with red hair and matching braces let us in. It turned out they were brother and sister. The Maple twins, the Dreaded Redheads. They looked as if they had just stepped out of a SpaghettiO's commercial, but actually they had been dealing drugs since the seventh grade. The boy, Andy, wore a green snake T-shirt; Angie wore the blue.

"Give 'em hell," Andy roared, slapping me on the back.

He pulled the door closed and resumed his watch. Nervous political hopefuls paced in random bunches, mumbling phrases to themselves and fretting over note cards palmed furtively in their hands. We dodged them all and climbed a short flight of steps to another door. Nu Tran repeated his three-part knock and again a door opened to us, this one leading onto the backstage area. "Ah, good," said Peggy, peeking at us from behind the opened door. "You're here."

The backstage area seemed a vast secret jungle illuminated only by the naked bulb of a work light overhead. Black metal poles fixed with spots and klieg lights perching like buzzards crossed the ceiling. Ropes thick as vines hung from the ceiling. Others were festooned from the superstructure or fastened tightly to stanchions set along the walls.

Tangles of cable nested on the floor, twining and knotting their sleek skins, orange and black, while yellow wires, thin and flat as tapeworms, slithered against the back wall. Peggy led us over the knotted cables to a tall, narrow room opening off the farthest corner.

"We'll stay here until it starts," she announced. "Homeroom will be over in fifteen minutes."

"Why here?" I asked. "Are we hiding or something?"

"Of course not," Peggy muttered unconvincingly. "Just concentrate on your speech. What are you going to say?"

"No idea," I told her. "I tried writing something about twenty different times, but nothing really grabbed me."

"Stephen, you're hopeless," she told me. I had heard that before. She pulled me to the floor, and we sat leaning against a stack of flats, sets from old school plays, painted to resemble castle walls. Or maybe dungeons, I thought, imagining the weight of iron manacles tugging at my wrists and ankles. "Tell them why you're running. Be honest." She took my arm in both hands, massaging it almost. I suppose she was trying to loosen up my instincts for honesty. "You must have some reason for wanting to be class president."

"Not really," I said. "You're the one with the reasons. Remember? It was your petition, your campaign. My only reason is you."

"I'm your reason? I can't be a reason. Don't be idiotic."

"Sure you are. If I have a reason, you're it. Even from back last year, with that Rasmussen disaster, you were the only bright spot. Maybe it was your dumb buttons," I said, looking at the front of her Save the Snake T-shirt. She had only one button. It said: "This Space Available." I gave it a tweak, and she dropped her head as if to look at the button herself. Embarrassed, she held it there a count too long before defiantly bringing it back up with a snap of the neck. "And that thing you do with your hair, like you just did, how it all lands over one shoulder or the other. That absolutely wipes me out. Like that." And I popped my neck in imitation.

Peggy blushed. I was getting to her. "Really. Wipes me out. And those leg warmer things. And battered-wives workshops. And how you noticed the porpoises on the cafeteria walls at the same time I did. And I don't find you the least bit unattractive, if you really must know." She dropped her head again, this time with the corners of her mouth pinched into the commas of a reluctant smile.

"And so," I said by way of conclusion, "*that* is how *you* are my reason for running. Shall I tell them that?" Her hands went limp on my arm. I grabbed her right wrist as though feeling for a pulse. "Plus of course all the other usual reasons one runs, like power, prestige, posterity, sex . . ."

Suddenly her hands clamped my arm with a vengeance. She dug her nails into my flesh. "That's disgusting, you're disgusting," she shrieked, pulling at my arm until I practically had to roll over on top of her. We were nose to nose. "You disgust me," she whispered. "You really are a snake." Then she closed her eyes and her face became a lovely silken mask, until at last I caught on. I angled down to meet that mask and felt it move against my lips.

Elections, suspensions, biology teachers, and counselor profiles all went poof. Suddenly the cluttered floor of the backstage prop room had become a white hard beach on a small island in, say, the Lesser Antilles.

# Chapter 20

"Imagine that," said Peggy finally. "I was beginning to worry that you didn't like girls."

"Too much bother," I said. "Only somehow I figured you were . . ."

"Different. You bet I'm different. Nice of you to notice." From a distance we heard the drone of the bell signaling the end of homeroom. Doors opened and closed somewhere, metal chairs scraped the wooden stage, squealing underwater voices echoed in the auditorium.

"Let's go," said Peggy, once again the intense campaign manager. We stood and dusted each other off, then peered out the doorway. We crossed the maze of wires to downstage and followed a velvet curtain to the edge of stage left. We peered from behind the curtain onto the apron of the stage where the candidates were now gathering themselves by grade levels. Predictably, Roy Bedoya stood composed at the center of the sophomore contingent, a rolled cylinder of yellow legal papers clutched in one hand, his shoes polished to lustrous black to match his brilliant hair. He was practicing being gracious, accepting everyone's best wishes with a "Who me?" shrug of the shoulders and an "Aw shucks" bob of the head.

"You'd better get out there," Peggy warned with a nudge to my tailbone. "And make it good. We'll be ready for you out front."

A knot of latecomers swelled onto the stage just beyond the curtain. I took the opportunity to fall in among them and found my way to a row of chairs filling with the sophomore hopefuls. Roy was leading a group in single file from the far side. I vaulted one row and came at Roy from the blind side, taking the end chair he seemed intent on having for himself. Finally he turned around and caught himself before falling fully into my lap.

"Oh, Douglass old man, it's you," he stammered. He turned back to his following. "We're uh, one short here. Try back here, Stace." He pointed Stace to the row behind us, and she fell from the ranks and, looking abused, settled for back row center.

"Say, Douglass, this is quite a campaign you're putting on." Roy crossed his legs and started buffing the toe of a loafer with the sleeve of his jacket. "This snake thing is brilliantly conceived, although the Truelove part is a bit dodgy. Still, best of luck." He thrust a hand at my solar plexus, and I took it, let him shake it, actually. He was one of those guys who thought a real vise-like handshake grip was a sign of masculine well-being or something.

But what did he mean about the "Truelove part"?

104

We sat onstage like children waiting to be fitted for new shoes at Thom McAn's, stupidly upright and proper, worrying perhaps that our socks might smell. Below us, the rising bank of velvet seats was filling with students. They jostled down the aisles and collapsed bonelessly at random points. They didn't seem especially intent on finding leadership. Entertainment more likely.

From behind us a rather official-sounding contralto voice begged attention and started reading off candidates' names. The woman, over six feet tall and bristling in a tweed suit, strolled along our rows, checking off names as she called them. When she had exhausted the names of the sophomores, I realized that mine had been skipped. While I momentarily pondered the significance of the oversight, Roy Bedoya pointed me out to the woman and announced my candidacy. I would have voted for Roy myself right then. He was such a straight-arrow.

The woman mumbled to herself. "Douglass, Douglass, Douglass, . . . ah, right here. Sorry, Stephen, you were crossed off for some reason. Very well, you'll follow Roy. Thank you, Roy." Roy nodded to the woman and patted me on the knee.

Finally the woman approached the microphone, *zweet zweet zweet,* her stockings contending with her tweed skirt, static electrical charges building perilously between her thighs. She stood ramrod straight at the podium and stared the entire student body into submission. After a squeal of feedback, she announced herself as Ms. Wilberforce, assistant principal for student affairs. She welcomed us back to the

105

best high school in the Carolinas, welcomed the best-looking sophomore class she had ever seen, and thanked us all for the best start-up of a school year she had ever been part of. Consider yourselves fortunate, she told us, that we had fielded probably the best group of candidates ever to run for student office, and with hard work and a whole lot of pulling together, we could make this the best year ever at Cable Hall High School.

Bloodied by Wilberforce's salvo of superlatives, the audience sat basking in the afterglow and oozing from every seat with self-congratulation. After letting that mood ripen, Ms. Wilberforce goosed herself up an octave and proceeded to what she called "the business at hand, namely, the political process." We would progress office by office, from secretary to president, one class at a time, starting with the sophomores. At last, "without further ado," as she put it, having already exhausted all the ado she could muster, she presented the first candidate, Jayne Ellen Albritton, and so began the battle of the secretaries.

Jayne Ellen testified to a cumbersome sense of responsibility and was followed by two perky contestants who shared a fondness for altruism and robustness: candy striping, gymnastics, day-care volunteering, diving, tutoring, riding, church work, volleyball. A close race. Next up were the candidates for treasurer, all male this time, all members of the Future Bankers Club. They had little to say, the tradition of treasurer oratory being well-nigh negligible.

Julie Faraday, running for vice president, reminded us that the gym was named after her grandfather, the man who put three wrestling cups in the school trophy case before disappearing over Burma during World War II. Her opponent was a guy who had just transferred from Wheaton, Illinois. He mostly told us how great Wheaton was and about how he was running just to make some new friends at our school.

Finally, it was Roy's turn. Roy was very good. You could just see him at home before the mirror practicing his moves. The head swivels left, the right hand stabs the air; head swivels right, left hand stabs the air; head forward, voice solemn, both hands clench the podium; rise on balls of feet and bounce to the closing cadences. It was so good. But I couldn't recall what he had said.

Ms. Wilberforce glided to the microphone, and out of a muzzling of amplified noises I finally recognized my name, echoing like thunder throughout the vaulted auditorium. I rose mechanically and approached the podium. "This is it," I mumbled to myself, then, "This is what?" came the question just as fast. I was empty, an utter void, standing before the assembled numbers of my supposed peers, but to no apparent purpose. I was a joke, perhaps, or a martyr, perhaps, a bright and shining hope. I tried to trace the sequence that had brought me there. It was a strange lineage going from Peggy to Truelove to Peggy, to Rasmussen, to Mustero and Cheddaster, to Mrs. Flatner to Miss Means, and back before that to Butter Rum Lifesavers, and beyond that to the Douglasses' bright little boy in the Winnie-the-Pooh windbreaker, asking questions without answers.

"Do a good job," Peggy had said. So all right, I will, for you, Peggy.

# Chapter 21

Plywood, I thought, looking at the podium, just a simple slab of good old American plywood: tissues from old trees, glued and pressed together. Heat and pressure and the flesh of old trees. I held the podium in my hands, a solid thing, and studied its bright lacquered surface and its grain: whorls and ripples and a giant thumbprint; it was taken from an old tree. I thought of Dad's bar.

But say something. Speak.

I looked up from the podium, out across the auditorium. Heads nodded and twitched, restless, ready to hear something. I opened my mouth, curious to hear what would come, when suddenly I caught some movement from the back, the upper seats. People were standing, obviously bored. Were they leaving? Pouring to the exits? A great green-and-blue tide moved from the seats and rolled, no, downward, down the aisles, toward me. The swell of green and blue filled the aisles, green and blue T-shirts, those serpents on the front, of course. And they swept downward, chanting rhythmically and growing louder and louder:

Save the snake save the snake save the snake save the snake save the snake SAVE THE SNAKE SAVE THE SNAKE SAVE THE SNAKE SAVE THE SNAKE SAVE THE SNAKE

until those still seated, those in neither green nor blue nor T-shirts of any kind had taken up the chant and were rocking, swaying in their seats. "SAVE THE SNAKE. SAVE THE SNAKE. SAVE THE SNAKE."

Just as suddenly, teachers appeared, standing in knots of twos and threes, scanning the auditorium for help, for direction. Cautiously they singled out students and sternly pointed them the way back up the aisles. Others merely stood and waved the students to their seats.

Ms. Wilberforce brushed me aside from the podium and commandeered the microphone. "Please, will everyone return to your seat? If everyone is not seated at once we will ring the bell and begin classes. Be seated immediately or we will ring the bell."

That did it. Slowly, the chant lapsed into a harmless murmur, the tide went out, the greens and blues receding up the aisles to take their seats. Ms. Wilberforce descended the steps from the side of the stage and chased a few stragglers. Finally all was order once more. Ms. Wilberforce returned to the stage and issued one more warning about outbursts and the value of the political process and so forth. She called me back to the podium and told me to get on with it.

"My fellow students," I began. My voice boomed like a great wind filling the room. I listened to it rattle through the auditorium.

"First of all, let me begin by saying that I . . ." But what would I begin by saying? Why was everyone staring so intently? ". . . that I have been to better-looking leper colonies." Yes, I said that. Jerk, smart-ass, self-destructive dink. Say farewell to Peggy Klecko.

"Whoops, wrong speech," I said. A thousand teen-agers exhaled and crossed their legs. Some tittered.

"My name is Stephen Alexander Douglass, and I am running for sophomore class president." There, this was really quite simple. "I have never held class office before. In fact, until a week and a half ago I didn't even know I was running. You might say I was railroaded into this whole campaign thing, so now that I'm up here don't hold me responsible for anything I might say." More appreciative chuckles. Maybe this straightforward sincere stuff was working.

"I have never done volunteer work. I do not play in the band. I have never played any sports. Actually, I should say I have never *participated* in any sports because, as you probably realize, some sports cannot be played as such. For example, how many of you have ever played track? Can you play the hundred-yard dash? And you can't play wrestling. You can participate in wrestling, you can wrestle, you can run track, even though you can't track, of course, unless you're a hunter, or an Indian, or more properly, a Native American.

"So anyhow, oh yes, I was talking about playing.

111

For example, you can't play bowling, and you can't play swimming, and you can't play fencing. Anyhow, my point is, I have never played *or* participated in any of those things, sports, so if you measure your candidates by their pectorals, forget about me." A few snickering girls in the front row were misinterpreting my remarks about measuring pectorals. Everyone else seemed stunned.

"I am not running because I think I can bring some great and dramatic changes to your lives. I cannot guarantee that you will all pass your courses with straight A's. I cannot restore jelly doughnuts to the cafeteria menu, nor can I promise you doors on all the toilet stalls. I doubt if I can get the sophomores invited to the senior prom." Well, at least that was all true. Still, I couldn't just stand there and tell them all the stuff I couldn't do. I'd better come up with something fast.

"So you might ask what my platform is. That's a fair question, and it deserves an answer." Now if only I had an answer.

"This T-shirt that I'm wearing, that many of you are wearing today in support of my candidacy, is a symbol. It represents something that I did last year, some would call it a mistake, that has become a part of my reputation. Not necessarily a good part, but I'm stuck with it. And I'm stuck with something that happened last week, something that many of you know I've been suspended from school for. I guess you could say that school and I just don't get along. At least not always.

"I know many of you feel the same way. Like me,

112

you do something one year, and it follows you the next and the next. And you're stuck with it. And how does it follow you through school? Very simple. They write it down and put it in your folder. You know what I'm talking about. Those folders that follow you from grade to grade, from school to school, hovering over you like a dark and dismal cloud. They stain your reputation, they prejudice your teachers and principals against you, they dog your every move.

"That's why my platform is called the Fresh Start platform: If I am elected, I promise each and every one of you that I will work for a fresh start. A clean slate. How would it work? Very simple. Each year, as you move to the next grade, you would be provided with your folder. Any records, test scores, psychological profiles, discipline or suspension reports that you found personally objectionable, you would have the option of removing. Of course, your grades would have to stay. That's only fair. But all the other stuff—the excess baggage that follows you around, if you want it out, it's out. Then each year would have a fresh start, a chance to begin again, a chance to put past mistakes behind you."

Scattered, reluctant applause rippled through the audience. Oh well, I tried. Maybe not enough of them had felt the old-folder curse; maybe I had grabbed the wrong issue.

"Of course, it won't be easy. Nothing this important ever is." That had a familiar ring to it. What was I thinking about? "But with a concerted effort of students and parents, we can work toward this goal through the school board and through the school ad-

113

ministration to achieve this fresh start for all of you."
More polite applause. Had I galvanized the elector-
ate? I suppose not. Was Peggy impressed? Too early
to say. Did they want blood? Probably.

"In conclusion, I can only say that as your sophomore class president I would work to serve you, the
students. If you have concerns, I would be ready
to help. If you have complaints, I stand ready to listen . . ."

*"Then listen to this . . ."* came a shriek from the
back of the auditorium. A thousand heads swiveled to
the rear as two figures in green T-shirts unfurled
what seemed to be a bed sheet. They held it aloft like
a great banner and came running down the aisle
toward the stage. As they approached, I saw the
drawing. Suddenly Roy's comment about "the Truelove part" took on sinister meaning. A rude carica-
ture of Truelove, looking like a great tumorous
potato in a lab coat, adorned the bed sheet. Sketched
in angry reds and blacks, Truelove floated in a giant
mayonnaise jar, himself a specimen pickled and em-
balmed, *X*'s where his eyes should have been. The jar
bore a label, *Paedagogus biologicus.* And below that,
across the length of the sheet, was written "DUMP
TRUELOVE."

When the two figures reached the front, I could
see that they were unfamiliar to me, rather big for
sophomores, more likely upperclassmen, seniors.
They held the sheet high overhead, a hand on each
corner, and floated the banner back and forth until
it bellied out like a spinnaker catching the wind.
"Dump Truelove," the two boys yelled hoarsely back

114

at the audience. Voices from the back seats took up the chant first, obviously prepared. Quickly, the others caught the rhythm and joined in, "Dump Truelove, dump Truelove," until the chant became, instead, the three syllables each separate and distinct, roaring through the hall: "DUMP TRUE LOVE DUMP TRUE LOVE DUMP TRUE LOVE DUMP TRUE LOVE DUMP TRUE LOVE DUMP TRUE LOVE."

Ms. Wilberforce had bolted from the stage and was joined below by a cadre of male teachers entering the auditorium from the side doors, where they had probably been taking a cigarette break in the outer corridor. They encircled the two boys, pulling at the banner until they had wrested it free. The crowd muttered a few suppressed boos and turned instead to a steady insect buzzing. The two boys were escorted out through the side doors and were gone. Ms. Wilberforce returned to the stage and, leading me by the elbow like I was a blind pedestrian, pulled me down the steps stage left. There stood Wilfong, materialized out of thin air, with a look that could wilt rhubarb.

"Okay, Smartass Douglass," he growled, "you're down for the count."

# Chapter 22

"The count" turned out to be three more weeks. Mom and Dad got identical letters from Wilfong. There wasn't even any conference. The letters cited a violation of my first suspension and creating a disturbance. Peggy, of course, was sorry. She had urged the wearing of our T-shirts, but the chanting and all that she claimed was spontaneous. As for the banner, those guys were lowlifes, she said. Senior dirtballs grabbing a chance to rouse rabble. They had each gotten a week's suspension for their efforts. Still, Peggy loved the speech, my speech. She seemed a bit repentant, calling me her sweet warrior, but raging at the school for injustice, for tampering with the political process.

I won the election in a landslide. Wilfong said no dice, I was an outlaw candidate, and he gave the whole thing to RoyBoy. Dad cried foul and his old ACLU buddy got a hearing scheduled. "We'll teach them a thing or two about the Constitution," Dad kept saying. "We'll show them they're not dealing with just anybody. Nils Steiner may be a *pro bono* pushover, but he's no slouch in a courtroom. And your old dad turned a few heads when he was on Law Review. They'll see. . . ."

Peggy was delighted to be in litigation. She told her parents, and they were delighted. Her father, a professor of economics and apologist for socialist agrarian reform in third world nations, was delighted. Her mother, an illustrator of nonsexist kids' books for the Little Sister Press, was also delighted. Together they mobilized the PUGS.

PUGS stood for Parents United for Gifted Students. They were a sort of child-advocacy group for the best and the brightest, comprised of parents who thought their children fit that description. It was a large and vocal group, as many parents in a university town tended to qualify as bright, and it seemed only natural that their children should also. The Kleckos, Peggy informed me, were among the prime shakers and movers, responsible over the last several years for expanding the gifted program into the lower depths of the grade schools. They had, of course, also instituted the program in high school. We had them to thank for honors biology, for example. We had them to thank for Truelove.

So Mom joined the PUGS at the Kleckos' invitation. She came home from a meeting one night, eyes lit by a special fire.

"Those people have clout, Stephen," she told me. "I like people with clout."

She was happy to have a cause again, something besides midriff bulge. She hadn't felt this alive since

117

the night she had kept a vigil for Bobby Seale. I was glad somehow to be now linked, however obliquely, in my mother's mind with that estimable gentleman. Perhaps that meant that she had forgiven me my trespasses.

With the hearing approaching, my dad was reanimated with a fascination for the law. The undergrads were back guzzling his beer and the Mother was going full bore, but Dad's real joy came after hours as he pored through school law and state statutes on student rights with his ACLU buddy Nils Steiner. He even unpacked the old law books one night and stretched them end to end on the bar, dusted them off, and buffed their plasticized leather bindings with saddle soap. Nils Steiner had to laugh. Together they stacked them one at a time in Dad's office, swapping stories about the professors who had dragged them case by case through each of the several books.

I was glad to have brought so much joy to so many.

Next Monday morning Jamie picked me up at home and drove me to the university. She parked behind the education building and took me inside to a second-floor seminar room where I was scheduled for my interview with the gifted lab school admissions bunch. Jamie introduced me to the committee, three professors from the ed school and a resident in adolescent counseling.

"How would you describe your relationship with your peers?" the counselor asked me.

"Polite to nonexistent," I answered.

"Is that your choice or theirs?"

"Never thought about it. Both, I suppose."

"Describe your closest attachment, any personal relationship at all."

"Well, there's this girl," I began, launching into a description of Peggy. "She's the one got me to run for president. She started it as a kind of joke."

"Does she think *you're* a joke?" he broke in, pouncing like a leopard on a hobbled kudu.

"I suppose at first, maybe. Now she imagines me as some political activist type. I think she's putting that all on me, 'cause I'm really not the least bit political, but she comes from this radical family. They vacationed in Cuba once and lost their passports."

He gave a subtle nod to his colleagues, and eight eyebrows rose as one.

"Any relationships with males of your own age?" He turned a page of the steno pad in his lap and started scribbling.

"Well, there's this Vietnamese kid. We're not superpals or anything like that."

"And what do you like about this young man?"

"He's good at art," I answered. But that wasn't really it. "Well, he's sort of like from another planet. Could be his accent. But, I mean, he doesn't do jerky stuff. He doesn't tell everyone to suck shit." Lots of interprofessional eye contact on that one. "He doesn't play grab ass. He wears socks under his sandals. He belongs to himself."

"And do you?" the counselor asked.

"Not as much as I'd like."

"And why not?" This guy had an amazing faith in the power of rational explanations.

"Beats me. I guess everybody lately has been lay-

119

ing claim to little chunks of me. Like you guys, even."
I smiled and pointed broadly at the four of them. A
little whimsy, but they weren't buying.

"Tell us about your parents," he said, shifting the
inquisition away from himself. I gave him a thumbnail sketch of Mom and Dad, trying to keep pretty
antiseptic.

"They sound like very clever people, Stephen."

"Please, not that word," I shot back. He wrote fran-
tically on his little pad. Everyone else sat humming
and tapping and wiping imaginary dust off their
chair arms.

"It's just that someone once called me that, in not
so nice a way. Never mind."

"Oh, I see," said the counselor. But of course he
didn't. Then with a wink down the line, the counselor said, "All yours, Larry," and Larry took over.

Larry extracted a folder from his briefcase on the
floor. My folder, as it turned out. Collusion with the
enemy.

Again I sat through the recitation. Superior test
scores, yes, extraordinary IQ, yes, mediocre grades,
yes, unusual attitude, strange discipline, psychological referrals, yes, yes, yes.

"I imagine you're a very frustrated young man,"
Dr. Larry concluded.

"Not especially," I answered, as frustration
clouded Dr. Larry's face.

He tried again. "What I mean is that you must feel
. . . puzzled that so many people expect so much from
you, and you haven't . . . well, delivered, as they see
it."

"That's their problem. I haven't been trying to deliver. But I did deliver. I got elected, didn't I? I delivered all those scores. I delivered my IQ. Face it, if it weren't for that, I wouldn't be here. Maybe those are wrong and I'm perfectly normal. Deliver that!"

"Of course, I didn't mean to imply . . ." He turned to Jamie, who sat dumbstruck beside me. I was blowing it.

"So, what are your hobbies, Stephen?" They always ask that. I never had hobbies. Hobbies are for twinks.

Still, for Jamie's sake, I decided on some hobbies. "I enjoy working with my hands. I carve things out of soap."

"What kinds of things?"

"Oh, seabirds, dogs. I once did a manger scene from two six-packs of Ivory bath-size bars." I figured that mention of Christian iconography would soften him up.

"That's lovely," he said. "Do you still have it?"

"No," I told him. "We put them too close to the lights on the tree once and they all melted. Except for the camels. They were Camay; it's harder."

"Yes," he agreed, "Ivory is quite soft. That's a pity." We had found a common ground. It was quite heartening the way everyone perked right up. I decided to throw in an extra hobby.

"Summers I like to do rock climbing. That gets me outdoors, you know."

"*Oooohhhhh,*" went Dr. Larry. "That can get mighty dangerous from what I hear."

"Yes sir, it can, if you don't know what you're

121

doing." Wham, that did it! You could have heard a piton drop.

From there it was all downhill, very steeply so. They warmed to the task, while I fired back some really terrific stuff. The last guy wrapped it up by asking me how I saw myself twenty years from now, what I thought I might be doing.

"Twenty years from now, I see myself somehow serving my fellow man. I imagine myself perhaps encircled by children, young children and some in their teens, children very much like myself." Here I paused both for dramatic effect and to recall more precisely the exact words of Charlotte Melody Ziff. Miss Ziff, you see, had been a finalist in the Miss Teen America pageant back in July, during one weekend when I wasn't out rock climbing. Those words, her telegenic image, and an uncanny knack for acrobatic dancing had won her the bejeweled tiara.

I continued, paraphrasing loosely. "These children have come to me seeking what I myself am seeking today. Answers, yes, answers to the questions and challenges that young people of today, and of every day, must somehow confront. Wracked as we are by sudden, even cataclysmic, personal growth, puzzled and perplexed by a rapidly changing and increasingly technological society, we struggle vainly, blindly, to know who we are, what we will become. The fortunate find answers to the eternal questions, yet the troubled and unfortunate never do. For them the search continues, leading often and tragically to crime, unhappiness, despair.

"I have seen this tragedy among friends and others

in my community, and even through troubling accounts on the contemporary media, and have pledged that someday, when my quest is finished, I will share with others, the generations to follow, whatever small wisdom I might have gained. Of course, every truth is a personal private truth. Every struggle is a solitary war. And yet, I know that my truths, my struggles, can become the touchstones, the bellwethers, to somehow ease the troubled tread of those who must follow in my steps."

Or something like that.

"Tell me something," Jamie said as she drove us to the Mother for a postmortem. "Was that you, or was that a performance back there?"

"I don't know. I'm not sure there's a difference anymore. Or ever was."

"You're a strange fish, Stephen Douglass. You don't add up." I had never been called a strange fish before, but I liked it. "So your theory is that everyone's performing, is that it?"

"Not exactly," I said. She wanted a theory, I would formulate a theory. "I think people feel better when you tell them the safe stuff, the comfortable stuff. Honesty is scary. I think we all walk around afraid that someone might blow our cover. We're all freakin' crazy, is my point. They only send away the ones who drop their guards, who don't work hard enough at keeping the lid on. Normal is just a disguise some people learn better than others. Like table manners. Tell me the truth, Jamie. Did you ever catch yourself, say, in the middle of brushing your teeth? You look right into the mirror. You're foaming at the mouth.

And suddenly you get this strange urge to look yourself right in the eye and scream your lungs out. And maybe if no one's home you do?"

"God, Stephen," she said. "You can be scary when you want." She angled her chin upward ever so slightly, as if it were being pulled by a fine thin thread from above. And she stole a quick look in her rearview mirror.

My last few days as an obscure private citizen passed rather uneventfully. Jamie came by Mom's house daily, first to announce I had passed my interview, then to bring a schedule of selected courses the lab students could choose from. I still wasn't sure about that. Sensing she might lose her best subject, Jamie was upset when I told her. I was the linchpin of her dissertation. She needed me, or so she said. She really wanted to see me interact with other gifteds.

The day before the hearing, Jamie came by the house again to monitor my mood. She spent the afternoon in the exercise studio in the basement and then bounded into my bedroom, invigorated by her workout. Her face was glazed with sweat, beaded like the simonized hood of a rain-drenched Ford.

She gave me a little peck on the top of my head. "I'm gonna take a shower now," she said. "Be right back." She bolted down the hall and I heard the shower start, when suddenly she reappeared, wrapped in a towel. "Give me some clothes, brilliant thing. Jeans, shirt, whatever you got." I grabbed a pair of jeans and a T-shirt from the drawer and draped them over her shoulder. "And carve this, if you get a chance," she said, lofting a bar of Camay over her shoulder as she turned back through the doorway. "Make me a camel," she hollered from out in the hall, and her laugh, deep and liquid, disappeared into the whispering rush of the shower.

Finally Jamie returned from the shower. "Where shall I throw these?" she asked. I took her things and stowed them in a gym bag left over from a failed attempt at tennis camp three summers past. Jamie slung herself across my bed while I pulled a chair alongside. She plucked my Babar off the shelf above the headboard. She placed him upright on her stomach, where he did a little tap dance, and studied him as though he were about to say something quite clever. "He's very cute," she said, and pinched his trunk.

"Cute isn't the half of it," I told her. "I should give all this stuff to Goodwill, but it would kill my mom." She surveyed the shelves of ducks, bunnies, Smurfs, robots, race cars, and rockets. "She won't part with this stuff. It's like living in a time capsule that's stuck back in the years when I was just an innocent youth."

"And when, exactly, was that?"

"It's just a figure of speech, like." I watched her stretched out there, a sly sleepy smile focused for no apparent reason on Babar. Babar remained inscrutable and she replaced him on the shelf, blindly lifting her arm straight back over her head and dropping him heavily on top of Roadrunner. Together they tipped sideways and stared vacantly across the room.

"You're like your dad, ya know? He's a doll, believe me. But it's like he's been in a sort of fortress all his life. He's afraid to go beyond the little world he's made, to throw away his toys."

"Please, Jamie, I get this stuff all the time at school. No offense, it's just too easy to sling the old diagnosis around."

"Sure, I can understand in your case, Stephen." Jamie sat up in the center of the bed, her legs lotused beneath her. "You've heard about the bar, haven't you?" I knew that the night I had "met" Jamie in the bathroom, Dad had been exploring offers from some people interested in buying the bar. Jamie explained that a new federal highway funding law had put the screws to the states. Last fall they'd had to raise the drinking age for beer to twenty-one. Otherwise, she said, the states would have to fix their own damn potholes. The law had meant disaster for the busiest undergrad beer bar in town. And left my dad inconsolable—"well-nigh" inconsolable, is how she put it.

"Even if he doesn't sell, he won't be happy," Jamie continued. "It's the kids, undergrads of nineteen, twenty, that's his crowd. Still green and waking up, he says. I think anyone else he calls over the hill. Pretty strange for a man pushing forty."

"Peter Pan with a liquor license," I said.

"Could be, Stephen. That bar is a little never-never land. It's like this room, except instead of Babar and Roadrunner, it's sophomores with pitchers of beer. There were always sophomores, like the lost boys, fresh waves of them every year to take the places of those who grew up and moved on. But by then, they had become invisible to Wilson. He chose not to see that. So now it's like they've pulled the

126

plug. He's gonna have to come out into the daylight, and he's more than a little scared."

"Sounds grim. But I mean, you know all this, and he's got you. After all, can't you—"

"He hasn't got me." She pulled herself to the edge of the bed and grabbed the pillow.

"Well, he's always got his law degree, if he wants to use it bad enough."

"Bad enough, Stephen, that's just it." Jamie's voice rose a pitch, filling with exasperation at me, or at Dad's quandary. I couldn't tell. "He didn't want it so bad that he went out and built himself a little playland called the Mother Won't Know. Think about that name for a minute. Sure, he was brilliant in law school, but it was still school, after all. It was play, a contest where he got to be the brightest boy of all and the winner got the best grade-point average. And your dad was the winner. But that was the end. There would be no more numbers, no simple ground rules. The game was over. The brightest boys get no guarantees, Stephen."

# Chapter 23

Then I became a personality. It happened after the hearing as I stepped from the shaded porch steps of the county courthouse into the slanting glare of the afternoon sun that Friday in September. It must have been a slow news day. The *Five Alive* mobile news van straddled the curb, its rainbow stripes and mini satellite dish causing a stir among the cluster of pedestrians gathering at its flanks. This was, after all, the same van that had brought us live remotes from Green Falls Lake the day they found the scalps in thermos bottles floating by the boat ramps. This van warned us of nematodes on the tobacco farms, of cantaloupes grown fast by toxic waste dumps, of migrant workers locked in moving vans.

The Kleckos, I found out later, had tipped off a friend, an associate producer at the station. The Kleckos promised an event, something visual, a good student-rights story. Sure enough, on cue, a file of mothers from the PUGS came tramping from around the van, marching in time and singing "Teach Your

Children Well" *a cappella.* They wore pastel sweat suits and carried placards. Peggy and her mother led their ranks, and my mom anchored the militant snake dance, waving a sign that read "Spare the rod, spare the child."

This was a bit much, I thought, considering it had been merely a hearing and not a trial. It had lasted barely half an hour. Nils Steiner argued quite simply that five straight weeks was an unconscionable penalty, that I had an entitlement by law to an education and five weeks at the beginning of school seriously impeded my right to learn. The judge agreed, pretty much dismissing the school attorney's argument that I was a disruptive influence. Truelove and the lab were never mentioned. For me, it meant back to school on Monday and reinstatement as sophomore class president.

But for *Five Alive News* it was fresh meat, a story with national implications. It was a hot year for stories about our schools. That's what Janice Whitney called them, "our schools," when she read the lead into her story. She interviewed Mrs. Klecko, speaking for the PUGS; Nils Steiner for the defense; and finally it was my turn. The camera stopped, and Janice Whitney checked her face in a compact mirror. Lean, black, and a rising star, Janice Whitney treated every story with the intense reverence due a mass execution at, say, Bloomingdale's. Her director, equally intense save for the bamboo frames on his sunglasses, positioned Janice at the foot of the courthouse steps and checked angles.

"Could we have the PUGS up here chanting again,

please?" he asked, indicating the steps behind Janice. "And don't march, just give us a little sway, like this." He planted both feet and rocked slowly side to side.

Obediently, the PUGS took up their places and renewed their song. "A little softer, please," he warned, checking sound levels on Janice's mike. "Tell you what," he shouted at the militant mothers. "Start with the song, nice and loud, and when I cue you, let's bring it down to a hum. Any problems with that?" There seemed to be none. "Good. Janice, get the kid."

Janice pulled me alongside her and the camera started to roll. I switched into my performance mode. So Janice peppered me with questions and I fashioned stirring and eloquent responses and that was that.

"Dynamite stuff," yelled the director, and we all went home to watch the news.

# Chapter 24

The happy band of celebrants, minus my mother, of course, arrived at the Mother Won't Know just as the dinner hour was proceeding apace. Solitary undergrads hunched at the bar, nursing their beers and feasting on beef jerky, Slim Jims, pickled eggs from a two-gallon jar of brine. Dad relocated them all to booths and sent Corky, the afternoon barkeep, back to the kitchen for Motherburger baskets all around. Dad manned the tap and drew three pitchers and scattered a brace of pilsners up and down the bar in front of us. Nils took the first seat, next to the elevated TV. I sat between Jamie to my left and Peggy to my right. Beside Peggy sat her mom and dad, followed by selected activists from the PUGS.

"So you've been vindicated. That's terrific," Jamie said. "But don't let it go to your head. I really think you'd enjoy the lab school, with kids like you from all over the state. You'd pretty much design your own program, believe me. It's not just my dissertation. I could always get another subject."

"Hold on," protested Peggy. She slid her elbow onto the bar and pivoted to join our conversation. "You can't run out on us now. Rub their noses in it, Stephen. Old Wilfong, that tightass. And Truelove. He was back this week and meaner than ever. Everyone knows what a joke Truelove is. Besides, the guy can't teach. He lectured us on morals this week, can you imagine?"

"Sounds like a good reason to leave," said Jamie. "Of course, it's your decision, isn't it, Stephen?" She grabbed me by the chin and swiveled my head around to stare me right in the eye. "Isn't it, Stephen," she repeated, this time without the question.

"One doesn't walk out on a class presidency," Peggy growled.

"Oh, doesn't one?" Jamie's husky voice went shrill, mocking Peggy's tone and pronoun.

"Oh look, our burgers," I announced.

"Who is this person, really?" Peggy hissed in my right ear. She reached for the mustard, and I took refuge in a mouthful of Motherburger.

Dutifully, we sat at the bar and ate our meals, saying very little. Dad skipped the eating part and prowled the length of the bar, delivering a stirring play-by-play of the hearing. To listen to him, you'd have thought he'd just sprung Sacco and Vanzetti from the Suffolk County jail.

"Remember the moots in Chicago? You and me, Nils, taking on those fruits from Yale?" I had never heard this one. Dad never talked much about law school. It all had something to do with a mock trial competition, some case about an exploding lawnmower wiping out a nanny on the sidewalk.

"Sure, the fruits at the moots," Nils agreed, dabbing a freckle of catsup from his tie.

"Remember how I whipped out the old *Dufresne* v. *General Mills*, how the judge waffled on the limits of an implied warranty, and how the Yalies stood there shitting bricks?"

"Bricks, right," Nils nodded. "But didn't we lose that in the end? Still, good fun. Chicago was quite a town."

"It toddled," said Dad. "Yeah, the damn Yalie bastards with their prissy little briefcases, and their goddam matching ties, and those smarmy Ivy League smirks. The way they looked at you like they were sorry for you. The way they sucked up to the judge. Remember what they did at opening arguments? Christ, they practically genuflected in his damn lap, and then—"

"Drop it, Wilson, that was seventeen years ago. Just drop it," Nils said sharply. He leaned across Jamie and gave me a conspiratorial wink. "Wouldn't play if he couldn't win. You know the type, Stephen, takes his ball and goes home."

"Stephen knows nothing. Butt out, Nils." Dad snatched an empty pitcher off the bar. I thought he was going to smash Nils across the jaw. Instead he spun and set the pitcher briskly beneath the tap. "Flow gently, sweet brewski, our throats have gone dry. Flow gently, sweet brewski, let's drink 'til we die," he sang, his voice hollow with good cheer. Finally he plunked the full pitcher back onto the bar. "Who's ready?" he asked. "Come on. This stuff is baked fresh daily, right here on the premises." But he couldn't raise a smile. He stood, his head bent, watching himself in the glossy surface of the bar. Slowly his face managed a smile, the drawstrings tightening unseen somewhere behind his ears.

"Could you turn it up, please?" asked Mrs. Klecko, pointing to the TV. The *Five Alive* news team sat on-screen, preening and shuffling pages of script, arrayed behind a curving bank of desks in the pale studio lights.

Then, lights up, zoom in. "This is YOUR *Five Alive News* at six, and I'm Bryson Hunt." The big voice with the silver hair and the confidential eyes told us about power rate hikes and legislative bickering. It announced footage on underground cable projects and dried-out reservoirs. A commercial for seafood nuggets followed.

"They'd better run it or I'm calling the station," threatened Peggy. Much fidgeting. Then Bryson Hunt:

"It seems Collier County Courthouse was the setting as one Cable Hall High School student fought back for the right to be in school. Only two days into the new school year, Stephen Douglass, a sophomore, was excluded from classes for a total of five weeks. Janice Whitney filed this report from the courthouse steps."

Janice did her walking lead-in, descending the steps one at a time, looking occasionally at her feet.

"Bryson, our schools today have become a battleground—teacher against student, student against administrator. Today that battle spilled over into this court of law [free hand points at brick building behind her], the Collier County Courthouse. The hearing focused on the case of one Stephen Alexander Douglass.

"Described by some as a brilliant oddball, Douglass was expelled after only two days of school for a run-in with a biology teacher that resulted in some destruction of school property. Suspended for two weeks, Douglass nonetheless returned to school the following week to campaign for class office. For violating the first suspension and for causing an uproar with his speech, Douglass was given an additional three weeks' suspension, for a total of five weeks altogether. Douglass and his father decided to fight back. Nils Steiner, of the ACLU, counsel for the youngster, explained the case this way."

Terse and professional, Nils explained the case as simple good sense. The school's right to exclude was exercised without full and proper due process. Plus my right to learn superseded their immoderate application of school discipline codes. Or something.

"But some see a larger issue at stake. These marching mothers behind me [pause for a chorus of their song], these women call themselves the Parents United for Gifted Students. We talked to their spokesperson, Margaret Klecko."

Peggy's mother, flushed and panting, raised the stakes. "What's happened to this young man is happening all across America. Stephen Douglass epitomizes the gifted student's fight for recognition in a society and a school system that encourages only the mediocre. This boy has talents and intelligence well

135

beyond his years. Kids like this sometimes have a hard time fitting into the ordinary classroom. Often they run afoul of the system."

"But what do you propose to do for them?" Janice broke in. "What can a group like yours hope to accomplish?"

"We hope to change the system. We want the schools to bend a little bit, to adjust a little to our brilliant sons and daughters, for they are our best hope for the future. We're talking special classes, we're talking enrichment, we're talking understanding. Otherwise, the schools will continue to process these children. Or, as in Stephen's case, they will just spit them out whole, a sad admission that they have failed with our very best."

And then it was my turn. There I stood, shoulder to shoulder with Janice Whitney as behind us the PUGS chorus line swayed in unison, militant Rockettes.

"Stephen Douglass, you have been a young man very much the center of this controversy. Are you satisfied with the outcome of the hearing?"

"Yes, very. Gratified, actually. While the school may feel the decision is somewhat less than equitable, it would seem that we now have a beginning for the process of building a rapprochement with the administration, if they are willing to wipe the slate clean."

Curious performance. Gratified, actually. Equitable. Rapprochement. Wipe the slate clean. From the mouths of babes, the stiff and oily words, tumbling from that boy up there. His thin lips barely part for these words, yet they trace a wry curl skewing across the face, inching up the right cheek and squeezing a twinkle from the dark right eye. Who is he kidding? Everyone, perhaps. Maybe just himself.

"Do you feel that your giftedness has made your adjustment to school difficult at times?" asked Janice.

"Certainly it's been difficult at times." The young man brushed aside a shock of black hair and folded his arms with great certainty across his chest. "Public education in a democracy is still a great and noble experiment. Sadly, however, such a system puts the premium on the happy medium, the great numbers of the middle ground. We are looking, I suppose, for serviceable citizens, and so our schools are pushed to spew out products, tidy bundles of neatly packaged and measurable, predictable human beings. Some of us don't fit the machinery, and there have been times when I've felt like one of those spare parts. While I'm certainly not espousing institutionalized elitism, I do think our schools need to consider alternatives for students who might need something more, or at least something different."

"And what about Stephen Douglass? What's next for him?" Janice Whitney asked the young man.

"Ah, well, for Stephen Douglass, it's back to school on Monday, classes, and starting his term as class president. And trying to get along the best he can. Besides, he's got a lot of catching up to do." Warm smile.

"Indeed he does." Janice posed as the camera pulled in to frame her fully on the screen. "And when that school bell rings Monday morning, it will

137

ring for Stephen Douglass as well. That's it, from the Collier County Courthouse. For *Five Alive News*, this is Janice Whitney."

"Bravo," yelled my dad, waving a bar rag in circles over his head. "Bravo, bravo," came lesser voices up and down the bar.

"God, Stephen, you were so fine." Peggy glowed. She clamped my right knee in her left hand and gave it a pincer squeeze. "That little thing you do with your mouth, like this," she said, forcing a droll exaggerated tic on the left side of her face, "just like that Kevin guy in *Shaky Faces.*" I hadn't seen the movie, but that Kevin guy had been all over the tube all summer, even guest-hosting *Star Search.*

"That was some exceptional performance, kiddo," Jamie said, her voice thick as pudding with irony. "I don't know where you get it, but you get it."

"It helps not to think. Plus I read a lot of 'Dear Abby.' "

"Same difference," she said. She looked at me. I looked at her. Together we stifled the giggles.

My right thigh wrenched in Peggy's squeeze. "That was me just over your left shoulder, did you see? I was in the lime green, just over your left shoulder."

"No, sorry," I told her. "Maybe we can try again at eleven." She held her grip on my knee and twisted it around till my back was to Jamie.

"You know what you have now?" Peggy asked. I told her I didn't. "Credibility, you have credibility. They can't push you around anymore."

"Just the women can do that, right, Steve?" It was

Nils, standing behind us, ready to go. "Take care of yourself, Stephen, and keep your nose clean. And watch your old man for me, too." He shook my hand and then reached across the bar to grab Dad's. "Sorry about—well, you know," he said, dropping his voice as Dad nodded, understanding.

"No harm, no foul," Dad said. "Let's talk sometime." Nils left and the Kleckos and associates stood and made farewells. "Don't be too late," Mrs. Klecko told Peggy, and they were gone.

# Chapter 25

Finally Dad switched the TV set back to the game. The Braves were losing with dignity—a double-header on the coast. The Friday nighters started rolling into the bar, so Peggy and I excused ourselves and went upstairs to my room.

"Do you actually know how to work this thing?" Peggy sat at my computer, her nose wrinkled in mild disgust.

"Only when it's on." I stood behind her and switched on the machine and the monitor. There was already a disk in the drive, so I punched up the file. "Now hit A, and watch the screen."

Suddenly the screen filled with cursive scrawl in green letters. "Stephen A. Douglass presents COMP-ACCOUNT, an active variable accounting program for small business."

"You present what? Do some more." Peggy's hands floated over the keyboard. "What do I hit?"

I told her what to hit, taking her through all the displays one by one. Accounts receivable, accounts payable, deductions, monthly billing, thirty-day ledger, payroll, double entry, and all the rest.

"They're so pretty. What are they for?"

"Just a program for bookkeeping in small businesses. Dad uses it for the Mother, and Mom uses it for her spas. It's got a few bugs still, but I'm cleaning them up. Once they're gone, Mom says I can sell it. She's got this client at the spa who works for Data Bank. They're always looking for new stuff."

"*Gawwwww*, who isn't?" she said, staring into the monitor at the small distorted oval of her face. "I mean, who isn't looking for new stuff? You are so fine."

That phrase again had become her refrain. Was I really that fine? I had blown them away on TV, and only Jamie saw through the glorious glib. And now computers. I had figured she would laugh. But now, strangely, she was charmed, as though the green blips and the electric hum and the genie of imprinted circuits locked inside that plastic box had somehow commingled their parts into a high-tech aphrodisiac.

She switched off the computer and sat herself on the padded bench of my Body Flexer exerciser. Letting her legs straddle the sides, she gripped the torso power bar and brought it up and over her head, extending to the full length of her arms.

"They say Baryshnikov lifts," she puffed, letting the words escape on the downstroke.

"Baryshnikov's a man," I answered.

"A dancer's a dancer," she wheezed. "Strength is important."

"I just meant the men lift the women. The women

141

are more elegant or something." I jumped to my top bunk. Stretched out belly down, I watched Peggy straining at the machine. "Too much muscle makes you bulgy and stiff," I warned, "like weight lifters."

"Old wives' tale," she said, releasing the bar. She reversed herself on the bench, attached the foot-locks, and started doing thigh presses. "Wow, you can feel those flexors like anything. This is great. I could do this all night."

"Try it; you'll go home in a wheelchair. Besides, your mom said not to be out late."

"Oh, please," she moaned. "That's just for public consumption. I go home when I'm ready. Ted and Margaret are into trust."

She released her feet from the stirrups and lay back full upon the bench. Finally her breathing returned to its normal rhythm. With the little fingers on both hands she sorted out the stray threads of hair that had plastered themselves to her forehead. Her hair tumbled free over the bench's end, just reaching the carpet, enough to tickle the brown-flecked shag.

"Maybe you're right," she said. "That just kills the legs." She lifted her legs into the air, bicycling her feet in small circles. She sat upright on the bench, spun sidesaddle, and grabbed her thighs underneath. "Hamstrings feel like rope." She jiggled both legs on the floor as she massaged their undersides.

She stood and wobbled her way to the lower bunk, where she collapsed in a heap. "I think I'll stick to the barre, for now."

I mumbled something about that being a good idea, and then we both fell silent for a good stretch. I was ready to see if she had fallen asleep, when suddenly she looped first one shoe, then another. The second one caught me across the face.

"Hey, watch it with those things," I yelled.

"Bunk beds are fun, but kind of . . . you know."

"Babyish. Say it. I agree." Still, I defended my dad's logic in buying the beds. "Be good for having friends over, buddies and all that."

"How many buddies have you had over lately?" Peggy asked.

"Well, none. I'm not the buddy type, sad to say."

"Then I'm the first. Does this mean we get to go camping and stuff?"

"Look, if you're going to get an attitude, maybe you should go. No one forced you to stay," I told her.

"You're so insecure. Why can't you just relax? REEEEElax. I meant it when I said you were so fine. Can't you take a compliment even? Get down here." Now she was giving orders.

"I'm fine up here." So it had resolved itself into the battle of the bunk beds. I was going to play it territorial. At least I would be able to say I had never budged.

Suddenly the lights snapped off. It was after eight, already fully dark outside. Only the beams from passing cars now filled the room, moving walls of light reflected off the street below.

"Move over, shithead," came Peggy's voice. She had pulled herself up to the top bunk and rolled across me heavily, squeezing me to the outer edge. "What was that word you used today, Stephen? Remember, the one you told Janice Whitney you'd have to develop with the administration?"

"Uh, *rapprochement* you mean? It's French."

143

"*Mmmmmm*, yes, that's it. Now put your arms around me and say it again."

"*Rapprochement,*" I whispered, holding her close, my mouth next to her ear.

"Now softer, slower, say it," she urged.

"*Rapprochement,*" I said again, syllable by syllable. "*Rap-proche-ment, rap-proche-ment.*"

I could have thrown in *détente* or *savoir faire* or *joie de vivre* or *tête-à-tête*, but I don't think any of them would have helped much. Besides, it was *rapprochement* that I'd used in the interview, *rapprochement* that somehow seemed to stir Peggy's deepest urges. . . .

*Quelle rapprochement!* . . .

"There," said Peggy, breaking what must have been an hour's silence, "buddies." And she threw back the covers and offered her hand. I shook it. "Check that out," she laughed, pointing to the exercise machine in the corner. Her shorts hung from the topmost bar, one leg slipped perfectly over its plastic sheathing. The rest of our clothes littered the floor like things washed up by a storm tide.

"Serious damage." I laughed. "Are you all right?"

"Of course I'm all right," Peggy answered, appallingly matter-of-fact. I should have known. No big deal. She turned toward me on her side and flicked her palm toward the ceiling. "See, good as new."

I took the floating arm and ran my hand down its length, over her shoulder, tracing the planes below her neck. Above her right breast there was a shadow, a smudge of color, and I tried to brush it off.

"That's attached, if you don't mind," said Peggy.

144

"It's just a unicorn." She propped herself up higher on her elbow. As the occasional headlights from below illuminated its outlines, she told me the story of Kees. Last summer in Amsterdam, she had met him. Musician, poet, metalsmith, part-time tattoo artist, eighteen years old. It was a farewell gift, she said. I wondered what it had cost her. Suddenly I was jealous of some guy three thousand miles away across the North Atlantic.

"It's swell, if you like unicorns" was all I said.

"Kees did," she answered, and tucked her unicorn back under the sheet.

I could think of no delicate way to get out of bed and retrieve my clothes. Peggy, for her part, showed no interest. She lay quietly on the bed in a meditative trance, humming airs from her favorite ballets. *Les Sylphides*, she would announce, then *Swan Lake*. I thought I recognized *The Nutcracker*, but when I said so she simulated retching and pronounced me hopelessly sentimental.

"You'd better outgrow that bourgeois mind-set by Monday, mister, or we're cooked."

"Bourgeois, see, you can do it too! *Bourgeois, bourgeois.*" Then I pulled out the heavy artillery. *"Bourgeoisie, bourgeoisie,"* but it didn't have the tingling sensuality of *rapprochement*, and her mind was racing ahead to other matters.

"So what's the proper Monday mind-set, anyway?" I asked.

"Mission Truelove," she said. "We've got to get him . . . out of that school . . . fired . . . gone. He's a menace."

"I'm not so sure. It's not my place, anyhow. Things

go haywire, especially when I'm involved. I've already had my fill of that. Last year—"

"You're talking about Mustero, aren't you?"

"Yes, that, him," I admitted. "It was wrong, a bad situation. I need to steer clear of bad situations. Today, the hearing, the news thing—that's enough for me, forever. I guess I want it to end. The whole snake thing, this celebrity stuff, this gloriously clever fellow nonsense . . ."

"Exactly. See, that was him, Truelove, did that to you, picked you apart, humiliated you in front of everyone. That's why he's got to go. So he won't do that anymore—to you or anyone, ever again."

"But it wasn't me. He doesn't hate me." How could I explain something to Peggy I was only barely beginning to understand. My Truelove hypothesis. It needed more observation. It needed a conclusion.

"He doesn't hate me," I tried again. "He doesn't even know me well enough to hate me. He's just . . . full of something, brain poison . . . or hurt. For what, from what, who knows? But it's there, like a land mine waiting in the jungle. I was reading the petition, he called my name, I didn't answer—and *blam*, he was off."

"And *blam*, he could be off again, anytime, and who knows what'll happen next. It's scary."

"Yes, it is scary," I admitted. "Scarier than even you imagine."

"Than I imagine?" Peggy propped herself up on an elbow and repeated, "Than I imagine?"

"Than any of us imagine, that's all I meant." But of course it wasn't. I wanted to tell her, someone, about

146

the lab, about Truelove's fit. Eventually. But it wouldn't be Peggy, I realized—not only because I'd already taken the "credit" for that one and become her martyr. But because, as much as I wanted to, there was still some small corner of Peggy that I couldn't . . . well, trust. And I guess that made me sad.

". . . sexist," Peggy was saying. "I sure don't have to imagine how sexist that horrible man is. Calling me a sweet young thing, a vessel of procreation, a fox, a trick."

"I think it was 'hot ticket,' " I corrected. "He never called you a 'trick.' "

"Defending him now, are you!! Sticking up for your sex! How predictable, how—"

"I'm not defending him. I was just . . . It's not important."

"My mother was outraged, just outraged, when I told her what he called me. She's gonna run for school board. She says the classroom is no place for sexist attitudes. If Truelove doesn't go, she'll make him go. It won't be the first time."

"For Truelove?" I asked. "How do you—?"

"For my mother. She got rid of Johnson. She and her contemporaries."

"Johnson who?"

"Lyndon Johnson. LBJ. They had a kind of chant: 'Hey, hey, LBJ, how many kids have you killed today?'—you know, Vietnam and all that."

"Yeah, all that. I know. I guess I just don't listen to the oldies radio station enough. I've never heard that song. Is that by the Lovin' Spoonful or something?"

"Snide. Be snide. My mother was in SDS before it

147

was fashionable. Days of Rage. Chicago. 'Hell, no, we won't go.' She led the student strike at Wisconsin. They planted little white crosses all over campus. She has photographs!"

"Family album stuff. Yeah, I know. My mother was into that too. Pretty heavy, I guess. Let's just drop it."

"Drop it?" Peggy bristled under the sheets. She grabbed my ear and pulled my face toward hers. "Drop it? Now? No way."

"Then slow down, let's just . . . slow down." I reclaimed my ear and pulled away. "At least for now."

"Slow down, now you say slow down. Half an hour ago you didn't want to slow down."

I wondered at the logic of that connection. Was it simply the heat of argument, of passion, as they say? Or was she making some bizarre connection between her campaign against Truelove and our recent breakthrough at redefining the buddy system?

"The man's not fit to hold a piece of chalk. He was out a week after you got the boot. Finally he comes back and for a week it's been shit work."

"Like what?"

"Like Monday we wrote down all the organisms that begin with *A*, *E*, *I*, *O*, and *U*. Tuesday he read to us out of the textbook. Can you imagine fifty minutes of arthropods? Wednesday he gave us a crossword puzzle on tropisms. Thursday we checked it, and Friday he gave us a test. On bivalve reproduction, for god's sake."

"Maybe he's just, like, seeing what everyone knows. Some classes take time to get cranked up." I put the best light on it that I could. Still, Truelove was

148

edging closer to the abyss, from what Peggy described. But I couldn't see the bottom, even though I had had a glimpse of his hurtling downward. But that had become my secret.

Peggy described the efforts to mobilize our class and other classes in an attempt to drive the man from the school. They were getting petitions to give to Wilfong. PUGS was meeting to call for his resignation. The students took turns dropping books, putting stink bombs in the sinks, rolling pennies across the floor. Kid stuff.

They must have thought they were doing this for me.

"Let's drop it, if you don't mind," I said, interrupting her recitation. "Maybe what we need to do is develop a *rapprochement* with Mr. Truelove." I took hold of Peggy and tried once more, half teasing, really. *"Rap-proche-ment,"* I whispered.

She ripped the covers off the bed and jumped to the floor. "School night," she announced. "Gotta get our rest. Don't ruin it. We're counting on you. Stay hungry!" She gathered her clothes and dressed without a further word. I buried my face in the pillow.

I never even heard the door. A quick slab of light from the hall, there and gone across the room, and she had left. I bit hard into the pillow. Then I unloosed a toothpaste scream right into its Dacron polyfill heart.

# Chapter 26

*SCREEEEEEEEEEEEEEEEEE!!!!* The shrill squeal cut through sleep. Now half awake, I wondered at its source. It came again, muffled and distant—*screeeeee*—then died around a distant corner, rubber on pavement, Detroit and Akron conspiring against sleep.

The green block numbers on my clock said 1:09. Closing time. A final promenade for all the barflies, weaving and bleary, on foot or in cars, back to dorms, or frat houses, or those square bungalows up and down University Avenue.

I jumped from the bunk and looked out the front window, down to Mifflin Street where the nightly migration filled the streets. Die-hard party animals filled the sidewalks, feinting at cars and retreating. They circled and fluttered, uncertain as moths when the porch light goes off. They swarmed at crosswalks where the police cars idled by the curb.

The floor beneath my feet was pulsing, the shag almost electric with the thunk and thud, the beat of music coming from below. I dressed and checked Dad's room. No Dad. No Jamie either. I walked downstairs, through the office, and opened the office door. The lights were up full to signal closing. Yet the bar's stereo was blaring in top range, so loud it was impossible to make out more than the chorus. "Baby, what's the use? Baby, you'd be wise to cut me loose." A guy in a silk shirt danced up and down along the booths by the far wall, eating pretzels out of an ashtray. The shirt had hibiscus stamped all over. Across the room, near the bar, a pack of undergrads stood in a semicircle bouncing to the music, a drunken half beat behind, applauding and hooting at some figure standing on the bar.

Dad! Old Dad! Bare to the waist, his shirt still tucked in but hanging limp over his rear end like a cockeyed apron, Dad stood above this knot of admirers, swaying and balancing as though he were perched on the tip end of an eight-foot canoe. In his right hand he held a ten-pound slab of a book, split open almost to dead center, thick red binding bent back to make a small red tent above his hand. His left arm stretched out from his shoulder at a right angle and his left hand cut at the air for purchase, to balance the mass and weight pulling from the other side.

Corky handed him up a pitcher of beer and he guzzled from the side, beer washing over the rim, down his ears, his chin. It glazed his chest and soaked a dark corona from the waist of his pale beige slacks. Finally, the pitcher half drained, its weight counterpoised against that of the big red book, Dad stood

151

fixed, balanced and triumphant save for a thread of spittle stretching from his bottom lip.

"Okay, okay, okay, how did we leave off, your honorables?" Dad shouted above the stereo. "Corky, terminate that muuuuuzzzzzzziiiiiik, if you would be so kind." Corky obliged by turning the volume to a low murmur, and Dad continued. "Now, what was it, assholes? Let's see, you wanted to hear about *exxxx*-culpation?"

The assholes assured him, gleefully, that they did. "You were up to insanity, remember?"

"Ah, insanity, yes, yes, yes. Let me tell you about an English gentleman, if I might presume to call him that. An old boy name of McNaghten. Thought he'd kill himself a prime minister, but got the old boy's secretary instead, fellow name of Drummond. Bulldog Drummond, ever heard of old Bulldog?" He paused and held the book face up. "Sure you did!"

"The problem with this old bullywipe, McNaghten, you see, is that the court found that he had, and I quote, 'an obsession with certain morbid delusions,' which, if you'd like me to interpret, means that McNaghten thought he was a plum pudding. And of course you don't give a plum pudding a gun, do you?"

"Or a fruitcake!" hooted one of the crowd.

"Manners, asshole," Dad hissed at the interruption. "So anyhow, their judgeships said that in all cases every man is presumed to be sane," and he paused to gulp more beer. "Butttt"—and the spit exploded over the heads of the audience—"the presumption of sanity can be obliterated if the defense can show that the defendant didn't know what he was doing or—and see if you can catch this difference—didn't know that what he was doing was wrong. Or did know, but it didn't make a difference. Ha! There it is."

"Give him more beer, get the old fighting DA another pitcher. This is going to be a long case," shouted one of the mob. Dad dropped his left arm to his side, and the dregs of the pitcher came spilling out across his shoe tops. Corky reached up from behind and relieved him of the empty pitcher.

With his newly freed left hand, Dad flipped the pages of his book. "Ha! *McDonald* versus *United States*. This is where the shrinks get into the act. Ya see, they figured normal old everyday people on juries couldn't figure out who's insane, so they had to leave it to the experts. They needed psychological analysts who specialized in crazy people. Eggggspert witnesses, yes, yes, yes. Crazy was no longer in the eye of the beholder, so to speak. Ordinary people like you and me—"

"Not like you, counselor. Tell us about *Michelob* versus *Heineken*," shrieked a squat blond figure waving a mug over his head. His fellows lifted their mugs too. That was a good one, they thought. They howled in unison, sounding like twenty steam whistles shrilling for a lunch break. They clinked their mugs together and howled once again.

I pulled the office door closed behind me and walked to the far wall. I found the dimmer switch and turned it all the way down. Just inside the entrance the fish tank floated in the darkness, glowing like a box of blue-green light.

"*Out*, everybody get out of here, it's closing time,

get out," I shouted hoarsely in my deepest voice, struggling for a trace of authority. I had had enough.

"Okay, buster, hold it right there." Someone grabbed my arms from behind and pulled them back. I craned my neck to see. My captor was only Corky.

"Corky, dammit Corky," I yelled, "get these bums out of here. Let me go, and get these bums out of here."

Corky obeyed without a word, and then I heard my dad's voice from above. "That you, Stephen old boy? Come on here with your dad and show these peckerheads what a real intellect looks like." I felt a hand groping for a fingerhold on the back of my neck. Then Dad's voice rose in formal introduction. "Gentlemen, I'd like you to meet my young associate and the real bulwark of the firm of Douglass, Douglass, and Debunk—my son, Stephen Alexander Douglass, JD, LLD, PhD, and RSVP. Come on up here, Stephen, and address the jury." But the jury was being sequestered by Corky. They were finally disbanding in bunches and pushing out past the blue light of the aquarium. They spilled in mumbles onto the street outside.

I reached blindly above me to where I had heard Dad's voice. I caught an arm and pulled; then *thunk*, he fell headlong across the bar and settled lengthwise, resting on his stomach. "Jeez, kill me, why dontcha? That you, Stephen?"

"Yes, Stephen," I answered. I heard his breathing, labored and heavy, and found his face mouth down on the bartop. "Come on, let's go upstairs," I said, turning his head sideways, out of the puddled surface of the bar.

"Close it up, Corky," I yelled into the darkened room. Just as suddenly, the lights came on. Corky stood in the corner, his hand on the switch. I climbed over the bar and started pulling Dad off, knocking down three stools as I did. The hibiscus shirt—Corky had missed him—came dancing over and wrapped Dad's left arm around his neck. I did the same with the right, and together we dragged him across to the office.

"Casebook, Stephen. I need it. Criminal law casebook," Dad gurgled, head wagging loosely from the shoulders. We leaned him against the doorjamb while I retrieved his book, and then, pushing and pulling fore and aft, we coaxed him up the stairs one at a time and into his bedroom.

The floor was stacked with old casebooks, brown ones and blue ones and red ones, all in separate piles. His bed swarmed with notebooks, yellowed and faded and much worn, their pages open to notes of cases, briefs, the lines of each page cluttered with yellow highlighter, red asterisks in the margins, big green question marks, and cryptic doodles. The room stank of the mildewed dust of old books that had been stored in dark, moist rooms for decades. I nudged a pile with my toe, and silverfish scampered into the carpet at my feet.

"Just a second," I told the hibiscus shirt. I pulled at the spread, like a magician doing the old tablecloth trick, and flung the covers aside. A clutter of notebooks thumped onto the floor. "Now," I said, and we gently draped my father's wilting body across the bed.

Dad's eyes snapped open. "Sweet shirt, Jack. Petunias, right? Give you twenty bucks for that shirt."

"No, hibiscus," said the guy. He took off the shirt and dropped it on the bed beside my dad. "It's yours, man. Keep your money."

I tried to offer the guy my shirt and thank him, but he left in a flash, his hairy back disappearing out the door.

"Nice guy, nice shirt," said my dad. "Where's the criminal law book, where'd you . . . ?" I dropped it on the bed beside him. He wrapped the shirt around the book as if it were wee baby bunting and clasped it to his chest.

I went to the bathroom and returned with a washcloth. I sat beside Dad on the bed and scrubbed his back where the beer had dried in sticky patches of crumbs.

*"Whoo,"* he yipped.

"Too cold, sorry. I'll let you sleep in a second. Just wanna get this mess off you. Roll over."

He did, and I pried the hibiscus-wrapped law book off his chest and scrubbed him down as best I could.

"You were really good today. I'm proud of you, son," he said, letting his eyes close. I returned the book to him, and he pressed it once more to his chest.

Suddenly the eyes flashed open, wide and staring. "I did it this morning. I shouldn't . . . I didn't want anyone to know, but what the hell, you're my kid. I registered for the bar exam, come May. It's crazy, but what the hell."

"I'm proud of you, too, Dad, in that case. No fooling."

"Seventeen years late, forgot it all, everything, gotta really bust my tail for once. But ya know, deep down . . ."

"You feel real good deep down, right?" I finished for him.

"No." He paused and let his head drop back on the pillow, eyes closed. "Deep down, I'm terrified. Scared shitless. Absolutely shitless. And do me a favor, will you?"

"Sure, anything, Dad, name it." I reached to his feet and pulled a sheet up over his arms, his chest, over the book.

"Our secret. Tell noooooooobody. Swear."

"Okay, I swear," I told him.

"No, really say it like you mean it," he urged, his voice rattling in his throat, frantic and pleading. "The whole thing, say it."

"I swear and promise that I will never divulge your intention to take the bar examination to anyone, ever, so help me God."

"There you go," Dad said. He curled onto his side and coiled beneath the sheet.

"Now go to bed," he told me.

I leaned over and kissed him on the left temple. It tasted like beer.

"Bed," he repeated. "Bed."

# Chapter 27

On Monday I returned to school a minor celebrity. When I entered biology seventh period, I circled around the first two rows of tables back to my seat, feeling the heads, the eyes, tracking me like radar. Truelove sat behind us at his desk, his large head tilted down as though he were pondering something in his lap. Other students entered, each set of eyes searching me out, it seemed. Finally Peggy skipped through the door just before the bell sounded and sat beside me.

"Mitosis," Truelove announced as he walked to the board. He drew an oval in yellow chalk and filled in the necessaries of one-celled life. He showed us how the nucleus stretched itself and split and how the geometric duplication of cells replicated endlessly the first. "The mother cell, god bless her, has no babies, only more mothers," he explained. "This is asexual, remember. We'll get to sexual reproduction later." Smiles blossomed here and there among my classmates. Two seats up, Buddy Autry cast sly glances right and left over both shoulders, desperate for female eye contact.

Truelove's lecture continued, organized and precise, and amply illustrated. Yet slowly, as the class progressed, I began to see the plan. He would turn to the board, and coughing would erupt around the class. Every pause, and there weren't many, was punctuated with a fart, a belch, a hawking in the throat. From behind me came a hail of raisins every time his chalk touched the board. The raisins would rattle off the board and scatter over the floor. One landed in the fold of shirt at Truelove's shoulder and nested there for the rest of the period. Books were dropped on occasion, just often enough to tell it was intended, yet infrequently enough to seem accidental. *Smack* they would land full flat against the floor, and everyone would shudder and bounce off the seats.

And through it all Truelove never blinked. He plowed on, relentlessly, through cell structure, through one-celled organisms, day after day, as raisins rattled off his paramecia, as farts rolled in thickening clouds across the floor, as books cracked on the new linoleum like gunshots from an unseen sniper. There was no discussion, no question and answer. He called on no one, asked no questions, simply stuck to his lesson and carried on. Likewise, no one raised a hand, asked for clarification, asked for anything, not even to go to the bathroom. It was a siege.

I studied Truelove as hard as I studied his one-celled organisms. His head seemed overmatched for

159

the short thin neck that held it. The face was un-marked, unlined. The body moved while the clothes went their own way, the voice droned on above the ragged belches of the class. He seemed, well, unused, a body barely lived in, barely touched.

He wore his hair clipped close at the sides and back. The bark-colored hair on top was oiled slightly and brushed off the forehead. At times, under the illumination of the fluorescents overhead, it seemed to glint darkly green and mossy. When he twisted his head toward the board, his pale neck and scalp shone white. By midafternoon stubble darkened his jaws like smudges of graphite.

He was a study in control. He rarely slipped. Some-times, at the board, his free hand would start flutter-ing across a drawing, pointing and gesturing. But it would freeze at once floating in midair, and then slowly, deliberately, he would return it to his side or confine it to a pocket like a parakeet under house arrest.

The daily routine of biological warfare had settled into an unnerving stalemate by the time Truelove finally returned that first test, the one I had missed, on bivalve reproduction. The class sat stunned, silent for the first time. Beside me Peggy let out a low hiss of dismay. I stole a peek at the test, and she pushed it in my direction.

"He's not for real," she whispered, her finger pointing at the 100 at the top of the test. There were twenty questions about bivalves and a diagram re-quiring labels. Peggy had written "carburetor" for number one, "exhaust" for number two, "piston" for number three, and so on. For the questions she had supplied a number of ballet terms as answers: "plié," "pas de deux," "grand jeté," et cetera. All were marked correct.

"Way to go," I told her as we walked out into the hall. "You really know your bivalves."

"What don't you make a joke about, I swear?" she snapped.

"Now, now, Peggy dear," I said. "You've got to learn to take your bivalves with a grain of salt."

We were drawing a crowd. "Lovers' quarrel?" asked Buddy Autry in a nasal whine.

"What'd you get?" Peggy asked him.

"A hundred, no sweat," Buddy glowed. "Me too," announced RoyBoy. Others clustered around, admitting to the same results. Nu Tran was just sliding out the door when I shot out an arm and grabbed him by the shirtsleeves. "How'd you do on the test, Nu Tran?" I asked.

He pulled the test out from among his books and held it under my nose. "I made very well on the test," he said. I took a quick look and discovered that he too had made 100. But even more amazing was that he actually seemed to have real answers, written in his meticulous printing. And at the bottom, strangest of all, were four painstakingly printed monosyllables in square block letters, all written in the same red ink as the score at the top.

"What's that say?" I asked Nu Tran.

Nu Tran obliged, but in his native tongue, a rapid fire of throaty bursts.

"In English, please, Nu Tran," I said.

"Oh, sorry, Stephen. Of course, for you." He studied the characters with his dark-brown eyes, moving his lips with the torment of the effort. "Something like 'Over you shines sun.' But you would say something like 'Way to go!' That's all."

# Chapter 28

All that afternoon, that night, I thought of Truelove's cryptic phrase: "Over you shines sun." Way to go, indeed. The test grades had put a strange chill on everyone. Peggy had left for ballet without word one. Buddy Autry practically swallowed his gum and then just slithered away. Only Nu Tran had seemed unfazed, tickled, in fact, to judge by his prize-winning grin as he tucked his quiz into his spiral notebook.

When I entered the biology lab the next afternoon, I saw Truelove stationed as usual at his desk, head down, contemplating his lap. Nu Tran sat up front, drawing eagles on a sheet of notebook paper. Behind, Buddy Autry watched me circle around the tables, then gave me the thumbs up. In the back, nearest Truelove's desk, Linda Zagouris bathed her contact lenses and giggled to her seatmate, Cheryl Zipperian. They bent their heads together like Siamese twins joined at the eyebrows. I sat and watched the rest file in.

Peggy finally settled beside me as the bell rang. After the usual three- to four-minute delay, the ritual stillness descended. Finally Truelove stood, and like a weary soldier, trudged to the front of the class. Only this time he walked unaccompanied by the chorus of flatulence and dyspepsia. No books slammed the floor. He turned briefly to the board, but no salvo of raisins ricocheted off its milky gray surface. Everyone sat rapt and expectant. Truelove stalked the floor, posing finally in front of the board. He lifted an eraser from the tray behind him and extracted his silver chalk holder from his breast pocket. He spent the next minute wiping at the board with the eraser, his butt wagging like a spaniel's as the board filled with a chalky rainbow of arcing smudges. At last he stopped stock-still, and his right hand wrote on the board "Test," and he circled that. Then underneath he wrote "Tomorrow" and circled that. When he turned back to us again his face seemed dusted a shade paler.

"What that means, children, is that you will have a test tomorrow. You did so well on the other one that I assume there are no objections?"

As usual, when confronted so directly, the class dropped their heads and shuffled awkwardly at their seats. But not me.

I raised my hand. Truelove stared back at me, more stunned than disturbed. Slowly his eyes widened, his eyebrows pushing upward until three creases lined his brow. He was waiting.

"Will this test be on one-celled organisms, mitosis, and like that?" I asked. My voice came out a squeak.

"Yes, like that," he squeaked back. The eyes narrowed again, the brows dropping to half-mast, the forehead again smooth and white.

And then I delivered it. I had heard the word, that title, so many times from his lips on that strange afternoon when I had sat hunched in the lab. Now I wanted to hear it again. Try it out, on my own. Maybe it was my way of letting him know. Maybe a start at getting even. "No objections, then. Thank you, Doctor Truelove." That was all—just "Doctor Truelove."

No, he did not hurl fragile objects through the air, did not rant or foam at the mouth or hose us down with formaldehyde. Did nothing, in fact. Stood rigid, stiff, only his eyes moving for a minute, maybe two, only his eyes moving over us, from me, around the room and back to me, again around the room, two pale eyes in a blank worn face, studying us, memorizing us, it seemed.

Control. I had studied his control before, but this unnerved me. So still, until at last the left hand lifted stiffly to his side and groped to find the pocket there and disappear. Yet realizing in his failure that he still held the eraser with that hand, he let it drop again slowly to his side. A rectangular imprint of white now marked the place just above his pocket. He then rotated slowly until he faced the board. Both hands rose to the aluminum tray at its bottom rim. Almost imperceptibly he deposited the eraser, then dropped the chalk and holder with a small, hollow *clink*. Then both hands grasped the tray as he stood leaning from the waist, clutching the tray, bent toward an invisible chalk horizon like a passenger on a cruise ship, gripping the railing and staring out to sea.

"You may study for the remainder of the period." The voice came out hollow, bouncing off the board one word at a time. Then he straightened and turned crisply to the door and left.

"God, was he crying?" said Linda Zagouris.

"Bullshit, crying," popped Buddy.

"What'd you call him, Douglass?" asked Roy.

"Called him 'Doctor Truelove,'" Peggy answered for me, proudly.

"Maybe he's sick, you guess?" Nu Tran offered.

"Sick in the head, no kidding, Neutron," Buddy said.

"How'd you dig that up, anyhow?" Roy asked.

"Yeah, how about that, Douglass?" Buddy seconded.

"He's not telling, are you, Stephen?" Peggy said.

"Nothing to tell," I added. "Just call it a hunch."

"Hunch, shiiiiiit," Buddy groaned. "Come clean, Douglass."

"Stick it, Buddy," came Peggy again, my protector once more.

The chatter rattled along like that for the rest of the period. Everyone seemed to agree that we had Truelove on the run at last. I was again proclaimed their hero and savior, but no amount of praise could squeeze any more out of me. I had done my little bit for the crusade. I had no interest in doing much more. I could still feel Truelove's presence in the room, those pale eyes watching us from that chalk-white face.

166

# Chapter 29

"Call this number. But wait, read this first."

"Mom, it's you!" I had arrived home on the bus with no idea that Mom would be home. She was never home in the afternoon.

"Well, scrape yourself off the ceiling and read this. It looks big." I was halfway into my closet, standing on one leg, yanking a shoe off the other foot. A hard posture from which to levitate in fright, but I had managed.

"Do that again, Mom, and we'll have to put a bell around your neck. Why are you home so early?"

"I live here, Stephen. Besides, we canceled the taping today. No show."

"So they finally closed you down. Bound to happen. Too much heavy breathing." But she was in no mood for teasing. "What's wrong?" I asked.

"It's Rolf," she said. "He's leaving. He's in Atlanta right now, the S.O.B. He's opening his own spa with some German fairies. Imagine."

"Maybe they're just elves. The Black Forest is crawling with them." She didn't even smile. She sat on the edge of my bed and folded her arms across her stomach. "I'm sorry, Mom. I never much took to Rolf—guess you knew."

But she had, maybe more than I realized. "German bastard. Know what he called me? Imagine."

"What, Mom?"

"He called me a handsome woman. A smart, handsome woman. 'Privileged to work with such a smart, handsome woman,' that's what he said."

"Well, his English was never tip-top," I offered. "Maybe he just meant that you . . ."

"He meant I'm old, Stephen." Her voice grew high and brittle. "Old women with blue hair are handsome."

"Mom, you're not old. The guy's a feeb. He's got strudel for brains and he's a feeb. You're not old. Hell, you'll never be old."

"Come here," she said, and patted the bed beside her. I sat, and she held me tight. "Thanks, Stephen. You're a good son. You're worth ten Rolfs, a hundred Rolfs."

I might have suggested an infinitude of Rolfs, but I got her point. Finally she released me and forced a cheerful note. "C'mon, c'mon, c'mon, open this, or I'll open it for you."

She thrust an envelope at my chest. I clutched it and read the—no, I didn't read, I just looked at it, at the seal, the wreath of stars circling the eagle rampant, one talon clutching the arrows, the other lightning bolts. Curling inside the wreath, the legend "Seal of the President of the United States."

"Holy gaw, holy gaw, holy gaw." I ripped the envelope open. It even smelled presidential. A little puff of Oval Office air burst like a ripe bouquet and drifted up my nose.

"What's it say? What's it say? Read, read, read," Mom prodded, bouncing on the edge of my mattress. I was still unfolding the letter inside. Such creases, such stationery, pebbled and rich to the touch, the official stationery of the highest office in all the free world. Damn. You coulda sliced cheese with those creases.

" 'Dear Stephen,' " I read. "First-name basis, see, Mom. Shall I go on?" A sharp elbow to the ribs suggested that I should.

Dear Stephen,

First, we want to thank you for your wonderful lyrics to "Hail to the Chief." The First Lady and I were deeply moved by your efforts, and especially by the inspiring sentiments expressed in your words. It is heartening to know that a young man like you is participating in the rebirth of patriotic feeling currently sweeping this great land of ours.

My staff advises me that yours is the first effort ever to put words to "Hail to the Chief." Although ceremonial and state fanfares are traditionally intended for brass instruments, I feel that your remarkable words should somehow be remembered. Accordingly, I have referred your lyrics to the U.S. representative from your district, the Honorable Bennett W. Thornton. Congressman Thornton pledges to introduce a resolution to adopt your lyrics as the official

169

words to "Hail to the Chief." Regardless of its outcome, this resolution will allow Congressman Thornton to read your stirring words on the House floor and enter your name into the public record. He will then forward to you a copy of the appropriate Congressional Record to keep as a memento of this occasion and of your achievement.

The First Lady and I would like to express our personal gratitude in another way. As you probably know, we annually invite four high school students from each of the fifty states to be our guests at the Freedom Scholars weekend in November. By recognizing the talent and achievement of our students, we hope to focus the nation's attention on the extraordinary promise of our next generation of Americans. We would be honored to include you as one of these 200 Freedom Scholars.

Again, thank you for sharing your inspiration with us. You are a clever young man and a credit to your nation.

Yours truly, [signed].

"*YYYYEEEEEEOOOOOOWWWWWWWW!!* Can you believe it, an invitation from the president. Holy cowdung!" I handed Mom the letter and she read it all over again, throwing in those little head twitches, just like he does in the press conferences.

"It's wonderful, Stephen, but what's he talking about? Lyrics to 'Hail to the Chief'?" She folded the letter and handed it back to me.

"Just a goof, something I did on the word processor. This is biiiiiihhhhhhhhhhzarrrrrrrre." I told her

170

about the day at the Mother Won't Know, the day Peggy showed up with her petition and everyone greeted me with a chorus of "Hail to the Chief," and how I got to thinking about that old bee joke, how they always hum because they don't know the words. Mom said she'd like to see a copy of the lyrics, but I didn't think I'd even kept one.

"Well, then, we'll just have to wait for the Congressional Record." She grabbed my head like it was a great melon and smacked me a kiss in the ear. "I'm so proud of you, my little boy. Imagine!"

I guess I could forgive her the "little boy" routine one last time, but Babar sat smirking at me from behind the bed.

"Did you say something about calling a number, by the way?" I could see she had one of her little "From the Desk of Eileen Douglass" memo slips smashed between her fingers. When her euphoria had passed, she held the rumpled pink slip toward me.

"Oh, sorry," she said. "Here. You're supposed to call this number. Maybe it's the queen."

"She wants me too?" Mom smiled at that one. Maybe she was forgetting about Rolf, about being a handsome woman.

She handed me the phone and moved off the bed while I dialed the number on the pink slip. A pleasant, secretarial voice answered. "WRBR, channel eleven," she said, and I identified myself. She told me to please hold.

"Hello, Steve, Steve Douglass" came an intense, glottalized voice. I pulled the receiver a couple of inches away from my ear.

171

"Yes. Stephen, that's me," I answered.

"Steve, this is Donnie Pitella, executive producer, channel eleven. We're involved in a major project, and we'd be interested to know if you'd like to participate. Let me explain." He was doing a documentary on public education, something in the area, a tie-in with the recent studies on public education. "A Nation at Risk" kind of thing, he called it. Their show was going under the name "The Shame of our Schools." A catchy title, but maybe a bit slanted. They were looking at schools statewide, interviewing teachers, students, parents, administrators, school boards, assorted experts. They wanted to do me.

"We caught you on the competition a few weeks back. That channel five piece with the Whitney girl. We liked your look. We liked your sound. You're articulate, you're bright, you're right there on the cutting edge of things, you've been on the hot seat already."

*"Mmmmm hmmmm, mmm hmmmmh,"* I said.

"We'd like to send a crew over sometime. Follow you around, to classes, like that, do a pre- and post-interview, get your slant on things. Joe Student, like that. What do you say?"

"Well, I'd have to check it out with, you know, the principal and all that."

"No problem. You do that. I'll have an associate call the school. She'll have some releases to sign, strictly pro forma. We'll set a date, run through your schedule, *blah blah blah, blah blah blah.* What do you say?"

"Sure, Okay, I suppose."

172

"Peaches," said Don Pitella. "Don't sound so luke-warm, Steve. You could be national. ABC has us scouting talent. They're doing three hours in January. Be good." And that was that.

When I gave Mom the details, she was delirious. "Let's check your chart," she said. Every time something amazing happened, she wanted to get out her old guide to the stars. To her credit, she only used it for enlightened hindsight.

"Aw, Mom, give me a break. That's voodoo," I protested. She sprawled out on my bed and grabbed Babar.

"O mystical Elephant King," she intoned, waving one hand in front of his glassy little eyes. "Speak to us of the future. Tell us of your visions of Stephen to come."

"Careful, Mom, you might get Jacob Marley." She used to read me *A Christmas Carol* every year and do these great keening ghost voices for all the weird spirits.

"Bless you, Stephen, you still remember." She nuzzled Babar nose to trunk, then sat up on my bed and studied Babar's face.

"My little Stephen." Again with the "little Stephen." Then, "My god, Stephen. Look!" She held Babar right up in front of my face. I was expecting the Hope diamond to come dribbling out of his abdomen. "Look," she said, this time jabbing a finger right at Babar's trunk. I looked at his trunk. It was tipped with a dark gray-brown smudge, its plush slightly crusted and stiff.

"Dat's your little 'Babasniff,' remember? You used

173

to wear this thing right under your nose. Come nap time, I'd give you this and you'd take a couple good whiffs of your 'Babasniff' and pass right out. God, it was agony for you to give this up. You were eight. I hid Babar in the fridge, right in the crisper, for a month. Finally, you broke the habit, but what misery. Your little 'Babasniff.' "

"But I never sucked my thumb," I reminded her. "Now can we please give Babar a little respect?" I removed the stuffed creature from her hands and replaced it on my headboard. She was definitely being weird. I was afraid she was going to go into the old breast-feeding routine. She never tired of telling everyone that she founded the Cable Hall chapter of the La Leche League. Even in my company.

Later we dressed fancy, and she drove us to the Good Thyme Restaurant to celebrate. Its two claims to distinction were its vegetarian menu and its fortuitous location at the corner of Rosemary and Sage streets. I had the spinach lasagna and Mom supped on marinated hearts of palm. We split a carafe of wine. Mom explained as how it made her feel naughty and European to see her young man partake. The waiter thought otherwise and removed the coffee cup out of which I had been drinking.

Later we stopped for ice cream, but when she suggested a movie I had to beg off. I did have a biology test in the morning, and I thought it might not hurt to read a few chapters in my book, just on the outside chance that anything in there might show up on the test.

I settled in my room when we got back, and Mom

said she was going to stretch out and read. So I read the chapters on microorganisms and looked over mitosis one more time.

It was past midnight when I finished. From somewhere, from beyond my room, came a whoosh and a rushing sound, as though the house had found its voice, a strange sonic complaint, barely audible but present, part metallic and part something else. I walked down the hall and checked on Mom. She wasn't there. I followed the noise downstairs, and the rushing grew louder. Now, in intervals of quiet, I could hear a voice, what seemed like a voice, then a whoosh, and the voice slid beneath the sound once more. I followed the sound, its volume rising, down to the basement. A light came from beneath the door. Of course—the room, the exercise room, and the rushing of Mom's rowing machine. I tried the knob, but the room seemed locked.

I decided to go outside. I crept along the back and slid in behind the azaleas where two rectangular windows at ground level allow some daylight to intrude into the exercise room. I peeked in just enough to see that Mom had pulled the machine up to the mirrored wall. Even as she rowed she kept her head up, her eyes fixed intently on her image in the mirror. She wore shorts and a sweatshirt, stained, saturated completely with sweat. Stranger still, her hair had been braided into pigtails barely long enough to hang of their own weight and bound with small pink ribbons. Through the window I could hear the rush and snap and whoosh of the machine. Mom seemed to push it, straining at its limit. For how long, I wondered? I could see her lips moving, speaking at her image in the mirror with an anger I had never seen before.

I was ready to run inside, knock at the door, and interrupt. Yet suddenly she released the grips, let the oars fall to the side, and collapsed forward from the waist, her head falling full against her knees. Her body convulsed, fighting for breath, even as she bent double over herself, unmoving. She remained like this for probably five minutes, then slid off sideways and lay with her back flat against the floor. When her breathing seemed fully back to normal, she sat, then stood, still watching herself in the mirror. She grabbed the bottom of her sweatshirt and peeled it off. Then she watched herself, studied herself in the mirror, naked from the waist up. She turned sideways and inhaled, then backward, awkwardly staring at herself over her left shoulder. Then full front once again, now breathing deeply. Her lips started moving until I could hear her voice filling the empty room. I put my ear to the pane. "Handsome woman," she kept repeating, then stopped. "The big four oh," she said. Finally, more gently, she started singing "Happy Birthday," removing the pink ribbons one at a time and letting her hair fall back around her face.

I ran up to my room as fast as I could and grabbed my Babar. I scribbled a quick note and rushed into Mom's room. I stuffed the note into Babar's vest and sat him proudly on her pillow. It said, "Happy Birthday to my all-time favorite mom. Love, Stephen."

It wasn't much, but at least she'd think I'd remembered.

# Chapter 30

I woke up late the next morning. I had barely gotten on my underwear when the bus passed outside. Mom was still asleep. I decided not to bother her for a ride. I hitched as far as I could and walked the rest of the way. I had already missed homeroom and would need a late pass to get into first-period English, so I stopped by the office first. Suddenly Wilfong poked his head out, ducked back in, then popped it out once more. I thought he was going to go "Cuckoo" and announce the hour. Instead, he saw me and forced a waxen smile. "StEEEEphen, Stephen, just thinking about you. Come here, son. Let's talk."

I followed him into his office and sat across from his desk. "Got a call from channel eleven this morning. Sounds like they want to make you a star. Did they talk to you about it yet?" He picked up a Lucite cube with a butterfly trapped inside and started rolling it around in his right palm.

"Yes, sir, yesterday. They said they'd call. They're fast."

"Yes they are, yes they are." He studied the butterfly. "What'd you tell them?" he asked.

"Well, I didn't tell them much. But I said it was fine by me, as long as the school—as you—didn't mind."

"Ahhhh, yes." He smiled at the butterfly. "There's always a catch. I'll be honest. I'm not fond of the idea. You know how I feel about disruptive influences in our school. Bad for learning, bad for learning." He chuckled and plunked the butterfly back on his desk, tugging at his beard. "But, I think, here's an opportunity, opportunity knocking, so to speak. Opportunity for you, of course, and an opportunity for us to showcase our school."

"Yes, sir," I agreed. But had he been told the proposed title of the documentary? "The Shame of our Schools"? I supposed not.

"Look." He shot a quick glance outside his office. "Can I have your assurance that anything we say here will not go any farther than this office?"

"Sure," I said. "Not a word."

Wilfong sprung from his chair and eased the door closed all the way. He plopped back into his chair. *Huuuuusssshhhhh* it went under his weight.

"How's your biology doing these days?" he asked.

"Better," I said.

"Oh, is it really? That's not what I hear." He reached into a drawer and pulled out a folder. I looked for my name on the tab. But it was blank. And half as thin as mine. Wilfong opened the folder and started leafing through its contents. He pulled out a lined sheet filled with signatures and scanned its contents. "Ah, Eileen Douglass. That your mom?"

178

"Yes, she's my mother. Did she write you about me?"

"Indirectly, you might say." He dropped the paper to its folder. "She's one of eighty-eight signatures here. These gifted parents are asking for Truelove's dismissal. What do you think about that?"

"Sounds serious. But, I mean, isn't he on tenure?" I remembered something about Mr. Mustero. He'd had no tenure. He'd been teaching only two years.

"Tenure, yes, Mr. Truelove is tenured. He's been with our school ten, eleven years now, I think it is. Frankly, he's been losing his grip lately. But to dismiss a teacher on tenure is messy business: courts, attorneys, it can drag on for months. And proving incompetency is no bed of roses. Everyone comes out looking a little messy—the school, the administration . . . even the teacher. It's not pleasant."

"No, sir, I'm sure it's not." I kept waiting, waiting for Wilfong to arrive somewhere.

"Maybe a student could help some. You know what they say about a fly on the wall. Listen to this." He shuffled through the folder once more. "Number one: Classroom management. Total lack of control, chaotic class learning environment. Number two: Curriculum management. No course syllabus, no apparent organization, no regular homework or classwork pattern. Number three: Student evaluation. Tests on uncovered material, arbitrary evaluative instrument, arbitrary and capricious scoring of same." He paused and handed me a sheet of paper from the folder. "Have you ever seen this before?"

It was a Xerox copy of the test on bivalve reproduction. Peggy's test, in fact. "Yes sir, just briefly. I was out of school when he gave it."

"And do these, uh, does this list of grievances, let's call them, do they seem reasonable to you?"

"Oh maybe, some yes." I wanted to explain them, explain the student siege of Truelove. But Mr. Wilfong wouldn't have been interested. "But I think he does know his biology. When he gets to it."

"Let's be frank." Wilfong put his elbows and his beard back on the desk. "You seem like a sensible boy with a bright future. Class president. My, my. You'll want to go to college someday. That was a good speech you gave, all that about fresh start. I can see why you'd want your folder cleaned up a little. Any college takes a look at some of the shenanigans you've been through, and they might want to run the other way. So let's say we tidy up your folder a little. And let you do this TV thing. And maybe we could forget about that three-thousand-dollar IOU. Certainly all that should be worth something?"

"Yes, I suppose it might be worth a lot," I admitted. "But what, exactly, do you want from me?"

"Just what you know. What you've seen. I'd want you to be a . . . witness. Of sorts. Tell the school board, share your observations."

"Of Truelove, you mean?"

"Yes, of him. It'd be strictly closed session. Just you and me and the board. Kept in the utmost confidence, of course. They don't ever take minutes in closed session."

"And would I be your only witness?" I asked.

"Maybe. Depends on what you tell the board. It

might be enough. He could be out by Christmas."

"But why me? Especially after all the . . ."

"The suspension? The hearings? No hard feelings on that score, Stephen. Besides, that gave you credibility, recognition. Put you in the limelight. Your little channel five speech was an impressive performance. Made me look like a piker. Even Mrs. Wilfong thinks so!" He held out a hand, palm up, as though to introduce the invisible Mrs. Wilfong.

"That's nice. I'm flattered and all, but there must be a hundred kids who could do the same thing. . . ."

"Ah, yes, but maybe you have better reasons to want to," he purred. He sat smiling at me, stroking Truelove's folder. "We think you might have some extra-special insight into Mr. Truelove, no? Maybe you'd like to tell your side of the lab thing, your side of that day in front of the class. I still don't feel . . . comfortable, exactly, with what went on that day. It bothers me."

"Me too," I shot right back. But what bothered me more was what Wilfong knew that he wasn't saying. Or maybe he was just guessing lucky. I didn't want to know right then.

All I knew was that here was the chance. A real fresh start. Maybe Truelove deserved his walking papers after all. I had been the martyr long enough. It was time to let that go, to let it all go: My observations of Truelove were going nowhere, really, other than in the direction everyone suspected—that he was a certifiable bull-goose looney, or at least a mid-life crisis teacher burnout. It happens.

181

And then we could see afterward if Peggy liked me for my native charm or only for my credentials as radical provocateur and much-put-upon boy wonder. And Mom and Dad could take their monthly turns being glad that I had gotten onto the straight and narrow at long last.

Why not? Uncomplicate.

"Let's say I do—" I began. I was speaking hypothetically, I thought, but Wilfong took it as all-out consent.

"All right, son, we'll say you *do.* It's the right thing. I know you won't regret it."

"No sir," I said. "I hope not."

"I knew I could count on you. Oh, and let your teachers know about this TV thing. It may be a month or more. I'll put out a memo. They like to put their best foot forward too, you know."

"Could you write me a pass, sir? That's what I came for in the first place. I need to get into class." And the bell rang. Time for second period. "I didn't have a note, but I can get one if that's a problem."

"Note, schmote. Look at this." He ripped a sheet from his phone memo pad and scribbled his name in a large generous hand. "Howard Wilfong. Excuse Stephen Douglass." "You'll want to hold on to that one, son. Use it whenever. Come by and talk."

I told him maybe I would, but I didn't really believe it.

# Chapter 31

But I didn't go to second period after that. I walked straight out through the cafeteria and settled behind an overstuffed dumpster, where the lunchtime potheads came to play. I sat with my back against the huge green box and watched the flies gather in lazy squadrons on yesterday's lettuce. These were October flies, ponderous and slow, mostly baritones, ripe for the first hard freeze. Little did they know.

Then back to the rest of my second-period class, and third, and so on. I tried to explain to my teachers about the TV thing. Most made a big deal about how eager they would be to open their classes to the media, but there was small terror in their eyes. Telling Truelove was another thing. Maybe we could skip that altogether.

When I got to seventh period, I remembered about the test. The class sat properly at attention when the bell rang. Peggy greeted me with the warmest smile in her repertoire, shades of the courthouse steps. The bell rang and Truelove surprised everyone by lunging from his desk and walking to the front of the room. He held a bundle of papers in his hand. The test.

"Okay, let's get started," he announced. He waved the bundle at us and approached the first row of tables. He licked his thumb and prepared to pass out the tests.

But suddenly heads turned, front rows looking to the back, back rows looking at each other. Buddy turned toward Peggy and nodded, then scanned the rest of the class. Most were watching Buddy, not Truelove. He bobbed his head—one, two, three—and slid his stool backward. As he did, Peggy did the same, and then the rest of the class, most of the class I should say. Up front, Nu Tran sat still under Truelove's elbow.

Again Buddy bobbed his head one, two, three, and the entire class stood at their tables and . . .

*"Good afternoon, Doctor Truelove,"* they said in unison, or almost in unison, Buddy's voice leading the others in a mocking singsong.

They had found it, Truelove's weakness, or a part of it, and I had given it to them. Peggy sat back down beside me, poker-faced, the blankness hiding her passion for the right cause. What did she feel?

Truelove was shaken. He seemed barely able to get the tests passed out. He averted his face from the class, as though he could hide in front of twenty-eight pairs of eyes.

He did not give me a copy of the test. He returned to his desk, and I heard the chair scrape back. I didn't watch. I sat, as the class bent to their tests, wondering. Then a hand appeared from behind me, ghost-like, and dropped a paper in front of me. It was a test, folded lengthwise. I opened it and read. There were twenty true-or-false questions and an essay question on "The Miracle of Mitosis." Not exactly a superior evaluative instrument, in Wilfong's phrase. But it wasn't on bivalves.

At the bottom, in pencil, was a message. It had been written in such a cramped, microscopic hand that I almost missed it. "Green Torino, south lot, at four. Important. Tell nobody. Can you be there? Please?"

I did the test. My hand shook so much that my essay was almost unreadable. I finished early. It was a short test. I sat and stared at the blank wall for twenty minutes. When the bell rang, I wrote "yes" at the bottom of the test and turned it in.

# Chapter 32

Peggy was waiting for me in the hall outside. "Come on to the studio with me." She took my arm and tried to lead me down the hall. "Stephen, come on." I resisted her pull. "You can come home with me. Ted and Margaret are at group tonight. I'll make you dinner. You like Greek? I'll stuff some grape leaves." She lowered her voice into a sultry whisper. "You'll love my stuffed grape leaves. Come on."

"I would love to, believe me," I lied. And then prepared another lie. "But I have to see a doctor today. I have a four o'clock appointment. I gotta get going."

I broke away from her grasp and backpedaled five steps, apologetic. Peggy spun away in a sulk and took off. "You're a loss, Stephen," she called to me. "Anyway, tell your doctor hi!"

I collected some books from my locker, deposited some others, and headed for the south lot out beyond the auditorium, where the teachers parked their cars. As I walked through the exit doors by the auto shop, the dead weight of fear settled on my shoulders. My knees trembled, my calves seemed to wither. But I dragged myself to the south lot and sprawled on the bank at its edge. With my backpack under my head for a pillow, I closed my eyes and listened to the buses exiting on the road above me, their engines straining.

After the last bus had whined beyond hearing, I watched the football team assemble on the practice field below the south lot. They gathered into ranks on a bare clay oval they had worn into the grass and went into their warm-ups. *"Hunh, hoo, hee, hoorrr,"* they chanted. Volume seemed to count for more than effort. It rose to a higher pitch as they saw the coaches approach, whistles twinkling in the afternoon sun, clipboards wielded like blunt clubs. Finally the athletes broke into groups by specialty—linemen, receivers, backs, and so on—and ran through their drills. Blocking sleds went scudding over the bare dirt. *"Drive drive drive those legs, you pansies"* came the voice of the line coach. The backs pumped their legs, knee to chin, and the receivers traced smooth curls and sharp breaks under a wobbling rain of footballs. Soon everyone was lathered in a healthy sweat, polished pink or brown or somewhere in between, like rough stones tumbled to a glossy hard.

Right then I would have traded my nifty IQ, my high-tech toy chest, and a year's supply of smart remarks to be down there with those guys. It wasn't that I was dreading my rendezvous with Truelove (which I was), or that I wanted to develop my weak American thighs. I just envied those guys right then.

187

Not so much for their football-hero status, but more for the simple joy of the game, the chance to find some sweet release for the brain.

Finally teachers started appearing in the south lot and settling in their cars. Some eyed me suspiciously and kept their windows up as they drove out of the lot. As the cars left, I finally decided which one of those remaining was Truelove's. It sat at the very center of the lot, a faded Torino in a pale lime green, a color fashionable during the avocado heyday of major home appliances, maybe ten years back. It had a vinyl top, once black but now gray with age and too much sun. The vinyl poked up in ragged triangles, like some bird had pecked across its width and length in a misbegotten search for worms.

Truelove appeared from around the far end of the auditorium and shambled to his car. He held a brown grocery bag from Food Lion in one hand. He entered the Torino, put the bag on the backseat, and rolled down the front windows. When he started the car and steered toward the exit, I swelled with relief. He had forgotten. Thank God. But instead he circled around and pulled the Torino alongside the curb, stopping right in front of the bank where I sat. He leaned across the front seat and popped the door.

"Get in, Douglass. I won't bite," he said, and patted the seat beside him. I slid down off the bank and stared into his car. Bulges of foam swelled from the seats through torn seams.

"Get in, it's okay," he repeated.

I threw my backpack onto the seat and sat down so near the edge that when I slammed the door it bumped me another six inches closer to Truelove. The car rumbled to the end of the school road, but he turned left, away from town. He was taking me out to the country somewhere. They would find me in a week with an ax in my brain.

"Another day at Hatred High, eh?" he said to himself. "Can you get me that bag back there?" I retrieved the shopping bag from the backseat and set it between us. "Reach in and find my cigarettes. There should be a pack of Camel filters in there somewhere."

I found the cigarettes and offered him the pack. He took it, removed one cigarette, and lit it with the dashboard lighter. He threw the pack onto the dash. "Cookies in there. Help yourself." I looked into the bag and saw a bag of iced raisin bars. But I wasn't hungry.

Instead I watched out the window, ravenous to record every detail of this strange southern landscape I had never really seen before. I knew it wasn't mine, didn't belong to me with my wise-guy Yankee heart. But it would have to do, might be the last I'd ever see. I might have to remember it for a long, long, time: this open country with miles of withered cornstalks and tobacco stalks stripped bare as spikes and curing houses bunched along the roadside, high, rough-timbered shacks with tin roofs rusted orange. Soon we had passed under the interstate and through the town of Verner Mills where the Great Toneco River drove the state's first textile mills. The river still flowed in its flat banks, more rusty orange, the universal color of piedmont clay and water and old tin roofs. But the town had withdrawn from the river, leaving the ruins of century-old brick mills to tumble down its banks.

"Be there soon," Truelove declared, pulling himself up from the seat and hunching over the wheel.

"Soon" stretched out another fifteen minutes, and then finally we passed a lumber mill, an auto yard selling TV satellite dishes, and a Christian academy called New Hope Day School. We bumped over some weed-covered railroad tracks and entered a two-stoplight town by the name of Hawleyville. Main Street was two blocks of hardware stores and beauty shops, most closed. Faded cardboard signs in the windows boasted hairdos ten years old. Overhead, power lines held lights and tinsel garlands. Foiled letters proclaimed the joys of Christmas: "Season's Greetings." I knew I would miss that season of the year the most.

Truelove continued on out through town to where a gas station sat squeezed up against the road. A big plastic Coke sign announced this as the A & G Superette. We turned there onto a crumbling black road, its ragged shoulders dissolving into clay and weeds. We came to a row of small brick houses, all homemade from the same orange brick. One was two stories, as high as it was wide, with a flat roof and a seam where the second story met the first. A short walk led straight from the front door to the road. The right side of the walk was close-cut lawn, a sparse growth of something more brown than green. Its centerpiece was a birdbath, a great plaster ocean shell resting atop the heads of three rigid seahorses posing back to back to back.

To the left of the walk, bare clay with two shallow ruts suggested a driveway. Truelove steered his Torino down these ruts and pulled around behind the house. Two kids of maybe ten or eleven stood shooting baskets at an orange rim fixed to a pole—no backboard, no net.

"Hey Willis, hey Jimmy," Truelove called from the car. The boys held the ball for us to pass and waved back at Truelove. Finally he parked behind a half-collapsed swing set. A rectangle of weeds had grown between its legs, a wheelless lawn mower resting at the thicket's very center.

"We're here," Truelove announced. He grabbed his shopping bag and I grabbed my backpack. "This way," he directed, walking to the other side of the house. A rickety Z of stairs led to a landing at the second-floor entrance. Truelove pushed his way through an unlocked screen door and waved at me to follow. I felt that I was entering the very heart of the mystery.

"Feast your eyes on this, Douglass," Truelove said. I surveyed the late-afternoon gloom of his apartment. A room filled with stacks of magazines turned, at its far end, into a kitchenette. Along the back wall two doorways framed a bathroom to the left and a bedroom to the right.

"This is where you live," I said. It was more statement than question.

"Right, Douglass. Even I have to live somewhere." He walked to the kitchenette and plunged his hand into a sinkful of dishwater. Two roaches floated on its surface, struggling against the pale gray tide. He plucked them out just as the water guzzled down the drain. "Order Orthoptera. Family Blattidae. They will inherit the earth." He smashed them against the sink and scraped their remains into a garbage bag under the sink. "Not those two, of course, but their descendants."

He rinsed his hands and sat at a small drop-leaf table against the wall. "Go get a chair," he ordered, pointing at a canvas slingback across the room. I pulled the chair over to the table and sat. The table was set with a mismatched pair of salt-and-pepper shakers and a brown cube of meat loaf drying on a plate. It had a paring knife plunged into its top and a small dew of grease at its base. Beside the meat loaf a stick of margarine slumped on a paper plate.

"We need to talk first; then we can eat," Truelove announced. Neither choice seemed very appealing.

"What about?" I asked.

"I brought you here to talk about us, way the hell away from that school. On my territory. Now let's talk about us, about Doctor Truelove and the clever young man. First of all, where'd you get the Doctor part? Let's begin there."

"Got it from you, if you must know." I described for him the afternoon I had sat hunched under the table while he trashed the lab and ranted about being Dr. Truelove. I even recited it almost word for word.

"So you were there? I figured as much. That girl, the Klecko girl, bending over. I chased her out, and she was talking to you all the time. Damn. You mean you just fell right down on your butt . . . ?"

I nodded. "You reamed me out pretty good. No

breath. Couldn't get my legs to work. So, yes, congratulations. You chewed me up for real."

"For real, eh?" He raised both hands to the tabletop and held them thumb against thumb, as though measuring his nails. "And so they kicked you out for two weeks. Pity. And you never made the first peep about me. I suppose I should thank you. Odd, though, you never said 'boo.'"

That did it. "Oh, don't count your blessings. It wasn't for you. I wasn't trying to save your lunatic ass. I didn't owe you cowpie, and I still don't." I was ready to spring from my chair and out the door at his first move.

But he just sat, staring at his thumbnails, nursing a chuckle in his throat.

"Cowpie. No, I suppose you don't." Then he stared right into my eyes. "Scared stiff, that's more like it. Musta been scared stiff, a boy like you."

"Sure," I admitted. "At first maybe. Still am, some. But there was more. There were advantages, so to speak. That girl Peggy, for one. And everyone took me . . . seriously, for a change. Class president, then TV, it just grew, and I rode along. Maybe too far, but I did. Besides, I should've trashed your lab. I had every reason to. So, when they said I did . . . well, all right. I'd take the blame as long as I got the credit. It gave me . . . a kind of weight, you see. Credibility."

"You became an estimable gentleman, a rogue without portfolio. Well, I'm glad."

"Oh, don't be," I snapped. I didn't really want his understanding, his approval. "Besides, I wanted you to myself. You had your turn with me. Now it's my

193

turn. Hypothesis, observation, conclusion. The scientific method, remember, lesson one? So maybe I felt a little more observation was what I needed."

"And here you are." He spread his arms, palms up, in welcome. "Have at it, I'm all yours."

"Oh heart, be still," I declaimed, hand to sternum, an old favorite of my dad's.

Truelove ignored the wit.

"And you must have assumed I was crazy," he said.

"Well, yes, I figured you were really cracked, right then."

"And maybe I was, maybe I was," he repeated. "But am I now?"

"I don't know anymore." Then I remembered what I had told Jamie. "I once told this woman about how you've gotta scream into the bathroom mirror every once in a while. I guess she thought I was pretty far gone, too."

"Are you?" He smiled for the first time. He took the plate of meat loaf and spun it on the table, edging his fingers around the plate's circumference, smiling into the meat loaf as though it were a crystal ball.

"Far gone? Not yet, but I can feel it, how easy it would be. When I scream into the bathroom mirror it scares me. I look around to make sure no one's watching. Or sometimes, at night, under the covers, I cackle until I have to stuff the pillow in my mouth."

"As long as no one sees you, is that what you mean? If a tree screams in a forest, it's not crazy until someone hears it?"

"*Mmmmm*, yes. You do know. In public, at school,

even with my mom or dad, I feel as if I really have to work at it, at playing this normal person I'm supposed to be. I mean, you see these crazy types downtown, spitting at parking meters and pissing into those instant-money walk-up teller machines and you . . . at least I . . . feel ashamed."

"Ashamed to be watching them, you mean?" He started wiping crumbs off the table, invisible crumbs. I was making him nervous.

"No. Ashamed that I'm not out there with them going 'la la la' and eating magazines. Ashamed that I am better at keeping it all a secret and they've given up trying. Like I've betrayed them, if you can imagine."

"I can imagine," Truelove repeated. "God knows, you sure caught me with my psychic pants down, so to speak."

His psychic pants. Here I was, grinding away at how I really felt, and suddenly he turns cute. "Your damn psychic pants were pretty ragged the day I saw you. Pretty damn threadbare. I'd say you'd gone so far over it amazes me you're able to sit here and talk without drooling on your shoe tops. I'm sure I'm not the first, won't be the last, to catch you with your so-called psychic pants down. Fact, I'd almost have been willing to say the damn emperor has no psychic pants, is about the way I saw it."

"Your point is taken, Mr. Douglass." Truelove rolled his head back, stared at the ceiling. His right hand rose to his neck, kneading the loose skin there one palmful at a time. "Maybe you need to appreciate how it is to have lived, say, maybe half your life or more and realize you've come up empty. Very empty indeed . . ."

"Well, maybe I have," I said. "In the last couple of months I've learned maybe more than I should about that kind of stuff."

"I can imagine what you've learned," he growled at the ceiling.

"I'm not talking about you. You don't have a copyright on that. My mother just turned forty. It was hard. She spent the night all by herself and when I went downstairs—it was after midnight—do you know that she was absolutely—"

"Stop!" Truelove called out. He threw his hands up, palms out, like a traffic cop. "Don't. It isn't worth it. You shouldn't tell. You owe her your silence more than you owe it to me. Tell me that, and you'll have more reason to hate me later on. And you have enough already. So just don't."

He dropped his hands to the table and exhaled heavily. I knew he was right. It was the first, the only time I had reason to respect him. He had saved me from that and from unloading about my father, too. He didn't need to know, and he'd said so.

"It's her pain," he continued. "Hers. And there are so many kinds. You're finding out so early." He rose from the table and walked across the room, circling in and out among the piles of magazines stacked around the floor. When he reached a desk by the side window, he sorted through its center drawer and removed an envelope. He returned to the table by a direct route, hurdling the piles until he stood behind me.

196

"This is my pain. Take a look." He dropped the envelope on the table in front of me. I picked it up and pulled a stiff cardboard from inside. It turned out to be a photograph, folded in half. I opened the picture and smoothed it out on the table in front of me. The picture showed a group of children standing formally in front of a green wall. They seemed a strange new species, mostly Oriental, but not quite. There were twelve or thirteen kids, aged maybe seven to fourteen, dressed in loose-fitting white shirts. Their hair was cut at a uniform length around and below the ears. It was impossible to tell which were girls. Although they all shared a dull blank stare directly into the lens, the differences were even more remarkable. Three had tightly curled black hair and dusky complexions suggesting some black blood. Others differed in details of eyes, of skin, of shape even. Some noses seemed a bit too sharp, some faces too long or angular. Others showed a glint of red hair that couldn't merely have been the photograph itself.

"What are they?" I asked.

"One of them's mine. My son." Truelove paused, and now I knew why he was standing behind me. When he continued there was a catch in the voice. "One of them. One. Maybe this one here." He tapped the picture with a thumb, indicating a tall figure in the back row. "Of course, I have no way of knowing for sure. You're holding fourteen . . . fourteen years of effort there . . . fourteen years of letters and dead ends." He breathed deeply and attempted an apology. "That picture came the first afternoon of school, the day before . . . I mean, it doesn't excuse anything, but I wanted you to know, that's all."

"No, it doesn't," I agreed. "After . . . what? . . . fourteen years you ought to mellow out, you know, get some control." So he was all stressed out about the Amerasian kid he said was his, and he had decided to use me for his whipping boy. Hardly a fair trade.

"Well, control's a funny thing. They give you prescriptions for control: Quaaludes, deseril. You can end up comatose or fat or forever in hock to the pharmacist. Control has a price, son." He reached a hand across my shoulder. I folded the picture back into its envelope and handed it to him.

"Besides," he continued, "I'm in the wrong game, teaching science to children." He spit out the last word like it was a spoiled piece of meat.

"Like stress, burnout, sure, it's in all the magazines."

"No!" he almost shouted. "It's you!" He collapsed back into his seat, and the weight of his forearms drove the table flat against my solar plexus. He had me pinned. "It's you," he repeated. "Every year, it's you, always the same, with your braces and your backpacks and your smirky little faces and fifty-dollar running shoes and your hair, just so . . ." He cocked his head like some twelve-year-old coquette and did this strange primping thing with both hands, flouncing imaginary hair just below his ears. "And your little summer vacations at the beach, I hear you talking, don't think I don't. . . ."

"I hate the beach, sir," I fired back. "And I don't

198

have braces, and so what if I have a backpack. You want me to carry a briefcase, for god's sake? I'm only sixteen. Ya want me to go barefoot and eat rice just so you'll feel better, like it's all my fault."

Truelove sat stroking the envelope, smoothing it against the tabletop. "I guess I was trying to say something about American children . . . teenagers, whatever you call yourselves."

"Sure, crucify me. Like I chose to be American, like it's my fault, like it's some original sin. No one chooses that stuff." I planted both my hands against the table edge and shoved it back at him, firmly but gently. This was becoming a fight for territory.

"Fair enough," he conceded. "No one, as you say, 'chooses that stuff.' It's like everything else—blind dumb luck, good or bad. All the same . . ."

I caught myself trembling again, my leg shivering. I planted my feet against the floor and clamped a hand on each thigh. Fear drained through my toes and emptied into my fifty-dollar running shoes.

"So look, I'm sorry about your son," I offered. "But why didn't you bring him back? And the mother. There was a mother, wasn't there?"

"Yes, of course there was. But we had to get married first. The Army was very particular about those arrangements. Meantime An Le—the mother, I mean—was being relocated from Long Binh. That's about the time that I became, uh, indisposed."

His voice dropped another ten decibels on "indisposed." He reached across the table and lifted the meat loaf, using the paring knife for a handle. He walked to the sink and dropped the meat under-

199

neath, into the garbage bag, on top of the roaches. Putting the knife into the sink, he turned on the hot water and let it run. The sink filled, and steam rose from the basin.

"Indisposed how?" I asked. "Were you wounded or something?"

"Or something," he said. "Confined to quarters. I was being investigated, a bunch of us were. *Newsweek* had done a story on certain doctors, yours truly among them. And the brass had to clean house. Too generous with the drugs, they said."

"Were you? Was it true?"

"Of course it was true," he answered, and turned off the hot water with such force that the pipes shivered beneath the floor. "The original Doctor Feelgood, M.D., O.D., Doctor of Overdose. I just couldn't handle their pain, that's all, the burning, all of them in the end just pink and burning. And dying. At least without pain, if I could help it. But the Army didn't think it was cost-effective. And I was losing interest pretty fast in what the Army thought. And that's when I excused myself."

"Excused yourself from what?"

"From the Army. The war, what was left of it. My ass was grass already, is how I figured. So I went looking for An Le. Long Binh was a zoo. Saigon was worse. They were talking evacuation, they were lining up for days. I saw children fighting over cardboard boxes. That's when I knew."

"To get out?" I asked.

"Yeah, out. Americans were getting pretty scarce. I didn't want to stick out."

"So you flew back home? To the States?"

"Not a chance. Couldn't fly military. I'd already been over the hill, what? Maybe three, four weeks. I paid a small ransom to be smuggled to Thailand. Bangkok. I figured maybe I could keep on looking from there.

"Any luck?"

"Just that I met the guy who sent me that picture. He had contacts. Everyone in Bangkok had contacts. It was kind of a growth industry in those days. You paid them, they bribed the V.C. Guess I paid enough to keep an entire regiment in pajamas and cigarettes."

"But you never found An Le?"

"No. Oh, there were crumbs. But by then I guessed she must've had the kid. And I was running out of funds. It took all I had left to get to Hong Kong, get some British papers, and finally make it home."

"British papers? You mean you had to use a fake passport just to get back?"

"Just so. Right as rain, mate." He clipped it off in a proper limey accent. It convinced me.

He explained how he had stayed on the West Coast and gotten his master's degree in teaching somewhere in Oregon, then slowly worked his way east, as far away as he could get. Finally he had taken the job at the high school. He had cast off most of his past and at first enjoyed the anonymity of teaching, the relative seclusion from the adult world. Until the last few years, he said, when it had begun to engulf him. All he had left was the company of sixteen-year-olds. That, and his long-distance search for a son.

201

"And this is as far as I got," he sighed. He picked the photograph off the table and jammed it into a back pocket. "Now for dinner. You've earned it. What do you like?"

I told him I was flexible, but not to make a fuss.

"A fuss, Douglass? Don't worry about a fuss. I'm just walking down to the A & G. It'll be a surprise." He let the screen door slam behind him and creaked his way down the makeshift Z of stairs. I watched from the side window as he reached the bare clay where Willis and Jimmy were still playing horse.

Truelove grabbed the ball from one of the kids, dribbled maybe twenty feet away from the basket, then spun and shot. The ball left his fingers with a perfect spin, arced into the air, and dropped without a sound through the orange hoop. He caught nothing but the net that wasn't there. Sweet shot.

# Chapter 33

Now by myself, I played archivist at the Truelove museum. I didn't think of it as snooping. I was simply conducting more observations on the Truelove phenomenon. I wasn't sure if it was time to revise my hypothesis, but at least it felt good to know I would probably survive my visit.

I scouted through the stacks of magazines, some of them going back more than ten years. There were *JAMA (Journal of the American Medical Association)* and the *New England Journal of Medicine.* One pile was devoted exclusively to pharmaceuticals and drugs, thin pamphlets published to announce the wonder drugs. Another tilting stack contained *The New York Times Magazine,* and others the newsmagazines, a mix of *Time* and *Newsweek* and *U.S. News and World Report.*

Instead of a tub the bathroom had a stall shower, its door stained nearly green with mildew. The medicine cabinet held three glass shelves lined with empty prescription bottles.

The bedroom was a square, barely ten by ten, with pink walls and a fine powder of grit on the linoleum floor. A mattress sat on the floor, with sheets turning gray in a tangle in the center and a navy blanket folded at its end. Above the mattress a large American flag hung against the wall. A patriotic touch, I thought, until I noticed that little white skulls had been sewn where the stars should have been. Instead of a closet, an arrangement of RC cola boxes stood against the wall. They contained the wardrobe, the three spare pants, the strange array of short-sleeved shirts and those V-necked T-shirts folded and stacked in a tidy pile.

Two of the boxes sat back to back beside the bed, serving as a nightstand. A stoneware lamp, like a whiskey bottle, sat on top. Leaning against the lamp was a snapshot framed in perforated brass. It was a picture of Truelove and a woman. Truelove was leaner and younger and more tanned. He wore fatigue trousers and a baseball cap shaded his eyes. He was grinning. He leaned against the end of a picnic table, his legs crossed at the ankles, his left arm around the woman's shoulder. The woman was probably Vietnamese. Her long black hair was gathered to one side and fixed above the right ear with a bolo clip, two pink plastic balls on elastic. She seemed embarrassed, staring not at the camera but downward somewhere beyond her feet. Her T-shirt said, "War is not healthy for children and other living things." Beneath the words was the figure of a rifle with a single flower sticking in its barrel.

Behind the picture, wedged between it and the

lamp, was a sheaf of stationery, pale-blue mottled paper with stripes around the borders. I pulled the papers out and examined them. They unfolded into letters. A PO box number was the only thing I recognized in English. I sorted through the lot of them, but each seemed identical to all the others. Carefully I refolded the letters, and wedged them once more behind the lamp. When Truelove walked through the door, I had just settled into the canvas slingback at the table in his kitchenette.

"Here we go," Truelove announced, putting a shopping bag down in front of me. He removed four recently microwaved Stewart's sandwiches, a bag of taco chips, two cans of Vienna sausage, and a jelly roll the size of a small pine log. He then reached across to open the cabinets above the sink, where a small TV sat on the bottom shelf. He turned it on and together we watched *Jeopardy* and lit into the food.

"Always wanted to go on that show," Truelove declared as we hacked our way through the jelly roll. "But it's not the same without Art Fleming. All these new guys have mustaches."

He answered all the questions before the contestants even buzzed their buzzers. "What is the Magna Carta?" he shouted at the TV as a spray of jelly-roll crumbs exploded from his lips.

"You oughta try out for it some summer," I told him.

"But someone would probably see me," he mused. That would seem a logical outcome, I figured, but he at least seemed to know what he'd meant. "I should hardly imagine I'll have to wait for summer at any rate, Douglass," he added. "The wolves are circling. They can smell the blood."

"Wolves? You mean seventh period, I guess. I'm sorry."

"Oh, don't be sorry, Douglass," he shot back. "My goodness, it was your contribution with the 'Doctor' routine that really opened the biggest wound. Consider it a public service. Think of yourself as a savior of public education, right up there with Dewey and Horace Mann and Captain Kangaroo. . . ."

"Mr. Truelove, look, don't go dumping all that on me." I thought we had gotten past the nasty stuff. I stood up and went for my backpack. I could hitchhike back to town if it took all night. "It wasn't my idea. The doctor thing, that, just happened. It had been rattling around in my brain for so long, it just slipped out."

"Douglass, sit down. Come on back." He reached his leg under the table and kicked the chair in my direction. I sat. "I wasn't being sarcastic. I was being honest, in a way. My time has come. I should have quit three years ago. I can't . . . I don't have the will, five times a day, thirty kids times five, times one hundred eighty days, times years, ten years, it comes to . . . what? I can't pretend I care anymore, driving the same load up the same hill, year after year. And you kids, your breath reeking of watermelon bubble gum, wearing your jeans like you just discovered sex, smiling from behind your goddamn braces like you believe, yes, believe in the perfectibility of the human smile. Good god, I just don't belong in there anymore. I don't. There was a time I thought it would be a sanctuary, and it was.

I was, I was good at one time. But who really cares anymore about bilateral symmetry in *planaria*, annelida, and god, I hate those flatworms. I do hate those flat ugly worms. . . . Do you see what I mean? Do you?"

"Yes, I do," I told him. He started pulling at the cellophane around the remainder of the jelly roll, tearing it into thin strips.

"There's been no one, Douglass, no one to tell it to. Excuse me. I'm . . . you must think I'm . . ."

He dropped his head to the table and rested it across his arms, staring in silence across the room, over the piles of magazines stacked around the floor. I reached out a hand to touch him on the shoulder. He recoiled, shrugged away from my touch, and sat upright once again.

"Why not resign?" I asked. "Just quit, go somewhere else, and start again? You're not chained to this job, are you?"

"I haven't saved very much. It's the money. I can't afford to give it up." He waved a hand around his head, indicating the apartment. "I've got to live, you know. Jelly rolls don't grow on trees. They have to eat in Bangkok, too." So he was still sending money over there. And after fourteen years!

"Still, better to quit than to let the bastards fire you, sir. That's what they're after, you know. I've heard Mr. Wilfong wants it." But I couldn't tell him that Wilfong had recruited me for the offensive, to be his eyes and ears, to testify before the school board.

"Wilfong is a man of vision." He smiled. "Wilfong is a worm. Still, he's probably right. I've got to go. Just not on their terms."

207

"What terms are those?" I asked.

"They freeze you out, string you up, and hang you out to dry." He explained what happens when someone, a teacher, gets fired. They lose it all: salary, insurance, still can't collect pension until age sixty. "But on the other hand . . . yes, there's always the other hand." He rolled his eyes around the room and then sprang from the chair to pace his small apartment.

"A nice little medical leave . . . with salary, of course. Hold on to my benefits, just sort of disappear. Why, I could live off my disability for a good . . . I'll have to check my policy. It's gotta be a year or two at least, long enough to make a fresh start anyways, without having to walk Wilfong's plank."

"Medical leave. Don't you have to be really sick?" I turned to watch him leaping his stacked magazines.

"Really sick," he cackled. "Yes, really, really, really sick. *Bleaahhhhhh.*" He posed astride his *Newsweek*s, lolling his tongue from the corner of his mouth. When he finally settled across from me in his chair once more his voice fell into a hushed, conspiratorial tone. "Look, Douglass, if I'm as crazy as everyone thinks I am, it should be a piece of cake. Besides, given your reputation with that episode last year . . . What's that guy's name?"

"Mustero," I offered, "but I'd rather not . . ."

"Yes, with his scalp on your belt, what's another? We could do an encore performance. I could get you up in front of the class and . . . well, let you have it again. We'd be great. Only this time it would be different, see?"

"Different how?" I asked.

"Because this time I wouldn't spare the lab for after class. I could let fly with the specimens. Oh, just enough for everyone to get the point. Think of it. You could even clear your name, tell them that's the way it went the first time around. And then . . . *poof* . . . I'd be out, and you'd be . . . what do you call it?"

"Cleared?"

"Vindicated. You'd be vindicated. Everybody wins. It's perfect. Perfecto. Whadda ya say?" He thrust a hand across the table. We were supposed to shake on it. Instead, I twisted sideways in my chair.

"I don't think so," I told him. "I'd like to help you, but it's . . . crazy, pardon the expression. Maybe if you just went in to Wilfong and explained your idea, he could see that for himself. It might spare both of us the bother."

"Douglass, I'm disappointed in you, son." He slid his hand back across the table and gave it one thump with his palm for punctuation. "I thought you were a gamer. Would've bet my eyeteeth on it."

"Well, sir," I admitted, "that's just the problem. Everyone thinks I'm a gamer. I'm trying to tone it down. I promised them I'd try to go easy. It gets pretty old pretty fast."

"Promised them? Them who?"

"My parents, the school," I answered.

"The school? You mean Wilfong, don't you? Sure!"

"Maybe. What of it?"

"And what's the payback? There's always a payback, isn't there?"

"No payback," I said. "Just, like, peace of mind.

209

They'll drop some stuff from my permanent record. Plus the thing at channel eleven."

"Channel eleven? What thing is that?"

"You were supposed to get a memo from Wilfong," I explained. "They want to do a story on a kid at school. They chose me after that hearing, when they saw me on channel five."

"No kidding?" Truelove grinned. "No, I didn't get a memo yet. Or if I did, I trashed it. I may have to start reading my memos again. No kidding? The *Wunderkind* on the telly." He thrummed the table, pondering something. "Ya know, that would've been perfect. 'The mad biology teacher' live on tape. That would really have cinched it for us. Incontrovertible evidence. Damn!"

"Look, Mr. Truelove." I wanted to finish it, to put a lid on his harebrained scheme. I wasn't going to be a part of it. "Don't get all manic about it. Ask me, the only thing really nutty about you is expecting me to help bail you out. It's taken you, what, ten, fourteen years of hard work to get into this fix. I don't think any little rampage is gonna make it all right again."

"Yeah, so maybe I am a nut. Still, might have been worth a try."

Truelove swiveled in his chair and watched the *CBS Evening News* come on. He wore a sly, twisted grin on his face and then pressed his fingertips against his mouth and puffed out his cheeks, as though holding back a small eruption building inside. He studied the news with his eyes squinted, his head screwed toward the small TV.

About halfway through the newscast he stood and

snapped the TV off and slammed the cabinet doors shut—*bam bam*—against the small white circle still shrinking in the center of the screen and dropped back into his seat.

"Sorry, Douglass," he blurted, "this can't be very enjoyable for you." It had never occurred to me that he was shooting for "enjoyable."

Suddenly Truelove turned into this sort of activities director for some long-lost summer day camp. He disappeared into his bedroom and came back with an armload of toys and junk. He whipped out this antique Rubik's Cube and started putting it through its paces, swiveling and twisting until finally he had all the right colors aligned. Then he made me do it, like it was some major thrill when I hadn't even touched one since maybe third grade. Then he did it again, then me, timing each of us, and declared himself the winner. Next he whipped out this pocket version of Pac-Man, of all things, and made me stand behind him and watch his little guys gobble power pellets and blue ghosts. Again, I had pretty much peaked out on Pac-Man sometime in third grade, but I told him "way to go" and all that, since he was really having such a good time himself.

Finally his batteries ran out. He slapped a Scrabble board on the table and produced the letters from a sandwich bag he had sitting on the floor. Well, at least it was something two could play, I figured, so I indulged him for a couple of games and he won them both, blitzing me at the end with *anorexia* on a triple word score. He was so ecstatic his voice went into that little squeal again. He sat there in his chair, jig-

211

gling up and down, saying, "Triple word score, triple word score."

I figured maybe it was time to leave. I started yawning, and the Truelove's big face sagged once again into its slack, blank look, and he wiped *anorexia* off the board.

"I don't mean to gloat, Stephen. You must think me a rude host," he apologized. "Yes, I suppose you need to get back. I would like to ask you one favor, however, and please don't think it peculiar of me."

He reached into the silverware drawer beside the sink, groped around for a minute and withdrew, finally, a dull metal rectangle hanging from what looked like a chain of silver BB's.

"Put it on, son," he said. "I want you to have it."

I slipped it over my head. No harm in obliging the guy, I figured. Then I pinched the rectangle and read the letters stamped across its surface: "Truelove, Burton R." And below that, a string of numbers in a long, straight line.

"Geez, it's your dog tag. Thanks." I tried to sound grateful.

"No, not mine." He tried an uncomfortable smile. "But he was a good kid, Truelove was. And I think you're . . . you're one, too."

"Not yours? But it says . . . Truelove."

He shook his head. "Never was. Just borrowed him for longer than I planned. What you said tonight about getting out of . . . this hole I've dug. . . . You're right. It'll be hard enough. You can help by taking that, can set him free."

"Setting you free, don't you mean?" I asked. "Whoever you are. Who the hell are you, sir? If you don't mind my asking, that is."

"No, I don't mind. I'm not going to tell you, of course. Besides, it's not important." Truelove exhaled as though a millstone had just been lifted from his chest. "Let's just say I'm still missing in action. Hope you don't have any major problem with that."

Well, maybe I had problems galore, but it would take a lot of sifting through just to get it straight. But no need letting on right then. He had been playing Truelove so long, maybe he wasn't so clear on who he was anyway. He was a ghost, looked like a ghost, a chalk-white tourist from the war zone.

"No problem," I said. "After all, we broke jelly roll together and that's gotta count for something." And he actually laughed for the first and last time. He was a strange fish.

And so he drove me home in his Torino through a yellow, moon-filled night. It was October. The air was so clear and sharp that the radio picked up Fort Wayne, Indiana. They were playing the Series. I could hear the crowd behind the announcer's voice rising like a tidal wave caught in a bucket. They were playing nearly three thousand miles away, third inning on the coast and the bases were loaded.

"Follow baseball?" Truelove asked.

"Not much," I said.

"I used to, some," said Truelove. He turned the radio off, and the noise snapped away into the air. The count was three and two and it would have to stay that way. He rolled down his window and the rush of air filled the car, blotting out the quiet that had fallen between us. We drove that way right into Cable Hall and on out to Newgate Estates. I thanked Truelove for the ride because I didn't know what else to say. He told me to let him know if I ever changed my mind. I said it wasn't likely, but okay, I would. He pulled into the driveway and let me out. I had just put my key in the door when he pulled his Torino back onto the street and drove away. Then he hit the horn, two shorts and a long, *WA WA WAAANNNNHHHHH,* and the noise followed me into the house as I shut the door.

"Those your friends, making that racket?" Mom asked as I entered the living room. She sat, half asleep, with a copy of *Business Week* spread across her lap.

"Yeah," I answered. "My friends. Sorry I'm so late. We got involved in a game. Scrabble, if you want to believe it."

"Scrabble, really?" She stood and stretched and dropped the magazine on the couch behind her. "I'm going to bed. You'd better get some sleep yourself. You're leading such a wild life now."

"I know," I told her. "It takes its toll."

# Chapter 34

The first Sunday in November was moving day for me once more, but it rained so hard all morning, it was two in the afternoon before Mom pulled her Volvo in front of the Mother Won't Know. I ran one load of stuff up to my room while Mom idled at the curb. She had gotten my sweaters out of summer storage and was forcing me to take along all the ones that still fit. As I came back through the bar after my first run, Dad saluted from the corner underneath the TV.

Dad stayed put. Mom honked outside. Dad still stayed put. The etiquette of moving day was like this. Mom stayed in her car outside on Mifflin Street; Dad idled at the end of the driveway in Newgate Estates. It was understood. It was a given.

"Get a move on, honey," Mom yelled. She made a point of yelling honey at me, especially downtown where the college kids could hear it. Or in grocery stores, where the checkout girls were working their way through high school.

I dragged two suitcases and a duffel bag out of the Volvo's rear end and slammed the tailgate closed. I slid them down the walk and bent my head through the window to tell Mom good-bye.

"Stephen, did you know anything about this?" Mom asked. She pointed back past my ear. I turned my head to look. Over the door of the Mother a metal FOR SALE sign had been fixed to the lintel with sheet-metal screws: COMMERCIAL PROPERTY, OFFERED FOR SALE, CHOICE LOCATION. CALL 769–7817. It was Dad's number.

"Oh, no, I think he really means it," I said.

"What's he up to, Stephen?" Mom asked. "Running away to join the circus?"

"It's the new law. The drinking age is now twenty-one. He told me he was thinking about it. Didn't want a bar for old folks, he said."

"Grown-ups, adults, not his peer group, that's for sure," Mom joined in. "But what's he got else to do, the bastard?"

"He's not exactly hard up, Mom," I told her, repeating the same wisdom I had heard from her ever since the divorce.

Mom set her jaw like a Batman also-ran and dropped her shades from on top of her head. "He had better not be running out on, uhhhh . . . on you." She wrung the steering wheel in both hands until I thought it would soften like taffy.

I opened the door and slipped in beside her. This was no way to leave her, in this mood, so soon after Rolf, after her midnight ride in the exercise room.

I rolled up the window. "Mom, don't be this way,"

I pleaded. I reached across and took the sunglasses from her eyes and nested them atop her head again. Her eyes were stained with brown, the bottom lids speckled with iridescent powder like the fine dusty scales from the wings of moths. She wiped at her eyes and turned away from me.

"Strike me dead," I said, "but maybe you have a right to know, maybe more than me." So I had become a soft touch and a bad risk when it came to secrets, but this was a worthy cause. "I promised Dad I wouldn't tell, but . . ."

"Tellllll?" Mom echoed me, her *l*'s drifting up like hawks in a thermal draft.

"He's studying for the bar exam, this spring." I watched her eyes roll up to the roof of her Volvo. She fell back against the seat. "He got the books out, all that stuff," I continued. "Ever since my hearing, he's been going through his old notebooks, everything. I swore I wouldn't tell, so don't ever let on that you know. I think he's kind of scared, to tell the truth."

"Good," Mom said, a smile returning to her face. Good that he was scared, or good that he was taking the exam? Mom wasn't saying. She sat unmoving with her back against the seat, her grip now loosened on the steering wheel, running her fingertips around its circumference.

"Seventeen years, almost seventeen," she chanted to the roof above her. "Jesus, what a late bloomer, a late-blooming bloomer."

Finally she turned to me. "Don't worry, Stephen. It's safe with me. Thanks." She put her right hand against my face, kneaded behind my ear. "You'd better get going. Get settled in. Hang those sweaters up to let the wrinkles fall out. And call me before you leave for Washington. I want to hear your schedule."

I tried to act like it was no big deal, but I'd call anyway. I kissed her good-bye, and she pulled me back for another one, just a quick one.

At last I stood on the curb among my suitcases and was about to slam the door.

"Hey, Stephen," she called to me, and I bent my head down to see what she wanted. She was pointing at the for sale sign once again. "What do you think? We could have a couple of racquetball courts, a steam room, jumbo coed Jacuzzi. Get the downtown crowd, strictly upmarket and professional. Maybe a salad bar. Do you like it?"

"Sounds perfect," I said. "We could call it Eat and Run."

# Chapter 35

Two days later, Dad came upstairs for dinner early—
I had made my famous fish sticks and beans. We were
knee deep in tartar sauce when I finally told him I
thought maybe I had a buyer for the Mother.

"Buyer? Who?" he asked.

"Mother," I told him.

"Your mother?" he asked.

"Yes, my mother," I said. "Eileen Douglass, remember?"

"Yes, your mother, buying my Mother. Are you
serious?"

I assured him I was. I explained Mom's idea about
turning it into a downtown lunchtime spa. I wondered what he would do with the bar top, the old
many-layered slab of oak with its "Wilson Douglass,
beerhead" inscription, a shrine, a legend. And who
would get custody of the fish tank? A world in flux.

"Flux?" Dad said. "Flux deluxe." He couldn't re-
sist. In fact, he hardly seemed bothered, just leaned
back and launched into a chorus of "Who Knows
Where the Time Goes."

I was taking the night off for current events. It was the first Tuesday in November, an off-year election in other words, and Dad wanted me to watch the results on TV with him and help him study a little law. The apartment had been transformed into a law library. The casebooks had escaped the confines of Dad's bedroom. They sat piled around the living room floor and out into the kitchenette. Each book was surrounded by a little orbit of index cards, numbered in the corners and arranged counterclockwise.

Dad flipped on the TV. Dan Rather was wearing a vest. Dad stretched out on the couch. Dan Rather was bragging about the CBS computers. I said I was hungry, and Dad said, "Help yourself." I found a box of garlic-flavored croutons and stretched out on the floor. Dad dropped a law book in my lap, a five pounder on civil procedure.

"Call these out, just the names," Dad said, showing me the index in the back.

*"Pennoyer* versus *Neff,"* I said, and Dad launched into a three-minute monologue on jurisdiction over nonresidents.

Dan Rather turned into a computer graphics American flag. A little box in the lower right corner said "CBS projects a winner with 63% of the vote," and then a check mark floated across the screen.

Dad lunged up from the couch. "Smug bastards," he yelled at Dan Rather. He crossed to the TV and switched to ABC. Some guy in a bow tie was explaining how the Republicans had become a juggernaut. Dad turned off the sound and fell back across the couch. "Juggernaut, my ass," Dad grumbled. "Ask me another one, Stephen."

"*International Shoe Company* versus *Washington*," I said.

"Delaware Corporation," Dad mumbled, arranging the facts, "Fourteenth Amendment, Chief Justice Stone, due process, due process, oh, yeah, here goes . . ." and he took off on another monologue on the mysteries of jurisdiction.

By midnight we had finished civil procedure. Dad sat on the couch singing "Help Me, Rhonda" into the empty crouton box while I washed up and put the law book on the floor with the others. Dad finished up the chorus—"Help, help me, Rhonda. Help, help me, Rhonda," then did the big finish where he puts his fist through the bottom of the crouton box and sprays the floor with a powder of fine crumbs.

"Think I've got a chance?" he asked, wearing the box over his forearm like a bracelet.

"Maybe if you work on your adenoids and buy some striped shirts," I told him, and he said, no, he meant with the law boards. I told him sure, he'd got it down pat. He was planning next week to review torts, he said.

"You'll like torts," he assured me. "I'm gonna save the rough stuff for March and April—the trusts and estates, the corporate taxation. First things first," he added. "Remember, not a word to your mom about this law-board stuff. Okay?"

"Absolutely mum city," I pledged, borrowing a phrase from old Truelove.

"Good boy, Stephen," Dad said. He pinched my

chin and tilted my head back till our eyes met. Then he squinted real mean, like some B-movie cowboy. I guess he wanted this next to come across with extra texture: "Ya see, son, I want it to be a surprise. I want to surprise her with it and all, 'cause I been thinkin' how we could all use a second chance, if you know what I mean. How your mom and me never really got a chance to finish up some things once we got started. Like law school. Like you, kid. Like us, your mom and me. Loose ends, I reckon. I was figurin', who knows—and don't dare to laugh, neither—I was figurin', just maybe, things go right and all, maybe come summer, I could talk your mom into us getting hitched up again. So say your prayers and think pure thoughts, and good Lord willin', this time next year, who knows, we might be hitched again."

Hitched. Good Lord. I was sure he'd rehearsed it. It was strictly cowboy from start to finish. And despite all that, I think he meant it, every bit of it, lock, stock, and barrel. Shoot.

"Do you really think you stand a chance?" I asked.

He straddled a chair backward and considered the question seriously, chin resting on his forearms. "I'd give it a fifty-fifty chance at best. Where's the harm?"

"Well, she's become a pretty independent woman," I warned him. "And pretty successful." And pretty lonely, I could have added, recalling her fortieth birthday party.

"She has that," he admitted. "Only this time's different. I'll have the law board behind me—I hope. And your mom won't be pregnant with you. I won't be draft bait."

"Hold on—she was pregnant when you got married? With me?" I started calculating my birth date, subtracting from their anniversary—but what was their anniversary? The kid's always the last to know.

"Whoops." Dad covered his face. "I thought for sure she'd told you about that. Ask her sometime. She's much better at that stuff than me." He dropped his hands from his face. "Ask her how she saved me from the dreaded ax, pal."

The dreaded ax. Sometimes Dad thought life was a cartoon. What had Jamie told me once—the bar was his playground.

"And you won't have the Mother to . . . worry about anymore." I had almost said "hide out in."

"Hell, son, I never had to worry about the Mother. It was my sanctuary, my therapy. Damned old saloon saved my life once. Course, like any strong drug, it sorta became habit-forming."

"Saved your life how?" I asked. "Mom always said it was your ruination."

"Ruination! Stephen, be careful, you're beginning to sound like one of these red-clay crackers." Dad gave his best, boyish, ten-dollar smile. But when I didn't give it back he dropped the act and continued. "I was seeing someone about the time I married your mother, off and on during that last year of law school."

"Someone? A woman?"

"A man," he said. "A doctor."

"A shrink, you mean."

"A shrink's a doctor, Stephen."

"Did Mother know?"

"No." He squinted his eyes shut and remembered. "No, she thought I was working on Law Review. And mostly I was. But then I had to see someone. I couldn't sleep, awake all night, staring at the ceiling, watching your mother sleeping, hating her because she could sleep. My head was jammed with precedents, rulings, cases. I was afraid to turn it off, to let it rest. Obsessive behavior, failure anxiety. I had always been the best, the quickest, Mr. Tip-top, and I was afraid to let it go, all that brilliant deadly momentum I had going for me. . . ."

"But you were first in your class, no?" I asked.

"Sure, number one, the head barracuda. They hated me."

"Who hated?" I couldn't imagine anyone hating my dad.

"The whole school—students, professors. I hated them right back, but they sure as hell couldn't keep me off the mountain."

"Mom didn't hate you."

"Ah, Mom. She was in the school of social work. I was her first and best client—a career project."

"So you married her, right?"

"She married me is more like it. Something else to fail at, I discovered. Marriage. And a kid coming along—scary proposition." He stuck a hand out, sort of dusted across my hair. "Still is, amigo. No hard feelings."

"None," I answered.

"Good," he said. "And then on top of all of it there was the draft, the army breathing down my neck. . . ."

"And you didn't want to fight in a senseless war, right?"

"No, I never thought that far ahead. It was just the Army scared me shitless. I'm talking cold midnight sweats. I'm still not sure why. Afraid of failing in a different way, is how it was explained to me. No control over myself, over being number one. Just put on the uniform and march and shut up. That terrified me. Course, that just might be a fancy way of saying I'm a coward."

"And so you bought the Mother and started hiding out?" There, I'd said it after all.

"That's your mother's line, isn't it?"

"No, Jamie's—don't tell her I told."

"Jamie—huh? Anyway, the therapist said just to put all that pressure—those obsessions—aside, put them"—he looked sideways at the smudged brown plates we'd left on the table—"put them on the back burner, like a pot of beans. The Mother was my way of doing that. So the Army, the law boards, and all that got set aside."

"And Mother and me . . . set aside, too?"

"Your mother, yes. You, never. Bimonthly maybe, but never more than that."

With that, Dad stood, cleared the table, and set to washing the dishes. I sat and watched as each knife and fork and plate and pan left the sink and nested in the strainer, spotless and shiny. Just like new. If it were only that easy. Dad must have thought it was, scrubbing his old obsessions spanking brand clean. Mr. Tip-top, the barracuda. Wilson "Beerhead" Douglass. Then who was that man who had stood on the

225

bar not so long ago, blathering about the insanity defense, the McNaghten rule? That had looked like Dad, too. The old obsessive Dad? Or only the drunk one? I watched him at the sink scouring the bean pot, scrubbing away with a mission until I thought his hand would plunge right through its bottom. The man really did believe.

I sure hoped he was right. Set those pots aside. Scrub them later. Get them nice and clean. If he could manage it, then why shouldn't I? Who was really farther gone, after all? Farther gone, further gone, father gone. Was I that far gone? Was anybody? I mean, what's the real problem? Where's the real rub after all?

Scrub a dub.

Burned-on grease. Ground-in grime.

# Chapter 36

Christmas comes but once a year, a wise man once said. But then, he was probably not a product of a broken home and had never enjoyed the extravagance of alternating parents in a split-custody divorce settlement. For me, Christmas had been coming twice a year, once in November with Dad, and once December-style with Mom. It was like dueling parents, a wretched excess of competitive good cheer. But nice, in its own way, I suppose.

So by the second Sunday in November Dad was brimming with yuletide cheer, skipping around the apartment in his red p.j.'s like a distended elf. He had a small tree sitting on a coffee table, a tree he had bought already-decorated at a nursery. "A timesaver," he had called it the night we spiraled two strands of blinking fairy lights around its perfect branches. Dad twinkled and so did the tree.

"Let's get going, sport," he announced as I staggered from my bedroom. He threw a bag of Krispy Kremes right at me and produced from the kitchen two pilsners filled with eggnog.

I tore into the bag of doughnuts and split one open like a clam. I ate the half with the jelly and threw the other half back in the bag. Dad messed around behind the coffee table for a bit, then produced a package and handed it over to me.

"This one says 'To Stephen from Santa.' Merry Christmas, boy child." He dropped the box in my lap. Of course, it said no such thing.

"Oh, for me?" I said. It was this little family joke. "Shall I open it?" Lots of foreplay, kinda.

"Yes. Yes," Dad cajoled. "It's those new pajamas you've been asking for." Another family joke. We were a jolly bunch.

I opened the package. It was a radio-controlled formula-one race car. Dad said we'd have to try it out in the driveway. Dad was excited; he loved toys. I told him it was swell, and we moved on to package number two. It was as big as a suitcase. "Too big for socks," he said. It turned out to be a compact disc player. More cutting-edge electronics stuff. He loved it.

Packages three through six turned out to be equally neat stuff. A pocket television. A real leather bomber jacket. A waterproof surfing camera. A solar-powered beach radio.

"What, no socks?" he said. "Try the closet by the fridge." So I picked my way through the crumpled piles of wrapping paper over to the pantry closet where Dad kept all the brooms. But when I opened the door, I saw only a pyramid of sleek white cardboard boxes. All stamped IBM.

"Too big to wrap," Dad yelled from his chair by the

fireplace. I slid the boxes out, one by one, and pried their flaps open. A computer. A double disk drive. A full-color portable monitor. A modem. A letter-quality printer. State of the art.

"Dad," I hollered. "I mean, you didn't have to. This is incredible."

"Santa likes you, sport. We'll set it up in your room here for good. You can keep your old one at your mother's."

I sat there in the middle of all those boxes, breathing in that fresh perfume of cardboard, Styrofoam, molded styrene. My fingers ran chittering across the keyboard like mice on a holiday.

"Now, one more, sport," Dad announced. He walked over to me and dropped a pair of battered slippers in my lap. I told him they were just what I'd always wanted, and he told me to shut up.

"Just put them on and follow me," he added, and I did as I was told. He led me downstairs to the bar, and suddenly I'm thinking, like, hold on to your purse, Marie, he's gone and done it. He's gotten me that new BMW, and now I can be one of the kids at last. And I still hadn't gotten my license.

Well, close. It was German, after all, but it had only two wheels. It was black and silver and stood out on the sidewalk chained to his front door and cocked at a jaunty angle, a spanking-new moped with the legend PUCII painted across its flanks. A cherry-red helmet hung like an ornament from its handlebars.

"It's a sweet machine," Dad said, stating the obvious. "I wanted you to have some wheels. Save a fortune on taxis, is my point."

Dad snapped the chain free. I sat on the moped and rolled it down the walk, did a figure eight out into the street, then walked it back up to where Dad stood in his red pajamas. He had started sleeping in his pajamas again. Just for me, I think.

We decided to go in, put on shoes, and try it for real. In the meantime, we assembled the computer and ran through a quick instructional program. Then we watched Oral Roberts from the Prayer Tower on my pocket television, and it was very moving even though we had never really been terribly devout and the reverend seemed incredibly petite. It was still early when I slipped on my new bomber jacket over my pajamas, and we went back to the driveway. We took the radio-controlled racer and put it through a few turns, until we totaled it dead center against a parking meter.

"Let's pray that Andretti comes out of this alive," Dad said, holding the shattered toy by the tip of its antenna like a flattened, day-old possum.

Finally, Dad poured a pinch of petrol in the Puch and took off. He rolled it along the walk cranking its pedals until the motor caught, and the bike sputtered off down the street sounding like this basso profundo hummingbird in a sandstorm. After maybe three, four minutes he came whining his way back up Mifflin Street, right up onto the sidewalk, and squealed to a stop at my feet.

"Take it for a spin, Joe Bob," Dad yelled above the shrill engine. He slammed the helmet atop my head and showed me the hand brakes and how to hold my feet so that my toenails wouldn't come off on the pavement. I gave him this dumb salute, then rolled down the drive and took off.

Not bad, I thought, and I cruised the neighborhood like a free man, born to be free, and all that, up Mifflin, down Bradley, around University Circle, all over lower campus. Dogs barked, kids on roller skates stopped and stared, a boy on a skateboard wiped out along the curb. Power, I thought, flight, speed, curve, lean, bank, glide, zoom, whoosh. The mild November air slipped beneath my jacket under my pajamas, slid beneath my helmet, rushed up my nose, and it was as if I were breathing air, real air for the first time ever, good old premature yuletide air, so I leaned my head back and let my eyes close just a little while. I listened to the engine thrum, and my helmet filled with the noise, and I realized it was me, too, humming right along with my 2.4-liter Puch, silly little German toy imitation motorcycle, and when I opened my eyes I was rolling up Mifflin again, and Dad was standing by the Mother Won't Know waving his arms like a flight-deck guy from the SS *Coral Sea*, and I squealed to a stop at *his* toes this time. He said, "So whaddaya think?" and I said, "Not so bad for a start, I suppose," but I was really thinking how in maybe another year or so we could spring for a Harley and really kick us some ass out on the blacktop.

"C'mon, Ace, still two more to go," Dad announced. Imagine my shame! So Dad stowed the moped inside the bar, and we went upstairs to prolong the mirth. He darted into his bedroom and returned with two more packages, one in each hand.

231

"Here," he said. He squinted at the card for maybe ten seconds, real high drama. "This one's for you, Stephen." He was having fun. "It came to your mom's house, but she thought you should see it right away. You'll see what I mean. Go ahead, open it."

I took the gift and tore into the paper. It was a frame, something in a frame, matted in this tawny cardboard. It wasn't a picture, not even a snapshot, but all print, a microscopic print almost. I read across the top, the words above a thick black line, and discovered what was up. It was a page from the Congressional Record. He'd gone and done it, that congressman. He'd gone and read my name into the Congressional Record. I was described as a "patriotic sixteen-year-old," followed by assorted glowing epithets. And then came the lyrics. Imagine that.

No kings or princes, no barricades or fences,
Can stop up the voices of people speaking
    free. . . .

And all the rest of it, just like that.

"If you could've seen the look on your face just then! I'd give a million dollars to see that again." Dad was really coming out with the gems. "Just think, you're part of history."

"Yeah, but which part?"

"Well, you're in the official record of the greatest legislative body on the planet." That was strong stuff, coming from Dad. Still, he was proud. He came up behind me and took the frame, holding it out at arm's length in front of us.

232

"Where shall we hang it, Stephen? We'll have to think of a place."

"We will. No hurry."

But he was in no mood for filial nonchalance. He pranced around the apartment, floating from wall to wall to wall. "Here? No. Maybe here. What do you think? Or maybe here?" I just kept nodding and Dad kept floating.

"Oh, no hurry, you're right. We'll find a place." He produced the second package from beside the sofa. Then, "Oh look, one more."

It was a big one, wrapped in silver foil shaded with snowflakes. "Oh, it's another one for you, Stephen," he trilled, jamming it into my chest. "Open it, open it."

As soon as I released the first bit of tape from the end flap, I had a vision. It was a suit, I knew.

A charcoal-gray, wool-blend, three-piece suit, in fact, with reversible vest and trouser legs that seemed to run on forever. "We can take those up," Dad said. I was holding the pants by the waist, way over my head. The cuffs just tickled the floor.

"It's a terrific suit," I said. "Banker gray, real grown-up. What's it for?"

"Now try the inside pocket. That might explain it. That's where you keep important papers and things." One hand clamped across his mouth trapped a beginning smile.

I ran a hand up inside the jacket, across the cool, sleek lining. I felt the label, beneath that found the vent, and plunged my fingers into the pocket. They met with something stiff, paper with a hard, straight

233

edge. An envelope. I pulled it out. Plain white, sealed tight.

"Open it, open it," Dad whispered.

I ran a finger along the flap, tore it open, and withdrew . . . a ticket. Piedmont Airlines. I fluttered its leaves open and read, "Round trip to Washington. Leave November 21, return November 24. Coach. $89.99."

"Washington, D.C. I'm flying to Washington? Oh, right! Washington! How'd I forget!"

"The pocket, the pocket," he was saying. "Stop farting around and try the pocket, Stephen."

I slid my fingers in there once more—another envelope, smaller, I could feel. I pulled it out. A square envelope this time, pebbly to the touch, with this bumpy embossed patch under my thumb. It was addressed to me, jet-black ink, a fountain pen I figured, and since it was so fancy I took extra care not to rip it open. So finally I pulled out this stiff white card folded in half, and on the outside was that bumpy seal. I recognized the presidential seal. Inside, more black ink, curly letters and printed so they just rose right out of the glossy hard paper, inviting me to the Freedom Scholars weekend, absolutely, to join the Freedom Scholars of fifty states "as an honored guest of the President of the United States. . . ." And there was my name again at the bottom, resting perfectly straight and even across this fine horse-whisker of a black line.

"Merry Christmas," Dad bellowed. "Just imagine, my boy, Stephen, a guest of the president." He grabbed me by the scruff of the neck and squeezed.

"But do you think it's safe?" I asked, pulling away.

"What's not to be safe? Fear of flying, Stephen? Good heavens, no. Commercial flight is much safer than . . . well, than that moped sitting downstairs, for example."

"Not the flight," I corrected. "I meant, you know, the president."

"The president, safe?" Dad collapsed onto the sofa and folded himself up to consider. "I should imagine he's safe. Bodyguards, G-men, security tighter than a turtle's behind. Probably the best-protected man on the planet!"

"Never mind, Dad. I meant if I . . . if it was safe for me to be . . . there."

"Safe as anywhere. Don't worry, you'll be fine." Finally he caught on, his head lifted from the sofa. "Oh, that. You're still worried 'bout that snake-boy stuff. Son, you really are such a worrier. Just wear the suit. A kid in a suit like that is ironclad guaranteed not to screw up. Wear the suit—a nice maroon tie, I'll let you take one of mine, polish your shoes, smile, and just say yes sir and no sir. And you're golden!"

"Or lobotomized," I added. "Anyway, let's keep this just in the family. Until we see how it goes."

"Gee, no sound trucks, no brass bands at the airport?"

"No, none of that," I said.

"I was gonna call the paper, Stephen. I mean, hey, the old Douglass clan is making a comeback. We gotta go public, no?"

"No, Dad, no paper."

"'S your party, son." He sat up, poised on the edge

235

of the sofa, unbuttoned his pajama top. Finally he stood and surveyed the room. The floor was a tangle of ribbon, wrapping paper, boxes, odd bits of molded Styrofoam.

"It's a mess," Dad said.

"A mess, sure is," I answered.

"Let's go get changed," he said.

"I wish," I said. "Don't I wish."

# Chapter 37

When the Piedmont jet finally rattled down the runway, taking off for Washington, I sat staring out the window, relieved to see that after takeoff the wings were still there, and beyond them the earth was sinking away in dull-brown rectangles. We lifted over acres of slash pine, their green tops receding like herb gardens, then blending into a feathery green down there, like chalk.

At last we sifted through the thin clouds. "Goodbye, earthlings," I said at the window. I leaned back in my seat, pushed the button on my armrest, and sank backward.

I returned my seat almost to upright when a hollow *kerchunk* shuddered through the plane. I waited to hear the captain's voice announcing doom. It didn't, so it must have been the landing gear retracting. Down there, somewhere in the plane's belly, folded up with my new gray suit, itself folded up in Dad's Slimline garment Travelall. He'd lent me that and a bottle of after-shave. He'd said to enjoy myself, but don't spit off the top of the Washington Monument, you'll get an eyeful, treacherous winds. I didn't even know they had windows.

Mom had said to be sure to get lots of pictures and then hadn't packed the camera. She'd remembered that on the way to the airport, but by then it was too late. I told her I'd buy lots of postcards, but she wasn't convinced. She said to be sure to call once I got there, and to be nice to the president.

I straightened up and read my emergency procedures card. My seat was a flotation device.

"Sandwiches" came the voice from above.

"Yes, sandwiches, thank god," I said.

"Excuse me, sir?" she said. "Chicken salad. Tuna."

"Chicken salad," I said. "And ginger ale."

"You sound hungry," the stewardess said. She dropped two triangular wedges into my lap. They were wrapped in clear plastic. I lowered the tray, and she plopped a glass down, dropped some ice inside, and poured some soda over the top.

"Hungry? Guess so." I smiled up at the stewardess, floating above me like a dental technician. Only prettier.

"I can bring more," she said. I dropped the emergency card to the floor. So relieved.

"Bring all you can," I told her. "Tuna, too."

# Chapter 38

When we deplaned in Washington, a guy with a red-white-and-blue armband snagged me right off the exit ramp and whisked me to a VIP lounge filling up with kids. They were doing a lot of whisking that afternoon—people, luggage, flight bags, buses—but then, airports are for whisking. So when they had a busload of us, they whisked us off to the hotel, the Hyatt Regency, and checked us in. I had a room with a guy from Ohio who had started a drug hotline in his basement and a guy from Oregon who'd saved three kids from a mudslide. They had a poker game going in a room down the hall and asked me to join, but I begged off. Instead, I called home to tell Mom I was fine. Then I brushed my teeth when suddenly the tuna caught up with me. I pulled the curtains closed and stretched out on one of the beds to let my stomach settle. I ate two mints from the ashtray and stared at the cherry-blossom mural on the wall beside the mirror, mock-Monet, all pastel and watery.

It was after five when I woke up. I showered and

put on the gray three-piece and went downstairs to the lobby. The place was crawling with Freedom Scholars by now. I followed them into a "Function Room," festooned with braided crepe paper, and it wasn't black and orange, either.

A woman behind a card table asked my name. "Douglass," I told her. "Stephen A." She produced a name tag from a file of plastic tags arranged alphabetically on her table. "Here, put it on, mingle a little. Dinner's at eight." She handed me a mimeographed schedule, with the names of all 200 Freedom Scholars alphabetized on the back.

I stuck my tag to my left lapel—they had left an *s* off *Douglass.* Dad would have been incensed, but I could manage. I slid into the room ready to mingle. The room was vast, with a sea of tables already set for dinner, napkins flounced up on their haunches, crystal goblets upside down, silver arranged in various ranks from right to left, and a perky carnation sprouting from some hidden source behind each pepper mill. Along the far wall a makeshift stage on risers held a stand of microphones, a nest of drums. Above, suspended from the ceiling, a net pouch crammed with balloons waited to erupt over the stage. A banner against the wall said, "Freedom Gala—Welcome All."

Along each side wall, banquet tables stretched end to end. My fellow Freedom Scholars seemed to be fussing over these tables, browsing some displays, so I crossed the room to the first table to see for myself. Some tables had newspapers, framed, recounting our accomplishments. I saw my roommate smiling out at

240

me from the front page of the *Youngstown Vindicator* under the headline "Teen Fights Drugs from Home Basement." Other clippings told of tornado heroics, charity work for teen alcholics, ballet students doing prison recitals, gutty stuff like that. A girl from northern California had even started a wolf patrol to spot renegade wolves slipping into suburbia from the lower elevations of the Sierras. And then there was my name on the framed page from the Congressional Record, just like my Christmas gift, with an AP wire blurb inset: "Student Pens Patriotic Tribute for Presidential Fanfare." It called me a sixteen-year-old straight-A student. I had been writing songs since grade school. My dream was to meet the president. So much for the news.

Farther along, the tables held other displays. An Indian-looking kid was waxing a wooden eagle carved from a tree trunk. Beside him, a girl wearing a black sweater down to her knees stood smoothing out a quilt along an entire table. It had all these red, white, and blue squares. Each of the white squares had an embroidered president. Franklin Pierce had all this black hair, like Fred Flintstone. John Kennedy looked like Howdy Doody.

I practically tripped over the next girl, squatting on the floor over a suitcase. She grabbed it by the handle and slammed it atop the next table.

"There," she exhaled. "Give me a hand, how about it?" She was staring at me, at my name tag. "Oh, I know you. You debated Lincoln. Great debates."

"Oh, my name, Stephen A. Douglass. I have two *s*'s, actually."

241

"Ya got two hands, too, actually. Here, press down. These latches stick." She tapped the corners of her suitcase, a ragged cardboard number worn through the fraying paper at the corners. I pushed down as hard as I could while she snapped the latches.

"There, good work, Stephen A. Douglass. With two *s*'s."

"Pronounce it with a burr, like 'Douglasssss.' It's Scottish."

"Okay, Douglassss," she burred right back. She stuck out her hand. "I'm Regina Steadman-Greenlaw. Pronounce it with a hyphen. Mom gets pissed if you don't. She's the Steadman. You're talking to the pride of Waterville, Maine."

I shook her hand. "Pleased to meet you, Regina." She had red hair flying in every direction, eyes green as envy, and when she laughed, her teeth bucked out in gappy rows straining against a moist infrastructure of criss-crossing rubber bands.

"Just call me Reg," she said. "Come on, I'll let you help." She opened the suitcase, and a mound of paper plates swelled out and spilled onto the table.

"Paper plates?" I said.

"Damn straight. Paper plates. Chinet. The best. My dad designs 'em. They make 'em right there in Waterville."

"He must be the Greenlaw," I said.

"Sure is," she said. "Old Maine name. Might be Scottish, too, but who really gives a shit? Here, take a look." She lifted a plate from the table and handed it to me. I turned it over. Behold, a lobster cut from stiff paper, glazed bright red, sprang in three-D from

242

the very center. It had piano wire for feelers. Across the top Reg had painted "MAINE" in bold blue capitals.

"Hope you like it," she said. "I have one for each state. I call them the Plates of the Union. My art teacher got me started, sent a photo to the prez, and *voilà, ici.*" She handed me another. I flipped it over. A great black-and-gold honeybee, with "IOWA" across the top.

"These are gorgeous, really," I told her. "United Plates of America."

"There's no plates like home," she fired right back. She was terrific. She caught right on. "What are you here for, anyway?"

" 'Hail to the Chief,' " I said. "Sort of a fluke. I put it to words. . . ."

"You mean you put words to it? No kidding, let's hear."

So I recited my heroic lyrics, line for line, verse for verse, and when I finished Reg was doubled over, laughing right into her suitcase.

"Excuse me, Douglass . . . I'm sorry . . . that's the most ridiculous thing I've ever heard." Finally she straightened up, staring at me with her lips pulled tight across her mouth. "Then again, paper plates of the states are pretty sucky, too, when you get right down to it." And she practically fell into her suitcase again. And me with her.

So after we sobered up some, I helped her display her plates across the table. She had one for each state and one for the District of Columbia. And a little Lucite stand, homemade, for every one. We traded

243

inspirations, me telling about the time I came home after being elected class president and everyone in the Mother was humming "Hail to the Chief." Reg's inspiration made more sense—at first. Her art teacher had taken her to a traveling exhibition in Boston to see the works of feminist sculptors.

"Shouldn't it be 'sculptresses'?" I asked.

"I'm not sure. That might be sexist," Reg said. "Anyhow, her name was Judy Chicago—"

"Chicago, like the city?"

"Yeah, she's from there. I guess she liked the name. Otherwise she'd have to use her father's name. . . ."

"And he's a man. I get it. Like Malcolm X."

"Is he a sculptor, too?" she asked. I just shook my head. "Well, anyway, she had all these ceramic plates, like a table setting. Except hers were of great American women: Molly Pitcher, Emily Dickinson, Susan B. Anthony . . ."

"And she had a picture of one on each plate, right?"

"Well, not a picture, exactly," Reg said. "C'mere," she said. She took my head and swiveled it and started whispering. At first I thought it was some joke, but Reg seemed to know what she was talking about.

"Their . . . parts?" I said. "Private parts on a plate?"

"*Ssssshhhh.*" Reg tried to quiet me down. Her display had drawn a crowd. They were all staring at me. Reg pulled me to the next table, to the quilt.

"Yes, on plates," she continued. "But it's not, not . . . obscene. I mean, that's the point. They're very abstract, very stylized, all highly glazed and colored.

244

They're beautiful, organic renderings, like little wedges of lettuce."

"But Molly Pitcher, a wedge of lettuce? I guess I'll have to see it for myself." I left her there by the quilt and retrieved her suitcase from the next table. "Let's get rid of this and go somewhere. Dinner's not for two hours." I took her by the arm, but she pulled away and took me by the arm instead.

"Let's eat dinner together too," she said. "You'll join me. We can sit at the same table."

"Terrific," I said. "If I get there first, I'll save your plates." That's when Reg took the suitcase and slammed me over the head. I fell across the card table by the door, knocking the plastic name cards to the floor. That woman at the table just looked down at me, staring into my nice gray vest.

"Can I help you?" she said.

I pushed my lapel up under her nose so she could focus on my little name card in its plastic sheath.

"Well, you can get me another *s,*" I said. "I'm supposed to have another *s*. It's not for me, it's for my father. He insists on two *s*'s. It's important to him. Parents are like that." I slid off the table, Reg picked up the cards, the woman straightened her hem. Reg jabbed me in the ribs, I apologized, and we left. The woman was still shuffling through her cards, looking for another *s*.

245

# Chapter 39

Reg got an orange parka from her room and said we should go walking 'cause she'll probably never get to see Washington again and she should see as much as she can while she's got the chance. Outside it was getting dark already, and had turned so cold the sidewalks sort of crackled underfoot. The bitter wind was the only traffic on the streets. The town seemed empty, full of cold white buildings, all empty too, but all lit up, like window displays, like toys in a museum.

"This place is dead," I told Reg, but she just lowered her head and leaned right into the wind. We turned a corner and saw the Capitol, like a frosted cake, pushing its dome up into one dark candle on top, and Reg headed right toward it.

"I'm sure it's closed," I shouted into the wind, but Reg just kept pushing onward. We marched up the long slope to the Capitol's back side, past the Supreme Court, until we could see the long brown stretch of nothing, now in darkness, straight across to the Washington Monument.

"How about that," I said to Reg, but I noticed that

she was staring down at her feet. We were standing on a grate, a huge cross-hatching of metal where the warm air flows up from the Metro, the subway, underground. "Damn," Reg said, "they're gone."

"Who's gone?" I asked, staring down at the toes of Reg's boots.

"The vent people, the ones who have to camp out over the hot-air vents. Barbara Walters said they sleep in the shadows of the Capitol building."

"Really. Maybe it's too cold. Maybe they've been cleared out. Come on."

I tried to pull her off the vent and get moving again. She snapped her arm away and stamped her boot heel on the grate. It rattled and echoed beneath us.

"But Barbara Walters said . . ." Finally, Reg spun and we headed across an intersection. "It's just . . . I wanted to see some bums. We don't have bums in Maine, not in Waterville."

When we reached the other walk, Reg bucked up once into midair, then bolted off down the sloping walk at a full gallop, me following her orange blur of a parka maybe five feet behind. At the bottom of the hill we collapsed onto a bench, breathless, wolfing gusts of cold air into freezing lungs. Reg's face glowed pink as a new blister under the streetlight. A drop of clear liquid gathered at the tip of her nose, a jiggling crystal bead.

"*Woooooohhhh,*" she said. She put a hand out and grabbed a chain suspended between iron stanchions. The drop fell from her nose, leaving a dark spot on the tan leather of her boots.

"Let's move along here, kids" came a voice. We

looked down to see a policeman bundled against the cold. He had on a ski mask and gloves the size of bear paws. "Get moving," he said, waving one paw down toward the empty street.

"Where are the bums, the vent people?" Reg tried again.

"All on a vacation," the policeman said.

"We were just doing a little sight-seeing, officer," I tried to reassure him. "We're guests of the president, just doing a little sight-seeing."

"So's my mother," he said. "Now get going, you be freezing your asses off. Come back tomorrow." He pulled a flashlight from his hip pocket, and I took that as a threat.

"Yes, sir," I told him. "Could you point us the way back to the Hyatt Regency please?" He snapped on the light and pointed it off into the darkness across the street. He said something about making a zigzag diagonal "thataway" and keep on going.

"Guy's a jerk," Reg said.

"Yeah, well, they must get lots of death threats, stuff like that."

"No wonder," she said. "I bet they put them all in jail, the bums. They always do that when it gets this cold. They put the bums in jail."

"The crazies, too," I said, "to keep them off the streets. The FBI has files on all the crazies. They round them up for stuff like this."

"Not all of them," Reg said. "They can never get them all. Just way too many. New ones every day." She let her breath out in a giant plume, and we walked on together as it hung behind us like a silver beet.

# Chapter 40

By the time we got back to the hotel, the dinner was half over. A man with a clipboard and a Styrofoam straw hat checked off our names.

"Thank god you're all right. You kids had us worried," he said. "We were about to call the police."

I go to the bathroom and run hot water over my hands until I can move my fingers some. My face feels raw. I pat water on my nose, hold it between my hands; no better. I am afraid I will lose my nose.

Back in the dining room, I spot Reg at a table. She has saved me a chair, her orange parka hanging from its back like a flag. Everyone is eating baked custard already. Reg introduces me: "This is my friend Stephen Douglass." I tell them all hi, then just hold my hands clamped against my nose and everyone stares at their custard.

A waiter brings us plates of chicken wrapped in ham and covered with a gray sauce. Cream of mushroom soup. I pick out the mushrooms, unwrap the chicken. It has no bones, is still pink inside, and shines in the light like a toy badge. They bring baked potatoes. I pick up mine. It is still hot, so I hold it in each hand in turn, then flush alongside my nose until I can feel my nose again. Reg grabs my wrist and pulls my hand away from my face.

"Would you like some sour cream?" she asks. She takes the potato from my hand and drops it on my plate. She splits it open with her fork, and the steam escapes in a gush. I lean over the potato and inhale. It would be good with a spoonful of Vicks, I think, all that eucalyptus oil. Mom used to make me breathe it in a bowl of hot water. "VapoRub," I say. But Reg drops a clot of sour cream on it anyhow.

"Just eat your potato," she says. "They're getting ready to begin."

Already the waiters are clearing the tables. A Dixieland band has taken over the small stage, warming up. Everyone swings chairs around to face the stage. I see only backs of heads. I scoop out my potato and eat the skin. No one sees me. The band is playing "The Muskrat Ramble," and wearing those same flat Styrofoam hats as the man with the clipboard. When they finish, they throw their hats at us, into the audience. They are wearing gray vests, too, and white shirts with sleeve garters where their biceps should be. Next they push their stools to the back of the stage. They play a big fanfare, and the guy with the clarinet steps forward to the microphone and introduces Ben Vereen. Ben skips up onto the stage from a door I had thought went into the kitchen. He is wearing shoes with tassels and a black suit pulled in at the waist. A ruffled shirt spills out beneath a butterfly tie. He spins backward to the mike and starts singing: "If they could see me now, with that old gang of mine . . ." and slides around the little stage until I can see it swaying back and forth.

Reg leans over to me. "Isn't he great?" she says. "We don't have many black people in Maine."

He is good, I tell her. But I am confused. Why is he here, I wonder. Why is he black? Why is Reg from Maine? Why wasn't the chicken cooked? I want to ask her, but Ben finishes, and the applause drowns out everything.

Ben is joined by Sandy and they sing a duet. They sing "Side by Side." And the guy with the clarinet steps forward to do a solo while Ben and Sandy do a soft-shoe with this really cute bit where they're marionettes and they hang from strings and their arms flop down at their sides. Reg likes it too. She hangs her head real loose from her neck and bobs along in time, smiling at me right over her plate. So I bob my head and smile back, all of which is pretty stupid, but it's getting so hot in there, and Reg is from Maine and probably hardly ever gets to do this stuff, so I figure it's okay because nobody around there knows me anyhow. More tremendous applause follows another song, and I excuse myself and go to the bathroom again.

It's so hot that I take off my vest and unbutton my shirt and splash cold water this time all over my face and down my neck, and sit on the toilet, mostly because I need to sit down for a while. When I get back to the gala, Reg is gone but her parka's still there, so I sit down, and it's really quiet. A man is standing at the microphone, just talking, and at first I'm not re-

251

ally sure who he is. He's tall, dressed in a gray suit, too, very elegant, with a red tie knotted so perfectly it could be a clip-on. His face, his jaw, might have qualified for chiseled once, but now seems a little fleshy—still dignified and heroic. A generous nose slopes hawkishly to a fine sharp tip, and on either side high cheekbones glow a ruddy pink under the bright lights. Otherwise, his face seems a healthy tan, browned and creased, and even for November, strangely healthy.

He's telling us how important we are.

". . . You are America's future. You will lead us into the twenty-first century, and looking around at your faces tonight, I know that our nation will stand strong in the world community as long as we have the talent and the wisdom of people like you to show us the way. Ya know, they keep telling us how the younger generation is letting us old folks down, but golly, just between you and me, they've been saying that since Hector was a pup. Tonight, looking into this audience, I know that isn't true. . . ."

He smiles, and the audience gurgles with warm laughter that turns into applause. He crinkles his head to the side and cracks this huge grin spilling over with teeth. He has the kind of hair that never moves, even in a wind tunnel, just stays right where it's supposed to. He's perfect, reassuring, fatherly, wise, tall, groomed, resonant, composed, noble, folksy. . . . He is, in other words, presidential. Why has it taken so long to register? That voice, that face . . . of course, he wanted to surprise us.

Well, he sure has caught me off guard.

252

As the applause dies down, a flashbulb pops up front, and then another, bunches of them suddenly. I see a legion of kids, squatting at the stage's edge, cameras pressed to their faces. Reg is there among them, her bristly red head like a nest bobbing in a windstorm. The president puts out his hands, palms down, to hush the crowd. He tells us to enjoy every minute of our stay, and to be sure to dress really warm tomorrow. And if we have any questions, he has a little time, and he'll try to do the best he can.

Some kid against the wall sticks up a hand and stands. "Do you prefer TV shows to movies?" So, all right, this is a gala, but what a jerky question to ask a president. I can see he's embarrassed, the way he tries to smile and look down at his shoes.

Finally, he looks back at the kid and asks, "Do you mean to make or to watch?" Well, that does it. Everyone roars, and the kid melts into his chair, and the flashbulbs pop, and the president just pinches his lips together and waits, gracious as can be.

Finally he says into the mike, "Shall we try again?"

This time I put my hand up. Ordinarily I'd just sit quietly. People who always have to ask questions usually like to show off how much they know all the time. Anything to be noticed. But I figure maybe I can restore some dignity to the occasion, especially since we've just been told how talented and wise we are, and this first kid comes along like a complete airhead.

So I put my hand up and stand, the way they do at those press conferences. The president nods in my direction. All the kids pivot in their chairs, since I'm toward the back of the room.

"Uhhhh . . ." I begin. But what question? Taxes, terrorism, defense spending . . . too depressing. Give the man a chance to reflect, I decide, let the guy wax historical.

"Uhhhh, yes, I'd like to know what you consider the greatest accomplishment of your first term . . . and what has been the greatest challenge of your second?"

"Second what?" he says into the microphone.

"Term," I call back across the room, suddenly dead quiet.

"Term?" he says. He stands back from the microphone smiling, scratching at his chin.

"Your presidency," I try reminding him. "First term, second term. Your accomplishments." I'm almost shouting now. Must be the acoustics.

A slow boil of coughing, giggles, ruffles through the room. I look at the faces watching me, staring. Something is wrong. Wrong planet. Wrong language. Something.

I wipe at my face. My nose is warm. I'm sure I can feel cellophane across my face, around my ears.

A hand clamps my elbow, pulling me backward from the table. I grab for balance, get my water goblet. It spills across the floor.

"Apologize," I hear, "apologize to Mr. Heston." A man with a flat, desperate face, his sour breath against my nose, repeats the command: "Apologize." It's the man with the clipboard, without his clipboard. Something is wrong.

"No, no, please, that's all right." It's him, still. Even

with my back turned, his voice is coming through the speakers. "No harm done. They used to think I was Moses. I'm flattered, but maybe the president's the one who needs the apology. From me." Hilarious. Whatever it means, it's hilarious. The room swells now with laughter, so loud against my eardrums, rattling against the cellophane there, and beneath that I hear the voice in my face say, "Charlton Heston! Get ahold of yourself, son," but I seem to be falling sideways.

"The actor?" I say.

"Charlton Heston, yes, the actor."

"Well, why didn't he say so? Who put him up to it? Who the hell is Hector? He shouldn't do that. Impersonating presidents. Imposter. Imposter." But I can't hear a thing, the cellophane is so tight around my face now, the sounds aren't getting out. "Moses, God, president, Moses, God, imposter, he should have said so." "Actor, actor," I remember yelling, but no sound came out. Just the yell "actor" and floating sideways above the tables. I remember tearing at the cellophane around my face, so hot, so hard to breathe, and asking them to take it off. "It's hot, the cellophane is hot," I tried to yell, scream, but my voice was gone, down a dark, long hole and sinking faster than sound itself, than light.

# Chapter 41

"There now, that should feel some better." The voice came faint and small. I opened my eyes to darkness, and it was wet.

The wet and the darkness went, and I was staring at the surface of the moon. I closed my eyes, and when I opened them again Reg was bending over me, holding a wet washcloth wrapped around her knuckles. Above her head the moonscape was a ceiling, pocked and stippled white plaster. Her pale face glowed like moonstone wreathed around by hair, sparking red and gold in the cold light. She is my angel; she has come for me, I thought. I floated up to her.

"Stay put, you're in your skivvies." I sank beneath the weight of blankets, back to the bed, a bed, as the sheet against my back pulled me down like a wet second skin. I tried to lift my head, but there was a stone resting on my forehead. I tried again, angling my head up off the pillow. Better this time. Only my brain stayed behind, curling into the pillow like a dead cat. Beyond the bulge of my toes I could see across to the desk, and above, to where the TV hung from the wall, glowing blue. A face floated up behind the screen, a man's face.

"Stephen, good to meet you. You've had a nasty fever. It's coming down a bit. Rest, liquids, the usual. Tomorrow you'll be absolutely first-rate. You've got Regina to take care of you. Aspirin there if it goes up again, but it shouldn't. Call the desk if you need me. Doctor Dunston. I'm here till eight." He smiled and left. He had brown teeth. He might have been British.

"Isn't he nice?" Regina said. She stuffed another pillow under my head. I tried to smile back at her but my knees hurt. "Here, drink this." She put a glass to my lips and I swallowed. Ginger ale. The bubbles hurt going down.

"Where am I?" I asked. My tongue felt like a flounder.

"Your room. Your roommates were moved out. Me, I don't care if I get it." She sat at the edge of the bed and brushed the washcloth across my face. "Look, there he is." She pointed to the TV. A man was standing at a spray of microphones lashed together like bunches of broccoli.

"It's him again," I said. "I think I dreamed about him. He was talking about Moses, and I . . . Something bad, something about cellophane."

"That was Charlton Heston, silly. Look." She disappeared and came back with a spray of daisies in a brass mug. "He sent these," she said. She plucked a card from the mug and read: " 'For Stephen, my toughest critic. Hope you're feeling better real soon.

All my best, Chuck Heston.' Now try telling me Mr. Heston's not a class guy, huh?"

"A class guy," I repeated, and Reg put the flowers somewhere above my head. "Then who's that?" I asked, nodding toward the TV while something sloshed in my skull.

"It's the president, Stephen. It's a press conference, remember?"

"But we're not there. We're supposed to be there."

"No one's there, just them, in the White House."

"But *they're* there."

"But they're dignitaries and reporters and stuff. It's over. We had breakfast with him. This morning. You were here. Sorry, Steve."

"But I was supposed to be nice. Mom said to be nice to the president, and now . . ."

"They were afraid you'd croak. Too damn cold. Like Maine out there." She sprang to the TV and turned up the sound. The president's head was down now. You could hear feet scraping on the floor. Someone was coughing.

I shot up in bed. It was obvious. "Of course, how can I be nice to him if he doesn't exist. He's not a real person. Why do you think they kept me here? So I couldn't meet him, that's why. They keep sending out imitations, all these presidential imposters, thousands of them in identical suits. They make them in a laboratory. Walt Disney makes them. Have you ever been to Disneyland? Have you ever seen Abe Lincoln? He seems so real. So real . . ."

*Zam*, in a second Reg was at the bed, pushing against my shoulders, pushing me back into the bed.

258

"It's okay, Stephen, try to rest, get some rest. Here, just watch. He's going to talk now. You'll see." She studied the screen, and the camera panned the reporters. "Look," she shrieked. She pointed at the set, snapping her fingers at it, saying, "That's, that's, that's, with the hair, that's the guy on TV."

"Sam Donaldson," I said. "ABC."

I pulled my arms out from under the blanket and folded them across my chest. I was feeling better. I said, "See, I told you it's not real. Why do you think he's there? They put him in there to make the other guys seem real. Look at those eyebrows. That's all. It's simple common sense. Two and two. Add it up."

"God, Stephen, you're impossible." She stamped her feet against the floor and stood, then threw the blanket over my face. "Just stay right here. I'll be right back." She tromped out of the room, snapping off the TV as she went, and slammed the door behind her.

I lay back in bed and shut my eyes. Behind my lids I rolled my eyes, hot and dry, and listened to the sounds they made, the capillaries whooshing like the tide going in and out. I rubbed my eyes until they flashed red and cosmic flecks of light came streaming at me from the darkness, all jiggling and Brownian, like things in pond water under a microscope. The door slammed and they swam away.

"I'm going out now. Will you be all right?"

It was Regina, back again, this time in her parka just barely oranger than her hair. Her boots reached almost to her knees, where gray wool socks turned down and over, making a cuff above the boots. A

259

green scarf looped around her neck and hung to her waist. She had a small blue bundle tucked under one arm.

"Out where?" I asked. "I thought you were taking care of me."

"I am, will, you need your rest. They're giving us a tour of the city, us and some band from Kansas. So we won't miss everything. The band washed ten thousand cars in Coffeyville just to get here."

When I asked about the bundle under her arm, she stood on the bed next to mine and unfolded a flag as big as a queen-sized sheet. It was faded blue, with a seal, State of Maine, a bear rampant pawing a fish beneath some pine trees. It was torn at the corners and smelled like the inside of a shoe. Reg stood completely hidden by the enormous flag except for where her fingers held it pinching each corner at the top.

I told her it was a terrific flag, and she draped it over the bed and started refolding it, half, quarter, eighths, sixteenths, until it was a tidy blue bundle under her arm again.

"Are you taking it for a shawl, or are you just proud to be from Maine?" I asked her.

"Neither," she said. "I'm supposed to leave it somewhere."

"Why not just give it to me?" I asked. "It'd look good on my wall at home."

"Sorry, Stephen. The school board wants me to leave it at that Vietnam memorial wall they built. It's our old school flag, and two guys from school are buried there. They died in the war or something."

"They're not buried there. It's just their names, a bunch of names."

"Whatever. So I thought this might be my only chance. The paper back home said they'd run my picture if I got one. I brought my camera just in case." She patted the pocket of her parka, where the camera bulged at her side.

I threw back the covers and sat up in bed. "I'll take your picture. Let me come, and I'll take your picture." The room was spinning around me. Finally, I focused on Regina and tried again. "I'll take it. I'm coming with you."

"The hell you are. You're sick, you'll catch your death out there."

"The hell I am so. I've already caught my death. Where'd you put my suit?" I was out of the bed that fast and prowling the room. I found my suit hanging in a recessed closet by the bathroom. I slipped it on, pants, shirt, vest, sweater over the vest just in case, jacket. I sat on the edge of the bed trying to remember how to tie shoes. Bunny ears, bunny ears, damn, I couldn't get my fingers to do the bunny ears. I just tied a square knot and tucked the laces into my shoes. "Let's go," I said, standing up. Reg stood there with her back against the door, swaying her head from side to side. *"Tsk, tsk, tsk,"* she was going. Then she smiled and opened the door like a footman. She plunged a hand into her parka and withdrew a camera dangling from a strap. "Here, go on and take it," she said, slapping the camera smack against my fragile sternum. "And remember, bud, it's your funeral."

261

# Chapter 42

The lobby was swelling with Freedom Scholars stuffed into ripstop nylon parkas, sliding around each other like fingerlings in a tank, going *zish, zish, zish.* The more prosperous parkas among them had ski-lift tickets hanging from their zippers and enough goose down to repopulate Ontario. Reg and I pushed to the entry door. We could see three white buses idling among drifts of white exhaust, their doors closed against the cold. A Republican matron took our names and told us where to stand. A line wound behind us into the lobby. When the driver in bus one flashed his lights, we bolted in an orderly queue through the doors and onto the bus.

"Hurry 'em up, I'm losing all my heat," the driver complained.

The band from Kansas was already plunked down in the back half of the bus. They were sitting in each other's laps, taking pictures of each other, eating hard-boiled eggs out of white boxes and throwing their shells on the floor. They had bad complexions and gold jackets with "Coffeyville" embroidered across the backs and blue cornflowers under that, and they actually looked like they'd just washed a thousand cars.

Reg and I found a couple of empty seats toward the front on the curbside. I pulled out the camera, and Reg ran me through its intricacies, like how to aim it and where to look through and complicated stuff like that. The bus rattled out onto the street, and as we turned onto Massachusetts Avenue this lady in a blue blazer sprang up from behind the driver and announced herself as Estelle.

"Good afternoon, ladies and gentlemen, and welcome to the Potomac Capital City Bus Tours, and thank you for choosing Potomac." She clutched a little microphone in her mittened hands and nasalized her monologue.

"Washington, District of Columbia, is actually the third site of our nation's capital, after New York City and Philadelphia. In 1791 Pierre Charles L'Enfant was commissioned to design a capital here in the marshy coastal plain at the confluence of the Potomac and Anacostia rivers. This site was chosen as a compromise between those who favored a northern site and those who felt a more southern setting was appropriate to our emerging nation. Not coincidentally, this new capital was to be located on land once owned by our nation's first president, George Washington."

Well, she had an awesome command of her facts. But I knew what was coming next: the part about L'Enfant's design, the wheel, the spokes, all that. I gave Regina a nudge.

". . . in perfect geometrical fashion, the streets

263

radiating like the spokes from a wheel, and at the hub of this wheel sits the White House, the very center of L'Enfant's design."

"Radiating like spokes from a wheel, see?" I said to Regina, but she didn't, not quite.

". . . overlaid by a perfect grid of intersecting streets," Estelle continued. "Much of the surveying and design was done by a Baltimore mathematician and engineer, Benjamin Banneker, who was also black. . . .

"See," I whispered to Reg, "he was also black."

"Was L'Enfant?" she asked.

"No, he was French. Also French."

"White?" Reg asked.

"Also," I said. "Also French and also white."

"But Banneker was black? I don't think I . . ." Reg paused, fluttered a hand, then dropped it to her lap. "I don't follow," she finished.

"What's to follow?" I said.

The bus whizzed down Massachusetts Avenue and around a bunch of circles and Estelle took a couple hits of nasal inhaler and then twittered to life. We circled around a slope of brown grass with a white storybook kind of house at the top.

"These are the grounds of the Naval Observatory, and if you look to your left you will see the residence of our vice president, the second white house, if you will . . ."

"Also white," I said.

And then we cruised by the Washington Cathedral with its reasonably impressive mock-Gothic tower, and Estelle went into this rapture about its carillon.

264

Finally, after a bunch of stoplights, we hit Connecticut Avenue, and Estelle put a hand on the driver's shoulder. The bus pulled over and stopped alongside a curb.

"Across the street you see the distinctive wrought-iron gateway to our national zoo. We invite you now to take a brief stroll through the grounds. The zoo houses one of the largest collections of fauna in the world and is open all year round. Of course, most animals are inside at this time of year, but you are still welcome to take a look. Please be back in thirty minutes."

"C'mon, Steve, man, let's check it out." Regina stood in the aisle and nodded toward the iron gates across the street. "C'mon. And bring the camera, too. We'll get some shots."

So we got some shots of the empty hippo pond and a monkey island where some bare tree parts stood in the middle of an empty concrete moat. I thought I heard an elephant trumpet from inside some distant building, but it was getting too cold to bother. So I just grabbed Reg by the elbow and started steering her back to the entrance, back the way we came.

"Yooo, slow down, wait up," Reg protested, pulling away and walking off down a walkway branching to the right. I found her standing there, in front of a low gray building with a recessed entrance. A chain hung from one side to the other, across the entrance, with one of those embossed plastic signs: "Sorry, No Visitors Today."

Reg stood at the far end of the building, with her hand reaching back to me, fingers opening and closing. "Gimme the camera, Stephen, I gotta get one of this, and then we can go."

I put the camera in her hand. "One of what?" I asked.

Reg just put the camera to her face and tilted it up. "One of this here," she said. "Read it for yourself."

I looked up to where the camera was pointing. A small TV monitor stood on a post just below the building's roofline, behind a fence put there to shield it from the tourists. Below the monitor, another plastic sign: "Ling Ling, giant panda, donated by the People's Republic of China."

"Doesn't she look sweet?" Reg said. I stared at the monitor. Ling Ling sat in the gloom of her concrete den, slumped into a corner. Her great head tilted to the side, her arms seemed stuck to her sides, her legs splayed out as though she had been dropped from a great height and left there. Between her legs three stalks of bamboo sat neglected, their leaves sticking to the floor in a puddle shaped like Argentina.

Reg twisted the camera into her face and leaned toward the monitor.

I reached a hand out and pressed it against the lens. And closed my fingers around the camera. "Don't take her like that, off the TV. It's an act against nature. Just remember her in your mind's eye."

"Hey, know what?" Reg asked. "I think you're a Muslim or something. But hey, I can respect that. I don't have a hang-up about Muslims. No, really. No pictures, if it means that much to you."

So Regina pocketed her camera and tried to push

me once more up the walkway toward the bus. Suddenly two steps up she halted, pivoted, and hoisted an arm back in a salute to the monitor.

"Hey, you take care now, Ling Ling. And be a good panda."

She yanked me around beside her and lifted my arm. She said she was taking me back to the nice warm bus, but shouldn't I say good-bye to Ling Ling, too?

"Good-bye, Ling Ling," I said, "and be a good panda."

# Chapter 43

So after that I was ready for anything, and we rode in the bus along the Potomac River, Reg beside me with her flag folded in her lap, and me beside her, starting to warm up some, especially at that spot on my chin. It felt like someone had driven a burning cork through to my bottom gum. We got to the Lincoln Memorial first, and there sat Abe, a vision of composure, hardly aware of the cold, old Abe, probably the last of the real presidents before they started using imposters. I know because I've seen the snapshots by Mathew Brady. Estelle had the bus lap the memorial once, and then she let us out for some quick pictures.

Then back on the bus and across the mouth of the tidal basin, where we did another quick lap around the Jefferson Memorial. We stopped once more for what Estelle kept calling photo opportunities. Estelle pointed out the classic open portico and the wonderful columns so characteristic of Mr. Jefferson's passion for Greek architecture. Everyone produced a camera and snapped away like crazy.

And finally we got on the bus, all of us, and the bus rolled by some very official-looking buildings that turned out to be the Department of Agriculture, according to a plaque at ground level on one of its corners. Then the bus bisected what Estelle called the Mall, but it was just a wide space lined on either side by the Smithsonian museums. Up at the far end we could see the Capitol again, sitting on its frozen brown hill. To the left stood the Washington Monument, so close that its top rose out of view, and far away past that the Lincoln Memorial, again like a block of white ice rising from the cold Potomac.

We turned onto Constitution Avenue, and ahead was the White House across a wide space of bare trees, the Ellipse. And the bus turned once more, into a drive that opened to an oval of pavement. The bus rolled beyond some cars parked diagonally and shuddered to a stop. We sat on the rear flank of the Washington Monument. Estelle announced another photo opportunity, and Reg bolted forward from our seat and conferred briefly, her flag tucked underarm.

Reg skipped back down the aisle, bent her face down into mine, and whispered, "Estelle says we should get off here, but not be too long. I can get someone else if you want to give me the camera. You don't have to come."

But I was already standing up. "I'm coming," I said. "I want to."

"Well, come on then," Reg said. "If you think you're warm enough. If you can hang on for a little longer."

"Hang on to what?" I said right back, but Reg was already off the bus.

I followed her off and caught up through a clot of blue band jackets walking in all directions. We were heading for the Washington Monument. I looked up to find its top, a brilliant white blur, with the sun halfway down in the sky, hanging like a cosmic tetherball from its blunt-sharp end.

I was heading right for the base, the entrance, when I heard Reg yelling from a distance, "Not there. We don't have time. This way, over here." She was pointing across the grounds toward a broad street and beyond, toward the Lincoln Memorial.

Suddenly Reg broke into a sprint, clutching the flag in her hand, running across the avenue, up onto the hard brittle grass, with me right behind, panting to keep up, and gulping at the air, so cold I felt my lungs shrinking with every breath. I pulled up behind her and she slowed to a jog, and I slowed to a crawl. Finally we hit a sidewalk sloping down in a straight line beside the wall, the Vietnam Memorial, with black granite slabs standing maybe ten feet tall and edge to edge. They went on almost forever until the straight line of the wall and the walk broke back at an angle toward the Lincoln Memorial at the other end.

Reg stood just ahead of me, studying the wall, a white index card crumpled in her hand. I stood beside her and looked back along the walk. A dull white stripe seemed to run the wall's length along its bottom, maybe one foot up. But it moved as I backed away, and I realized it was only the walk

270

itself, reflected in the hard black luster of the granite. Behind us the sun floated over our shoulders, reflecting off the wall through a bare stand of trees at our backs.

"He's not in this section," Reg said to her index card. "Clay Ronald Pelletier, 1969."

"Sounds French," I told her.

"Frog, Canuck," she said. "Waterville is sixty percent Canuck."

We stood squinting at the names, hard to see at all, more like a pale etching of frost on the slick black wall. There were just endless names forever, each separated from the other by a dot in front and back. No ranks, no titles. I liked that.

"Here, see, it's chronological. This is sixty-two." Reg fluttered her card at a spot to her left. A date, 1962, had been chiseled midway down a slab. It was bigger than the names.

We followed the wall farther along the walk until Reg found the 1969's. She checked her card again and squinted at the wall. I stood beside her, looking for Pelletier, the frog, Canuck. From the walk to the wall was maybe two feet of stiff brown grass. Reg and I both looked down at the same time. The base along this section was littered with trash. Handkerchiefs, a pair of soiled gloves, what seemed to be some Christmas cards stuck through with spikes to hold them on the frozen ground.

Reg walked down to the next section, and turned something over with her foot. "Yuck," she groaned. "Can you imagine someone leaving this?" It was a six-pack, Heineken Dark, in thick brown bottles, the frozen liquid pushing up through the necks like dark fingers of ice, scattering the metal caps to the ground.

"Whatever happened to flowers?" Reg wondered.

"They'd freeze, too. Some guys like beer better. It's a fact of life. To each his own."

Reg told me to stand still, to block the glare so she could read the names where my shadow fell against the wall. We walked slowly, in tandem, until Reg knelt at the bottom of one stone.

"This is him," she announced. "Clay Ronald Pelletier. Get the camera."

She unfolded the flag and draped it across one shoulder and down over her knees like a kneeling Lady Liberty. I focused on her through the lens and knelt myself, five feet away, to get a straight-on shot. I told her not to smile, and she said don't worry, she wouldn't. She pointed to the name, so the homefolks might see at least where it was, and I snapped the picture.

We headed off to find the next guy after that. Reg read his name off her card: Albritton W. Singletary, 1973. I told her that should be easy to find since it probably took up a whole row by itself. She said most likely.

We got to the vertex, where the wall angles off in a different direction, and stopped to admire a sort of war tableau. Statues of six soldiers had been grouped maybe forty feet off from the wall beneath some trees. They stood in a tight pack, holding not guns but signs. I pulled Reg over so we could get a closer look. That was when they came to life. I was ready to turn and run, but Reg grabbed me by the sleeve and said, "Hey, it's just a bunch of old veterans. Let's check it out."

So we headed over, and all six veterans turned to face us, just staring and suspicious. The fat one tweaked his beret and said, "Hello, younguns. What can I do you for?"

His face was full and white, sagging with jowls. Sideburns reached down to the end of each jowl and angled off in straight lines like knife blades. Like the others he was dressed in rumpled camo fatigues, worn and faded, the pants tucked loosely into boots laced twice all around the tops. He had a dog tag hanging from the lace.

Reg explained how she had brought the flag from her school in Maine, and they thought that was a pretty good gesture. She told them the names and no one seemed to know her soldiers from Waterville.

"Lots of boys gone," Sideburns said. "Big war, long war."

"Here for the weekend?" I asked the big guy.

"We alternate," he said. "Want to remind the feller in the White House we're still here. But he welshed on us. Like they all do." He removed his beret—it had a feather in it—and stroked the pale smooth top of his head. When he replaced the beret and twisted his head around, I could see an earring hanging from his left ear. He looked like a pirate; they all did, more like pirates than any war veterans I'd ever seen.

"Y'all haven't seen any cameras roundabouts, have ya?" he asked.

273

"Sure, got one right here," I said, holding Reg's camera out by its strap.

"No, boy, I mean TV, television cameras. We was planning a media event. But they'll welsh on us too. We tipped them off and everything, even threw in a little violence just to pique they's appetite, but no go, I bet. Too cold. Too cold and old news, screw it all." He turned and faced the others. They shouldered their signs indifferently and shuffled up behind.

"We was expectin' lotsa others, plenty more of us too, but it's not comin' off." He spun and led his men off in a slow broken march. I read the signs the last two carried, upside down and tilting toward the ground. One said, "Still Missing"; the other said, "Honor the Living Too."

"Those guys are . . . pathetic," Reg said, once they were out of earshot. "I mean, why don't they go home, live, stay with their families?"

"Not everybody has one," I told her. "Sometimes it's hard to give up on the past and all. I don't know." We resumed our search for Albritton Singletary, for the slab from 1973. Reg wrapped the flag around her shoulders and held its corners out like wings, to shield against the sun, to read the words, the numbers. Finally she found it, this time at the top. She stood, lifting up onto her toes.

"Come on, let's take it and go back. I'm freezing out here. The others are probably to the White House by now."

She arranged herself in front of the black granite, this time with the flag draped full across one arm,

Dracula style, while the other stretched upward to the name. I backed around to find an angle where the glare would disappear. The sun had settled almost to the horizon now, slicing by the trunks of trees until the wall seemed streaked and spotted, vandalized by sun.

"Will you take it, for god's sakes. I can't stand like this forever."

I put the viewfinder to my eye and swept the camera around to Reg until the thin red line inside bisected her face. I pushed it a touch more to the right, to get the name, and snapped.

"Thank god. Let's go," Reg said, slipping out of the small rectangle. But I just held the camera to my eye and read the names.

"I said, Stephen, we got it. Enough!" Reg shouted, her voice far away down the walk.

But I just pulled in closer, reading the names, hypnotized by all the names.

Then I found the stone marked 1974, the final stone, and scanned the names. I knew it would be there.

Truelove. Truelove. Truelove.

"No," I said. But nothing came out. I inhaled, then tried again. "Noooo. Can't be. Can't be. Just can't."

But it was. Burton R. Truelove. With a dot at the front and a dot at the back.

*"Bastard. Crazy bastard. You're dead. You've been dead all the time."*

"Who's a bastard? What's the shouting for?" It was Reg's voice coming from over my shoulder.

"Look, it's him," I said, pointing at the name.

275

"Funny name—who is it?" Reg asked.

"It's him. It's my biology teacher. He's dead."

"When the hell did you take biology, Stephen?"

"This year, just this fall, with him, Truelove. But it's not him at all, see, because he's been dead all the time. It was never him. They're trying to get him fired, and he's already dead. He was always one ahead of us. Smart crazy bastard."

"Stephen, this is so incredible." Regina pulled the camera from my hand, from behind. "Stay there. I'll get your picture. This is so cool."

"Cool?" I leaned against the cold stone and slumped against it to the ground. "Cool?"

"Yes, it's so cool, like on *Saint Elsewhere*, when this doctor comes here and finds his brother's name. And that Magnum guy finds his old buddy. They were both helicopter pilots, and Magnum comes here and sees his buddy on the wall and he just cries and cries. It's been on all the shows."

"Regina," I began, and then I looked up at her and she was pointing the camera right at me. "Regina, put it away. I haven't seen those shows. It doesn't matter."

"Oh, but it's not just the TV, Stephen. It's real life. And even books. There's one where this girl comes looking for her father and sees her own name. It's very moving. It's full of agent orange."

"But look, Regina, I only know, I mean, I know him better than any of them. He wanted me to know. Just me, one person, that's all. I knew him better than any. His room, his kid—he has a kid over there—the jelly roll. Doctor Feelgood, that must have been it.

276

Doctor Feelgood, hiding behind Truelove. It had to be . . ."

"His real name is Feelgood?" Regina asked.

"No way," I said. "That's a kind of a . . . private joke. His real name he never told me. I think he switched names with this Truelove guy the day he died."

"Maybe you can call the Army, straighten this all out."

"I don't think so. I think if he decides it's time, then all right. If he wants me to know. Even if it has to be on *Jeopardy*."

"On what?" Regina dropped to her knees and put a palm against my forehead. "So friggin' cold I can't feel anything right now."

"Me either," I told her.

So all right. The stone was cold and hard and real behind my head, and that was probably the only thing I knew. The other stuff I knew I didn't know at all. But how does life stop, twenty years ago, fifteen, sixteen? It had for old True, too, and the pirate veteran with the sideburns, and Albritton Singletary and Clay Ronald Pelletier, one way or another, it had stopped for them all. Even Dad, behind his bar, and even Mom. Something had happened that wouldn't let them go. Some had gone to fight, a bunch had died, some were still missing in action, some were still in hiding. None had let that something go or freed themselves of it completely. Maybe they couldn't. But now at least I was beginning to feel, to see, the shape of their lives, like some distortion or some twist in the bone apparent only in their X rays.

They marched alongside walls or exercised by mirrors, but they were cold, pale shapes in dark water, moving slowly under winter ice. Strange fish.

From far off I heard the counting—"hut, hoo, hee, hore"—the scraping grit of boots on concrete. I looked to my left to see a dark clump of men, marching two by two by two.

Regina stood up first. "It's them," she said. "They're coming this way. They're marching."

I stood beside her and watched. The veterans, their ranks now swollen to a dozen or more, came marching down the walk right at us, holding their signs and dragging their boots to sound like thirty, forty men.

I stepped in front of them and put up a hand. Sideburns stopped his men.

"Problem, kid? Make it fast."

"Just a second. Do me a favor." I walked to the wall and pointed to Truelove's name. "You wouldn't know this one, would you?"

Sideburns stared at the name, then turned to his men. "Any you grunts do duty with a Truelove, Burton R.?" They searched one another's faces. No one had. "Sorry, kid. What's he to you?"

I looked at Sideburns and his men, then back at Reg. I knew she would understand.

"He's my father. I was hopin' you guys would let me march for him, for Dad, I mean."

"Stephen, you shouldn't," Reg began to blurt out. I grabbed her by the wrist and squeezed.

"Let me do it, Reg. I'll tell you later."

"How do we know? I mean, the men don't want

some kid, some imposter, messing their ranks." The men stood behind Sideburns, eager to march, shifting from side to side and twirling their signs.

I threw off my jacket, my sweater, my vest, and popped the top button of my shirt.

"You'll freeze, Stephen. This is dangerous." Reg threw the flag over my shoulders like a cape, but I already had my hand around the chain, the beads running through my fingers, until I found it, the tag. I pinched it between two fingers and pulled it out from beneath my shirt so that Sideburns could read.

" 'Truelove, Burton R.' Looks good enough to me." He turned to his men. "Boy's dad's on the wall. He's for real, wants to march too. Problems?" Some murmured, but none complained. "The more the merrier. You stay up front with me."

He bellowed out something like "Ready, HAAAARRRRCII," and we set off as Reg ran alongside.

I fell in step, and we marched down to the end of the walk, as far as the wall went, snaked our column around, and came back, Sideburns counting cadence and singing out verse:

We been back a long long time,
Folks back here still think we're slime.
Sound off, ONE TWO, sound off, THREE FOUR.

Each guy took a verse, and some of them were pretty filthy and some were just angry as hell, and we marched back down the walk. But I didn't feel it hard enough—not hard and cold as the wall, as Truelove did. Not even close.

"Bare chested," I yelled to Sideburns. "Let's do it bare chested." I ripped off my shirt and threw it down where we turned, so that I was marching there naked from the waist up, except for the flag still around my shoulders and the dog tag jangling back and forth, slapping hard against my cold, stinging chest.

Sideburns turned to me and leered. "Boy, you're plumb crazy, owl shit in a fruit jar." He threw his head back and roared over his shoulder, *"Let's take 'em off, boys!"* He shed his jacket and two sweaters under that, and he was down to a T-shirt, but not just any T-shirt, one of those Truelove specials with the V necks. I looked back at the others. They were all down to their V-necked T-shirts, and I thought, bless us, I hope old True is watching this somewhere. And finally they were down to bare skin, pale as fish and jiggling. Sideburns beside me pushing a stomach out in front like a sack of wet bread, rising yeasty and falling flat with each breath.

Reg stood there yelling, "Idiot, idiot, put your clothes on," but when I got right up by her I scooped her out to the walk and threw the flag over her.

"Come on with us, show a little spirit for once. Do it for Maine. Do it for Waterville. Do it for all the people making Chinet plates."

And god bless Regina, but didn't she finally break down and join right in, running out ahead of us, holding the flag flat over her head, a corner in each hand. I could see the bear. I could see the fish. I could see the pine trees waving on their sides.

So I just marched along and stared at Regina

prancing up there, like a winterized hood ornament on a '37 Hudson, all of us marching and counting, *"Hut hoo hee hore, hut hoo hee hore."*

We marched like that up to the end again and back, *"Hut hoo hee hore, hut hoo hee hore."* My chest was feeling cold and hard as the wall I was walking beside, my nipples hard as acorns. It was lucky I didn't have any Butter Rum Lifesavers right then. They'd freeze right up and snap like frozen O-rings. Then I'd never find out what they're for.

But at least I felt it, finally, cold and hard enough.

# Chapter 44

Come Sunday, they put me on an early morning flight back home and I drank ginger ale all the way. Reg told me to drink lots of fluids so that I would still be alive by Christmas. She said she would write. She promised me my own special paper plate—she was making them for gifts. It would come UPS, she kept telling me.

Somewhere over Richmond my fever broke. By the time we landed, I was dry and cool inside my new gray suit. Dad met me at the gate.

"Stephen, you're a ghost," he told me.

"You should see the president," I said.

Back at the Mother I crashed on my bunk and slept until Monday. I woke up, showered, and shuffled through school in a blur. It was Thanksgiving week. If I could make it through Wednesday, I would be plumb thankful.

Back at the Mother on Monday night I went upstairs, washed up, and admired the toilet. The toilet had been cleaned. It was full of blue water. The sink

had been scoured. The shower curtain had been replaced. Gone was its scuzzy, freckled, bubbled plastic face, years of mold cultures husbanded in vain. In
its place hung a sparkling new curtain covered with
flamingos rampant and braces of egrets winging it
south.

I went downstairs. Dad was spraying the cash register with Windex and dabbing it dry with a bar rag.

He handed me the bottle and the rag. "Hey, sport,
wanna get the back?" I sprayed and dabbed at the
register's back side.

"Health inspector coming by or what?" I asked.
"The bathroom upstairs looks like a Holiday Inn."

"Spring cleaning." Dad smiled. Spring cleaning in
November?

"Can't hurt to put a fresh face on things, give it the
old spic-and-span," he continued. "Guess who's coming by to look at the bar—guess who might want to
buy the old Mother."

"Ted Turner," I said.

"Not even close," he said. "Guess again. Someone
without a mustache this time."

I could see it coming now, but I wanted him to
sweat it a little. "Can't think of anybody without a
mustache," I told him. "Give me a clue."

"Think female. Think exercise," he hinted.

"Jane Fonda. No kidding, Jane Fonda's buying the
Mother Won't Know? That's incredible, Dad."

"Smartass punk," he said, snapping the rag about
two inches from my face. "It's your mother, Eileen
Douglass, *that* aerobics queen. She's interested in
buying the Mother!"

283

"See, I told you she's interested in the Mother."
Then it struck me. "So that explains the toilet."

"Nothing explains the toilet," Dad shot back.
"Why don't you mind your own business?"

"So is Mom coming over to see us tonight, or
what?"

He leaned across the bar, eyeball to eyeball, and
grinned. "What you mean *us*, white man?"

Something was definitely going on. He was dredg-
ing up vintage Lone Ranger jokes. He leaned across
the bar and a small cumulonimbus of after-shave bil-
lowed through the stale air. Fjord, I think it was;
essence of Viking longboat.

"What I mean is," Dad began to explain, "is that
this is, you know, strictly business." He pulled off the
apron he had been wearing to reveal his best sleeveless lamb's-wool argyle sweater vest. Mom had ordered it direct from Harrod's in London the last
Christmas we spent together. A spray of black and
steel-gray hair sprouted like fine moss above its neck-
line.

"Oh, and speaking of business—old business, channel eleven called last Friday. Did you see the note on
the fridge?"

"No, too dazzled by the john. What'd they want?"
I was hoping they would cancel, hoping they'd forgot.

"They'll be at school next Monday, November thir-
tieth. I told them that was fine. They'll meet you in
Mr. Wilfong's office."

"So soon. It's too fast . . . too—"

"Face it, champ, you're on a roll." Dad reached

284

across the bar and thumped an affectionate fist against my shoulder. "But that's old business. New business is behind you. There's someone waiting to see you." His voice became a whisper. "Don't panic. Stay cool. Look in the last booth against the wall."

I pivoted around. In the farthest, darkest corner, a dim figure of a female raised a hand and waved. Five pounds of gold chain slid from the wrist and settled at the elbow. It was Peggy. She smiled. I waved and turned around.

"What's she doing here?" I asked.

"She called, wanted to see you, I think she said. I told her to come on over."

"I wish you'd . . . I mean, I wish I knew. I mean she's so—"

"Stephen, relax. I think she likes you. Said you were a zombic today, worried about you. She strikes me as the kind of girl who really knows what she wants."

"You got that one right," I told him. "I'm just not sure that she wants—"

"You? Of course she does. Didn't you see that smile?" He reached into his hip pocket, withdrew something, and slid it across the bar toward me. When he lifted his hand I saw two twenties folded in half. "Go on, take it. Have a good time. And don't worry about it being a school night. You worry too much. It's not healthy. Now, go."

I pocketed the two twenties as subtly as I could, feeling like the little boy locked outside to meet the neighborhood bully. But Peggy was on her best behavior. She took my arm and we strolled Mifflin

Street. Where did she want to go? It didn't matter, as long as she was with me. What had she wanted to talk about? "But, Stephen," she said, "your dad said *you* wanted to see *me.* I figured you wanted to, like, apologize for brushing me off lately. And besides, where were you last week? Stomach flu or what?"

So, instead of pursuing the matter of who wanted to see whom, I took the cue and apologized. I said I had been sick. I mumbled about swine flu and held my stomach. I said I had been preoccupied. She said she understood. She said sensitive, deep types such as me couldn't be held to the same standards of behavior as just normal people. I said I supposed that she was right. She said I had enough to think about, what with channel eleven coming to school next Monday.

"Oh that," I said. "How did you know about that?"

"Your dad told me," she said. "And I think it's wonderful. I think you'll do just great. You've got something special, something that comes across on screen. I always said you did."

"It's just some news thing about schools," I told her. "Like they're always doing. You know, wife beating, child abuse, child pornography, latchkey children, drugs in the schools, drugs in the army, drugs in the locker-room, drugs in the studios, drugs in the nuclear power plants, drugs in the sewage treatment plants, drugs in the forest service, drugs in the pharmacies. Whatever's hot, they jump on it."

"Gawwwww, Stephen, you're so modest," Peggy said.

We strolled down Mifflin Street and sat on the brick wall in front of the post office. This was the ideal spot for ogling all the campus types who filled the sidewalks during the early evening. It was time to collect more specimens. Audubon would approve.

"Here, check this guy in the hiking boots," I whispered to Peggy. A compact Paul Bunyan type came toward us, short legs pumping on the sidewalk, jeans rolled into cuffs above the boots, each boot like a miniature Japanese sedan molded from finest calf's leather. A neatly groomed black beard reached just to the first button of his plaid wool shirt. "Probably a chem major, I would guess a junior, with a 3.7 average. Next year the beard comes off and he interviews all spring. He gets a job with Monsanto and moves to Atlanta. He starts putting on weight. When he's thirty he'll try jogging. By forty he has a kid in high school. The kid is ashamed of him, his chubby little dad who jiggles when he walks. But you see, this guy will remember sometimes this night when he walked down Mifflin Street, and though he can never explain to his kid how it felt, he'll at least have that. And maybe that'll be enough to keep him from someday going in to work and strafing the Monsanto parking lot with machine-gun fire."

Peggy stared at the guy as he brushed past us. We could hear his boots go *zwit zwit* on the dry grit of the sidewalk. "You don't know," Peggy complained. "You can't know anything of the kind."

"Don't think so, huh?" I said. "All right, then you take this one in the scarf." She was maybe twenty, with long black hair that fell forward over both shoulders and down across the lapels of a greatcoat, obviously imported, obviously quite old. The coat hung

287

open, billowing, as she leaned into the wind, lunging with each stride. The scarf was a wonder, maybe twelve feet long, a deep scarlet with blue and gold stripes. She had looped it once around the collar to her coat, then once again around her hair, which swelled over the collar like a soufflé edging from its dish.

"Radical scarf," Peggy murmured. "What about it?"

"The girl, not the scarf," I whispered. "Tell me about the girl. Take her through twenty years. What happens to her then?"

"All right." Peggy considered the girl as she strode past us. "Okay, she's a poet. She will be an important new voice. Colleges will fight over her. Instead, she will buy a farm, raise horses in the mountains, but continue to write. She will win a . . . what's that writer prize they always give?"

"Pulitzer, Nobel, Bollingen," I offered.

"Right, she'll win one of those by thirty but refuse the money or give the money away, like to the Indians or some third-world guys, and then she'll marry some guy, like, say, maybe some stable hand or the local blacksmith, and they'll have this incredible physical animal relationship, like this incredible sexual bond. So anyway, she'll give up poetry and concentrate on breeding."

"You mean horses?" I asked.

"Of course horses. Get your mind out of the gutter." She smacked me on the shoulder and continued. "So anyhow, I don't know, I guess they'll just breed horses and stuff. What do you think?"

"I think, if she's lucky, she'll get a nice job in a travel agency. Bus tours to Gettysburg. I can see it now: 'The Blue and Gray Getaway Weekend.' Three days and two nights in the blood-soaked cornfields. Reenact Pickett's charge with water balloons. 'We recommend that you bring a raincoat. Only $299.95 includes a box lunch at Devil's Den.' "

"Old fart," Peggy yipped. She clenched a fist and aimed for my left ear. I decided to excuse myself and ran down Mifflin Street as fast as I could. Sure enough, she was right behind me, fist still clenched above her head. The light was red when I got to the corner. The pedestrian light had a red palm held up against traffic. Cars turning off Mifflin were bunched bumper to bumper. I turned and Peggy was on me. I ducked beneath her wild punch and grabbed her in a bear hug.

"Babies," I whispered to her. "We're acting like babies. I'm sorry, Peggy."

She buried her face in my shoulder. "Is anybody watching us?"

A semicircle of coeds had gathered around us, waiting for the light to change, trying to pretend that we weren't there. A guy with a leather beret and a Labrador on a chain had pushed in front of us. The dog was wearing a bandanna around its neck.

"Naw, whatta they care," I told her, and she mumbled something about being so embarrassed. Finally the light changed.

"C'mon," I said, "let's dance."

I pulled her down an alley by her sleeve. Like a three-wheeled calliope came the chunky back and forth of electric bass and drums. I forked over a ten to the girl at the door and we went inside The Rhythm Method.

"Well, okay, but try to act grown-up," Peggy hissed into my ear. So I sucked in my cheeks, frowned like a maniac, and got dead sinister as hell.

"That's better," Peggy shouted. We walked through the clot of sound and tables to a half-empty booth at the far wall. Smoke hung at nose level, like angel hair twisting on a string. The band stood on a raised stage at the far end, bending into their tunes, syncopated island music full of choogling, plinking, gurgling, like amplified tidal pools. The musicians were black, island types, some with knit mushroom caps, others sporting dreadlocks, Medusa style. Rasta men.

Peggy grabbed me by an elbow and pulled me toward the floor. "Come on. I wanna teach you how to skank."

It was sort of like skipping in place. Just bend from the waist, pump one knee at a time up to chest height, and be sure to swing the arms at the side. It was easy.

And the band played on, steel-drum breaks trilling in among the guitars, with the lead man sweeping up across the strings with a thunk just a slight beat behind, driving the music like a flywheel just off center, pushing it all uphill.

But somewhere in there I began to hear the words, just me I suppose, since the whole crowd kept smiling, and Peggy danced in a blurry, grinding trance. But there was this song:

Fall on de knife, boy, jump on de knife,
Cover de silver or dey come for your life.
Been sixteen too long in dis tin part o' town,
Dey find you some day and dey follow you down.
So run, boy, run. Run, boy, run.
De sheriff got silver, too, all in his gun.
So run, boy, run.

And so I took my skank down a notch or two and
started listening to the lyrics. Beneath all those Afro-
Caribbean polyrhythms, there was something dark
and desperate. Dying mothers, hungry babies, crossing the water to Babylon, even some more run, boy,
run, lullabies of despair.

I watched the band. Their faces seemed frozen into
stiff tribal masks. They stared at their own hands
indifferently, then out into the smoky air above our
heads. At one point when the keyboard player did a
solo break, I watched the bass player instead. He lit a
cigarette, dragged in heavily, and then stuck the cigarette, ash tip up, into his strings, just down from the
end. The smoke fanned up across his face like a veil of
fine threads, and his mask crumpled into a grimace.
He turned to face the lead guitarist, and when their
eyes met he let his face, the left side facing me at least,
draw full up in a squint. Maybe it was just the smoke, I
thought, or maybe I was making it all up, and maybe it
was no big deal at all. But I thought I saw the squint
become a wink, a quick flicker of a wink like the
shutter of a camera. And the two shared a smile, sly
and tight lipped, hardly a smile at all. But to me it said
that they knew, and we didn't, and the joke was on us.

*"Dance,"* came Peggy's voice over the music. "Dance, come on, move."

I was standing dead still, both feet planted on the floor. Peggy skanked around me like I was a Maypole or something.

"No," I said.

"I said, why don't you dance, move, *do* something?" Peggy shouted. She stopped moving and leaned her face into mine. "I can't dance with a corpse."

"No, you can't," I answered.

"Well then, *dance.* This isn't the national anthem."

"Maybe it is," I said.

"Is what?"

"Is the national anthem, this song, maybe it's the national anthem."

"Sttttttttrrrrrraaannnnnnge." Peggy threw her head back and rolled her eyes up at the haze of smoke. She took me by the hand and led me to the booth. She pushed me in against the wall and slid in, trapping me in the corner.

"Now why don't you tell what the problem is *this* time?"

" 'This time'?" I said. "What's that supposed to mean?"

"It means you always find a way to ruin things. You get silly, just plain stupid, or you start to, I don't know, you get weird, like you drift away into your own little—"

"World," I finished for her. "Sometimes I wish I could. It might be a relief."

"And where would your own little world be, if you

292

could go there?" Peggy crossed her arms and pinned me with her elbows more tightly against the wall. Maybe it was just the music, but when I closed my eyes, I conjured up visions of Jamaica, of blue waters and brown boys and palms bending like question marks over lagoons.

But then I opened my mouth and said, "Maine."

"Maine?" Peggy asked. "Maine?"

"Well, they have such a nice flag," I said.

"Where's your head, Stephen?"

"It has a bear and fish and pine trees and it's all blue—"

"Get your head on straight," Peggy ordered. "You've never been to Maine."

"But they have lobsters and mooses, and canoes and paper plates, and—"

"Get a grip, Stephen. You've got Maine on the brain," Peggy said.

"Cute rhyme," I told her, but when I looked into her face I wanted to see red hair and braces, wanted her to be the white-faced girl with the two last names.

I shut my eyes and tried to remember Regina. Suddenly the band stopped playing, but the music seemed to hang in the air thick as the smoke. My ears rattled like steel drums.

"I was *thinking*, that's all. I started hearing the words to those songs they were playing, and it got me thinking. Listen." I needed to get my head back to Jamaica. I started tapping out the rhythm on the table, trying to catch that island feel, and when I thought I had it, I started singing the words to that

293

song about the kid with the knife. Peggy pushed about four feet away to the end of the bench and turned her head.

"Anyhow," I began, "the point is, they don't fit. The words and the music, they don't really go together. The song is about this guy who's killed somebody or something and the music"—I stopped to hum a few bars—"see, the music is all like bouncy and bubbly and full of warm breezes, like."

"Like your brain," she said.

"Cute, Peggy, but listen." I pulled her closer and tried to sound real calm and reasonable. "Like nothing really fits together, if you think about it. Take my father. He's a bartender. But say he's really a lawyer. I bet lots of lawyers are bartenders, but what does that explain? Nothing, see."

But Peggy wasn't really listening.

"Or take my mom. Exercise, right? Aerobics, right? But not really. She's really other things. I mean, of course she's a mother, but she used to be this family counselor, and in college she used to do all these antiwar marches and civil rights stuff. She was really into that—"

"Really? Your mother was into that?" Peggy brightened.

"Yeah, everything, to hear her tell it. Sit-downs, lie-downs, boycotts, hunger strikes. She marched on Washington maybe three, four times. But I mean, you see her in her leotards, and you'd never guess. See what I mean?"

"Maybe—and you got that all from a song?" Peggy

pulled her blond hair over one shoulder and twirled it between her hands.

"Yeah, one song. I started to see how these people here are working at it too, trying out being somebody else, at least for a night. I mean, you never know about a person, is all. Like a teacher might really be a doctor, say—" Suddenly I realized maybe I was saying too much, or maybe this was where it had all started in the first place. Peggy's eyes snapped with a dim recognition, so I hurried on. "Or a doctor might be a poet, or a poet could sell insurance, or an insurance salesman could be a welder, or whatever."

"So you could have one job but really be better at another job. I see."

"No, you don't see. It's not jobs. Don't get the idea I'm talking about jobs. Look," I said, pulling her hands away from her hair and closing them between mine. "Take you. You scare me. Always have. Even back in junior high. Terrified. Even while I liked you, you scared me. And when I called you last August, that first time, I mean, I was crazy, that's how much you scared me."

"Me?" Peggy asked, suddenly all innocence. We had finally found a subject that interested her.

"Yes, you, because, well, there's your looks, and beautiful girls are always intimidating as hell to begin with, and, I don't know, all those buttons, like you wanted everyone to know to stay at arm's length. But mostly, it's like you're so, not intense exactly, but so definite. Who you are, what you want, what you ought to do . . ." I gave that a minute to sink in and then added, "And even what I ought to do, like you *know* what I'm supposed to be, when I don't even have the foggiest—that kind of scares me."

"A gutless wonder," she laughed, and then slipped her hands between mine.

"I just figured it was time you shaped up," she said. "I mean, I agreed you had this potential, and nobody seemed to wanta shape it up. You were so out of it last year, but you always seemed to know something you weren't saying."

"Maybe I still do," I said. "Like, I know about your unicorn tattoo, see, and that didn't quite seem to fit either, or maybe it did, like a permanent button, even though it bothered me to think about some guy in Amsterdam. But maybe you were just making that up."

There. I had given her an opening, but she didn't take it. Instead, she pulled one hand away and touched herself above the left breast where the unicorn grazed in secret.

"And this Truelove thing, how much you want to go after him, that scares me a little, I suppose. I don't trust crusades is all. I never have. That's why the campaign and this president stuff . . . it doesn't fit me. I just really, *really* don't see the point to it all."

"That's why you need me," she said. "You gotta find a cause. It's just a cause, Stephen. It's right."

"Right is something else again," I said. "I will settle for a context in the meantime."

"Stephen, you're sweet," Peggy told me. She leaned over and gave me a kiss. "Sweet and crazy. Really."

"You're too generous," I told her, and grabbed another kiss before the moment passed.

Then she announced that all that skanking had dried her out, so I offered to pop for a round of naturally carbonated beverages. She said fine, just don't get lost.

# Chapter 45

I pushed through the crowd over to the bar, where a mob stood squirming itself into a line three deep.

"What you drinking, ace?" asked the girl behind the bar. She was pointing right at me. A chalkboard above her head offered celery soda, Kiwi Cola, or bottled water.

"The kiwi stuff," I said. "Two bottles, please." I pulled my wallet out and slapped two dollar bills on the counter.

"Say what, two what?" the girl shouted back at me.

"The kiwi stuff, two of them," I tried to yell. She thumped two bottles down. I reached a hand out for each bottle, got jostled from behind, but grabbed the right bottle firmly. The other bottle spun out of reach just to my left. Suddenly a black hand grabbed the bottle, now empty, and rolled it back across the bar toward the girl. "One more, Rachel," came the voice. When he turned, I recognized the bass player, the one with the wink and the cigarette, standing right beside me. "That Rachel, she's overworked, understand, Chief?"

He was talking to me. He smiled and put the back of his thumb against the side of his nose and pushed slowly up and down. His eyelids dropped and his smile vanished.

"Right, I understand, thanks," I finally managed. His eyes snapped open, and finally he pinched his nose and waggled it. He gave me a heavy-lidded wink and turned away.

"I like your music, by the way," I blurted out at the black leather spanning his back. I grabbed his elbow and tugged, suddenly determined to register my gratitude. He swiveled his head back toward me.

"I just said I like your music, man." I should have done without the "man" part.

"That's good," he said, and once more turned away.

"No really, I mean I *really* liked it, especially the lyrics." Again I pulled at his elbow until this time he came full around. His face eclipsed mine like a dark planet. "What I mean is, I was out there dancing and all, then I heard those words, the ones about the boy running away with the knife, and I thought, my god, these people are dancing out there, thinking this is some great good time and all, but you guys are out there, you know, your lives are in this music, all those hard times you must've had and all, suffering, and, oh, like hunger, I suppose, and now it's all just something for a bunch of white kids to be dancing to. And I started wonderin' how you guys must really feel about that, like other people getting off on what must have been your misery and all, but then I saw you wink at your guitarist. And that's when I knew that you knew better than all of us, us . . ."

299

He stared into my face. "So?"

"Well, so . . ." I tried to slow down and take it one thought at a time. "So, anyhow, I was wonderin' how long you've been in this country?"

"What country is this, anyway?" he said. He wasn't smiling.

"America, you know, how long you been in America?"

"Say, twenty-nine years."

"So you must have come here, what, pretty young?"

"Yeah, real young, boy." He said all this without even moving his mouth. "Born here, boy, in your country. Macon, Georgia. Momma, Daddy born here, too. And all before that, born right here in your country."

"But then you're not from the islands, from Jamaica?"

He said nothing.

"And the rest of them, they're all from here too? I mean, it's not my country. 'S yours too. I mean, that's not the point, is it?"

Again nothing, but the lips arched slightly, still not a smile.

"But I mean, you all sound so real. Those songs, those words about the boy with the knife, and the sheriff, and the tin part of town, that sounds so real. Where do you get songs like that?"

"Maybe we get 'em at K Mart. You get all kinds of things at K Mart these days, boy." By now the crowd at the bar had thinned and pulled away into a semicircle. The woman behind the bar stood glowing at the K Mart bit. A girl appeared from behind the

Rasta man. She had clamped onto his elbow and stared at me over his huge left shoulder.

I was amusing them all.

I would have one more go. "And what about the one where the hungry children wait for 'dey mudda' to come with the biscuits late, but she's already sailing to Babylon, which I suppose means she's dead. Did you get that one at K Mart too?"

Finally the guy smiled. "No, honey, we got that one from TV. You can get more from TV than from K Mart, if you watch real close. All of it is right there, every night, on the evening news. Check it out."

"Television?" I said indignantly. "Television. You're a fake."

Suddenly his hand took the bottom of my T-shirt and came up from inside until his fingers appeared at the collar. He had my whole shirt now squeezed into his hand. He pulled me right into his face. "And you're a butthead, see." He stuffed the handful of T-shirt right into my face, and I fell back against the counter and then slid down to the floor.

"And don't forget your drink, boy," he said from above me. He emptied an entire bottle of Kiwi Cola across my chest.

I sat there on the floor as the drink soaked into my jeans. I removed the T-shirt and leaned back against the bar. For some reason I had gotten into the habit of wearing Truelove's dog tag, and now it hung drying against my chest, sticking like a silver Band-Aid. I had suddenly become invisible. People stepped around me, over me, and the whole thing was over, just me in my kiwi juice.

"Still a damn fake," I said to no one in particular.

301

"Still a goddamn imposter. You're all damn fakes, specks, little specks, fly specks on the wall of time. Just ask Carl Sagan about that. Infinitesimal protoplasmic specks, specks disguised as Rasta men, phoney Macon, Georgia, Caribbean specks, and bartender specks, and lawyer specks, and teacher specks, and doctor specks, and goddamn television specks. Even you, Carl Sagan, you damn astronomer speck, you should know better, you speck—speculatis, spectacular circumspect specks, specks with spokes, specks with spandex, speculating specks, spackling specks, spotted Spam specks, health spa specks, specks with sex, secular specks, specks specks specks specks . . .

"*So run, boy, run, run, boy, run. De sheriff got silver and it's all in his gun. So run, boy, run . . .*"

And when I looked up, sure enough, the specks were skanking all over the place, thousands of bouncing, lunging specks, and the music thundered in the room. I pushed myself back against the bar and stood. I had to find Peggy.

But when I got to the booth, she was gone. I bobbled out onto the floor and wound my way through the skankers until I found her. Just in front of the stage. She was wearing a plaid shirt, red and black checks, wool, the heavy, itchy kind. And skanking with some guy. A short guy. He had a beard and suspenders. He had boots, hiking boots with red laces. It was the lumberjack from Monsanto.

"Let's go," I yelled over the din.

"Stephen, where's your shirt?"

"I lost it."

302

"What's this?" She reached for the dog tag.

"It's nothing, junk." I grabbed the tag and flipped it around my neck so that it hung down my back.

"You're all wet!"

"I know. Let's go."

"But you're all wet."

"The drinks . . . I spilled them."

"What happened?" Suddenly the lumberjack leaned his head into the conversation.

"Specks," I shouted back at Peggy and the lumberjack.

"You what?"

"Specks happened. Never mind, let's go."

"Let me finish the dance," Peggy said. But I had started skanking again, bare chested and sticky. The lumberjack seemed to relax after that.

"Hi, Barry Costas here," said the lumberjack. He held out his hand and I shook it in mid skank. Barry, I thought. Jesus.

"Carl Sagan," I shouted to Barry. "Pleased to meet you."

"Great band, huh Carl?" Barry shouted back.

The music stopped on a downbeat, so suddenly the floor beneath us seemed to bulge.

"Thanks for the dance," Barry said to Peggy.

"Thanks for the shirt," Peggy said to Barry. She removed the shirt and handed it to him. He offered it to me, but I declined.

"Itchy," I said.

"Whatever," said Barry.

I pulled Peggy away from the stage. We got our stuff at the booth and headed for the door. I put on my windbreaker, and we walked out into the night.

"What the hell did go on in there?" Peggy demanded.

"Racial violence in Soweto," I said.

My jeans seized up about halfway home. We were looking at a hard freeze. Kiwi Cola crystalized beneath my jeans. I hurried back to the Mother, Peggy shuffling double-time at my heels. She offered to leave me alone if I didn't feel like being with her. I assured her that wasn't it. I was cold, was all.

The Monday-night Mother crowd was watching a game from Denver. It was cold there, too—snowing, in fact. Frank Gifford was miffed. Someone had thrown snowballs at the field-goal kicker on the other team. He said they should let them have a do-over. "A do-over, did you hear that?" roared Corky to the warm approval of the patrons. "Holy cowpie," a patron mumbled. "A do-over."

I made Peggy wait in Dad's office while I checked out the situation upstairs. The only thing going up there was a light burning in the wall-hung Radarange. Everything else seemed dead quiet.

"It's all right," I told Peggy when I returned to the office. "You can come up if you want to for a while."

"Really, Stephen, do I look like I'm begging?" She picked a stapler off my dad's desk and started shooting staples all over the office.

"All right, then, won't you please come up for a little while? You're under no obligations this time."

"What do you mean, this time?" she snapped, aiming the stapler at my chest.

"I mean, like the last time. Like the first time, I mean."

"Stephen, you're still such a boy. Maybe I've been wasting my time."

"Doing what?" I asked.

"If you don't know, then you'll always be a dink." She slammed the stapler down and headed for the door.

"So hold on. Is that it? You're rescuing me from dinkhood? That's what all this is all about? Think you're a social worker, is that it?"

I went to the door and blocked Peggy's escape. She moved back from the door and collapsed in Dad's La-Z-Boy recliner.

"No, that's not it." She paused. "Or maybe that's only part of it. But look how far you've come since August, for god's sake. Class president, TV star, defender of students' rights, all in two months. Then you make that damn crack about obligations. I don't do any damn thing because of obligations, especially not—you know, sex or stuff like that."

"Sex for specks," I said.

"See, that specks crack again. Nothing gets through to you, absolutely nothing. 'Sex for specks.' Where do you get that junk? It just bubbles out of your brain like tapioca, for god's sake. Nothing's sacred to you, not even sex." She threw her arms out to her sides, and the recliner let go a notch. It schlumped out flat. Peggy pressed her lips together. I thought she was trying to avoid laughing. It would have been better to let it out, I figured. But not Peggy. She grabbed the back of the chair and tried

305

pulling it to upright. The chair ratcheted forward, *click, click, clitch*, and rolled over on top of her, smothering her fury on the floor.

I pushed the chair off her, over onto its side, and tried an apology. "Just tapioca," I began. "You're right. It just bubbles right out of me and I can't stop it. It doesn't mean anything. The words come, and I say them. If I ever stopped to think first, I'd probably never say anything. First I'd have to decide what I thought about something, and that's impossible. Then I'd have to find the words closest to it, and that's even worse."

Peggy sat up and ran her hands down both legs and seemed satisfied that everything still worked. "You make it too complicated, Stephen," she said. "You always do. It's a disease." She reached her hand out to me and I pulled her up and held on.

"Complicated, yeah, maybe so," I admitted. "But it happens." I explained how the old tapioca had just oozed out when I started talking to that bass player from the homegrown reggae band. "And that's when I got a lapful of Kiwi Cola, see?" I stepped back and together we admired the spreading, darkening stain running in crazy blotches from my waist to my knees. I was thawing out all over the place.

"Look," I said, "I gotta get out of these now or I never will. You're still welcome to come up. Or not. You decide."

I locked the door to the bar and then went up the apartment stairs without even turning the lights on, without even looking back. But when I turned the light on in my room, there was Peggy right behind me. I closed the door behind us, pulled a robe from my closet, and turned back to Peggy, who still stood in the center of the floor. I took her by the hand and led her past the foot of my bed to the wall. I handed her a shoe box of tape cassettes and pointed at my stereo on a shelf beside the dresser. "Music," I said, and left to get a shower. As I lathered in the gush of hot water, I pondered Peggy's Tapioca Theory of Unpremeditated Discourse.

Yes. Yes, the old brain, wonderful organ with a mind of its own, endlessly spewing out gibberish, bubbling over like a runaway pot of porridge, spilling through the windows and doorways, smothering hamlets and drowning small animals in its path. It turned on innocent musicians, blathered campaign nonsense for the assembled student body, rambled for TV cameras about *rapprochement* and *vis-à-vis*, gibbered about specks, sending out its weird protoplasmic pseudopods and encircling everything, everyone.

When the hot water finally faded to lukewarm, I killed the shower, dried off, and slipped on my robe. I left a cloud of steam rolling down the hall and entered my room. Peggy sat on the bottom bed. She had laid out six pairs of pants, my pants, side by side, their legs hanging down across the mattress almost to the floor. Above the pants, along the other half of the bed, she had arrayed about a dozen shirts, fanned out like cards in a poker hand.

"Having a yard sale?" I asked. I circled around the bed and closed the door to my ransacked closet.

"Something smells good. Is that you?"

307

"Yeah, heather thistle soap," I told her. "Dad's, I guess. Imported."

"Heather thistle. No such thing."

"Probably not. Don't worry about it." I smelled the back of my hand. "Look, what's the deal with the clothes, anyway?"

"No deal. Just picking something out for Monday, for you to wear, for the TV. Like, nothing too busy. No checks, 'cause they run on TV, and nothing too corny, 'cause if I know you, you'll go right for the *Sesame Street* mix-and-match look. And it's gotta be, you know, nothing too stark, or too bright, 'cause the color picture tubes can't handle that so well, but it's gotta have the right look. You gotta get something that has the right look to it. For you, the right look means something, well . . ."

And while she tried to explain the right look, I stood there, dreading Monday all of a sudden, and knowing that what I had in mind and what Truelove had in mind and what Peggy had in mind and what channel eleven had in mind and what Mr. Wilfong had in mind and what everyone else had in mind . . . it was all wrong, was the point.

I couldn't be all those things: not Peggy's stylish boy stalking-horse, not Truelove's champion and deliverance, not Wilfong's avenging fury, not Mom and Dad's bright-eyed malcontent, not channel eleven's clever young man. I would call it off. No go. Get a sore throat, get really nauseous—not so hard to do— but I would not perform for all the good folks out there, would not let the brain ooze in public, on TV or anywhere else, ever again. Not ever . . . Would not. Would not.

*"I said put these on. Is that so hard to do?"* Peggy was shouting over some music from the tape deck. I turned to face her, standing now by the bed. Suddenly, a pair of pants came flying through the air and hit me smack against the chest.

I turned my back to Peggy and stepped into the pants.

"Now hold the robe up and turn around, Stephen," Peggy commanded. Again, I obliged. I was wearing the Army fatigue pants, the ones I'd worn last summer to scrub out the hot tubs at Mom's—paint speckled, spotted, and worn at the knees.

"Great," Peggy announced. "Tough, bad, awesome pants. Now . . ." She sorted through the shirts on the bed and pulled out an off-white Oxford cloth with button-down collar. "First we lose the buttons," she muttered. She inserted a puff of shirt into her mouth, bit, and spit a button onto the rug at my feet. She did it once more, and another button nickered along the carpet.

"The P-S-duh-resistance," she announced, holding the shirt out to me. "Try this on, and you'll look like Misha."

"Misha who?" I asked.

"Baryshnikov," she informed me. "Misha, short for Mikhail."

"Him again," I mumbled, dropping the robe at my feet. I slipped the shirt on and buttoned it up.

"No, no," Peggy scolded. "Leave the top two unbuttoned. That's how Misha does it."

"Maybe we can just get Misha."

"Don't tempt me. Now tuck it in and blouse it out some here." She swarmed around me, pecking at the shirt until it puffed out like a wilted balloon. "There. Better." She stood back and studied me, her face pinched with cautious approval.

"It'll have to do. Maybe we can get you a vest. Misha likes to wear little vests, just loose and open. Did you see him on PBS last week?"

"No, sure didn't," I said. "So this is what I wear for Monday. Do I wear shoes too, or what?"

"I'm willing to ignore that." She picked my robe off the floor and came at me from behind, blotting my hair dry. She snatched a comb from the top of my dresser, and told me to stand still. She combed my hair straight back into a slick bonnet then, wielding the comb like a knife, came at me again, this time sort of dive-bombing from the top and sides. "There," she announced. "Check yourself out."

When I looked into the mirror above my dresser, I saw a pale-faced kid with an explosion of black hair. "A regular piece of work, Peggy, no kidding."

"You look like *somebody* now, Stephen," Peggy crowed. "We'll get some hair spray, in case it should drop. Or styling mousse."

"Styling mousse?" I said.

"Don't worry, they make some brands just for men, so it's okay."

"Men's styling mousse," I said.

"Yes, men's styling mousse," she repeated. "Now, do you know what you're going to say?"

"About what?" I turned around and looked right at Peggy. "You mean, thank you for dressing me, thank you for combing my hair, like that?"

"No, fool, I mean Monday. Have you thought about

what you're gonna say when they interview you about school and all that?"

"Nah, just thought I'd, you know, say whatever comes up. Whatever bubbles up. You know, old tapioca brain. It got me this far."

"Not good enough." Peggy stepped back and considered. "You haven't lost sight of what this is all about already, have you? I mean, why you're going through with this whole TV thing?"

"Because they asked," I said.

"But why did we say yes?" Peggy shot back.

"Because we're nice guys."

"And what else?"

"How about a hint?"

"Truelove," Peggy said. "Truelove, we're gonna put the heat on. Go public, so to speak. You've got cameras, you've got the six-o'clock news. You've got one free shot, so we can't afford to waste it. We could finally send him packing, him and his pop quizzes on bivalve reproduction. This is no time for tapioca. It's too important for that."

"So you want me to write a speech or what? Damn, you *do* want blood." I put a hand to my head and started raking my hairdo over to the side before the whole mess dried.

Peggy thrust the comb in my direction. "Here, take this." I took the comb and started pulling it through my hair.

"No, not that, forget the hair." Peggy yanked the comb from my hair. She arranged my hands in front of me and jammed the comb upright into my right fist, then pushed the fist up toward my chin

311

until the comb was about four inches from my mouth.

"Now, that's your microphone," she explained. "You be the reporter, and I'll be you. Now go ahead, ask me something. I'll show you what I mean."

Peggy arranged herself beside me and cleared her throat. I took one more swipe through my hair with the microphone and formulated my first question. "Tell me, Stephen, has anyone ever told you that you bear an uncanny resemblance to Mikhail Baryshnikov?"

When I moved the comb to Peggy's mouth she caught my good mike hand in midair and dug her nails into the back of it. "Fool," she muttered. "Try again. Be serious."

"Fair enough, Stephen," I said, not missing a beat. "Maybe we'll get back to that later. Let's talk for a minute about your classes, your teachers. Do you feel that you're getting a quality education here at Cable Hall High School?"

"No, not really," Peggy answered.

"Would you like to expand on that a bit for us, Stephen?"

"All right, of course," Peggy said, speaking directly into the comb. "I think it's mostly the teachers . . . some teachers . . . a particular teacher, to be exact. There's a biology teacher at this school, a Mr. Truelove, who is probably insane."

"That's a pretty strong accusation, Stephen," I said.

"Well, if he's not insane, at least he's incompetent. Second day of class, he stood me up in front of the

312

board and tried to humiliate me. When he lectures, he stares out across the room, never looks at anyone, just rattles along in this zombie monotone."

"You're saying, then, that eye contact would help?"

"Let me finish," Peggy answered. "One day it's cells, the next day it's starfish, the next day it's genes—whatever comes into his head. And he gives us tests on anything, any day, and other days he makes us answer questions from our book on material that we haven't even read yet. He has no plan, no logic. Everyone hates him. He dresses so grossly. You should see his shirts. They look like someone's drooled all over them. And he doesn't seem to care. Last week he just walked out of class with, like, forty minutes to go, just walked out in the middle of class. And once when . . ."

I pulled the comb away from her mouth. "Stephen, you're rambling. You're rambling and you're whining. A rambler and a whiner is not attractive. Get a hobby."

Peggy whirled and took a wild swing in my direction. I caught her arm so suddenly that the gold chains around her neck sloshed over her shoulder and hung down her back like overcooked pasta.

"Just slow down," I told her. "Just relax. It won't be necessary. I can't say that. I don't want to say any of that, and it won't be necessary."

"Let go of me" was all she said, trying to twist away. Instead, I took her other wrist and spun her around to face me. She tried to pull away; her legs went limp and she dropped to her knees. I let go of her wrists, but when she started muttering something about a dink under her breath, I'd had it. I dropped to my knees, faced her, and took her by the shoulders.

"Look at me, dammit. Look at me, Peggy Klecko." Slowly she raised her face to mine; her eyes were watery with defiance. "I'm not a damn dink and I'm not your fool and I'm not a jerk and I'm not a snake and I'm not Mikhail freaking Baryshnikov and maybe I don't have tapioca for brains. So maybe you'd better go home and sleep on that. And if that doesn't suit you, you can save your styling mousse for Mr. Right, or Misha Right, or whoever the hell it is that you think I ought to be."

Her face softened and her watery defiant eyes were suddenly just watery. "Are you sending me home?" she asked.

"I'm not sending you anywhere," I answered. "You decide for yourself. Like you always do anyhow."

She settled back on her ankles and dropped her chin to her chest. Slowly, strand by strand, she arranged her gold chains. Finally she lifted her head and stared at me with the practiced, soulful stare of a basset hound. Then she lay on her back, breathing deeply, her eyes closed. When she finally stood, after maybe three or four minutes, her face had softened, the anger and defiance now gone like a bad dream. She danced across the room to the tape deck.

She turned the volume up a notch and circled around me to the window. She did a few of those limbering moves, rippling her backbone like a cat unraveling from its tail to its head, and then stood looking out the window.

"I love these cold nights. They make you want to—mmmm."

"Drink warm cider?" I suggested.

"No, well, maybe. They make me want to stay inside. Like, curl up in front of a fire, stay warm, that kind of stuff. Mmm." She laid her cheek against the window, almost like she was hugging this double-insulated Andersen thermopane double-hung window. A spray like a Spanish fan unfolding grew where her breath fell against the glass.

I apologized that we didn't have a fireplace, but told her that if we got a VCR for Christmas maybe I'd rent one of those crackling fireplace tapes. Then she could come over and we could curl up in front of that. And drink warm cider. And eat doughnuts. And toast marshmallows. Or popcorn. But we'd have to get a bigger TV for that. Or a really hot tape. Or both. And so forth.

Which is about when she turned off the lights. She settled on the floor behind me, resting against my back, draping her head over my shoulder.

"Of course, we can start our own fire right now," she whispered.

I was reasonably certain that that sentence had been uttered before, somewhere, sometime. But then, I wasn't busy awarding points for originality. I was considering my alternatives.

"Could," I said—rather, I heard myself saying.

"Could do that," I elaborated, squeaking through a larynx knotted like old socks.

315

"MMMMmmmm, good deal, stay right here." Peggy nuzzled those last words right into my ear. Then she stood behind me, and I sat fixed to the floor, watching the wall to my right where the exerciser stood beside my desk. The moving lights from below, from outside, threw their shapes through the window and against the wall: triangles, rectangles, trapezoids.

From behind me music grew louder by degrees. My legs started a dance of their own against the brown carpet, but it had nothing to do with the music. Twitching, jiggling, nervous and electric, like two eels on their first date. My teeth started chattering.

"Chilly?" Peggy asked. She stepped in front of me. She stood wrapped in a comforter, my old Star Wars comforter, pulled around her neck and hanging to the floor. Even in the dim light I could still see the orange stain where I had spilled a bowl of Spaghetti-O's one Saturday lunch some eight years earlier, right on Chewbacca's face.

"Where'd you get that thing?" I asked.

"Closet," Peggy smiled. "Top shelf."

"No kidding. I'd almost forgot—"

"Look, never mind that," she interrupted. "I'm sorry." The Star Wars comforter lifted like two wings from around Peggy. Then, looming above me like a specter of contrition, she and the blanket floated, settled, to the floor beside me, on top of me. She still wore her golden chains around her neck, but that was it. Soon I had shed my Baryshnikov playclothes, and together we wrapped in the

316

blanket and huddled against the floor, against each other. Her gold chains were cold against my chest. She asked why I was twitching so much, and I blamed it on the chains, but I wasn't complaining. I lifted the chains gently and kissed where I remembered the unicorn had been. She grabbed a corner of the comforter and pulled it even more tightly around us. Wrapped like two bodies in a shroud, we rolled along the floor. At some point we found ourselves wedged against the wall, against each other, body to body. We stayed like that, quiet and still for the longest time, saying nothing. The music played, now all guitars full of air and rising like zeppelins. I remembered that time in the prop room before the speech, lying against the sets of palms and sand. Peggy was right about the warm part, it was that warm again, like a beach somewhere with the heat lifting from your body like bolts of flannel unwinding.

When the guitars stopped playing and the first tape ended with a click, we lay stiff against each other.

"What the . . . ?" Peggy lifted her head.

"Ignore it," I said. "We don't need it."

"But I like it," Peggy said. "Let me put another one on."

She pushed off me, her hands planted on the floor. But halfway up she stopped, snagged, and I felt something pulling at my neck.

"Oww," Peggy said, "I think I'm stuck."

"Hold still," I told her. "I'll get it." Her chains had tangled something and caught against me. I ran my

317

fingers through the strands and found my dog tag knotted in her golden chains. I had left it on, had forgotten about it in the shower, had worn it without thinking. This *hadn't* seemed an occasion for heavy thinking.

"Got it? Come on, my arms are getting tired," Peggy complained.

But I couldn't get the chains free. Instead I unsnapped my chain from around my neck. "There, you're free. Now take your chains off and give them here. I'll get it later."

Peggy stood and lifted the chains from over her head. But she didn't hand them over. She crossed to the window and found my chain hanging like a loose thread among hers.

"Get away from that window. Someone'll see you." But she didn't go for that.

"What *is* this thing, anyway?" She had traced the chain up to the tag and stood in the window, angling it toward the light.

"Put it down. It's private," I shouted. I rolled off the floor and went after her.

But too late. "Truelove, Burton R.," she read. "Truelove? *Truelove!* Mr. Truelove, it's *his* dog tag."

"It is?" I attempted.

"You know it is, Stephen. Where'd you get it?"

"Found it," I said.

"No way, liar," she shot back. "Try again."

"All right, look . . ." I held my ground, my head spinning with possibilities, none too promising. "All right, look, you've gotta swear this goes no farther than this room. Absolutely. Do you understand?"

"Oh, I swear, absolutely," she said, crossing her

heart, somewhere just below the unicorn.

"All right then, he gave it to me. All right?"

But it wasn't. "Why? When? Why would he give you this old thing?" She pulled the tag and chain free from her chains and held it out like a dead worm.

I gave her the short version. Said he'd given it to me the day I'd gotten back from suspension. He'd felt bad about the humiliation, about my punishment for trashing the lab, and wanted me to have something . . . personal, I called it, as an apology.

"Well, isn't that cozy," she mocked. "And now you're all buddy-buddy."

"No, not buddy-buddy," I said. "Now can I have it back?"

Peggy bunched the chain in her hand and held it behind her. "Maybe you should explain first. Are you going a little soft on that man? After what he did to you? He gives you a trinket, cries on your shoulder, and you're ready to switch sides, is that it?"

"Sides? You think this is a game of red rover? I'm not on anybody's *side*! Give me that chain." I took a step forward and Peggy slid along the wall, her hand still clamped behind her.

"You're going to weasel out. You're a weenie, aren't you? Can't stand up to Truelove. Can't tell the TV people the sick truth. You don't have it, Stephen." She was pointing at me with her free hand, finger like a loaded gun. I hate that stuff.

"Maybe I *will* tell the TV people everything. About you and Mr. Wilfong. You just show up seventh period, and you'll see what Truelove and I tell your blessed TV people! Maybe *we* have plans!" So much for bluster and idle threats. Maybe it just

319

sounded good. But wouldn't it be swell to let them all hang out to dry?

Peggy was stoked, going full bore. ". . . probably don't have the *nerve* to tell the school board beans, even in closed session."

"You know? How do you know that?" I shouted. She knew everything.

"My mother is *very* involved," she said.

"Well, tell your mother this isn't my game anymore. Tell *her* that for me. Now, hand over the chain." I started stalking her again.

"But wait!" She dangled the chain at arm's length. "I think some folks would be interested in seeing this, Stephen. Folks like Mr. Wilfong, for starters."

I took after her slowly, but she kept sliding away, along the wall. She climbed onto my home gym and stood triumphant like a toddler on monkey bars. Her head bent beneath the ceiling, she held the chain behind her and pressed against the wall.

"Keep away from me or I'll tell, swear to god."

I lunged toward her and caught an ankle. I tugged until her foot was off the crossbar. She teetered, arms windmilling at her sides, and then fell sideways, sliding down the wall onto my desk and full across the video display full-color monitor of my new three-thousand-dollar home computer. Her momentum carried down across the desk, and like a great caboose derailing, the desk lurched forward, hurtling Peggy and computer, monitor, and double disk drives onto the floor—*waaaaachhhhhhoooonk*. The floor throbbed beneath us. The computer cracked, high-impact-plastic bits bounding like small shells, high-tech debris and Peggy heaped together, elbow to microchip, circuit to circuit.

"Peggy, I'm . . . are you Okay?" I stooped beside her and swept the computer away from her, across the rug. I lifted the chain from her hand and skimmed it across the room to my bunk.

"This is all your fault," I heard Peggy say, her words muffled into the brown carpet.

*"Stephen, are you all right? Is that you? What happened? I THOUGHT I heard . . ."* Dad rapped at the door once and stuck his head in. He turned the lights on and entered. He was pretty much undressed himself, except where he held a pillow, fig-leaf style, in his right hand. His left hand clutched the tip of an umbrella. He held it looped forward and aloft, a blunt instrument against intruders.

"What's going on here?" he asked.

"It's not what it looks like," I said.

"Peggy, is that you?" Dad asked, circling toward us, pillow side out.

"Turn the lights off," Peggy pleaded, face still turned into the carpet.

"What you kids been doing?" Dad tried again.

"What's it look like?" Peggy snarled, turning her face upward for the first time.

"Strip tag?" Dad said.

"Close," I answered.

"Here, take this, cover up." Dad stooped and handed the pillow to Peggy. She sat up primly, clutching it to her coiled body.

"Thanks," she whimpered.

"Dad, do you mind?" I asked. Now pillowless, he

stood above us with his umbrella at parade rest. "Cover up. Give us a break."

Dad hit the trigger on the umbrella. *Ffff-wwwwoooooppp* it went, restoring his modesty. He backed away from us, the taut black bloom of his umbrella bobbing beneath his shoulders. He tiptoed like a naughty chorus girl to the back wall. He squatted to lift the Star Wars comforter off the floor and minced halfway back toward us.

"Here, better cover up your own bad self, sport." He lofted the blanket through the air toward me. I caught the blanket and handed it to Peggy.

"You take it," I said. "You sure you're all right?"

She just nodded as I let the comforter fall over her shoulders.

That's when my mother walked in, wrapped in a sheet.

"Mother, no, what are *you* doing here?" I asked.

"It's not what it looks like," she said. Peggy stood up. Dad lifted his right foot and picked a piece of plastic from his heel. Mom threw the sheet over her shoulder, like the bride of Caligula.

"So that explains the shower curtain," I said.

"Shut up. Cover up," Dad said.

"Take this," Peggy said, offering me the pillow. Mother turned the light off.

"How long have you been here?" I asked my mother.

"I'll ask the questions, thank you," Dad said.

"Take me home, Mr. Douglass," Peggy said.

"Expecting rain, Wilson?" Mother said.

"It's ruined," said Dad. He nudged the disk drive with his toe.

"What'd you do to your hair, Stephen?" Mom said.

"This is low farce," Dad said.

"You should know," Mom said.

"I'll get dressed," Peggy said. She walked to the bunk and retrieved her clothes.

"Use our room," Dad said.

"*Your* room," Mom corrected. She stepped over beside me and threw half her sheet around me.

"You've got some explaining to do," Dad told me. "After I take the girl home."

"Of what?" I said.

"Leave the boy alone, Wilson," Mom said. We hobbled toward my bed, a kind of Oedipal three-legged race, and Mom pointed to my clothes. "You get dressed too." I dropped the pillow and slid my camo pants on beneath the sheet. Finally, Mom released me.

"Now it's your turn, Mary Poppins," Mom said to Dad.

"That girl's in there. Just wait."

"Peggy, her name is Peggy," I said.

"That's all right, he's just upset," Mom said, patting my hair into place.

When she had finished dressing, Peggy stood in the door sideways and announced, "I'm ready. I'll wait downstairs, outside." Dad left to get dressed, and Mom sat on the bed. I started replacing the computer pieces on my desk.

"You should have told her good-bye, Stephen. That's no way to be to friends."

"Friends?" I said. "Really, Mother."

"I don't mean friend friends, Stephen. You know what I mean."

"Yeah, well, we're not that either. I don't know what we are . . . were."

Dad returned, dressed, holding a jacket. "I'm going. Where's the girl?"

"Peggy," I said.

"She said she'd wait downstairs, outside," Mom said. "And take my Volvo. I've got you blocked in."

"Keys?" Dad said.

"Purse," Mom answered.

"Square?"

"Round."

"Silver?"

"Right."

"Gas?"

"Hardly."

"Unleaded?"

"Super."

"Duper," said my dad. He disappeared and came back with the keys. He wore his jacket, his tweed cap nested on his head.

"Don't start it with the heater on," Mom said.

"Battery, I know," Dad said.

"Yes, battery," said Mom.

"Unh-hunh," Dad said.

"Okay," said Mom.

"'Kay, then," said my dad. Then, "You two get acquainted while I'm gone."

"'Kay," said Mom. She smiled across at the empty doorway. Dad went thumping down the stairs.

So I just knelt there on the rug, scraping up the last bits and pieces of my erstwhile home computer, all 256K of memory scattered to kingdom come, picking it up bit by byte, one K at a time. And feeling mostly rotten. Rotten for being compromised by Peggy, more rotten for letting it happen, worse still for realizing it was only Truelove that brought us together, worst of all for thinking that was the end of Peggy as we know her today.

But it was hard to concentrate on how bad I felt about Peggy right then, because it was all mixed around with other varieties of strangeness, like my mother sitting behind me on the bed wrapped in a sheet, reciting "Humpty Dumpty" just under her breath as my desktop filled up with bite-sized computer morsels. And the memory of Dad backing his way around the room, umbrella at three o'clock. And their little farewell exchange, a tease, like something familiar, an old song, a primal tribal grunt.

How did it go?

Unh-hunh . . . Okay . . . 'Kay then . . . 'kay.

Ten years ago, Dad taking me to the YMCA for the Saturday-morning Aquatots, and we'd stand in the doorway, my face squeezed between the door jamb and Dad's thigh, looking back at Mom, and they'd go . . .

Unh-hunh . . . Okay . . . 'Kay then . . . 'Kay.

Or Mom. Sunday-morning emergency milk run to the Fast Fare, Dad and I'd look up from the floor where we had Prince Valiant or somebody pinned under our elbows, and Mom would stop real quick, just to double-check before she left.

And they'd go . . .

Unh-hunh . . . Okay . . . 'Kay then . . . 'Kay.

So you never know.

You never know.

And when I'd finished picking up, I looked back

across at Mom, still wrapped in her sheet, looking back across at me.

She said, "Stephen Alexander Douglass, you have got the nicest smile. And to think the orthodontist wanted to slap you in braces."

And I said, "What orthodontist?"

And she said, "A girl. Honestly. My, Stephen, I hope you know what you're doing."

And I said, "Don't worry, I don't."

And she said, "Me neither."

And I said, "It's probably all over anyway."

And she said, "Unh-hunh."

Okay.

'Kay then.

'Kay.


She excused herself to get decent, and I excused myself to get something to eat. When she found me in the kitchen, she was wearing Dad's terry-cloth wrap pulled tight around her waist above a pair of his old sweatpants. She looked like a Zouave infantryman in retreat.

"Chili, canned stuff. Want some?" Mom didn't answer, just fetched two bowls and set them by me on the stove. "Crackers there," I said, pointing at the tin bread box by the sink. "Milk in fridge, glasses, spoons."

Mom fluttered around until all was ready. The chili bubbled like hot red mud. We sat across from each other, eating like prospectors, stooped over our bowls, eyes down, spoons rising and falling in silent regular strokes.

"Good," I proclaimed, and swallowed my milk in one gulp.

"You've got a mustache, Stephen," Mom told me. She always said that.

I apologized. "I'm sorry, Mom. I guess it's all my fault. Again."

"It's all right, Stephen," she said. "It's not a night for laying blame. We all look a little . . . silly. At least you can say you're young." She pushed her bowl to arm's length and sat staring into the spoon. Her face grew soft and round, dropping its sadness into the concave bowl of the spoon. "Young," she repeated.

"Young is no big deal," I said. I reached across and took her hand, pushing it slowly down against the table. I pulled the spoon away and held it in my fist. "Young is overrated. Young isn't always even young. Take Peggy. Sometimes I think she's twenty-seven or thirty-eight or forty-nine." I was being careful to avoid forty. "I mean, she's so sure of everything. How I should dress, what I should say. I mean, she really seems to know what she wants, even in this school thing—"

"Your teacher, Mr. Truelove?" Mom interrupted.

"Yes, that. She wants me to, I don't know, serve him up on a platter. She sees it like a holy war. Forget about who he is or what his life is, she knows what's right, and by god, she's going to get it. I mean, that's not young to me."

"Me either," Mom agreed. "The sad part is, that was me once, I suppose. Just ask your father."

"I did already. He told me about law school, about the bar. You were in there somewhere. But he said

327

to get your version. I was also supposed to ask you about the dreaded ax."

Mom considered for a moment. She stared down at her bare feet through the clear tabletop. "This floor is freezing," she said. Finally she lifted her gaze from the floor and studied my face for some hidden clue. She stretched her arms across the table, palms up, and took my hands like we were going to have a two-party séance.

Then she cleared her throat, hitching the voice up a notch or two into this bizarre kind of fairy-tale register. "Once upon a time," she said, "there was a bright young man who fled from the land of his birth, from his family and their gold, to a land of long summers and brown rivers where he would study the mysteries of the law. He had a special gift, a beautiful intelligence, and many people expected him to use this gift. They enticed him with promises of fame and money, and the young prince said, 'Sure, why not?' although he really didn't know.

"And there was at this time a great war raging in a distant land. And it came to pass that the prince grew sore afraid—"

"That's the Bible, Mom," I said. "Don't mix your genres."

"Shut up and listen," Mom said. "Anyway, the prince was scared, but not, I think, of fighting, or of dying, not that so much. Just afraid of guns or uniforms or maybe growing up. So the prince worked even harder and studied at the law. He thought he could become so brilliant that the war could not touch him. But his land said, 'Too bad. You have had a year to be immune from our call of duty.' Yet the prince still needed time. The law could not be mastered in a year.

"And so the prince was sent away, and his land measured him and weighed him and pronounced him fit for soldiering. They told him to go away and wait. They would call him someday, and he must serve.

"And the prince grew sore afraid some more and built a huge wall of books, of law books, and huddled behind this wall, listening and fearing the call that he knew would come. And one day he heard someone, footsteps, approaching."

"The draft," I said. Mom ignored me and continued.

"But when the prince looked up to see where the footsteps were coming from, he saw only a young girl—"

"And that was you," I blurted out.

"... a beautiful young girl who said, 'Arise, and stop your sniveling, young prince.' And the young girl explained to the prince that the war was wrong, was illegal. She told him about National Liberation Front and people's revolutions and corrupt puppet governments, for she had learned these many things, and they sounded good. So the prince said, 'Yes, of course,' and the girl explained that the prince could be a greater hero by calling the war wrong. And so the prince no longer had to feel scared, and whenever someone called him coward he simply told them the war was wrong.

"Soon they fell in love. And as their love grew, the

329

girl offered one last gift, a magic charm against the war. It grew inside her, a new life. And when the prince found out he made her his bride, and the charm worked its magic, for after that the war could not touch the prince. And so the prince went back to being brilliant for a year, and the child was born—"

"So that's how I—"

"Shhhhh, just listen. So the child was born and they called him Stephen."

Suddenly a thought occurred to me. "So Dad was right. I'm, like, a bastard?"

"Not officially. No more than your father," Mom teased. "Just think of yourself as getting an early start on legitimacy. Happens every day."

"But I did keep him out of the war, when you get right down to it. Imagine me, a war baby."

"More like a peace baby," she said, laughing, "if you want to get technical. Now where was I?"

"A child was born," I prompted.

"Yes, and they called him Stephen."

"And it was good," I offered.

"It was all right," Mom corrected, "at least for a while. The prince was finished with hiding behind his wall of books, so he tore down the wall and hid the books. He didn't need them. But he was still scared in a way. It wasn't really the war after all, the girl discovered. . . ."

Mom's voice had returned to its usual timbre, only slower now, halting.

"And so?" I tried to prompt her.

"And so the prince opened a bar. He discovered that he could hide behind a wall of beer posters and cheap mirrors just as easily as behind law books. And he never had to grow up. The girl ran out of miracles—"

"And what happened to the girl?" I asked.

"Oh, she came back one day and bought the bar." Mom pressed my hands together and clapped them for me, palm to palm. "She thinks."

"No kidding, Mom. Great. Are you really? Congratulations!"

"Thanks. Now that's enough stories for one night. Maybe I'll try again sometime when you're older." Mom stood up and snapped to attention.

"Hold on," I protested. "What about the dreaded ax? Dad said to ask about the dreaded ax."

"Too ashamed to tell you himself? No wonder." She settled in the chair once more. "He called it plan B at the time. This was before you came along and saved his neck. Before we were married. One day he stopped off at the hardware store on the way home and bought himself this glorious thirty-dollar Tru-Temper ax. He had designs on his toes."

"Designs on his toes?" I repeated, trying to imagine Dad with toe designs—little tattooed flowers, perhaps.

"He was going to cut some off. He was going to maim himself just to stay out of the Army. He'd heard a toe or two might do it. He was never sure how many. And if that didn't work, he figured there was always section eight."

"Section eight was about toes?" I asked.

"No, it was about heads." Mom tapped herself above the ear and circled a finger there until I got

331

the point. "He decided that if missing toes didn't exempt him, being an ax-wielding toe chopper would. On the day his 'greetings' letter came from Uncle Sam, he was gonna let fly with the ax, then march to the induction center with his bloodied ax slung across his shoulder."

"But the letter never came," I said.

"No, you came. He gave the ax to Goodwill."

"But he *was* getting pretty crazy, huh?"

"Well, he was *cultivating* crazy. He was clever enough to know the correct . . . behaviors. He practiced them, like manners. If you work at it hard enough, you can convince yourself of anything, I suppose."

"Maybe he should've been in therapy. Maybe that could have helped." I was pushing it close to the truth—but Dad said she'd never known. So I studied Mom closely. All I could see was that she was nonplussed as could be. Dad was right.

"Your dad in therapy? Yeah, it's funny he never thought of that. He'd have done that, too, if he felt he could get a note or something. 'Please excuse Wilson from the war, as he is under a great deal of stress. Sincerely!' Sure, that probably was next."

"Do you think that kind of stuff is, like, hereditary?" I asked.

"Stuff? Head stuff?" I nodded, and she cocked her head, thinking. "I don't know. That one was still up for grabs, last time I looked. Intelligence, looks, those are hereditary, in part. Lord knows you did all right in those departments. But the other . . . Sometimes I think you have to make your own problems for yourself, really work at it. But I don't know."

"Neither do I, Mom," I told her. "Just thought I'd ask."

She stood once more, grabbed the belt around Dad's terry wrap, and let each fist tug an end downward until her waist cinched in and down. "Here, rinse these bowls off and get to bed." She swept the bowls off the table and held them out toward me. I took them and ran them under some hot water in the sink.

Then she pushed me into my room, handed me my pajamas, and steered me back out into the hall toward the bathroom. I brushed, I peed, I spit in the sink. When I got to my room, Mom was in the top bunk, curled up beneath the covers.

"Hope you don't mind the company," she said. "Your dad's got my car and there's no telling when he'll be back."

"No problem," I said. "The pleasure's all mine." I gave her a little pat where a bulge rose beneath the covers halfway down. "Besides, that's what these bunk beds are for. Don't fall off."

I picked up the Star Wars comforter one last time and threw it over Mom.

Finally I settled in the bunk below, listening in the dark to Mom stirring above me. Across the room, the window was frosting up with an icy glaze around its edges. The exerciser sat slightly askew in the corner, and the shattered computer on my desk resembled, in the dark, a mound of broken pottery.

I was full ahead in dreamland when Dad came back. I heard him in the bathroom humming "Botany Bay" through a mouthful of toothpaste. Then something, something from an interrupted dream just barely there, now faint, but I tried to pull it back once more, something about a figure stooping in a flooded terrace, water to the knees, back bent, hand plunging a green shoot into the mud, and then, slow motion, the figure standing and turning, as if to face a camera, and the face, I think I see the face is mine, and someone says, "You have the most beautiful smile. You really do."

# Chapter 46

Nightlife takes its toll. Next day I sleepwalked through classes and dragged myself into biology by the second bell. Truelove stood his ground up front and droned into the air above our heads. We were getting to vertebrates, and who would like to introduce the unit with a report? he asked. I made a move to raise my hand. "You, Douglass?" he asked, in his best sardonic pitch. "All right, if you're the best we can do. So be it." And once again he jabbed at the board with his chalk until my name appeared in the top left corner of the board. He circled it and returned to his drone.

When class ended, everyone filed quickly out the door, including Peggy, who had spent the period looking through me, past me.

I hung back, waiting just inside the door. Truelove settled at his desk, was about to wipe a hand across his brow when he spotted me.

"Oh yes? Problem, Douglass?" His hand seemed stuck there on his forehead. At last he dropped it to the desk, muttering something about poor ventilation.

"The report, my report, could we make it Monday, sir?" I asked. "The TV people will be here then. I think it might be the best time to, for you to . . . do your encore. Like we talked about."

"Ah, an accomplice. So you're willing, are you?"

"Yes sir, I am, if you are?"

"Can I ask what changed your mind, Douglass?"

"Personal reasons mostly, sir," I answered.

"They always are. So be it. I'll be here. Come dressed for battle."

"I will, sir. You too." For some reason I caught myself beginning a curtsy and started backing out the door.

"Oh, one favor, Douglass," Truelove called across the empty room.

"Yes sir, if I can."

"You can. Don't call me sir. It isn't becoming. To me or to you."

I just nodded at that request and left. Truelove. Sir. I was running out of things to call him.

Over Thanksgiving I worked on my report. I sat at the table watching the Macy's parade from New York. The balloons seemed to get smaller every year. Bullwinkle's antlers looked frail as twigs. A big band from Maine marched by playing "Good King Wenceslas." I watched to see if Regina was in the band, but of course she wasn't. Then I watched to see which girl in the band looked most like Regina and none did. I couldn't even tell which ones were girls.

336

I closed my eyes and tried to remember Regina: her red hair a wild crown, her braces, her green eyes pale as glass, her easy smile . . .

"Swallow the canary, Stephen?" I opened my eyes. Dad stood in the kitchen peering into the micro-wave.

"No, swallowed no canaries, not today."

"That's good," he said. "You'll need all your room for this turkey." But I doubted it. He had never learned the art of browning poultry in a microwave. Last year he tried basting it in soy sauce. We had to call out for chicken wings.

Finally, Dad gave up on the master-chef routine and dismembered the bird. He cooked it part by part and we ate in stages, turkey parts, macaroni, Stove Top stuffing, and big bowls of pumpkin ice cream buried beneath nondairy whipped topping—in chunks, no less. Chunks because it was still frozen and I drew the line at thawing it out in the micro-wave.

After dinner I got back to my report and Dad sifted through notebooks filled with torts. The NFL played on all afternoon. The Vikings beat the Cowboys, the Chiefs beat the Lions. By evening my report barely filled a page:

"On the great biological tree of life, the verte-brates occupy those honored upper branches of com-plexity and specialization. Vertebrates are so named because of their backbones, a remarkably supple col-umn of vertebrae which enclose a spinal cord to serve as conduit of the central nervous system.

"This spinal column originates in a skull that,

337

among the higher mammals, allows for a capacious brain cavity. Indeed, the size of man's skull allows for a brain remarkable among all the animals for its intelligence and sophistication. Whether conscious or unconscious, it is a control center for the body; a receiver and transmitter of countless messages every microsecond.

"But it is this complexity that makes the human brain so slow on the uptake, so long in the achievement of mastery. No other animal has such an extended infancy, nor such a prolonged dependence on parental nurturing and guidance. But at its fullest powers, it enables man to surpass his fellow mammals in acts of genius and creation. Only man can paint the mystery of a country sunrise, can sing to the majesty of his own creation, can write poems to celebrate the ecstasies of love and longing—all, of course, if adequately inspired."

Of course!

That's as far as my report on vertebrates got for Monday. I guess I wasn't adequately inspired. Partly I suppose it was because I realized that I had volunteered for the impossible. A report on vertebrates must have been another Truelove joke. Like describe the Renaissance in twenty-five words or less. So there was nothing about organ systems, nothing about neural networks or cellular differentiation, nothing about bipedal locomotion, nothing about gestation or the miracle of the opposing thumb, nothing about vestigial tailbone parts, nothing about secondary sex characteristics. Zilch about nipples.

Plus there was this hollow feeling now, like a toothache that is dull and distant and hard to localize. I think it was because of Peggy, sad to say, knowing that that confusion was over with for good, but sorry that it was, yet savoring that sadness, rolling it around on my tongue like a sourball that refuses to dissolve.

And the other thing was Mom and Dad. For sixteen years I had thought I was just their kid. But now I had discovered something more. I was part of their fear, part of their falling apart, their souvenir, their conscientious objection, their secret, their pride and joy, their adorable filial shuttlecock.

It was good to know where you stood.

Monday morning Dad was up early, came in and said, "Go break a leg, sport." And Mom called up to wish me luck. She said to find out when the program aired. She said to smile. She said to make sure I didn't slouch and not to mumble. "And wear something nice, that green sweater with the sleeves," she added. By seven forty-five I was down on the corner of Mifflin and University, and in my head I was hearing this voice like E. G. Marshall's churning his way through another one of those *National Geographic Specials*, "Woolgatherers of the Enchanted Tundra," or something. He was saying, "Dawn breaks cold and gray across the vast piedmont, and the morning ritual begins anew. The sophomore Douglass emerges from his habitat after his night of rest. He awaits the vast yellow vehicle that soon will transport him to the village school where he will join other young men and women of his tribe in a series of ritualized lessons preparing them for adulthood. The green sweater young Douglass wears is a typical costume for this region of the world, where temperatures can sometimes reach well below freezing. Notice the distinctive pair of sleeves, reaching from shoulder to wrist, so characteristic of tribal clothing that weds function to form in a pleasing aesthetic of traditional design. . . ."

By the time we got to school, I had pretty much lost my appetite for stardom. Still, as I walked through the front door, a hand grabbed the strap of my backpack and pulled me aside. It was Miss Nevelson, Wilfong's secretary. "They're all in the office," she said. "Follow me."

Wilfong sat behind his desk with the channel eleven guys seated on his couch. He was saying something about dialoguing with the community, and rolling his head side to side with each sentence. His beard seemed shorter, newly trimmed for the occasion, and behind it he was wearing a bow tie, orange and black specks shaped like paramecia.

"You gentlemen go ahead and introduce yourselves. This is the Douglass boy." Wilfong leaned way back in his chair and sighted down his nose.

The news guy in the blazer stood and shook my hand. "Ronnie Pothos here," he said. "I'm the reporter. Nice to be working with you." He said he had caught a tape of my *Five Alive* interview, my monologue delivered from the courthouse stairs. "Just be yourself, Steve," he said. "It's just a day-in-the-life kind of thing. We're not looking for a performance per se. And say hello to my crew," he continued. He pointed at his colleague, Luis he called him. Luis stayed seated, weighed down by a lapful of black vinyl carrying cases. He flipped the top item over and unzipped it, pulled out a camera, and swiveled it on a strap in midair. The camera looked like two shoe boxes attached side to side but staggered to rest on the shoulder, like a weapon. He withdrew from a zippered pouch inside the larger case a piece of wire, like a necklace, with a small bullet kind of thing attached. "Here, Stevie, put this on. Now step over there by the door and say something."

I walked to the door as ordered and started to recite "Humpty Dumpty" for some reason. Luis opened a flap on the recorder jacket and twiddled some silver knobs as a red needle bobbed back and forth. "That's good. One more time," Luis said. I obliged with another chorus of "Humpty Dumpty," and Luis pronounced us ready.

"Not so fast," Wilfong announced. He stood and circled his desk, then went over to the door and pushed it closed.

"It's important that we remember we've agreed on some simple ground rules. First and foremost, this is a school, not a TV studio. Any disruptions to the normal routine of the learning process, and we'll have to call the whole thing off."

"Yes, sir. We have no problem with that," Ronnie Pothos answered. It was his on-camera voice.

Wilfong seemed reassured. He urged them to visit the new weight room in the gym, "the finest of its kind in the South." He told them to drop by the new horticulture classes' greenhouses, "a one-of-a-kind facility for a school of our size." He reminded them to drop in on the new theater arts auditorium, "a mil-

341

lion-dollar complex second to none in the state," and on their way, he added, they should visit the refurbished vocational arts center, "a real model program for the career-track kids, a special hands-on kind of place."

Ronnie and Luis said they'd try, time allowing, and Wilfong exhaled deeply.

Finally, Wilfong lifted his weight off the office door and pivoted, one hand balled around the knob.

"Well now, Stephen," he said to me, "here's your chance to shine, a brand-new beginning and all. Remember, we're all counting on you to make us proud, to get back on the right foot, so to speak. Now go on, and remember . . . let's make it business as usual."

"Yes sir," I said. "As usual."

"Business as usual" turned out to be pretty strange. In homeroom, Luis and Ronnie sat in the back taping me as I watched Miss Armias reading the announcements about cheerleading practice.

In English it got stranger still. Mrs. St. Paul made us open our books to page 243 and take notes while she stood at the board for the whole period explaining about the great chain of being.

In French, Madame Wiggins ("Vee-gannnh") greeted us with *"Bonjour, mes jeunes amis,"* and we answered, *"Bon jour Madame Vee-gannnh,"* and then we went right to the work sheets.

The point is, it was all very proper, very safe. We all sat like good children, and the teachers never flinched. They smiled a lot and stood by the board. That seemed the order of the day.

"So far, so dull," I heard Luis mutter from behind

as we wove our way to third-period Ancient Cultures.

Ancient Cultures also played it safe. Mr. Tuborgson had the slide show ready to roll. The bell rang, the lights went off, and soon we were wallowing in ziggurats.

We were on our way to the cafeteria for fourth-period lunch when Ronnie Pothos decided to stop for a smoke. As we passed through the open courtyard, Ronnie pulled us over to the rows of concrete benches where the "benchers" sat row by row huddled over their cigarettes. "These kids are great," Ronnie Pothos announced halfway through his cigarette. "Maybe we should talk to them. The dark side of the American Dream, whither youth, that kind of thing."

"Dynamite," said Luis.

"Absolutely," Ronnie Pothos agreed. "Lunch," he said, snapping his cigarette into a pile of discarded butts beneath the branches of a stunted rhododendron.

We went on into the cafeteria and waited in line to select between hamburger stroganoff or grilled cheese. We paid for our grilled cheeses, and I led the television team to a corner table where they could survey the whole room from a safe distance.

"Hey, look, friend, don't let us wreck your normal routine," Ronnie told me as we sat down. "But hey, where's your peer group? Your lunch-table buddies?" he asked.

"I don't have a peer group," I said. "Most of my buddies have second lunch, if you must know."

Just then I spotted Nu Tran Banh floating our way,

carrying his tray at waist level. I intercepted him, took his tray, and led him to our table.

"Join us for lunch, Nu Tran," I said, setting his tray at the empty seat. He sat, startled but polite, and I introduced him to Ronnie and Luis.

"Good to meet you," Ronnie smiled. "Listen, Nu Tran, maybe you could give us a little input from a different point of view. How long you and Stephen been friends?"

Nu Tran stared at me. "Two year. Is that what you say, Stephen?"

"About two sounds right," I agreed.

"How do you two spend your time together?" Ronnie asked.

Nu Tran stared at me blankly. Ronnie tried again, "I mean, do you guys hang out?"

"Yes, we hang out very much," Nu Tran said, desperate to begin his soup.

"But . . . doing what?" Ronnie wanted specifics. "Do you, for example, go biking, swimming, things like that?"

Nu Tran stared at his soup. "Yes, swimming, we do that. Stephen is excellent with the water." Ronnie wrote something on a pad.

"We do computers," I added. "Games, programs."

"No kidding," Ronnie mumbled, still writing.

"Oh yes, computers," Nu Tran added.

"Girls?" Ronnie said, and winked at Luis.

Nu Tran finally got to his soup. "I have a girlfriend in Maine," I answered. "We see each other in summer. Nu Tran still plays the field." Nu Tran filled his bowl with crackers and kept eating.

344

"The field, no kidding," Ronnie mumbled. "Okay, Nu Tran, how about you give me a thumbnail sketch of Stephen here, one friend on another? Say you're describing him to your mom."

"I live with my uncle," Nu Tran said.

"All right, to your uncle. What would you say?" Ronnie planted both elbows on his tray and hunched across the table.

"I would say . . ." Nu Tran pondered, began folding his napkin into small triangles. "Would say Stephen is a loyal friend, very smart sometimes, a good president, and unusual to know but very worthwhile. Sometimes maybe a puzzle with many solutions, to himself I think sometimes too."

"I see," Ronnie said, but he had already folded his notepad and put away his pencil.

"I'm sorry if you're not getting what you thought you'd get," I started to apologize. "I mean, it hasn't really been too exciting, and I'm sorry."

"Hey, it's been great, man," Ronnie tried to reassure me. "Some days you just come up empty, that's all. Hills and valleys.

"Tell you what let's do, kid," he went on. "Luis and me are gonna go back out to that courtyard place. We wanna get some tape out there, maybe talk to some of those kids, get a little different perspective on things. You two stay here and enjoy your lunch, and we'll catch you on the way out."

"Right, Okay," I agreed. "Things are bound to pick up. I'm giving a report on vertebrates seventh period. And the teacher there . . . he's a very unusual guy."

"Sounds swell, really great." Ronnie pulled his wallet from his pocket and sorted through its contents. Finally he slammed a dollar bill on the table and tucked it beneath my tray. "Tell you what, Stephen, here's a buck. Go get yourself some of those jelly doughnuts. And keep the change. No problem."

We watched them leave the cafeteria as kids flocked at their heels like duck babies. Everyone wants to be on TV.

"I hoped I could help them some, Stephen," Nu Tran said.

"You were great, thanks. Don't worry." I could've hugged old Nu Tran then. He seemed the purest spirit on the planet. I wanted him to know. "Listen, Nu Tran. I want to tell you something. That report I'm giving today in biology? If something goes funny, if Truelove jumps all over me . . . it's sort of like a plan. I'm in on it. It's all on purpose. However bad it looks, it's like a trick. I just wanted you to know."

Nu Tran stared at me again. "I don't see."

"You will. Don't ask me now. Sometime I'll explain everything."

"Why tell me, Stephen, now?"

"Because it'll be easier for me if someone knows. I won't be so alone up there."

"You are very strange, Stephen Douglass." Nu Tran smiled around a straw and drank his milk.

"But hey," I teased, "that's no way to talk."

"But hey," he mocked me, "good friends tell the truth."

"But hey," I answered, "maybe you've got a point."

After lunch I headed for math. Mr. Burger was wearing a jacket and tie for the first time that year, and when I sat at my desk he sort of sidled up to me and said, "Where are they, Stephen? I thought they'd be with you."

"So did I, Mr. Burger," I said. "Except they got involved in the courtyard. I doubt they'll make it."

Mr. Burger's face sagged with disappointment.

Finally the bell rang for seventh period. I slung my pack over my shoulder and went out into the hall, expecting to find Ronnie and Luis waiting. But they weren't. I took the long way to Truelove's class, down each hallway, but still no sight of Ronnie and Luis. I made a final swing by the back door to check the courtyard, but it was abandoned by now, a slow cold rain having chased the final smokers inside.

I headed for class, anyway, knowing the bell was just seconds away. Probably Ronnie and Luis would be waiting there, tucked in a corner, camera rolling away. But no, the room was the same, students filling the desks, Truelove himself predictably sitting at his desk in the back corner hunched over his pale-green blotter, eyes cast downward.

I took my seat next to Peggy. Instantly she turned her back and went about the business of ignoring me. Two rows up, Buddy Autry had his feet perched on the countertop. He was lining his books up along the counter's edge with his toes, positioning them to go slamming to the floor first chance he got.

The room was buzzing now. Chairs scraped, notebooks fluttered, the bell to begin classes rang, and two more kids bolted through the doors, shoulder to shoulder, checking the back corner to make sure Truelove wasn't watching. He wasn't.

Suddenly Nu Tran pops his head in the door, then yanks it back out again just as fast. Again he appears, this time sliding sideways through the door. He stares at me, nods, then twists his head back toward the doorway and nods again. Ronnie and Luis slide through the doorway behind him. Like a practiced usher, Nu Tran lifts his arm out, palm cocked gently upward, and leads the two back toward me. The room falls silent. "Over there," I hear Nu Tran say, and then he takes his seat in the front row. Ronnie and Luis push their way past me. Ronnie nods. Luis offers a crisp salute with his left hand because his right hand is already perched atop his shoulder-mounted camera.

I nod back and watch as the entire class pivots to see them settle in the back corner opposite True-love's desk. Luis hops onto a worktable and pans the room with his camera. Ronnie approaches True-love and mumbles something. Truelove ignores him. *Thwack*, the first salvo of books hits the floor. Truelove's head bobs over the green blotter in a silent three count. He pushes away from the desk and stands, then seems to topple forward over the desk. Its old joints creak under his weight, dry glue crackling. He catches himself, planting both hands against the blotter, then nimbly disguises the awkward moment by sliding one hand across the desk and plucking his roll book from beneath a pile of papers.

He walks slowly to the front of the room, a condemned man, taking care to trample across Buddy's books with full heavy steps that scatter them the length of the aisle. He seems to be humming as he approaches the board—more a low animal groan, a barely audible rattle in the throat.

Finally he faces the class and opens his roll book, holding it balanced in one palm like a hymnal.

"Dearly beloved," he begins, "before we join the lists of the immortal, let us record that on this day and in this place our numbers commingled to serve witness to the grandeur and mystery of life. And so we gather at this shrine in the name of biology. Please let history show that these were the parties attendant to this holy moment."

He starts to read off our names, to intone them, rather. No one responds with "Here," or "Present." That's not the point. It has become Truelove's show, and we wait. He is in rare good form, and the class sits hushed. The names become a strange, wry prayer of retribution, and Truelove is the priest:

"One Eugene Harley Autry . . .

"One Nu Tran Banh . . .

"One Sherrill Reynolds Bernier . . .

"One Christopher Raphael Collogi . . .

"One Stephen Alexander Douglass . . ."

And the names continue in perfect cadence, one after the other. You can almost smell the incense.

"One Margaret Angela Davis Klecko . . ." I should have known she'd have three names.

And still the names continue, almost to the end, but when Truelove gets to Frances Shannar Zipperian, a hollow crackling intrudes on the final syllables of her name. From the round, silver speaker recessed directly overhead in the ceiling's very center comes an electric tapping of microphone, and an edgy, distant voice mutters. "Is this thing on? Is it on?" Then, after a final *tap-tap-tap* comes a voice: *"Please pardon this interruption . . ."* It's Wilfong's voice, like doom, like Oz, multiplied by a hundred echoing classrooms.

*"We have just received a call here in the office advising us that there is a bomb planted somewhere in our school. We have no choice but to treat this as a serious threat. We are asking that all teachers move immediately with their classes to evacuate the building. We are asking that you remove yourselves to the bus loading area at the front of the school as soon as possible. Please move in an efficient and orderly fashion to this area. Do not stop at lockers, but proceed directly and quickly to the evacuation area. We are asking teachers to please make sure their rooms are secured. Again, this is a serious threat. This is not a drill. Let's clear the building."*

Truelove snaps his roll book shut and holds it out toward the door, waving his arm in a sweeping motion like someone parking cars at the state fair. He leans against the board and shuts his eyes. Buddy scrambles into the aisle to retrieve his books. Buzzing and squealing, everyone makes for the door, knocking over chairs and jostling for position. Luis has planted himself just outside the door and stands there taping the confusion of this exodus. As the class drains out through the doorway and into the hall, Peggy calmly stands beside me.

350

She says, "Fancy that, a bomb scare," then packs her books and leaves.

Ronnie Pothos follows her out the door, collects Luis, then spins in the doorway. "Coming, Stephen, or what?" he asks.

"Be right out," I tell him, and he seems satisfied when I shoulder my backpack and head for the door. But when I reach the door, I just push it closed and flip off the lights.

Truelove opens his eyes and stares right at me. "You staying?" he asks.

"Are you?" I ask right back.

He pushes away from the board and walks over to the windows. "It's raining out there," he says. "No, Stephen, I think I'll ride this one out right here. There's no bomb. This isn't Beirut."

"Or Saigon, either," I remind him.

"Saigon was always pretty safe. At least until the end." He rolls the window open a crack, and I come up beside him. We stand listening to the noise, watching the milling students. They cluster in bunches, some holding books over their heads against the rain, others with jackets, sweaters, pulled up like hoods. Ms. Wilberforce is out there in a yellow slicker, bustling around with a group of teachers, chasing kids back into rank, herding the stragglers onto the concrete from among the brown azaleas.

"Guess this puts the damper on your swan song," I say.

"Oh, that." Truelove smiles blankly out toward the gray drizzle. "Guess so. I wasn't sure I had the nerve, sad to say, to give it up, all this"—he turns back to the room, lifting both hands, palms up, toward the ceiling; it is very saintly, in a way—"this, this grandeur."

"I thought you were ready today. That roll call was great. I thought you really had it cranking up."

"Must have been the cameras, that," he chuckles. "I've been playing the madman so long. it comes right out sometimes. They want a show. It's sort of expected. Fact, I halfway enjoy it. Keeps me interested. After ten years it's probably the only thing that does, most days. Keep them guessing, let the stuff just come right out, make them adjust, I figure."

"Like tapioca," I say, but I don't think he hears me. "Anyhow, my report on vertebrates really isn't much of a report. Couple paragraphs of b.s. to be honest. All ready to go."

"You've got more guts than me, I think." He sticks his hand out the window to feel the rain.

"Damn overhang." Truelove pulls his hand back in and holds it against his cheek. "Look at Wilberforce out there. She's having a field day. Mother hen incarnate. God bless her."

Ms. Wilberforce is running the length of the sidewalk, now with her raincoat in both hands, shooing the kids off the asphalt turnaround.

"The Wilber Force. Kinda sounds like one of those Saturday cartoons. Like Omega Force, Strike Force, Eagle Force. You watch those things, Stephen?"

"Used to," I tell him.

I see him smile, just real faint, at his reflection on the window, and suddenly I'm wondering what kind of kid he was. I can see this doughy, white-faced kid with V-neck T-shirts watching *Jeopardy*, eating jelly rolls, tending an ant farm, hatching sea monkeys, that kind of stuff.

Truelove leans down to get a clear view of the scene out front. He's looking beneath the glass, where the pane tilts out from the frame, squinting. Small veins bunch around his eyes, but the eyes themselves are clear, the irises almost yellow from the side.

"Don't see the prince," he says.

"The what?" I say.

"The prince, the principal, Howard Wilfong. Just your journalist friends with the television station."

I lean down with my elbows on the counter, like Truelove's, and together we squint out the same opening in the window. Sure enough, Ronnie and Luis dash out the front walk, past the azaleas, right up to the wet and milling student body. Luis has removed his leather jacket; it's now draped over his head, over the camera, and he swings to pan the crowd, his slick wet jacket like a black shell.

Ronnie, meanwhile, has settled Wilberforce at the edge of the mob. He starts an interview, and Luis crouches maybe ten feet in front. Instinctively, the entire student body fans itself into a perfect semi-circle at their backs.

"You should be out there, Stephen. This is your show," Truelove says.

"*Was* my show, you mean. I bombed, a real nothing; my media star has set."

"Hence the bomb threat, Stephen." Truelove plunges a hand into his hip pocket. Outside in the rain, Ronnie has now started interviewing a clump of students. Suddenly the lights come on, the room comes up full bright. We turn, and there stands Wilfong, planted in the doorway, one hand still attached to the light switch.

"Perhaps you gentlemen missed the announcement," he says. "About the bomb scare. Let's clear this room."

"Mr. Truelove thinks it's a fake," I blurt out.

"That's not an option we can entertain," Wilfong says. "Can't I get some cooperation here today?" He leaves the door and walks toward us. "Could you move along, please, Stephen?" he asks.

I nod and Wilfong stares and I start watching his beard again, getting lost in his beard. Wilfong is in my face, smells like coffee, has a brown V beneath his lip where the beard begins. He puts a hand on my arm and tries nudging me toward the door.

"Don't touch the boy. He'll go," Truelove barks. "That's not necessary. We're going."

"Gracious, aren't we possessive," Wilfong coos.

Angry, Truelove stiffens with authority and marches toward Wilfong.

Mr. Wilfong releases my arm and retreats behind me, throwing up his hands in truce.

"Well, well, thick as thieves," he chuckles. "I heard you two were . . ." But then he pauses to pick his words carefully. I'm expecting him to come out with something foul, but I underestimate him. "Up to something" is all he says.

Up to something. He heard. I start rolling that around a bit, chewing on those words to get the fla-

354

vor. Heard. Something. Up to something. He heard.

"Look, if you want us out, we'll get out. It's that simple." Truelove walks back to his desk and pulls a jacket off the floor. "Come on, Stephen, let's do as Mr. Wilfong asks us. Get your stuff."

Truelove seems suddenly eager and obedient. He circles around the back seats and stands by the doorway, in Wilfong's earlier pose, hand resting on the light switch. Wilfong seems relieved, murmurs, "That's better," and joins Truelove by the door. I hook a hand through my backpack and hitch it onto my shoulder. I close the window behind me and head for the door. Wilfong and Truelove part to let me exit first.

"The room is now secure," I hear Truelove say, and then we're walking down the hall, down toward the lobby, the main entrance, but I'm still rolling those words around: *"Heard. Up to something."*

We're maybe fifty yards away from the main office, cruising by the dust-choked trophy cases, right on by the Freedom Papers (wall-mounted plastic jobs: Magna Carta, Declaration of Independence, Gettysburg Address, all the great ones), and that's when I say it: "Heard we were up to something."

Wilfong freezes in his tracks. "Come again, please, Stephen?"

"What you said back there," I tell him. "You said you heard we were up to something. You said you heard it. I was wondering just how . . ."

"Now hold on, boy. I don't know what I said back there, but I didn't say that." Wilfong's eyes are turning into birdshot, BB's. "I said I *figured* you two were

355

up to something. That's what I said. I said 'figured.' "

"You said *heard*," I answer him.

"You said *heard*," Truelove echoes.

"We *heard* it, Mr. Wilfong," I say. "And what I was wonderin' was where did you *hear* it, or better yet, *who* did you hear it from? So tell us, please, sir, *who*?"

Wilfong stands pulling at his beard, like it might suddenly grow, like it might suddenly swallow him up. "I don't think this is a fruitful dialogue. I think it's over right now."

"With you it's over, maybe so," I tell him. "But I'm sure my friends from channel eleven out there might like to continue this dialogue, once we get outside there. It's been a slow news kind of day, sir."

That does it. "Come, we'll go in here." Wilfong struts across the lobby and unlocks the office door. We follow him and he points us to a couch where the visitors usually wait.

"No thanks, I'd rather stand," says Truelove. So I stand right beside him.

Wilfong turns back to the door and locks it from the inside and pockets the keys.

"Is this detention?" Truelove asks. "Stephen asked you a question. Why don't you answer him?" Truelove takes a step forward, and I realize that, beard notwithstanding, Wilfong's basically an elf beside the pale, sloping Truelove.

"It was Peggy Klecko, wasn't it? Peggy Klecko who told you we were up to something? Did she tell you about the dog tag? Did she tell you that part too?" It had to be her. I watch Wilfong shiver beneath his beard and turn his back to hide his face. I know that I'm right. Peggy, peg o' my heart, peg through my heart, Peggy.

Now Wilfong runs behind the office counter, plops down in front of the PA console, picks up the office phone, starts dialing.

"Calling the police, are you?" I shout. "Well, good, this is a bomb scare, isn't it? Make sure they bring their bomb-sniffing dogs. Tell them to bring all the bomb-sniffing dogs they own."

Truelove grabs my elbow from behind as I race to the swinging gate where the counter nears the wall. "Hold on, Stephen," he whispers. "Let's see."

Wilfong punches up a number on the phone, pauses, then says, "Irv, let's run those buses now. The kids are all around front, in the rain. No use makin' 'em stand there. Let's call it a day. . . . Sure thing." Then he hangs up the phone.

"It's not the police," I whispered to Truelove. "He can't call them, 'cause then he'd have to explain about this fake bomb scare."

Wilfong flips about ten switches on the PA console and then starts spitting at the microphone.

"It's *his* bomb scare. Is that what you're saying?" Truelove asks.

"Of course it's his. He heard *something* was up, and he knew it was up for seventh period. We got bombed out."

"But he's the prince of the school. He's brass. And brass is brass. Wait. Listen."

The school erupts with popping and spitting one more time, and Wilfong mans the mike. *"Please par-*

*don this interruption,"* he begins, and I'm thinking, What the devil does this guy think he's interrupting, anyhow? *"We are sorry for the inconvenience of this evacuation and for the disruption of your school day. We have decided to go ahead and dismiss school. The buses will arrive at the ramp momentarily, so please stay where you are. Those of you with your own transportation may be excused to the parking lot at this time. We are asking that the staff remain on the ramp and help in supervising the loading of buses, as the search of school property has not yet been completed. Thank you, and have a pleasant evening."*

"You lying bugger," Truelove screams. He vaults the counter and wrests the microphone away from Wilfong, knocking him to the floor.

*"C'mere,* Stephen," he yells at me. "Get on this thing and tell them the truth."

I plant myself in the chair by the mike as Truelove straddles Wilfong's chest and pins his arms against the floor. Wilfong is trying like crazy to maintain his dignity.

"Hello," I say into the microphone, and I hear *Hello* come back at me amplified a hundredfold.

*"Hello, hello out there. This is not Mr. Wilfong anymore. Mr. Wilfong is indisposed,"* I say. *"This is Stephen Douglass, your sophomore class president, and I have an important update on that last announcement."* I swivel in the chair and look out the front office windows. The crowd settles from its celebration. The jostling and milling stop; the crowd, as one, turns to face the office. I rise from the chair and wave, but I'm not sure they can see me.

*"What Mr. Wilfong forgot to tell you is that this bomb scare is a hoax. Mr. Wilfong made it all up. There are no police, no bomb-sniffing dogs, no fire rescue units. None of that stuff. Now ask yourselves. If this were real, they would be here in droves, wouldn't they? And why did Mr. Wilfong want seventh period canceled so much he would do all this? Perhaps he would like to tell you himself."*

It seems like a good idea at the time, a little confession from the horse's mouth. But when I spin around, there lies Wilfong on the floor. His feet are bound and tied with the cord to Miss Nevelson's IBM Selectric. The machine itself rests on his chest. Truelove is busy wrapping his wrists together with strapping tape. It all seems kind of severe to me, but Truelove seems strangely inspired by the whole effort.

"Bring the mike here," Truelove grunts.

I stretch the cord as far as it will go and tilt the mike toward Wilfong's mouth. He lies rigid, his eyes fixed blankly on the ceiling.

"Say something," Truelove prompts. "Say something to your public, shabby bastard."

Wilfong flutters his eyelids with infinite disdain and mutters something inaudible until Truelove nudges his armpit with a well-placed toe. *"I said, this is all a mistake. This evacuation has been a . . . misunderstanding and we are sorry."* Wilfong gasps, out of breath, and the typewriter sways to starboard on his chest.

"Bullshit," Truelove explodes.

"Untie me now, and let me up. Or else." Wilfong conjures a feeble threat from the carpet.

"Or what?" Truelove asks, standing directly over Wilfong.

"Or you'll never teach again. Never!"

"Oh, pity the children." Truelove rears his head back and roars at the ceiling. "Don't worry, pal, it's a dead issue. Consider me resigned."

Truelove brushes by me, looks out the window. He's getting his game face on, is Truelove, and I don't want to wind up with a typewriter on my own chest. "Get back on that thing," he orders me. "Keep talking."

*"Friends,"* I continue over the PA, and a little madness overtakes me (maybe it's contagious, and I've been infected by Truelove himself, but I have another little score to settle), *"before we go on with this afternoon's programming, I'd like to dedicate this to a special friend, so let's send this out with extra feeling to Miss Peggy Klecko and all the gals out there with unicorn tattoos . . ."* And then, from out front on the walk, even through the hissing of the rain, I hear delighted howls, "OOOOOhhhh, Peggy, Peggyyyyyy," and other voices going, "Snakesnake-snakesnakesnake," until the rain takes over again and drowns them all out.

I turn around just in time to see Wilfong's feet disappear through his office. Truelove has dragged him in there. He reappears and slams the door shut, dangling a set of keys, Wilfong's, from his thumb.

"Hurry, they're coming," he shouts. Out front, the buses are rolling up the loading ramp. Most students still stand at attention, staring back toward the office. Ms. Wilberforce is marching briskly up the walk toward the main entrance, flanked by Ronnie and Luis, who still has his jacket poised against the rain. They disappear from view. Truelove bolts to the supply closet behind Miss Nevelson's desk. He fumbles with the keys, unlocks the door, and slides inside. "Say something," he hisses back at me. "Keep talking."

I reach inside my backpack and find my paper on vertebrates. *"On the great biological tree of life, the vertebrates occupy those honored upper branches of complexity and specialization."* Now they're booing me out on the bus ramp, but I figure what the hell, don't squander all this good effort in vain. *"Vertebrates are so named because of their backbones . . ."* I drone along, and Truelove emerges from the supply closet.

He slides two huge cardboard boxes out onto the carpet. They say, "Carolina Biological Supply" in black letters on the side.

"Ha, my pigs," he announces, and I know for sure he's lost it now. He tears into the boxes, dumping plastic pouches all over the floor. Inside each pouch a gray-pink thing is curled up in liquid, like a vacuum-sealed kielbasa.

*"This spinal column originates in a skull that, among the higher mammals, allows for a capacious brain cavity."*

A splash of bright yellow appears at the office door. It's Ms. Wilberforce, still in her raincoat. Ronnie stands behind her, Luis at her side, taping. Taping whatever it is Truelove's doing. Wilberforce pounds on the door. "Let us in here right now," she's hollering.

361

I get up to do just that when Truelove shouts me back into my seat. "Read it, Stephen. It's great. Read it."

I read, *"Indeed, the size of man's skull allows for a brain remarkable among all the animals for its intelligence and sophistication,"* and I think, how true—but maybe not for me.

"I want you away from the door and out of the building," Truelove is shouting at Wilberforce and friends. "I want you away from that door." He's carrying a can of duplicating fluid, wielding it like a bomb. Luis has pushed Wilberforce behind him and stands recording Truelove's every frenzied move through the door's window.

"I want that camera out of here. I want you out of here. You are all liars. You work for CBS, I know you do," he's shouting. He squats at the door. He twists the cap off the fluid and pours it beneath the door.

"Consider this your last warning, absolutely your last." Truelove pulls a lighter from his pants, holds it against the stained edge of the carpet near the door, and lights the fluid. A pale transparent blue flame climbs up both sides of the door. It reminds me of those desserts, cherries jubilee, peach flambé. Luis skitters backward from the door. Wilberforce is gone, and Ronnie.

I race to the supply closet, but there's no fire extinguisher in there. I pop into Wilfong's office. He's frantic, but tells me to check the bathroom. I go down the back way to the staff toilets, past Wilfong's office, but they're locked.

The stench of scorched carpet, blistering paint, fills

the office. When I get back to the front office, I see Truelove squatting behind Nevelson's desk, cranking open a window.

"They're out here now, Stephen. They think we don't know. They think they can slide up on us, but no way. I know how they operate."

He crouches on the floor, hunkering like a strange troll, and tears into the second box. More plastic pouches spill in mounds at his feet. Snatching up one in each hand, he pulls at the pouches with his teeth. He spits the plastic corners to the floor. His chin drips with formaldehyde; formaldehyde stains darken his shirt. Across the carpet he scatters their contents— specimens for dissection: crayfish, starfish, giant worms. The largest pouches, containing fetal pigs, he doesn't open.

The stench is overpowering. The sour, pickling smell of formaldehyde twists thickly in the office air. It joins the toxic vapor of blistered paint, stirring in the gray haze, layered in the room. My throat burns when I inhale, and I crawl to the front window, desperate to breathe the cold and rainy air outside.

There, out front, maybe ten feet away from the window, stands Luis, camera still running. He's holding it above his head now, at arm's length, trying to angle it down, to catch the action where Truelove crouches on the floor. A voice comes through the window: Ronnie Pothos. Even though he can't be seen, Ronnie must have huddled himself just below the windowsill.

"Would you like to make a statement to the press? Do you have any demands? Would you like to make a statement?" Then, like a silver toadstool, a microphone sprouts at the open window.

*"Here's a statement for you,"* Truelove shouts.

He rakes a hand across the carpet and retrieves a clump of crayfish. Holding them just below his nose, he lights them, one by one. Their tails sputter like wet fuses, smoking more than burning, and he launches them like small grenades out the window. "There's a statement," he screeches in his pinched falsetto. He continues this strange and cherished ceremony, setting the specimens free. Handfuls of worms, like blackened, tangled pasta, hurtle through the window out into the drizzling afternoon. Then he hurls the starfish out. They spin stiffly and settle on the wet grass. Even, finally, the pouches of fetal pigs. They land with a liquid thud, and abruptly Truelove stops. He pokes his head out to gauge the damage. Debris, smudges of worms lie in bunches as though brought by some pestilent rain. The crayfish smolder like the butts of wet cigars.

Luis and Ronnie have removed themselves a mere five feet off to the side. They are smiling. "Stephen," they shout when they see me through the window, "what's going on in there?"

But Truelove grabs me by the arm. "Get down," he says, then a final order. "More fluid, those cans of it in there." He points back to the supply closet. "Get as many as you can. We'll douse them."

On hands and knees I crawl to the closet. Like somebody's shooting at us. Like live machine-gun fire dances just above my head. So I collapse into the closet, and there's thirty-some cans of this fluid stacked along the floor. But wait a minute.

Wait. Hold on. You might scream through your toothpaste all you want, and even cackle some, strictly to yourself, under the covers at night after the lights go out. But that's kid stuff, make-believe, like playing dress-up or sipping on cooking sherry when Mom's away. I wanted to claim some of their lives for my own, to feel and know firsthand my mom's despair, my dad's fear, even Truelove's crazy anger at the world. I thought I could visit their lives, and know what happened fourteen years ago or more, how I came from that like an immigrant from another land. Sure, I've had my glimpses, made my observations, but I was only a tourist on a bus in a foreign country, ogling the past but not speaking the language. I wanted to feel like the natives there so badly, I chose sides and pledged allegiance to Truelove. But his madness isn't mine. I will have to have my own life, however weird or sloppy or uncomfortable it might be. It's time to get off the bus.

So let the buzzards circle for Truelove, I'm thinking, but not for me. Not yet. He's been working on this moment maybe twenty years, fourteen at least, the way I figure. It must take time to gather, to build and accumulate all those private miseries, like dust, like sediment, particles of grief, like mercury poisoning the bladder of a fish, speck by speck by speck.

It's not my war, I think, it's not my battle. Win or lose, it can't be mine. And so I stand up. I stand in the supply closet, and I swing around back toward the door.

"Not here," I shout. "Don't see it."

"There, it's on the floor, cans of it, god's sake, boy, look around."

"It's gone, then. This place is empty," I shout.

I hear him coming. He lunges through the door and falls to his knees. Swearing, spitting with fury, he sweeps the cans into a pile with his forearm. And I step back, back through the doorway, and push the door closed. The two bolts snap crisply against the strikeplate, and I turn the T-shaped lever horizontal.

"Nooooo," he rails. "You're one of them. Ohhhhhhhgod," and the voice trails away like the howling of a cat falling down an empty well.

I open Wilfong's door. He's propped up on his elbows and knees, scudding along the carpet, dragging the Selectric from his bound ankles like a ball and chain. I grab some scissors, free his hands, untie his ankles.

"I've got him. He's in the supply closet," I tell Wilfong. He says nothing, just stands massaging his wrists, straightening his jacket. Finally we walk into the main office. Outside the smoldering door Ms. Wilberforce stands behind Thomas, the janitor, who's spraying the floor with a foam extinguisher.

"They've got my keys," Wilfong shouts through the door. "He's in the closet. We've got him locked in the closet."

Thomas turns the extinguisher off. He pulls a loop of keys from his belt and struggles at the lock. The door opens; a wall of gray haze billows out into the hall. Thomas and Wilberforce stumble into the office, followed in close order by Ronnie and Luis, his camera still running.

"Quick, over here." Wilfong pushes Thomas ahead of him to the supply closet. "Careful now, stand clear, we don't know what he might . . ."

Thomas eases his great bulk up against the door. His bulging stomach flattens against it. He nuzzles the key silently into the door, turning with one hand while the other turns the lever back to vertical. He turns toward us, lifts his eyebrows with a shrug, and nods once. Luis pushes past us and aims his camera at the doorway.

Thomas swings the door open and hops backward, behind it. Luis lunges, lens first.

"Get back," shouts Truelove in his falsetto. I strain to see past Luis. In the middle of the closet Truelove sits cross-legged on the floor, bare to the waist, a pale roll of fat drooping over his belt like ripe cheese. He looks like the Buddha. He is slick, glistening, sitting in a puddle of fluid, empty cans scattered beside him.

"Keep back," he says again. He holds his disposable lighter right next to his saturated pants cuff. "I swear I'll do it—keep back."

But Luis takes another step forward, crouching for a low-angle shot.

"I swear," Truelove seethes. His thumb goes to the metal wheel atop his lighter. He pushes it, slowly. *Skriiiiiitch, skriiiiiiiitch*, it goes.

"Tell him, Stephen. Tell him you're not one of them. Tell him to get back."

"Get back," I tell Luis. "Turn your damn camera off for once, and leave him alone."

Slowly Luis retreats, but the camera still runs. Then Wilfong approaches the doorway.

"Put it down, Truelove," he urges. "Just put it down."

"I think it's time" is all Truelove says. He leans forward and pushes at the lighter, snaps the lighter, then furiously, vainly, snaps it again and again.

"Shit," he says. "Shit." He throws the lighter at Wilfong and collapses forward over his folded legs.

Wilfong flutters around saying stuff like "Let's go, the show's over," but no one moves. Wilberforce pushes Ronnie and Luis back into the hall, and Thomas stands by the office door, running his hand across the blistered paint.

I look out front, where the drizzle still falls across the slick black lot beyond the walk. The buses have all gone; the sidewalk is empty. Teachers gather in the hall, buzzing in low voices, peeking through the door. The bell sounds loud and cracking, and I realize that the PA mike is still on. It's three fifteen on Monday.

In the closet, Truelove sits alone, head lifted. He has spread his shirt on his lap, sits wringing out his T-shirt in his hands, twisting and twisting until it knots in the middle. I walk into the closet. The carpet squishes under my feet. I kneel beside him, catching my breath against the stinging air in there.

"School's out," I tell him. "It's over for you now."

He sits, silent, still wringing the shirt. I try again. "Mr. Truelove, are you there? It's over, Mr. Truelove, sir."

Slowly he loops the shirt around my neck. His big,

round face rotates like a reluctant moon. Something like a smile appears.

"Truelove's dead," he says, "as I should be." He takes my hand and pushes it up against my heart. "Do this," he said. He made an X across his chest, and so did I. "Stick a needle in your eye. Truelove's dead. Our secret. Absolutely mum city. It'll always be our secret, strictly on the old qt."

"Sure, anything," I tell him. "Secret, always has been."

"And ever shall be," he adds, and closes his eyes. "Amen."

# Chapter 47

And then I became a reindeer. Not Rudolph exactly, but close. I had a red ball sort of nose and little nubs rather than your full-blown antlers. My head and forelegs were molded of fiberglass and stuck out from the snowbank that smothered most of Santa's workshop, except for the chimney where you dropped your orphan toy money and a couple of stray mechanical elves who sat up there with their tiny arms swiveling, their hammers not quite making contact with the little wooden trains they were supposed to be building.

Mom got me the job that last day of November. She thought I needed a new interest. She knew the manager at the mall real well and set up the interview. Audition, rather. The manager, Mr. DeMent, asked me if I could stand being cooped up in a twenty-foot mound of fake snow seven days a week, till Christmas. I said it sounded perfect.

It took me a day to really get used to life inside Santa's Toy Fund Village. I parked myself in the director's chair behind the one-way glass window. A pair of handlebars stuck out across my lap. They controlled the reindeer's head so that you could tilt and rotate it into all these different authentic reindeer talking and listening positions. The talking part was through a microphone attached to the inside wall on a gooseneck stand, and the voice came out through the reindeer's mouth. It didn't have movable lips or anything, but after all, this wasn't Disney World.

It was all really straightforward and pretty depressing to think that a reindeer would ask for money, even if he did have his hindquarters frozen permanently into a fiberglass snowbank. Still, I played it pretty much by the book for a couple of weeks, and the money came down the chimney and rattled into the metal box. At the end of each day I'd let Mr. DeMent into my snowbank to unlock the box and deposit it somewhere in his office safe.

But I must say I enjoyed my reindeer period, a welcome relief after the rigors of my previous male-child incarnation. Oh, I was still in school, struggling toward Christmas break, posing with conviction as Stephen A. Douglass. This Douglass youngster finally decided to stick it out. He called Jamie one afternoon and thanked her for her interest in his case, but he couldn't accept a place at the lab school next semester. He didn't want to be a gifted specimen after all. It wasn't right, he felt, that Stephen be perceived as turning tail. She understood, she said, and talked at length about the virtues of "facing the music." They agreed to stay in touch.

For hours each day that snowbank was my sanctuary, my refuge, my cocoon. Free at last, is how I felt. Free from everything, like the last cords had been cut, even while, out there somewhere, Miss Armias read her announcements and Jenny Chatauqua buffed her nails and good old Nu Tran played the field and Peggy stalked the new Baryshnikov and Dad sold his last beer and brushed up on torts and Mom hawked megavitamins and stayed fit. And Truelove . . . Old True . . . well, he was free for good himself, I thought. Free at last, like me.

I could feel the old brain healing. I tried thinking like a reindeer, and that helped too. Damn heavy sleigh. Man, my hoofs are freezing in here. Gawd, these antlers itch. Stuff like that. But after a while even that got old. That's when I realized I was on a higher mission still. Or lower, I should say.

See, the thing is, I realized somewhere in there that my snowbank was really this elaborately disguised bathyscaphe, and I had been dropped not into an American shopping mall but into the very depths of the deepest ocean trench to observe and report back on strange bottom-dwelling life forms. And as luck would have it, I had been dropped into a rich and varied ecosystem of remarkable complexity. The morning creatures were slow-moving, hard-shelled forms, aimless foragers sometimes locomoting with the aid of strange wood or aluminum appendages. They left by noon, to be replaced by livelier species with great numbers of young, restless and squirming, with apparently voracious appetites. The larger of this species seemed primarily female and could often be seen carrying young on their backs. Then, by four o'clock, and lasting for maybe two to three hours, this afternoon group was replaced in turn by schools of young breeders, males and females of the same species, characterized by highly ritualized movements and gestures: bench sitting, zigzag maneuvers up and down the trench, giggling and whirling, feeding on great bags of cheese popcorn and chip-filled cookies bigger than sand dollars. Finally came the scavengers, gray solemn males with strange duck-billed carapaces on their head parts and pushing long ciliated sticks out in front until the floor of the trench sparkled dimly under the pale-blue glow of the ocean's night.

I surfaced nightly but offered no word of my findings. I feared it would be premature, second-rate scholarship, only partly formulated. Better to wait until later. Instead, Christmas afternoon I packed two turkey sandwiches into two Ziploc bags, bid Mom farewell, and went uptown. I walked through campus and entered University Hospital through the service doors. When I got to South Wing where they kept the crazies, I asked the nurse at the desk for Truelove.

"The teacher?" she asked.

"Yes, was," I said. "Biology."

She laid a black notebook on the countertop and shuffled through its pages. "Are you family?" she asked.

"Sort of," I said. She knew I was lying.

"He's gone, transferred," she said. "He's been moved to a veterans' hospital out of state." I reached into my pocket and pulled out his chain and dog tag and dropped it on the counter. "Can you at least give me an address where I can mail him this?"

"If you were family I could give you an address. Otherwise, we can't reveal . . ."

I didn't stay long enough to hear what she couldn't reveal. I just snatched up the chain, turned, and walked back downstairs, down all the stairs, didn't want any elevator just then. Walked back across campus, heading home as afternoon turned to evening, Christmas night. I ate the turkey sandwiches too. They were good, but I got heartburn. It's hard to eat when you're walking. Or maybe it was the mayonnaise. Too much mayonnaise, that can do it too.

At the center of campus I paused at the top of Braswell Hill and looked down at the long sloping lawn they call Old Quad. On four sides stood huge brick dormitories, empty and dark, abandoned now for Christmas break. Between the buildings and across the lawn, oaks and poplars interlocked bare, twisting branches into a ragged canopy above the quad. Some of these trees had been there two centuries or more, older than the university, than the town itself. Through their branches pale light sifted from a cold new moon.

Two cement walks crossed this quad, bisecting it corner to corner and meeting at the center. I followed one walk down to that center and stood in front of a statue. It was the principal landmark at the very center of the oldest part of campus, a soldier of the Confederacy, emblem of a conquered nation and envoy from the land of lost causes. He stood tall and proud, nonetheless, but slightly rumpled, with bayonet and canisters hanging from his belt, kepi smashed low and cocky across his forehead. He held his musket at port arms, slanting, barrel up, across his chest.

But he shone with a clean metal luster even under this pale Christmas moon. I remembered the news story last summer, how he had been hoisted from his pedestal and trucked to Connecticut. There he had been dipped in acid baths and scrubbed to a raw new sheen by craftsmen of Italian birth. It hardly seemed fair.

But he was home now, for Christmas, for good, to stand another hundred years on his pedestal. A blank pedestal, see, because the most famous thing about this statue was that he had no name, no rank, no anything, just an all-purpose generic Confederate soldier standing four feet off the ground on an empty granite block. Oh, sure, they called him Silent Sam. It was tradition, very droll, but not a proper name, hardly more than a joke.

"Sam, it's time," I whispered. I found myself standing on his pedestal, at his back. I shinnied up his calves and clamped my legs around his waist. I looped one arm around his neck and pulled myself up onto his back. With my free hand I reached into my pocket and fished out the chain and tag. In a minute I had it snapped and hanging from his neck.

I let myself down, shivering, frozen from hugging so much bronze in December. I stood in front and watched him, staring clear eyed and square jawed over my head and across campus.

"It's yours now, private," I said. "You be him as

375

long as you want. It's a strange name, but as good as any. It'll be our secret. Strictly on the old qt."

I moved back a step and watched. I was going to tell him other things, about jelly rolls and crayfish and *Jeopardy* and vertebrates—warnings, sort of. There was so much to explain.

But I could see he knew how to keep a secret, and he could find that other stuff out for himself, and that was the point, after all.

So I just saluted.

"Hang loose, soldier," I told him. Then I spun on my heels and started marching, running, all the way back home.